Preface

MW01172401

After WWII, Russia and the United States agreed to divide the Korean peninsula at the 38th parallel. The Demilitarized Zone, or DMZ, is four kilometers wide, stretching from coast to coast. On June 25,1950, over 75,000 North Korean troops stormed across the DMZ. When the fighting came to a close July 27, 1953 with the signing of the Armistice, the United States buried 36,880 soldiers, sailors and marines and over 100,000 wounded. South Koreans lost over a million souls, civilians and soldiers.

The 1953 Armistice halted the hostilities with rules limiting the number of troops and types of weapons carried in the DMZ. The ruthless communists refused to allow thousands of South Korean civilians trapped north of the DMZ to return to the south. Families were ripped apart. North Korean prisoners of war refused to be repatriated. Korea was divided socially, economically, and by ideology.

Over the years, the DMZ became a wildlife sanctuary. Rice paddy's abandoned for decades turned into swamps. Tree-covered hills provided ideal wildlife habitat. Civilians were not allowed in the DMZ. Wildlife flourished, but so did infiltration by North Korean agents and military units.

In November 1966, North Koreans attacked an American patrol, killing six men. In 1967-1968 eleven hundred clashes occurred in or near the DMZ. The DMZ was declared a combat zone. US troops began receiving hostile fire pay. For a second time, within fifteen years, South Korea was forced to defend its borders against armed intruders. The

Republic of Korea Army defended most of the 161 miles of theDMZ. The US forces protected 18 miles. Of the 50,000 US troops in Korea, only a fraction of them served along the DMZ.

As the war in Vietnam raged, fears of a second front became a concern. Was North Korea going to repeat 1950? Were they testing our resolve with the attacks along the DMZ? Did Kim Ill Sung believe he could create fear in the south and stop South Korea from sending troops to Vietnam? Did he think the United States or South Korea's troops would overreact, giving North Korea an excuse to attack with Russia or China's aid?

The US intelligence community calculated the risk for Kim Il Sung was too great. Denial by them of the possibility that North Korea would expand their operations, hamstrung the troops. The best equipment went to Vietnam. The US troops had to follow the Armistice rules , the North did not. Kim Ill Sung kept the pressure on the South, hoping to start a people's uprising.

The story about Hyun-ae Bae and Lt. Reed is fictional intertwined with the following historical events. The North sent commando's and special operatives to attack positions along the DMZ. In January 1968 they attacked the Presdential Palace. Also in January the North Korean navy captured the USS Pueblo.

The Jeju Island uprising caused thousands of civilian casualties. The April protest in 1960 resulted in 186 people being killed by the South Korean government. In 1983 a Korean Airliner traveling from Alaska to Seoul was shot down by a Russian fighter.

GARY C GABLE

ISBN:

ISBN-13

DENIAL OF CONFLICT

LAND OF THE MORNING CALM

Chapters

PROLOGUE

It was the second day of September 1983. I arrived at the office just as Alice went to get water to make coffee. The morning paper was lying on my desk, opened to the second page. Alice was prone to get to the office early and use my desk to read the paper. I glanced at the page, which carried a story from the front page about a Korea airliner. The phone rang before I turned the paper back to the first page.

"M-R Detective agency."

"May I speak with Mike Reed?"

"Whose calling?"

"Mark Kowalski."

"Screw You." I said shouting into the phone..

A voice from fifteen years ago. Kowalski and his cohort Dick Meyer were two people I wanted erased from my mind, but could never let them go. I held the phone out away from my ear, tempted to hang up, I hesitated.

"MIKE, don't hang up, just listen. Did you see the paper?" Kowalski asked.

"No!"

"The Russians forced a Korean airliner to land on a remote island yesterday. It was flying from Anchorage to Seoul. Bae was on the plane." Kowalski explained.

"WHAT? No, you're full of shit. What makes you think she's on the plane? You left the military right after me." Mike said.

"I stayed in the business. I work for the government. North and South Korea are my areas of concern."

"WHERE WAS YOUR FUCKING CONCERN IN 1968?" Mike yelled.

"Listen Mike, I shouldn't even be talking to you, let alone what I'm going to tell you, but you deserve an explanation."

"I'm listening."

"The information is sketchy. Russian fighters forced the plane down. It was flying over the Sea of Japan. The Russians are claiming it's a spy plane, and it had strayed into forbidden airspace. There's chatter that they may have shot the plane down but..."

"WHAT ABOUT BAE?" Mike yelled into the phone.

"She was on the plane with two intelligence officers. I'm not privy if she escaped or defected from North Korea. She was in East Germany for the physicist conference on generating electricity from nuclear energy. The CIA helped her to get out of East Germany. She is an important asset or had classified information that we and the South Koreans wanted. I didn't and will never know the importance of the information. It's above my pay grade. It's my understanding she was being welcomed back to Korea. Over the past several years, we have received credible information North Korea was attempting to develop nuclear energy and nuclear weapons. We had information on their research reactor at Yong

Yon before the rest of the world became aware they had the ability. I'm not privy to how she got the intelligence or if she's the reason. There's speculation Kim ll-Sung asked the Russians to shoot or force the plane down? Probably not, but?"

"Enough bullshit about her spying for you guys. You got her aunt killed. God knows who else!"

"Look, Mike, I'm sorry they screwed it up. Meyers and I had no control over what happened in 68. They kept us in the dark. The South Korean Intel guys controlled the operation. We were on the fringe. For all I knew, she wanted to defect, and Chung and Bae used you."

"FUCK YOU KOWALSKI." I slammed the Merlin phone onto the plastic base so hard the bracket holding it snapped. The base tilted, and the phone slid off and hummed the dial tone. Alice, hearing the ruckus, stuck her head in the door and asked.

"Everything alright?"

"Yea, close the door."

I let my mind slide back to 1967, the start of my thirteen month tour in the Land of the Morning Calm.

ARRIVAL IN COUNTRY
"No man ever steps in the same river twice, for it's
not the same river and he's not the same man,"
Heraclitus

"Lieutenant Reed reporting for duty, Sir."
The major gave me the once over without saying a
word. Cigar and furniture wax permeated the office.
The air-conditioned office chilled my wrinkled,
sweat soaked khakis. The ride from the airport was
miserable. Enlisted men and officers packed like
sardines on a green army bus. Only half of the
windows opened. The hum of the air conditioner
was the only sound as the major continued to study
my orders. I stood at ease, staring at a triangular
piece of wood on the major's desk. It stated who I
was facing in two inch high letters on a brass plate,
"MAJOR RAMOS." It was hard to picture this very
thin, short, balding man with crossed rifles on his
collar leading men into battle.

The major looked up, his eyes just clearing the
top of my orders when he said. "Do you have an
assignment in mind?"

"I have a choice, sir?"

The major chuckled before he replied.

"No, but we ask. I see from your file you played
football in high school and semi-pro football? A
couple of years in college. You then joined the Army.
Why didn't you stay in college?"

"College wasn't for me, Sir. The professors wanted to just teach their point of view. There was an undercurrent among the students pulling in different directions. You had to pick your friends based on whether you were for or against the war in Vietnam. I wasn't learning. I was just pissing my parents' money away."

The major chomped on his cigar before asking. "Enough bullshit. Why enlist in the Army?"

"I was going to be drafted. The recruiting officer suggested Army intelligence."

"Lieutenant, you see where that got you. Do you want to play football? We have teams in Korea, Japan, and Okinawa. It's great duty, when you are not playing ball, you'll manage a recreation center. Training camp begins in a week. You should be in good shape after OCS. What position did you play?"

"Outside linebacker."

"Lieutenant, you look the part. What's your weight?"

"About one hundred eighty pounds, five eleven." Reed said.

"We need a linebacker. I'm the defensive coach."

As the major continued talking, he pointed to a row of team pictures hanging on the wall. On the shelf below, six metallic players on blocks of wood in varying ball carrying poses, each claiming a victory. The 2nd Division had won the Championship six years in a row. Play football again? It sounded too easy, fresh out of OCS and gung-ho. I remembered an old army adage, don't volunteer. I spent two years learning to be a soldier. Why volunteer for a management job?

"Lieutenant, what do you say?"

"Sir, what are my other choices, sir?"

"You were commissioned infantry, lieutenant, if you don't want to play ball. No pun intended."

"I finished Army Intelligence school at Fort Holibird with a top secret security clearance, sir."

"Yes, but as an enlisted man. I have no open slots for military intel and besides, those assignments are determined stateside. Security clearance and all, we can use you up on the DMZ. The 2nd of the 23rd needs a platoon leader, lieutenant."

"Yes, Sir!"

"There's a steel pot, flak jacket, and a rifle in the front office. The sergeant will sign the gear out to you. I will hold you responsible for it. A jeep driven by Specialist Rimmer will take you to your unit. At your destination, you will return the gear to Rimmer. Your unit will assign your equipment. Understand, Lieutenant?"

"Yes, sir."

"Good luck Reed, and welcome to the 2nd Division."

"Thank you Sir." I did a smart salute, and then, about face.

The major shouted out.

"Sergeant Willis, the lieutenant is going up north. Lieutenant, close the door on your way out."

Back in the front office steam bath, Sergeant Willis, a recruiting poster soldier, walked into the room carrying the gear. His khakis, starched and creased, no sweat showing on his forehead or uniform. How the hell do sergeants do that? My wrinkled khakis were dark with sweat stains, my short cropped hair matted as beads of sweat reformed on my forehead. Sergeant Willis placed the gear on a desk as he said.

"Here's your helmet lieutenant, along with a flak jacket, M-14 rifle, serial number 2348763, and one magazine with twenty rounds. Sign here."He handed me a clipboard with a pen and one sheet of paper with the list of gear and several paragraphs of regs and lawyer talk. I looked at Willis with skepticism.

Willis smiled as he said. "It's states if you lose any equipment between here and there, the army will deduct the cost from your pay. Once outside, you may insert the magazine but do not chamber a round. Your chances of getting jumped by North Koreans between here and the DMZ are a million to one. You wouldn't believe the horror stories about stolen or lost gear between here and the DMZ. At your unit, you will return the gear to Rimmer. He will arrive in a few minutes. Don't ask him to take detours or make stops. He has strict orders. Do not ask him to deviate from his duty."

"No problem SARGE!"

"Lieutenant, the 2nd of the 23rd is in the thick of it."

"Thick of what? I haven't heard of any trouble with the North Koreans."

"The number of DMZ incidents, meaning firefights,

has been increasing ever since the ROKs started sending troops to Vietnam. The North Koreans don't want the South Korean army fighting against communism in Vietnam. North Korea has been sending small units into the DMZ and attacking our positions. On a larger scale, they attack the South Korean army or, as we call them, ROKs. They attacked a patrol and killed six of our guys last November. Since then, the number of firefights has increased. Your driver is here. Rimmer was wounded when he was with the 2nd of the 23rd."

"Thanks sarge."

"God speed, lieutenant."

MISSED OPPORTUNITY
"He who is prudent and lies in wait for an enemy
who is not, will be victorious." Sun Tzu

Kim was shivering. Was it because of being wet or their encounter with Chung? The team was to return to North Korea with Chung or eliminate him, which they didn't do. Comrade Choi will not be happy. Now, Kim had to concentrate on which route to take north.

Lee and Park were resting. It's been two hours since they crossed the Imjin river and hid in a thick tangle of brush on Crab Island. A spit of land that became an island at high tide only. They were a kilometer south of the DMZ. They made sure they brushed the tracks away in the sand.

Just before daylight, Kim had located the sand bar that crossed the one hundred meter wide river. They waded across at low tide, which made Kim happy. It wasn't the water that fostered his fears, but what swam in it. Kim was able to hide his fear of swimming during training.

Kim had two options. The original plan, which Kim decided against, was to cross where the Imjin turned north, passing through North Korea's part of the DMZ. They would be in North Korea after crossing the river, but swimming was the only way to cross. Kim didn't want to swim in what his mind pictured, a snake infested river.

As a young boy, he loved to go swimming in the Taedong-gang river near his village of Songnim. The river flowed into the Yellow Sea. After finishing their chores, Kim and two grade school friends rushed down to the swimming hole.It was a place where the river made a sharp bend and the current met the Yellow sea's tide. The slow current allowed Kim to leisurely float on his back. The deepest spot was up to his shoulders.

His love for the water changed in an instant. He was standing in the deep part, facing downstream, when something bumped against his back and slither around both shoulders. A ball of yellow bellied sea snakes, mating, had floated onto Kim's back. With sheer terror, Kim flailed away at the snakes, screaming. As Kim turned, one snake reared its head, eye level, inches away from Kim's. He swung at the evil serpent. He felt a sting, like a bee sting on his arm. The snakes reformed their ball and drifted away. Kim missed school for weeks, lyingin bed in a feverish stupor, dreaming of monster snakes and dragons chewing on his arm.

Kim snapped back to the present. The mission will be over in hours. So far, the intelligence gathered by prior teams was accurate. Training with the elite 124th Regiment has served Kim's team well. With luck, they'll be in North Korea tomorrow morning.

The spears of sunlight penetrating the brush warmed Kim's wet back. Uneasiness replaced the pleasant feeling. Off in the distance, he could hear men approaching. Kim didn't need to alert his men. They separated and were quietly pulling brush down on them for concealment. He wanted to avoid fighting. Any contact with the Americans will make the return North more dangerous.

Kim could see movement forty, fifty meters away. He slid his PPSh-41 submachine gun up along his side, his right hand gripping the stock, ready to bring the weapon to his shoulder. There were seven or eight GIs. They were a noisy bunch, talking and making no effort to be quiet as they moved through the brush. Kim's grip tightened on the stock. The patrol was walking right at them. Kim and his men had the element of surprise. Just as Kim brought his weapon to his shoulder, the patrol stopped. The man out front stopped in front of a thorny tangle of brush. He motioned with his arm to the left. He turned, and the men followed.

Kim breathed a sigh of relief as the noisy patrol faded out of sight. Kim's right hand cramped from clutching his weapon. Beads of sweat had formed on his forehead. That was close, too close. The GIs missed an opportunity. His thoughts returned to the mission. He was confident that they could get through the DMZ as he visualized their preparation.

They had trained for months at the regiment training camp. The 124th, a unit consisting of officers, was the best of the best. Their insertion by sea into the south two months ago was uneventful. They landed on the rugged coast between Sokcho-si and Goejeong. They used the difficult terrain of the Tae baek mountains for the journey to Seoul marching at night avoiding civilians. Linking up with their contact at a safe house north of Seoul was easier than Kim had expected.

Chung Jin Hein was the main reason for the mission. He had been in South Korea for five years and versed in the customs, the routine of the GIs, South Korean Army, and police. Chung moved around Seoul with ease. He told Kim the South Korean people were weak and suffered from unhappiness.

Kim didn't see it that way. Most of the people didn't want to start a revolution. They didn't have any passion for their "unhappiness." In the two months he and his team were in Seoul, Kim saw a thriving city, bustling with cheerful people.

Chung's contacts with the university students could be an opportunity. Dissent was growing. Chung said he could recruit from the ranks of the poor. Chung claimed he made several conversions among the South Koreans. He arranged safe houses for Kim's team.

According to Chung, thousands of North Korea agents, at the end of the war disguised as refugees, were still in place. Over the last fifteen years, others entered by sea or the DMZ. Chung was confident they would rise up and fight when the time came. Chung made it clear the members of the cells knew nothing about other cells. Kim noticed the crackdown on the cells by the South Korean government. Even though Chung omitted it, the Seoul newspapers did not.

But for now, it's secondary to the question at hand. He had to decide what route to cross the DMZ. They could return along the Imjin river to where it bends into North Korea. Kim didn't want to go that route. Chung also thought it was a poor choice. Kim motioned for his comrades to crawl closer.

"Lee, Park." Kim whispered.

"We will leave tonight, through the DMZ. The 17th Foot Reconnaissance Brigade will make a diversionary attack on the GIs. We'll enter the DMZ, where we scouted before we came south. Before we leave this evening, we'll go over the plan in more detail. We must rest now."

Lee who talked too much. Did so again.

"Kim, the DMZ? Why not follow the river, no fence to cut, no minefield to cross with GIs shooting at us?"

"Did you not listen to Chung? He told us they increased patrols along the river. If discovered, we're too far from the MDL. Chung's information has been accurate. I will not doubt it now?" From his expression, Lee didn't give up.

"The Americans are sloppy. We could get by the patrols."

"The Americans are even more careless along the fence, and part of our mission is to attack one of their positions. We attack and make our way north in a matter of minutes."

"But comrade, if something goes wrong, we may lose the information in the satchel Chung gave you."

"Look comrade, if we take the river route, we'll be

easy targets in the water. Besides, we would have to travel five or six kilometers to get to where the river bends north. Here, we're only a kilometer from the DMZ."

"A kilometer away from the GI's bullets, mines and a three meter high fence!" Kim didn't want to hear anymore. In a loud, gruff whisper, he said.

"COMRADE LEE, ENOUGH!"

"Sorry Comrade. I was just pointing out other options."

"Get some rest, Park, you're on guard. Wake me up in two hours."

Kim's thoughts drifted back to the mission, what he was going to tell his superiors? There was no doubt Chung had infiltrated into the South Korean society with the help of sleeper cells. The individuals in these cells had secured employment or started businesses. They assisted Chung in gaining employment at the Ministry for Food Agriculture Forestry and Fisheries. A low level position, but it enabled him to rub elbows with higher-ranking members in the other ministries. Especially after work hours.

Kim thought Colonial Choi will be pleased with the maps, photos and the information on the guard changes at Kimpo air base and the Presidential Palace, the "Blue House." What a stupid name for a president's house. The only part blue was the roof.

There are several weaknesses in the security. They changed the guard at the same time. The grounds of the Blue House had several areas with trees and shrubs, cover, and concealment. There were no heavy gun emplacements. The grounds ended at the foot of the forested Bukhansan Mountain. The security detail did not patrol the mountain. Civilians could hike on the mountain above the grounds. The mountain ridge pointed north, providing an attack or escape route. The Presidential so-called palace was an easy target.

Chung's actions last night still had Kim befuddled. Chung was told to return because he was needed to train new agents. But Chung had no intention of returning. If Chung refused to return, Kim and his team were to eliminate him. They were not told why Chung was a threat to national security. During the last two months, Chung gave the impression he had every intention of returning. The classified information gathered and the freedom of movement around Seoul made Kim wonder why his superiors wanted to lose such an important asset. Was Chung a double agent?

It made little sense, but maybe it did. One night, he followed him. Chung moved through the streets as if he was a resident, with no countermeasures. At a market, he met an attractive young woman. They talked for a couple of minutes, then went in separate directions. Kim followed the woman, but as she walked away, a man began following her. He had the telltale look of a South Korean security man. Was Chung a double agent? Was one of his contacts compromised?

Last night, Chung escorted them to a safe house

south of the Imjin river. The face off with Chung was imprinted on Kim's mind. Chung wasn't an easy man to stare down. He was taller than most Koreans at five foot nine. He was from a far north province of Korea. With Chinese blood? His face was rather angular, with a narrow nose and deep set, dark hawkish eyes. When he stared at you, a glint of yellow flashed. He had the movements of a tiger, graceful but dangerous..

As they were getting ready to leave, Chung handed Kim one of the two satchels he was carrying. As Kim took the satchel, Chung backed away. Kim's hair on the back of his neck bristled.

"Kim, I'm not going back." As Chung said the words, a German C-96 Mauser equipped with a silencer appeared in his hand. Kim was familiar with the pistol. The pistol's grip was in the shape of a broom handle. Its rate of fire could sweep the room, taking out Kim and his team.

"Look in the satchel. There are copies of classified documents and rolls of film. They will impress our Supreme leader. The information will convince our Comrades, I need to stay in Seoul. There's a detailed map of the route for crossing the DMZ. I'm sure you trained for your return through the DMZ. The map includes new information on GI patrols. Avoid crossing the river where it meets the DMZ. Too many patrols. Buried under the north corner of the house, you'll find weapons and grenades."

"Don't try to stop me!"

He backed out the door grinning, showing his

white teeth, dark eyes with a glint of the yellow, perhaps from the flame of the oil lamp, or a sea snake!

THE RIDE NORTH

Outside, the Turkish bath was even more torturous. The jeep skidded to a stop, creating a cloud of dust. The dust like flour, stuck to my skin. Specialist Rimmer jumped out of the jeep and saluted. His starched fatigues looked like he had just picked them up at the cleaners, looking just like the sergeant. I returned the salute.

"Lieutenant, you can throw your duffel bag behind the seat. On the dash, there's a clamp for the rifle. I suggest you hang on to your helmet and flak jacket. I'll secure your duffel bag so we don't get ripped off by a slicky boy."

"Slicky boy?"

"Yes, lieutenant, there're a lot of poor South Koreans and they see the US Army as a depot for stuff. They're fast and innovative thieves. Last week I was taking a Lieutenant to 1st of the 31st. We were driving through a small village. I was making a slow turn. The lieutenant stretched his arm. He pointed at a farmer with the piglet lashed on his bike. A slicky boy standing on the corner, as slick as a fuckin' whistle, slid the expandable band off the Lieutenant's wrist. Before the Lieutenant could yell, fuck, the kid disappeared in the alley. My orders are not to stop. That was a pissed off lieutenant. His girlfriend gave him the watch as a going away present."

"Where's the MP's?"

"They can't be everywhere, lieutenant. Don't get the wrong impression. Not all Koreans are thieves. Most are good people. The majority appreciate the GIs for saving their asses during the Korean War. Hop in sir, I'll explain on the way. The ride will cool you off. You don't have to put the flak jacket on till we get to Freedom bridge."

"Thank god, this thing is heavy." I said as I climbed in the front seat of the jeep, clamping the M-14 to the dash. Rimmer peeled out on the gravel and dirt. "Rimmer, is it always this hot and humid?"

"Well, Lieutenant, the monsoon starts soon, July and August, and it's fuckin muggy. July is the worst month, you'll get used to it. Winter is as cold as a witch's tit. Not much snow, just windy and damp. Chills you right to the bone."

"How long have you been in Korea?" I said, as I tried to position the helmet and flak jacket on my lap.

"Let's see the way I have it figured. Today is June 15, 1967. I have sixty-two days, twelve hours to finish up my full thirteen month tour. Unless Ramos, uh, I mean, Major Ramos extends my ass. I'm his personal driver. I get to cart around the brass. They fly in from Japan or the states. I act as a tour guide. Saves the Major from explaining the historical sites. We get dignitaries, congressmen and senators. They don't give a shit about what's happening here. I'm just keeping my fingers crossed that the North Koreans do nothing stupid between now and August 17th."

"Sergeant Willis said you were wounded."

"Sarge tells the new officers, I'm supposed to tell you how it happened and give you a half ass briefing."

"Ok, I'm listening."

"Lieutenant, you flew out of Fort Lewis, right?"

"Yep."

"Did you attend any briefings about Korea?"

"No, the only knot of knowledge came from the Sergeant Major at Fort Benning. He said Korea was better than Nam. I received my orders for Korea right out of OCS with thirty days' leave. After six months at Benning, I didn't read newspapers."

"Hell, Lieutenant, it wouldn't make a difference if you read the New York Times every day. My folks send me the paper often enough. Nam gets all the ink. What's going on in the Korean DMZ is small potatoes."

As we neared the main gate, I noticed what I had missed earlier. The gate had two sandbagged positions on each side, with armed soldiers in full battle gear. Men in and outside the compound did not have weapons, helmets, or flak jackets. A strange mix. Rimmer nodded to the guards as I returned their salute.

"Rimmer, why the sandbagged positions?"

"We are on a half-assed alert."

Rimmer got quiet and seemed to be in deep thought as he shifted gears. The moving air felt good on my sweat soaked khakis. The paved road was narrow and lined with small ramshackle shops. Even with the restricted roadway, everyone stayed on their side of the road, in tune with the crazy mishmash of bicycles, pedestrians, people pushing carts, oxen pulling wagons, and small yellow cars weaving in and out, like big bees.

"Rimmer! What are the yellow cars?"

"Korea's version of the New York city taxi. Cab drivers are the same everywhere."

Fatigue was setting in. Ten hours of hurry and wait while processing at Fort lewis, twelve sleepless hours on the plane, I was bushed. As I was nodding, Rimmer slammed on the brakes and swerved to the left, damn near tossing me out.

"Sorry Lieutenant, I didn't want to hit that kid. If you're going to fall asleep, climb in the back. I can't lose a lieutenant. The major will have my ass and extend it in the stockade."

"I'm alright, fill me in on the DMZ."

"Well sir, when the so-called 'Korean Police Action' ended with the Armistice in1953, Korea remained divided at the 38th parallel. The DMZ is a corridor across the entire Korean peninsula at the 38th parallel. It's not a straight line, it's irregular, follows the contours of the terrain, juts north, then south, it zigzags across the land. The Z is four kilometers wide, two kilometers on each side of the MDL dividing the DMZ. We stay south of the MDL. The North Koreans are supposed to stay north of the MDL. Most of the signs marking the MDL are gone.

What's left are a few rusted signs here and there covered with brush or tall grass. We guard eighteen miles of the DMZ. The ROKs have the rest. A fence defines the southern boundary. North Koreans don't abide by any armistice or boundaries."

"Any civilians live in or near the DMZ?"

"No civilians. Matter of fact, in the area you're going, no civilians are allowed north of the Imjin River. Only the good guys and bad guys. The North Koreans used the DMZ and the sea to infiltrate South Korea. The DMZ is a strip of wilderness, overgrown, long abandoned rice paddies fertilized with human crap for thousands of years makes for some serious thick brush. Couple that with being under-manned."

"We're spread so thin the gooks could drive a tank across the DMZ without getting noticed. The 'gooks' have been sending combat units into the DMZ attacking our men and the ROKs. Last November they ambushed one of our patrols, matter of fact, it was a patrol from your new battalion. They killed six good men, and we killed not one gook!"

"President Johnson was in the country when it happened. The press reported on the ambush because it happened during the President's visit. A couple days after the ambush, the ROK'S and the 'gooks' got into it, ten ROKs KIA and as many gooks. Since then, we have been on alert status. The details of the firefights in the ROK sector come from KATUSA'S."

"What's a KATUSA?"

"A South Korean soldier assigned to a US unit. They

must be able to speak English, thus we get the more educated Korean."

"Are they any good?"

"Depends on who you talk to. We are under-manned because of Nam. They beefed our units up with KOREA'S AUGMENTATION TO THE UNITED STATES ARMY, otherwise known as KATUSA'S."

"How many in a company?"

"Two to four KATUSA'S in a platoon."

"How often do the North Koreans attack us or the ROK'S?"

"That's the problem, Lieutenant, too often and then, not often enough."

"How's that?"

"When you first get to the Z, you're psyched, gung-ho, and all that bullshit. But after a month of walking your ass off, trying to stay awake on ambush and freezing in the winter or suffering from heat stroke in the summer, nothing happens. No enemy contact, just a walk in the woods carrying fifty pounds of gear. Days, weeks go by and nothing happens. It's human nature, lieutenant, you drop your guard. That's when the 'gooks' fuck with you. They know when a patrol becomes careless. It used to be hit and run, "gooks" pop up in the brush, fire a few rounds and then beat it back across the MDL, but that changed."

"What changed and what are the rules of engagement?"

"Contact with the 'gooks' used to be sporadic. The gooks have stepped up the intensity and frequency of the attacks. They've started ambushing our work parties and patrols in and south of the DMZ. The rules suck. You'll get briefed at battalion, but if a gook crosses the MDL, he is fair game. Shoot first, ask questions later. Once they cross north of the MDL, we can't pursue them, nor can we shoot them."

"What about the ROKs? How hard are they getting hit?"

"The rumors from the KATUSA'S who have friends or relatives in the military. According to them, the ROKs don't take any bullshit. Someone has rumored they sent an entire company across the MDL and wiped out a gooks guard post, killing twenty or twenty-five. That's one story you will not read in the Stars and Stripes. My buddy over in G-2 says that they have intel that shows that the attacks will increase. Matter of fact, the brass is requesting more troops."

"Your buddy at G-2 could get in trouble passing along classified information."

"Naa, he didn't tell me until they sent the info to the line companies."

Rimmer slowed the jeep to a crawl as we approached a parade of Koreans, on bikes, walking, running, fighting oncoming traffic, struggling to get around a wagon pulled by an ox. The wagon was carrying two large wooden barrels the size of fifty-gallon drums. They didn't have tops. An ugly-looking slop sloshed over the rim and sticking to the side. The stench hit me. The perfume from hell. Rimmer noticed me covering my face with my hand

and chuckled.

"Rimmer? What the hell is that smell?"

"The effluvium of Korea."

"WHAT?"

"SHIT, sir!. It's shit; the Koreans use the carts to haul it to the farmers. The farmers pay good money for it, so I'm told. There are no sewers here. The Koreans crap either in pots or outhouses with catch barrels. Then the honey wagon guys go around and collect the shit. It is part of the economy in the countryside. They use it in vegetable gardens. I recommend not eating raw vegetables."

"NO SHIT."We both chuckled at my half-hearted attempt to be funny.

"Up ahead, the road widens and we'll be able to get around one highlight of your visit to beautiful Korea. Once we get out into the country, it doesn't smell as bad. In a couple of weeks, you won't notice it."

We idled along. A boy runs towards the jeep. Dressed in dark slacks and a white shirt. I crossed my arms as Rimmer's story about the lieutenant's watch came to mind.The kid smiles at me, then yells.

"Hey GI, wanna buy good jungle boots made just for you? Stop, I got your size."

He had four or five pairs of boots laced together, slung around his neck. Rimmer yells something in Korean and the kid stops jogging, makes a contorted face and gives us the finger.

"I thought you said they like GIs."

"I said, 'most,' many of these kids have no family,

thus no family values. Many were born in slums. The parents may have died in the war. Their mom may have worked as a prostitute. Worse yet, their father may be a GI. Racially mixed children have little chance of being accepted in Korean society. By the time these kids are teenagers, they can hustle you out of your boots if they're not laced tight. Don't forget, Lieutenant, the war ended just fourteen years ago. This country is fucked, economically, socially, you name it! After the war, the country was a freaking mess. During the war, the front lines were fluid. Civilians fled the battles, it separated families.There's still thousands of aunts, uncles, extended family members stranded in the north. Picture your parents captive for fourteen years in Canada. The communist bastards didn't allow exchanges after the Armistice. You can't call, visit, nothing. You don't know if they were dead or alive. North Koreans consider them as citizens of the north. If you expressed a desire to go south, you end up in a labor or reeducation camp."

"Do civilians in the north try to cross the DMZ?"

"They do and sometimes make it. The gooks use more soldiers keeping their people in the north than keeping the ROKs out. Those that cross tell stories of starvation and brutality. The defectors say if you leave family behind, they're murdered or put in prison camps. Did you know that at the end of the Korean war, over twenty thousand North Korea POWs refused to be repatriated?"

"No. How did that work out?"

"The South Korean government accepted them as citizens once they signed a loyalty pledge."

"How much money does a Korean family need?"

"Thirty five bucks in MPC, military pay certificate, script given to US soldiers instead of dollars to combat the black market. The working class is making a comeback. Some farm, others with jobs with the US military. Hell, we hire Korean security guards for bases south of the DMZ. Koreans do most of the construction.The people in the slums and tenant farmers dislike the South Korean government. Animosity has been building since the end of the war. The regime promised the tenant farmers their own land. It hasn't happened on a large scale. Five miles outside of Seoul, you're in a third world country. Coupled with an unhappy working-class and rebellious students, you have an unsettled country. Students protest here as much as they protest back home. The government in the past responded, resulting in hundreds of death. That's good propaganda for the Commies. It provided them with an ammunition for creating dissent. The country is infested with corruption because of the amount of money we pour into its economy."

"What corruption? Do people have money to be corrupt?"

"Sir, every compound south of the DMZ employs civilians, working as houseboys, cooks, carpenters. They even do our laundry, so there is money exchanging hands. The US military contract the jobs out to an overseer. They charge the overseer with vetting local people to do the various jobs. They pay him a fee. Then there's the black market trading in everything from stolen GI equipment to MPC for US dollars."

"Why doesn't the government crackdown?"

"We have two KUTUSA'S in our platoon. They tell us the government looks the other way. The ill-gotten money helps fuel the economy. Our presence here is key to this country's recovery. Not just the houseboy jobs, but by rebuilding roads, schools, airports."

The traffic thinned out as we traveled further to the north. The terrain flattened out with rice paddies on both sides of the road. Every rice paddy had at least one farmer bent at the waist, ankle deep in mud. Gray sharp mountain peaks were off to the east. Along the road houses with mud or stucco walls with straw thatched roofs. There were other houses with rusted metal roofs. The roof material appeared to be a mix of corrugated metal sheets and small rectangles. "Rimmer the house up ahead on the left. What are those different colored pieces of metal mixed in with the corrugated roofing?"

"Those lieutenant are soup, vegetable, oil cans, any can the homeowner can get his hands on. They remove the top and bottom, cut the can along the seam, flatten it and 'ta dah' you have a shingle. Koreans don't waste a thing."

"How do you know all that?"

"I'm a history buff, especially Asian history. I learned to speak a little Korean. The Korean people are friendly and easy to talk to. I read everything I can. My buddy at G-2 gave me unclassified research material about Korea. It's great stuff. When I get out, I'm going back to school to study Korea, Japan and China. I learned a lot from my Korean girlfriend."

"Good for you. Where's home?"

"Princeton, New Jersey, and I went to Princeton, night school. I worked during the day. I couldn't pay my bills and go to school. My parents have no money, so I joined the army. Volunteered for Nam, but typical army, they sent me to Korea."

"Lieutenant, how did you end up in the army?"

"Not much different, I dropped out of college, enlisted, after two years signed up for OCS." A couple hundred meters off to the east side of the road small barren hills rose out of the rice paddies, no trees only spotty patches of grass. Near the top were pillboxes, like you see in old war movies.

"Rimmer, are those pillboxes left over from the Korean War?"

"No, we built them after the war. They placed them in strategic locations between here and Seoul. This valley is one of the best attack routes to Seoul."

"Where are the trees? I don't think I've seen a tree since we left the base?"

"The Koreans cut the trees as soon as they get big enough to burn. They use the wood to make charcoal for heating and cooking. You'll see plenty of trees in the Z." Rimmer stated.

We rode on in silence. The paved road turned to dirt with a bump, lifting me off my seat. A dust cloud swirled behind the jeep and hung there in the hot, humid still air. I was dead tired, but excited about my first assignment. Rimmer was lost in his thoughts. I wandered back home trying to calculate what time it was in Buffalo, New York.

HYUN-AE'S APRIL II

"There may be times when we are powerless to prevent injustice, but there must never be a time when we fail to protest." Elie Wiesel

"Hyun-ae, how many posters do we need?"

Jung-hee was setting up the mimeograph in the back room of the tea shop. As long as they did not promote violence, the owner allowed Hyun-ae's protest group to print up fliers and hold meetings after hours.

"No posters. Print two hundred fliers, word of mouth, and the fliers should be enough. "

Hyun-ae was worried. The police were questioning her professors about her activities and her studies. She was months away from getting her doctorate in nuclear physics. They wanted to know why is she was wasting her time leading student protests. She didn't give a fuck what they thought, but she was concerned for the safety of her friends.

Protesting against President Park's government could be dangerous. It was seven years ago when the April Revolution forced President Rhee to resign, but at a cost. One hundred and eighty students killed and thousands wounded when police fired on the mass of protesters marching on the Blue House. As a first year University student, she was among the marchers. The blood and screams haunt her at night, but she rationalized the protest worked. It made changes, more were needed.

Parks regime so far has tempered its use of force. Students were arrested but let off with a small fine. Besides, April II wasn't calling for the overthrowing of the government, just changes for the good of the people and less dependence on the Americans. She didn't want Jung-hee or anyone arrested or injured. Jung-hee interrupted her thoughts, giggling as she spoke.

"Hyun-ae, you have a secret admirer."

"Why would you say that Jung-hee?"

"When we were sitting out front having tea the other day, this handsome guy was watching you. He looked older, but dressed like a student. Maybe he is shy. I've seen him here occasionally. He always sits where he can watch you without being obvious."

Hyun-ae almost let out a gasp but caught herself. How did Jung hee spot him?

"If he's not being obvious, how do you know he is watching me?" Hyun-ae said.

"My sixth sense kicked in and I caught him glancing at you more than once."

"He probably is some bastard from the government trying to find a reason to arrest me."

Jung-hee extended her arms as if to be handcuffed. "He can arrest me anytime."

Hyun-ae laughed, Jung-hee was not traditional. She did not need a proper introduction if she wanted to meet a man. But April II's benefactor, Mr. Chung was getting careless. Why was he watching me? I've seen him here, but he always left as soon as we made eye contact. An uneasy feeling came over her as she thought of her next meeting with Chung. Was she getting in too deep?

MAJOR "SMOKE" GIBBONS

"Do your duty and a little more and the future will take care of itself."
Andrew Carnegie

Rimmer interrupted my daydreaming of my last days at home, partying and drinking beer on the shores of lake Erie.

"Sir! Another two klicks to Freedom Bridge. Farmers on the south side of the Imjin can work in the paddies until dusk. We have manned positions along the south bank of the river at night as a second line of defense. It is a waste of manpower. The positions are a couple hundred yards apart. At night, you could sneak a battalion of men between the positions. But who am I to say? It's not dangerous and ten times more boring than the DMZ." rimmer continued.

"Sir, we have to put on our flak jackets and helmets before we cross the bridge. Your flak jacket has to be zipped up or you'll catch hell."

Rimmer found a wider stretch of the road and pulled over. He jumped out of the jeep and flipped the windshield forward, snapping it in place. A couple of minutes later, we caught up to a stalled convoy. Rimmer stopped behind a quarter ton truck with eight men in the back. He stood up behind the steering wheel.

"Hey newbies, you are going to love your holiday in the sunny DMZ! You're looking at a short timer. I'll be back in the real world before you guys get used to the smell. Don't get your ass shot!" The GIs remained stoic. They didn't want to be in the back of that truck or going to where they were going. You would've expected at least one of them to make a wisecrack. The convoy started moving and turned before the bridge. A lone arm rose above the heads of the men in the truck. Perched on the arm was the universal bird, FUCK YOU. I chuckled. I would have done the same.

"Where are they headed?"

"To the 1/31, they're preparing to move north. Those men are replacements with no heart or soul. Did you see the look on their faces? They're still better off here than in Nam."

As we approached Freedom Bridge, two GIs dressed in full battle gear waved us through. Metal arches with a wooden plank floor made up the bridge construction.. We rumbled across as the planks flopped up and down. The north end of the bridge was protected with sandbagged positions. Everyone was wearing a flak jacket, helmet, and carrying a weapon. It was as if we went through a time warp, south of the bridge, pleasant scenery with farmers working the fields. On the north side, it appeared as if an attack was imminent. The hillside had a large redoubt.

"Rimmer, what's up on the hillside?"

"That's the 90 mm recoil-less rifle. We guard the bridge to prevent any sabotage. If the gooks tried to pull the 1950 shit again, the troops guarding the bridge need time to blow it."

We pulled into Camp Greaves, a fenced compound guarded with manned positions on each side of the gate. Several rows of concertina wire surrounded the compound. Other than the men manning the gate, there were few soldiers in sight. Rimmer pulled up in front of an unmarked quonset hut.

"Lieutenant, this is battalion headquarters. I will need the rifle, helmet, and flak jacket."

Rimmer hopped out of the jeep and unstrapped the duffel bag. From his side of the jeep, he stood the bag up on its end, making it easy for me to grab the canvas handle. He smiled and saluted.

"Good luck, Lieutenant! Thirteen months will be over before you know it."

I returned his salute with a smile.

"Thanks, Rimmer, for the ride and the briefing." As I was slapping the dust off my khaki's, the screen door to the headquarters banged shut. Walking towards me was a captain wearing a helmet, side arm and a flak jacket. Looking like a man in a hurry.

"I assume you're Lieutenant Reed?"

"Yes, sir," as I saluted.

He returned the salute, then extended his hand. "I'm Sanders battalion operations. Major Gibbons wants to see you." Nodding his head towards the door.

"He's in the office. I'd join you, but I need to go up to one of the forward positions. I'll catch you later. Nice to meet you." The front office was spartan, with a chair and an empty desk. There was a large floor fan humming away in the corner. A deep voice bellowed from a narrow hallway.

"Lieutenant!"

The mayor's office had paneled walls, a desk, and two chairs. The major stood as I walked in the room. A large, squared shouldered colored man. I stopped short of his desk and saluted.

"Lieutenant Reed reporting for duty."

"At ease, lieutenant. Welcome to the second of the twenty-third. I'm the battalion executive officer. Colonel Williams is at division headquarters for the day. How was the trip over the pond?"

"Long!"

"Get accustomed to it. You'll have many long days and nights. Have a seat."

"Yes, sir."

"Charlie company lacks a platoon leader. The CO is lieutenant Roseman, a West Point graduate and about to make captain. He is an excellent company commander and will get you off on the right foot. Charlie company mans the southern boundary of the DMZ, guard post Gladys and patrols. The platoon on GP Gladys needs a platoon leader."

"Sir, is the battalion on alert?"

"We're not! This is the normal state of readiness because of the recent attacks. No attacks over the past few weeks, that can change in an instant. One of the toughest aspects of this assignment is not to become complacent. You and your men will be on GP Gladys for a week at a time or on patrol. The North Koreans pick when they hit. There's no rhyme or reason to the timing of the attacks."

"The jeep driver said we can't give chase or fire across the MDL."

"He is right, lieutenant. The rules of engagement are convoluted. If a North Korea agent or soldier crosses the MDL, they're fair game. Shoot first and ask questions later. You can not fire on North Koreans if they're north of the MDL, even if they're shooting at you. You can return fire if it's absolutely necessary to cover your withdrawal. If a person is in the DMZ unarmed, you'll use your judgment whether the person is a defector or the enemy. There are no civilians north of the river. The North Koreans have beefed up their units. South Korean intelligence confirmed one unit is the elite 124th Regiment. They are trained to act as agents and or guerrillas. They use the DMZ to infiltrate or ex-filtrate South Korea. The 17th Foot Reconnaissance brigade supports them. The 17th is used to escort agents through the DMZ and to attack the ROK'S and the 2nd Division's positions. Last month B company from 1st of the 31st, the battalion to our east, trapped three of them. The North Koreans were well south of the MDL. The KUTUSA with the patrol tried to convince them to surrender, and they answered with bullets. One North Korean was killed, two made their way north, though one left a blood trail. Which unit they were from is unknown, but it shows they are tough and dedicated."

"Also, lieutenant, their weaponry is changing. Most of their weapons are Korean War vintage. The

ROK's got in a firefight and recovered two AK-47's. The rules of engagement are to be adhered to, no if and or buts, understand lieutenant?"

"Yes, Sir."

"I know it's a lot to lay on you, lieutenant, but Charlie company has a good cadre of non-com's and platoon leaders. Listen to them when they give you advice."

"Sir, when was the last time we made contact with the enemy?"

"Three weeks ago, a work party was cutting brush for better fields of fire north of the minefield. The patrol guarding the work party spotted three or four of the bastards. Apparently, they were on a scouting mission. A running fire fight ensued. Charlie company suffered one wounded. After the firefight, the QRF found crushed grass and a well-camouflaged hideout. It appeared they were there a couple of days."

"We have since changed our operations along the fence to foul up any intelligence they may have gathered. There are things we can't change, the fence and the lay of the land. One of our hurdles is accomplishing our mission while being short handed. Anything else, lieutenant?" "No sir." "Lieutenant Roseman and S-2 will brief you in more detail." The major continued talking as we walked out of the office.

"We have a month more duty on the DMZ before we rotate south. Enough time to get your feet wet. Charlie company is on the other side of the compound. Sergeant Gibbs will get someone to help you with your gear. It's 1400 hours, you should have enough time to be issued your gear and make the S-2 briefing. Charlie company moves up on the DMZ at 1900 hours." "Good luck, lieutenant." "Thanks, sir."

REVENGE

"In time we hate that which we fear." William Shakespeare

Comrade Colonel Choi, as commander of the 17th Foot Recon Brigade and the 124th Regiment, was going over the details of tonight's mission. The coolness of the underground bunker, five hundred meters north of the MDL, helped settle his nerves. He had a good feeling about tonight's attack and the recovery of Kim's team. The bunker was large enough to hold twelve men besides the Colonel and his aid. Wooden planks covered the floor. The walls were sandbags. A large table with chairs was in the center of the room. The wall at the end of the table held a large 1:25000 scale map of the DMZ, with stick pins of known American fixed positions. Blue hashes marked positions deemed easy targets because of terrain, time of reaction by reinforcements, and or easy withdrawal routes to the MDL. Red circles on the map showed areas the Americans patrolled.

Choi's intelligence section confirmed the American unit that killed Tae Song Su three weeks ago will patrol the same area tonight. The 2nd of the 23rd has been in the DMZ for several months. They were getting better at intercepting the forays of Choi's teams. He smiled as he recalled the number of infiltration and exfiltration his teams had completed. The Americans made few changes in the way they operated. Tonight, he will make them pay for Tae's death.

Choi's thoughts were on the after action briefing of Tae's team. He concluded bad luck came into play in the encounter that led to Tae being killed. Tonight was their opportunity to take revenge, one of his best team leaders and the son of a high ranking communist party member.

He was getting pressure from General Kwak to increase the number of operations and inflict more casualties on the Americans. A successful mission will relieve the pressure. Kim and his team were to return from Seoul with Chung and, along the way, attack an American position along the fence. The 124th will attack the American patrol in the DMZ, creating a diversion.

Chung has become a concern for the party. Kim's mission was to return Chung or eliminate the party's concern. After several years in the south, Chung had deviated from his assignment.

Choi checked the time. The fine Russian Vostok watch was a comfortable weight on his wrist. It was beautiful, yet a rugged, stainless steel timepiece designed for the military elite. The party gave him the watch in recognition of his leadership. He wondered if he failed. Would the Supreme leader want the watch back? Maybe with his arm attached? The men filed in for the briefing.

MORGAN ASHFORTH

"As iron sharpens iron, so a friend sharpens a friend." King
Solomon

"First sergeant, I'm Lieutenant Reed. Major
Gibbons sent me."

First Sergeant Jackson, puffing on a cigar, gave
me a once over as he leaned back in his chair. He
then stood and extended his hand. "Welcome to
Charlie company. We got the call you were coming.
Lieutenant Roseman is on his way. Ah, here he
comes now."

A jeep skidded to a stop outside Charlie company's
headquarters. The short skid created a cloud of dust
with enough momentum to reach the screen door.
First Sergeant Jackson crunched down on his cigar
and stomped out of the door.

"RAMERISZ, the next time a speck of goddamn
dust comes in the door from your damn jeep, I'll
have your goddamn ass and use it as a fucking dust
mop. Take your goddamn foot off the goddamn gas
pedal!"

Ramerisz sheepishly replied. "Sorry Sarge."

"Sorry ass is more like it. Take the lieutenant's gear
to his hooch. He'll be up after the CO finishes with
him."

Lieutenant Roseman walked into the office,
knowing his driver would get an ass chewing. The

company commander walked across the room with the air of authority. He removed his helmet and put it under his left arm, resting it above the holstered .45 caliber pistol. The helmet hid a shorter than short crew cut; the dust covered face broke into a smile. We shook hands. "Welcome to Charlie company. When did you get in country?"

"About six hours ago, sir."

"Reed, we are both lieutenants and I go by Rosie when the men aren't around. What about you?"

"Mike."

"Mike, you can get a shower and change into fatigues at your hooch. Rosie pointed to a hut on the side of the hill. Meet me back here in an hour. We can go over to the armorer and supply, get your gear, then chow before the briefing."

The quonset hut was dingy on the outside and stark on the inside. It was separated into four cubicles and a common area. Each cubicle contained a bed, desk, small table, foot locker and rack to hang your clothes. In the center of the hooch, a couple of threadbare stuffed chairs were positioned around a fifty-gallon drum converted into a heating unit. Clothes were hanging from the rack in three cubicles. Ramerisz had placed my duffel bag in the empty cubicle. On the rack there were a couple of towels and washcloths. The warm shower felt great as it washed off the grim. My fatigues had not left my duffel bag since OCS. The laundry at Fort Benning used so much starch, it felt like your fatigues were made of cardboard. They looked too clean and formal. Anticipation overtook my fatigue. I was looking forward to the rest of the day.

I met up with Rosie. We walked over to the armory. The armorer issued the basic gear, a steel pot, flak jacket, M-14 with bayonet, eight loaded magazines, web gear and a .45 caliber 1911 Colt. The armorer explained they issue grenades just before you leave on patrol. As I was being issued my gear, Rosie filled me in on Charlie's company's mission in the DMZ.

"Mike, we need a platoon leader for the third platoon. They're out on GP Gladys, they're returning tomorrow. Sergeant Hicks is leading the platoon, one of our best platoon sergeants."

"Is the platoon up to full strength?"

"Hell no, you'll have between 35 and 37 men. We are not near full strength because of."

"Yea I know, Nam."

"Lets go get some chow."

The mess hall was in a large quonset hut. There were three rows of tables, each covered with a blue and white checked oilcloth. The tables ran the same direction as the rectangle hut, with seating for about forty-five men. At the end of the three rows, there were tables and chairs facing the blue checked covered tables. Major Gibbons sat in the center. Two lieutenants sat several empty chairs from the majors right.

The men began filing in, picking up metal trays and moving through the chow line. Rosie motioned for me to take a seat.

"We wait till the men get their chow before we

eat."

When I got to my seat, Rosie introduced me. "Reed, Morgan Ashforth, known as Mo. The guy next to him is Mueller the battalion S-2 and, of course, you met Major Gibbon's."

I nodded before sitting. Neither of them offered their hands. We made some small talk. Mueller was a graduate of Clemson and ROTC. He had been in the country for eight months. Recently promoted to first lieutenant and battalion S-2. Ashforth piped up when he heard Mueller mentioned he went to Clemson.

"GO GAMECOCKS! We kicked stripes right off the ass of the so-called Tigers of Clemson in 1964."

"Seven to three is hardly an ass kicking."

"What do you mean, you didn't get a first down till the second half? I ran for over a hundred yards."

"Only because I wasn't on the field."

"Screw you Mueller."

The major interrupted.

"Hey Clemson and SCU, rivals in school are okay, on the same team here, RIGHT!

In unison, "Yes sir." Morgan Ashforth looked at me. He spoke loud enough for the major to hear.

"We have teamwork. What needs changing is the rules of engagement. We got to be more aggressive and shoot the little fuckers north of the MDL. Gook bastards shoot us and get away with it."

The heads of the enlisted men turned, obviously interested.

The major was quick to respond. "Lieutenant!

I know the rules of engagement are frustrating. Screw up just once and your ass is out of here. You understand lieutenant!"

"Yes sir, sorry, sir."

Ashforth leaned on the table and whispered. "We need to pursue the little cocksuckers across the MDL, like the ROKs. The ROK's attacked a gooks outpost with an entire company. Rumor has it they killed a shit load of gooks."

Mueller added his two cents.

"Come on Mo, we don't need to start another fucking Korean war. The gooks want us to step up our response. Then they can ask for more aid from their buddies, the Russians or the Chinese. Do you want to give them an excuse to attack South Korea again? If Major Smoke hears you, your ass will be in a sling quicker than you can say jack shit."

"Fuck you, Mueller and the ass you rode in on. We have to fight with one hand tied behind our backs. The brass are in denial that there is a conflict. Men are dying. Just wait Reed. It won't take long before you see what I'm talking about."

I had to ask. "Who's Major smoke?"

Pointing his thumb to the left at Major Gibbons, Mo quipped.

"When you screw up, he will tear you a new asshole and leave you smoked and vaporized."

Rosie cut off the argument.

"Mo, cut Mike some slack. It's his first day in the country. Mo runs the best Quick Reaction Force in the division. You can count on him. Even if he is a jackass sometimes."

Mueller added, "Yea Mo, as in Curly, Larry and MO, what's this man's army coming to?"

Morgan chuckled, "Not only am I the fore-mentioned personality, but I am a spectacular officer, gentleman and a ladies' man."

Mueller mouthed. "Crazier than a shit house rat."

I couldn't picture "MO" as a general or a gentleman. At six feet tall, lean as Jimmy Stewart, a million-dollar smile, bright blue eyes, a ladies' man? Was he someone I wanted to get close to, or was he going to be a pain in the ass?

Rosie broke up the good nature ribbing. "Let's eat."

The chow wasn't half bad: meat loaf, fake mashed potatoes and beans washed down with bitter coffee. No vegetables from the Korean gardens.

IF NOTHING CHANGED

"There is nothing permanent except change." Heraclitus

Kim rubbed the side of his thigh, a bad habit he picked up when he was anxious. The dangerous part was about to start. In a couple of hours, they would move to thick cover to watch the GIs move into their positions along the fence. How they breached the fence depended on changes by the GIs. The Americans didn't occupy every foxhole during the day. They switched positions with no set schedule. At night, they occupied every foxhole which were fifty to seventy-five meters apart. Kim knew the GIs didn't patrol behind the foxholes. He needed to find a staging area to lie in wait till nightfall.

In the mountains to the north, at twenty-three hundred hours, lights will flash on and off with a message. If the Americans see the lights, they'll have no idea what they mean. The lights have been flashing at random every night for the past two months. There was a code if the mission was on. The lights eliminated the need for the radio, increasing their odds for success.

Kim knew he could count on Lee and Park. They needed luck and for the Americans to have kept the same routine. Kim's team was scouting the north side of the fence three months ago. For two days, from their concealed position, they watched GIs occupy the foxholes south of the fence. Tonight, they will use the information to attack the foxhole that guarded the gate to the path through the minefield.

The foxholes were forty to fifty meters behind the fence. They were permanent sandbagged positions occupied by three soldiers. The foxhole was T shaped, the top of the T facing the fence. The GIs covered the tail of the T with a piece of tin or wood large enough to escape the weather. Kim was thinking the GIs also took turns sleeping under the roof.

There was no barbed wire protecting the perimeter. They could get close enough to toss grenades. The next occupied foxhole was at least fifty meters away. The night promised to be moonless. At fifty meters, there's little probability the men in the foxholes could provide accurate supporting fire.

Kim looked at his watch. It was fifteen hundred hours. The riverside hideout has been quiet for several hours, no more American patrols. Kim tossed a stick at Lee and Park to get their attention, then motioned for them to crawl closer.

"Listen up. In five hours, we move up to the DMZ. After we find a suitable position, we'll wait for the GIs to go to their foxholes. Then make our final plans. Eat what food you have, check your weapons and grenades. You two rest, I'll watch."

Kim again reviewed every detail of the mission. The training was relentless. The team practiced a hundred times attacking a mock up foxhole.

Several times, they tossed live grenades into the foxhole. They ran countless times through a dummy minefield. Hopefully, nothing changed.

ON THE FENCE

The briefing room smelled of cigarette smoke and sweaty men. The oscillating fan pushed the smoke and smell over the sergeants and lieutenants. Rosie and I sat in the last row. Mo stood in the far corner behind us. Mueller was up front. The wall clock hands inched towards eighteen hundred hours. Mueller's nickname was "Mueller." As Rosie put it, the briefings were as boring as hell. Nothing changes, Mueller is Mueller. Mueller called out.

"Listen up!" The chatter died, chairs squeaked on the linoleum floor as the men took their seats..

"New reports of enemy contact. Last night, the ROK's had their hands full. At approximately twenty-three hundred hours, the gooks attacked with about one hundred men. The ROK's suffered five casualties, two KIA and three WIA. A heavy machine supported the attack. The ROK'S destroyed it with mortar rounds. The number of enemy casualties is unknown. The ROKs confirmed the last incident involved North Korea's 124th Regiment, an elite unit. We have yet to confirm the 124th is in our sector, but it's likely."

Mo shuffled up behind me. "That's what I meant. The ROK's don't put up with bullshit."

Mueller said it's only a matter of time before the enemy attacks the 2nd Divisions sector. It impressed nobody. Most of the men seemed preoccupied, they heard it before.

Mueller yelled at the top of his lungs. "A TEN HUT!" Everyone jumped to their feet, thinking a high-ranking officer just walked in the door behind them.

Mueller acknowledged the ruse. A few 'fuckin bullshits' were muttered.

"Sit, look men, it's been quiet in our sector, we can't just assume they will not hit us. You've to keep your men alert. Make sure they know we are up against North Korea's elite forces. The monsoon season will give more cover for gooks."

Mueller gave the weather report, chance of showers in the morning, then the password, call signs and the radio frequency.

"Questions?" Apparently not, as everyone stood up and filed out.

"Reed, stick around. I need to fill you in on a few details." Mueller asked.

"Lieutenant Roseman wanted to give me a tour of the fence."

"He can wait a few minutes. I'll give you a heads up what to expect and what's expected of you. The men have been listening to the same briefings for weeks, so you may not have been impressed by their attitude. The only thing that changes is the weather and I'm no goddamn weatherman. It's difficult to keep everyone razor sharp. You're green, right out of OCS. Your probability of fucking up is one hundred percent. How bad you fuck up is going to depend on you and how fast you learn."

Mueller's voice became louder and more intense as he spoke. Lieutenant Don Mueller was not a happy man. He volunteered for Vietnam, hoping to get combat experience and make the military a career. Instead, he got stuck here in a half assed pissing contest with the North Koreans..

Mueller continued.

"Right now the North Koreans are hitting the ROK's more than us."

"Why? I asked. Don't they see the United States as interfering, screwing them out of taking over the South?"

"They do, but it pissed them off. The ROKs sent a full combat division to Nam to fight against communism. Kim Ill Sung thinks North Vietnam should lead the way in fighting American Imperialism. South Korea shouldn't be interfering. South Korea sending troops to fight 'Uncle Ho' must have ticked Kim, the Supreme Leader, off and it may be his idea of a way of diverting American Troops away from Nam creating two fronts dividing our forces.

"Why the hush-hush? Nothing in the newspapers. At OCS, they said nothing. Fuck, is another war going to break out?"

"No Mike,what's going on here isn't a flea bite on a horse's ass, compared to Nam. We have four or five casualties in a month, in Nam they have twenty a day. You'll never see a reporter anywhere near the DMZ. It's not gruesome enough and besides, Division wants this shit kept quiet. You need to know we're putting up a fence along the entire southern boundary of the DMZ. It's not a deterrent, but it helps. We still have instances where they cut the fence and get through undetected. The little fuckers are good. You'll see what I mean when Rosie gives you the tour. No matter how you cut it, the entire DMZ is a sieve. US forces man eighteen of the 160 mile DMZ with a brigade."

"What weapons are we up against?"

"Small arms, grenades. The gooks are still using Korean War vintage weapons. Their weapon of choice has been submachine guns equipped with a drum magazine. We follow the Armistice agreement, no automatic weapons or artillery support; operations in the DMZ are supposed to be conducted with platoon size units or smaller. The ROKs don't obey the rules.

There were twelve firefights in the last six months. Eight GIs killed, six in one firefight last November, and fourteen wounded. Not one enemy body to show for it. The ROK's killed thirty-nine gooks. I'm believing the North Koreans attack the ROKs to punish them and leave us alone so they can infiltrate through our sector. A lot more is going on in our sector than we know."

"Why not use more troops?"

"I don't know Reed, it's above my pay grade. Listen up, when you're in the DMZ, you must know the location of the MDL. It's an imaginary line running through the center of the DMZ. You can not cross it. Right after the Armistice in '53', they marked it. Since then, we have done nothing to update the markings. If you don't know how to read a map, and find yourself north of the MDL, you are fucked!. The terrain is rugged and in the summer you have to deal with dense undergrowth. Two thousand meters is the distance between the southern boundary and the MDL. The battalion is stretched out just over five miles along the DMZ."

"How long do the patrols stay out?"

"Twenty-four to forty-eight hours. Another thing, there are minefields left over from the Korean war. They're marked on the maps. Avoid those areas. There's no guarantee we recovered all the mines. The unmarked minefields are the real problem." Mueller explained.

"How many of those?"

"We don't know."

"We find them after a heavy rain or frost heave."

"Do the gooks use booby traps?" I asked.

"NO, not so far. Mike, the battalion mans three guard posts, Charlie company mans Gladys. It's a hundred meters south of the MDL. You and your platoon will sit there for a week observing the North Koreans. They have a GP five hundred meters to the northeast of Gladys. You watch the gooks and they watch you. You're to report any unusual activity. The high-powered optics at the GP allow you to see well beyond the DMZ. At night, occasionally, the gooks get close enough to the GP's perimeter to toss grenades. It happened three times in the last two months. Duty in the DMZ is not a cakewalk, but it's not Nam. Questions?"

I pointed to the railroad symbol on the map as I asked.

"Is there a railroad in the DMZ?"

"The railroad tracks were removed right after the war. There's a bombed out locomotive in the middle of Charlie company's area of operation. If no other questions, I'll see you at breakfast tomorrow."

I left the room, not knowing what to think. Maybe I should have stayed at Division and played football. This shit is for real, Seattle to Seoul to the DMZ in less than twenty-four hours. Rifle, ammo, grenades, loaded for bear! Rosie was waiting in the jeep.

"Mike, get in, we will head over to B company. Their tower is on a hill. You'll get a better view of the countryside."

From the compound, it was a scant mile over a dusty road. High brush bordered the road on either side. I kept a tight grip on my rifle, with thoughts of being ambushed. Rosie and the driver talked baseball.

"Rosie, do the gooks ever ambush vehicles south of the DMZ?" I asked.

"Occasionally, mostly in the ROK sector. We sweep areas south the DMZ and around the compounds."

We pulled up to Bravo company's tower, which was flanked by a ten foot high chain linked fence, topped with barbed wire. On both sides of the fence, ground cover was non-existent, fifty meters to the north and twenty meters to the south, just an ugly orangish dirt. The barren ground north of the fence was a minefield. Rosie explained the engineers sprayed a defoliant each spring.

The fifteen foot tall tower was on a knoll which allowing a commanding view along the fence and out into the DMZ. At the bottom, the supporting posts were surrounded by sandbags, creating a three man fighting position. The tower was occupied by the company commander and a sergeant.

Rosie and I climbed the ladder to the tower. The platform was ten feet by ten. The walls and roof consisted of heavy planks and sandbags. The four sides were open at chest level for firing and viewing.

"Captain, Mike Reed, my new platoon leader, Mike, Captain Mitch Sanders."

"Welcome lieutenant, don't be afraid to ask questions." Sanders said.

I could see a tank in a dug out position.

"Thanks Captain, I noticed there's a tank behind us."

"We equip the tank with one hell of a big searchlight. We have pre-arranged aiming points for the light. I can radio the tank and ask them to light up a specific point, then adjust the light."

The captain turned and nodded towards the corner, saying.

"By the way, this is Sergeant Bill Graser. Usually he's out with a patrol. Bravo's sector and Charlie's company sectors butt up against each other."

"Pleased to meet you Sarge."

He nodded back.

"I'm thinking it's a good thing the sarge is on our side. He looked to be at least six foot six of solid muscle."

Rosie walked to a small table and pointed to a spot on a laminated map.

"Mike, look to the left. You can see the Imjin river a klick away. Where it bends out of sight, the far side is North Korea. The MDL ends at the river's edge. The gooks try to cross there occasionally, but increased patrols have closed the route. On the right, Charlie companies sector starts two klicks from here. B company mans GP Beryl, but because of the trees and terrain you can't see it. You can see GP Gladys, using the binoculars."

Rosie pointed in a northeast direction. In the distance, I could see a hill with a flattened top.

"That lonely looking dirt pile is going to be your first assignment."

I used the binoculars to look further north.

"What's those white buildings farther to the north?"

"They supposedly house civilians. We call it propaganda village. The village is five klicks in front of Gladys. With the big spotting scope on Gladys, you can watch the so-called civilians. They're dressed in white uniforms, so the guards can keep a better eye on them if they try to defect. They work in the fields.

"Do the civilians get close to the MDL?"

"The guards keep them at least four or five

hundred meters away."

"Rosie, as I understand it, we prohibit South Korean civilians north of the river."

"That's correct. Back to the buildings. We believe they house men from the 124th Regiment. A month ago, Sergeant Hicks, your platoon sergeant, observed an unusually large number of white garbed North Koreans in the fields. They were cutting brush, apparently preparing a new rice paddy. Hicks thought it was strange, so he counted the number of workers.When the column of so-called farmers marched back, Hicks counted only seventy. We know the missing thirty one didn't defect. They used the ruse to get more men on their GP."

"For what?"

"Who the fuck knows? They know we have eyes on them. They are just messing with us, making us think something is going to happen. Out on Gladys, you will get a dose of psychological warfare. They use loudspeakers to broadcast their propaganda in Korean and not so good English."

"Do we have speakers?"

"No. The gooks do it on a calm night, and the sound carries. It's spooky. You're lying there in an ambush with six or seven men. It's pitch black, you're armed to the teeth, listening hard for the slightest crack of a twig or the rustle of grass. Then a foreign sounding voice cuts through the stillness, telling you to go home, defect or you will die in the DMZ. They say other shit and play music."

"The Beatles, singing Penny Lane?" I jokingly

said.

"Let's go Reed, it's getting late."

Trying to be funny went over like a fart in church.

The road to tower five ran parallel to the fence. As we rode along, men with rifles slung over their shoulders were stringing out along the fence, going to their night position. As the sun started its slow descent toward the horizon, I could a coolness washed over my sweat damp fatigues. My rifle across my lap, locked and loaded, felt reassuring. Charlie company's tower Five was the same as the one we just left. There were four men under the tower. There was no saluting, just a nod and a Hi lieutenant directed at Rosie.

We climbed the ladder. To the left, a large gate allowed vehicles to pass. The dirt road headed straight into the DMZ. I noticed there was no tank.

"Rosie, how come no tank?"

"There are not enough tanks for every tower.

"Where does the road go?"

"That's the one and only road to GP Gladys."

In the tower, a large spotting scope pointed north. Beside it was a loaded M-60 machine. In the corner were two PRC-25 radios, their flexible antenna folded and secured with tape. Guarding the equipment was Sergeant Jackson, chomping on a short ragged cigar, probably the same one from this afternoon.

"Hi Sarge."

"Lieutenant, your first day in country. What do

ya think?" He lifted his head and blew a puff of smoke towards the ceiling.

"I don't think anyone could guess what the DMZ was like. It's night and day compared to south of the river."

"You got that right, lieutenant." Jackson said as he blew out a ring of smoke.

"Rosie spoke.

"The two radios are for the battalion net and company net. Each foxhole has a radio. We have no night vision devices. We rely on flares. You can secure your rifle in the corner. The fields of fire are designated by the small posts nailed to the wall. We do not fire our weapon between those posts as they line up with the foxholes. If something happens, you will handle the flares. Sarge will man the M-60. Pop the flares towards the shooting and keep them coming till I tell you to stop. Got it?"

"Yes, Sir."

"You learn to pop flares in OCS?"

"Yes sir, Flare 101, the M127A1 white star parachute flare, 125,000 candle power, seven hundred feet of elevation.."

The illumination flares were easy to use. Remove the top, put it on the bottom and give it a hard rap with the palm of your hand. Sarge chuckled and gave me a thumbs up. As Rosie spoke.

"Ok wise ass, make sure you point the damn thing away from the overhang. I don't need one of those lighting up the tower. If the shit hits the fan, make sure you know where everything is. There's no light switch. There are more flares on the shelf."

I turned in the direction Rosie was pointing. Near the shelf there was a folded army cot. I forgot how tired I was. The effect of the strong mess hall coffee was wearing off. Rosie caught my glance at the cot.

"The cot is available, we take turns. Sarge and I will take the first watch. You can sack out for a couple of hours."

"Okay, but I'll to wait a while."

"Suit yourself."

"Rosie, as I pointed to the M-60 machine gun. I thought automatic weapons were banned in the DMZ?"

" We're not in the DMZ. We're on the southern boundary."

The sunset was a spectacular array of orange, yellow to purple to dark gray. Long rays of the sun stretched the shadows of the uneven terrain across the minefield, creating pockets of darkness. The sun set quickly, sliding behind the distant mountains to the west. The men in the foxholes faded into the darkness. A couple of birds to our rear were chattering, either complaining about it getting dark or happy they made it through another day.

The dusk turned to a dark I had yet to experience. The only light was the millions of stars. By twenty-two hundred hours, you literally couldn't see your hand in front of your face. It was eerie. The birds had gone silent. The only sound were the whispered voices from the foxholes making their radio checks.

"Foxhole charlie all quiet, out" "squirrel hole all

quiet," "sierra doing fine, out" "groundhog, ready for another long night." And then the unauthorized SHORRRRT!! A term I heard a dozen times since crossing Freedom bridge. Rosie pointed the flashlight's red filtered light towards the cot.

"Lieutenant, get some sleep. It's going to be a long night. I'll wake you at 0200 hours. If anything is going to happen, it usually does between then and 0500 hours."

I stretched out on the cot. My god, it felt good. The last thing I remembered was looking into pure darkness, wondering if I should remove my flak jacket.

FOXHOLE CHARLIE

"Man always dies before he is fully born." Erich Fromm

Kim's team moved up behind the foxhole they were going to attack. They crawled the last fifty meters, leaving three snake-like trails through the dusty soil. They could have been slithering through mud if the monsoons had started. They reached a small knoll that provided concealment. It was forty meters behind the GIs position guarding their escape route. Two other positions, one to the east, seventy-five meters away and the other to the west at sixty meters, were occupied. The set up was the same as when Kim scouted the route months earlier.

Kim watched as two GIs sat on the edge, then slid off the sandbags into the chest deep T shaped foxhole. The third GI stood outside the foxhole, took his helmet off, and set it on the edge. He stood with his rifle in the crook of his arm, smoking a cigarette. He was looking out across the minefield when he suddenly turned and stared at the knoll. It was a long look, Kim whispered.

"Slide back slowly." Each man inched backwards. Kim stayed as a clump of grass provided a straw curtain to observe. The GI took a long drag on his cigarette. His last, Kim thought, tossed it to the ground, then stomped on it before jumping into the foxhole. One man went to the north end of the foxhole and set his rifle on top of the sandbags. The other two were standing in the back corner talking. Kim motioned for Lee and Park to join him. It was time to go over the plan. Two magpies started their raspy chattering in a nearby tree. Keeping a low profile, Lee motioned with his thumb towards the birds.

"Kim, hear that. Good luck is upon our mission. The magpies talk to us, saying we'll have success."

"Lee, you still believe in superstitions?" Kim asked. Park laughed softly.

"Lee's right, those birds are making fun of the Americans and their carelessness."

"Enough about birds. We have to go over our plan. Lee will cut the lock on the gate. Give your grenades to Park. Park and I will crawl close enough to the foxhole to throw grenades. I don't want to fire our weapons unless absolutely necessary. Lee, you'll follow us till we get to the small depression. Follow it to the fence. As long as we stay on our bellies, they'll not see us. Lee remains at the fence until we throw the first grenade. Then cut the lock. Remember, the gate swings out. You'll be the first through the gate. We've got to assume the route through the minefield is the same."

"I hope I can cut the lock."

"You are better at using the bolt cutter than Park or me, you'll do fine. Cushion everything you are carrying, no noise."

As darkness overtook the knoll, the two magpies had moved to a small tree behind the GIs. They let out a fusillade of squawks and shrieks. Another bird must have invaded their territory.

****

PFC Tom Boyer had been in the country only two weeks and he didn't like it. When he got orders for Korea instead of Nam, he was thrilled. His platoon sergeant back at Fort Polk told him Korea would be a breeze. Boyd could picture the sarge grinning as he exclaimed, "Boyd, screw up in Korea and they will send you to Nam. It's an easy tour if you play your cards right.

The night was going to be long. He was tired, four hours of guard duty earlier today, little sleep last night. Some fuckin cake walk. Boyer slid into the foxhole. Specialist McElroy, the man in charge, trying to make sergeant, barked at Boyer.

"Put your goddamn helmet on and get up to the front. You and Cook are on watch till 0200 and you better not go fucking night, night on me. The sarge said they spotted gooks heading towards the river early this morning, near the bridge."

"Come on Mac! We hear that shit all the time and nothing happens."

"Keep your shit wired tight Boyer, you haven't been here long enough to mouth off."

Boyer thought, what a bunch of shit. Here he was in a foxhole named Charlie with a rifle, and a real chance of getting shot. It was dark. Cook was barely five feet away, whispering a radio check. He could barely make out the vague form of a human, and it was going to get darker. If it wasn't for the radio checks and the soft clink from the sling on the M-14's, he would feel alone.

Boyer tried to check his watch, but it was too dark. The next time he got to a PX, he told himself that he was going to buy a watch with a luminous dial. It had to be after midnight. Heavy clouds had moved in and now it was even darker. It was as dark as the inside of the cave in Kentucky. Boyer's thoughts drifted back to eight years ago. Cousin Billy had taken him and two friends to explore a cave he had discovered. Billy was three years older.

Billy and his two friends had flashlights. The cave was unknown to local residents. Billy stumbled on it, hunting for arrowheads in the brushy hillside. The opening was small. They had to get on their hands and knees to get through the narrow passageway. At first, he was scared. After crawling several feet, the cave opened into a large chamber. Boyer was amazed at the large stalagmites and the echoing laughter. The sound of their voices ping-ponged off the walls forever. They took turns yelling cuss words, laughing as FUCK, FUCK, FUCK, fuck, fuck bounced off the walls and faded away.

The dancing beams from the flashlights and laughter made Boyd feel at ease. He was having fun. The fun suddenly turned to sheer terror. Billy and his friends had drifted off just a few feet, then turned off their flashlights and stood perfectly still. Boyd screamed as he had never screamed, so terrified he pissed his pants and started bawling. After what seemed an eternity, the flashlights came back on. Billy and his friends ribbed him about his wet pants.

His cousin realized they were in trouble if they went back to the house with Boyd's piss soaked pants. Billy convinced his parents they waded the creek. Boyd and his cousin became closer as the years passed, he missed Billy. Cousin Billy stepped on a mine last year in Vietnam.

Time passed slowly. Boyer was about to ask Cook for the time when he heard a noise. What made it or how far away he couldn't tell. It was a soft noise, a rustle. Like someone swiping their hand across a piece of fabric. A breeze stirred. There it was again. The breeze and rustling sound didn't fit. The hair stood up on the back of Boyd's neck. God, it's got to be something or SOMEBODY, real close. Just as he uttered the name of his buddy, COOK! he heard the thud as a grenade landed inside the foxhole. After the flashes from three more explosions, Boyd and his buddies were dead. They never fired a shot. Boyd's last fleeting thought, he was back in the cave with his cousin and he pissed his pants again.

****

"Reed, wake the fuck up!"
"I'm up what th…"
"Flares, get the flares."

Flares popped from the positions flanking Charlie. Intense white light pierced the black sky. The M-60 machine manned by Sergeant Jackson began its ear-splitting rattling, the sound resonating off the tower ceiling. I was up and popped the first flare in the direction Sergeant Jackson was firing. My eyes followed the arc of the tracers from the M-60. I could see three silhouettes sprinting through the minefield. The tracers were desperately trying to catch them. The three shadowy figures suddenly melted in the darkness as they dropped into the ravine at the edge of the minefield. I popped another flare. Sergeant Jackson continued to fire, the tracers ricocheting in a vain attempt to find a target. Flares continued to pop as the firing stopped from the foxholes.

The M-60 stopped firing. The empty brass clinked as it rolled around on the floor of the tower. Rosie was on the radio's one mike in each hand. A large flare suddenly lit up the sky beyond the minefield. Apparently, he called for the mortar platoon to fire flares. The enemy had disappeared. It was over in a matter of seconds.

The flares drifting across the sky, the tracers, was I dreaming, it was surreal. The roar of the QRF's personnel carriers' diesel engines interrupted my thoughts. Here comes the cavalry!

The radio calls to foxhole Charlie went unanswered. "Rakin Ramsey, this is SQUIRREL HOLE, OVER."

Rosie replied, "go ahead squirrel, over."

"CHARLIE TOOK A DIRECT HIT WITH FOUR OR FIVE GRENADES!"

"Stay put squirrel, the QRF is on its way."

Just as another mortar flare went off, all hell broke loose further out in the DMZ with the thump of grenades and intense automatic weapons and rifle fire. The radio carrying the company frequency relayed the unnerving words, "RANKIN RAMSEY, RANKIN RAMSEY, WE ARE UNDER ATTACK, WE ARE TWO HUNDRED METERS WEST OF RP SNAKE BITE. NEED HELP!"

The frantic call was from a Hunter Killer patrol on ambush near the MDL. Mo's voice responded. "This is a flamethrower. We are on our way."

"Rankin Ramsey, we are going through the gate, eta in about a minute."

Sergeant Jackson yelled to the men under the tower. "Open the gate, QRF on the way."

The fighting continued out near the MDL. The APCs roared through the opened gate, their blackout lights casting a slit of light across the dirt road. Flares continued to light up the fence. Foxhole Charlie did not not answer the radio calls.

Rosie was back on the radio. "Squirrel and groundhog, over."

"This is squirrel over."

"This is groundhog over."

"The QRF is going to aid the patrol. We'll use the jeep to get to Charlie. More mortar flares are on the way. Do you copy?"

"Squirrel copy."

"Groundhog, affirmative."

Rosie was on the ladder. "Grab your gear Reed. You're coming with me."

The driver was manning the sandbagged position under the tower, as was a medic. The driver and the medic were in the jeep. I got in the back with the medic.

Rosie didn't finish the sentence before the jeep was barreling down the road to Charlie. "Mike, meet specialist Moss, soon to be your medic."

Mortar flares lit up the road to the foxhole. I gripped my rifle, thinking we're dead meat if there were gooks in the brush. We were at foxhole Charlie within minutes of the attack. The flares were lighting up the overhead. The four of us exited the jeep and cautiously half ran, walked towards foxhole Charlie.

The light of the flares extended our shadows. The driver moved off to our right and dropped to a knee, his rifle at the ready, watching behind the foxhole providing security. Heavy fighting continued deep in the DMZ. We didn't know what to expect.

THEY DIDN'T FIRE A SHOT

"No evil can happen to a good man, either in life or after death."
Plato

Rosie and I stopped at the edge. The medic jumped into the dark trench. He identified the first man as Specialist McElroy. Below me, I saw the top half of one man. His body slumped against the wall of sandbags. I laid my rifle on the edge and slid into the foxhole. Rosie went to the left. I put my hand on his neck for a pulse. There was none. A mortar flare drifted overhead, and I saw why the soldier's pulse stopped. The grenade landed next to his legs. As the flare drifted away, the darkness covered what was left of the soldier's body. Medic Moss moved towards me. More flares continued to pop, casting an eerie light on the anguished face of Rosie and Moss.

"He's dead Moss."

"He is private Boyer."

"Private Boyer is dead."

Rosie spoke.

"Specialist Cook is dead as well."

Moss screamed in disbelief. "THEY'RE ALL DEAD? FUCKIN' DEAD, DEAD DEAD! THEY DIDN'T HAVE A CHANCE, THIS IS FUCKED UP, THREE MEN DEAD AND FOR WHAT!"

It was a long and macabre night. Moss didn't want to move the bodies out of the foxhole till daylight. He arranged each soldier's body in a dignified pose.

The medic and Rosie did what they had to do. Rosie was on the radio talking to battalion, Sergeant Jackson and the QRF.

Dawn broke, with the battleship gray clouds hanging over the DMZ like a lid on a pot. Two magpies behind us were chattering away as they dive bombed a third bird. Two against one wasn't fair. Feathers were flying. Man, beast, and bird weren't safe in the DMZ.

I looked down at Boyer, who was a few feet to my left. Moss had placed Boyer's arms across his chest. His thigh bone showed through his shredded pants covered in purple black blood. A boot laid off to the side with part of his leg still in the boot. Boyer's rifle was still lying on top of the sandbags, pointing north. He never fired a shot. Cook and McElroy's did not fire their weapons, no empty brass in the foxhole. Rosie called out.

"Mike, take men from the tower and sweep around the foxhole. See if you can locate where the bastards were hiding. Start on the knoll behind us."

Before I responded, an APC, followed by a jeep, was heading for us. Rosie called out.

"It's the colonel and the QRF."

"Mike, hold tight till we find out what the Colonel wants to do."

Colonel Williams vaulted from the jeep and walked to the foxhole. He gave Rosie and me an angry, hard look. It felt as if I was guilty for not protecting the men. I couldn't imagine how or what Rosie was feeling. The colonel sat on the edge of the foxhole and slid to the bottom. For a second time, I looked at Boyer's shattered body. The colonel squatted and gently reached inside Boyer's collar and slid the chain through his hand until grasped the taped together dog tags.

"Who is this man?"

Moss, who was standing in the foxhole next to the colonel, said.

"PFC Thomas Boyer, the other two are Specialist David Cook and Jim McElroy, sir."

The colonel was standing with a clenched fist resting on top of the sandbags. When he addressed Rosie, his look had softened.

"Lieutenant Roseman, send a squad to recon between here and the river. I'm sending the QRF back into the DMZ to see what they can find. The bastards got away as slick as a whistle. Have Boyer, McElroy and Cook transported back to battalion. A debriefing is at battalion at 1100 hours. I need as much information as possible for the briefing."

"Yes, sir."

The sweep to the river was uneventful. We found several depressions in the dusty soil that were GI or gook footprints. On the small knoll behind the foxhole we found matted grass, but nothing positive to say who or what caused it. The sons of bitches were ghosts. Dark ghosts, the eerie images of three figures darting through the minefield still fresh in my mind.

****

Kim and his men reduced their pace to a slow, halting walk after climbing out of the ravine. He didn't want to run into a patrol. They were lucky, scurrying through the minefield, tracers hit around them. Maybe the luck of the magpies helped, though he'll never admit it to Park or Lee. Small trees and brush provided cover as they moved north.

Colonel Choi's diversionary attack was perfectly timed. It sent the GIs away from Kim and his men. The heavy fighting died down. Kim could hear the growl of the armored vehicles going to the beleaguered patrol several hundred meters to their east.

The 17th Foot Recon Brigade must have withdrawn when they heard the armored vehicles approaching. Kim and his men had only a short distance to travel to the command bunker. Part of the mission was a success, but without Chung, Kim didn't know what to expect.

THE BRIEFING

The clock above the large wall map ticked towards 1300 hours. Line company officers and battalion staff started filing in the Division headquarters for the emergency briefing. Captain Hunt, the 2nd Division's G-2 staff officer, stepped to the podium and shouted out over the din.

"Gentlemen, take a seat. The General will be here momentarily."

A murmur drifted through the room. Colonels, Majors and several Captains made up the staff officers of the 3rd brigade and its battalions. They continued to stand, talking, until Colonel Williams quietly started directing the junior officers to take a seat. Captain Hunt watched the men as they moved to their chairs. Most of them, he knew, few of the staff officers had combat experience.

He knew platoon leaders with combat experience made good company commanders and captains commanding companies in combat made damn good staff officers. This group of staff officers will have a difficult time understanding why a soldier falls asleep on ambush or fires a hundred rounds and not hit an enemy soldier. Hunt knew it was his job to convince the men that North Koreans were a tough and tenacious enemy.

He may make his point because of the three

men killed this morning. The 2nd Division's latest casualties made it eleven killed and fifteen wounded. The Roks had three times the number of wounded and killed. It's not a hot war by Vietnam's standards, but the fighting continues to escalate. It was demoralizing. Not one enemy soldier had been killed by American forces. There were blood trails in two recent firefights. But not one body we could, figuratively, throw on the table at Panmunjom. The gook bastards at Panmunjom continue to deny the attacks.

Hunt thought back to his 1965 his tour in Nam. Korea was similar. As the battalion intelligence, he spent weeks in the bush of Pleiku Providence, speaking with the head honchos of the villages, trying to get a handle on the political view of the people. An AVRN platoon accompanied him and his RTO as security. Contact with the Viet Cong was sporadic. Hunt thought about Ronnie, his radioman. Ronnie never firing a shot in anger.

As they neared the village so that they could speak to the head honcho. Shots rang out, and he and Ronnie hit the dirt. When he looked over at his radioman, he was face down and not moving. Lying between them was Ronnie's helmet with a neat quarter-inch hole in the front. At nineteen, he was too young to die.

They fired hundreds of rounds at the enemy, no other causalities inflicted on themselves or the enemy. The AVRN had their battle for the day, they withdrew. The AVRN officer said the village was too hot, "all Viet Cong." So they pulled back with no retribution for Ronnie. They withdrew because the ARVN didn't have the will to fight.

But Korea was different. Hunt had the sense the Korean people rejected communism. They felt good and respected the Americans. The ROKs were excellent soldiers. It will be difficult for the North Koreans to gain a foothold. Hunt was jolted back to the briefing room when someone called out.

"AT TEN HUT!" Everyone jumped to their feet. General Izenour walked to the podium. He wasn't an imposing, bigger than life general, more of a stout businessman in fatigues. He may not of looked the part, but he had earned the respect of his subordinates. His acts of leadership and valor in North Africa and Anzio may have earned him his general stars, but his devotion to his men and ability to get things done won him the respect of his men.

The General scanned the room before speaking. "Gentlemen, please sit. The following is part of a communique from Eighth Army Headquarters and forwarded to the Pentagon."

"I quote, *Actions along the DMZ are increasing with planned, small-scale attacks. Firefights are occurring almost every night. Last night, three US soldiers were killed. This year to date along the DMZ: fire fights 69; NKs 64 KIA, 2 captured; ROK/US 35 KIA, 87 WIA, unquote. In the last few weeks, the North Koreans are improving their kill ratio.*"

"To expand on those numbers, including attacks south of the DMZ, year to date, one hundred thirty-two firefights, of which sixty-three occurred south of the DMZ. In1966, there were thirty firefights in the entire country. It's only July, and the number has doubled. Casualties numbers are worse. The ROK suffered most of the casualties. In 1966, there were seventy-three WIA and KIAs between U.S. forces and ROK'S. This year to date, two hundred and fifty casualties. North Korea's known casualties, one hundred and forty-six."

Captain Hunt, standing at the map board, flipped an overlay. Marked in red, were the location of the firefights. The General continued.

"The North Koreans don't intend to start another conventional war. They are increasing infiltrations by sea and through the DMZ, intending to destabilize the government through sabotage and assassinations. We are making it difficult to infiltrate as we continue erecting the fence and improving radar along the coast. Units will undergo intensive counter insurgency training before moving to the DMZ. A platoon from each company will conduct hunter killer patrols. There will be fewer restraints regarding the rules of engagement."

Colonel Williams raised his hand. "General, will the training be at Camp Casey, and how long?"

"Yes, Camp Casey and four weeks of training. One more thing before I turn it over to the Captain. The big picture gentlemen is we must react to these intrusions by the North Koreans in a controlled manner. The fear is that North Korea will continue to escalate the attacks along the DMZ, underestimating the South's response. If the ROKs were to conduct a large scale attack in retaliation, North Korea's reaction could spiral out of control. "

"We know the communist are increasing their agent network in the south. They'll continue to use the DMZ and the sea to infiltrate, ex-filtrate. We think Pyongyang's has expectations are of starting a 'people's' war by spending material and manpower to upset the political stability. The North Koreans want to expand their subversive capabilities. They're betting on turmoil in South Korean politics."

"Our part will be to increase our effectiveness, limit our casualties, and inflict more hurt on the enemy. We want to make it costly for them to cross the MDL. This needs to be done without starting another war. Captain Hunt will give the details on last night's attack, along with the specifics on training, changes to improve our operations, and the new rules of engagement."

"Captain Hunt, you're up!"

CHUNG'S REAL NAME

While awaiting his commander, Kim's thoughts focused on the last twenty-four hours. They made it back. There was no hero's welcome. They were successful in pulling off the grenade attack on the Americans. They escaped without casualties and returned with classified information and the reconnaissance on the military bases and the Blue House. Still, Kim had a sense of foreboding. The information Chung provided was important, but the real purpose of the mission was to return with Chung or kill him. Park and Lee were witnesses to Chung, holding them at bay with a pistol.

Kim jumped to attention when the commander entered the bunker. Commander Choi was alone, a good sign. Choi was an intimidating man. He was tall and broad shouldered, with severe scaring on the side of his face. A toad's skin, dark brown and bumpy.

During Kim's first meeting, he approached the colonel from the right. When the colonel turned to greet him, the scarring startled Kim. Choi smiled at Kim's shocked expression. The Korean war veteran imposed harsh penalties for failure. Kim feared he would suffer for not taking care of Chung. Choi motioned for Kim to sit. Choi sat on the edge of the desk, staring at Kim. Kim wanting to look away. Kim stared back, hoping Choi didn't consider it an act of defiance.

"Comrade Kim, we consider your actions last night as heroic and well executed. Our intelligence section informed us you killed three Americans. The information you brought back is useful."

"Thank you, Comrade Colonel."

"Don't thank me yet. It disappointed our highest level of leadership that Chung is still roaming around in South Korea. You did not follow the plan to return with him or eliminating him."

"But colonel, how was I to know he didn't want to return? Was he aware of the plan?

"HOW DARE YOU, insinuate the plan failed because of my incompetence!"

"No Comrade Colonel, I did not mean ... perhaps myself or one of my men said something or our actions tipped him!"

"YOU KIM, YOU ALONE! It was your responsibility to anticipate his actions. You spent two months with Chung. You should've been ready for his response."

"Colonel, Chung is good at what he does, and deception is one of them."

"Yes, I am the one who taught him how to be treacherous and mendacious."

"Colonel?"

"To lie, but enough about Chung. What did you learn? We may want to filter the information before turning it over to our superiors. The satchel with the documents. Did he say how he got them?"

"No, he told us very little."

"Did he say why he wasn't returning?"

His words were, "I need to stay in Seoul to finish my work. He didn't define his work."

"His work, not his mission. That is an odd choice of words. What else did he tell you?" The Colonel asked.

"Chung said that he contacted a mid-level source in the South Korean government. He didn't divulge who the person was or what branch of government. Several South Koreans are friendly to our cause, and he cultivated them. He trusts his life to these people."

"Did he talk about the other agents?"

"No, it's clear that Chung has integrated into the everyday life of a Seoul citizen. He moves freely in the city. He taught us his methods. One important lesson is our manner of speech. Many of our words have a different meaning. We call a lunch box a 'bagwak' they call it a 'dosirak'. Our dialects are different. If you speak in a different dialect, you get reported to the police. Chung told us not to speak to anyone. Every day we practiced speaking in a Seoul dialect. Over time, the war refugees picked up the new dialect and blended in with the general population. The government saw a pattern. Agents from the north were being caught because the former war refugees recognized the northern dialect. The government started asking the public to report anyone speaking an unfamiliar dialect."

"Kim, we now let agents listen to radio

broadcasts from the south so they pick up on the differences. Did your papers get checked?"

"Only once. Two police officers stopped us for no reason. Chung's papers showed he worked for the government. The officers let us pass."

"What does Chung do for the ministry? What is it?"

"The Ministry of Forest and Fisheries, he compiles the tonnage of fish taken by commercial fishermen and the number of trees planted. The government has taken on reforesting South Korea. He does not handle any classified documents. He said he has friends in other ministries." Kim replied.

"Any reason to question his loyalty?"

"No, but, ah ah, no."

"What is it Kim?"

"One evening, Chung brought food to the safe house. He arrived dressed differently, in casual and colorful clothing.. He was in a hurry, he refused to eat with us. His demeanor was different. He was acting odd. So, I followed him."

"Kim, that was a dangerous decision."

"After a short distance from the safe house, he was easy to follow. He took a few surveillance counter measures, as he walked to a large open market near the University. There, he met an attractive woman. They stood in the market and talked for five minutes. In the lights from the market, I could see she was smiling and she let out a hearty laugh. Then, just before they separated ways, Chung leaned in closer and put his hand on her shoulder and whispered something. It was a strange encounter."

"Kim, you risked your life for little information. Did Chung know you followed him?"

"No! We would've lost his trust."

"More likely, he would've murdered you."

"Colonel, there's more." The Colonel slid off the desk and pulled up a chair next to Kim.

"I noticed another man watching Chung and the woman. He was an older man. He could be a policeman or an intelligence agent. When Chung and the women separated, he followed the woman. I couldn't follow the woman. The man followed her into a narrow alley. I followed Chung. He moved through the city, taking no counter measures. He was carefree, as if he was back home."

"Were you concerned he might spot you?"

"No, it was early. Shoppers and students filled the streets. The university is a busy area."

"Where did he go?"

"He walked to a nightclub. It is called the Pui Lai something or other. He was inside for a few minutes. He came out, walked a short distance, and stepped into an alley. Several minutes later, a middle-aged man came out and walked towards the alley. As he passed the alley, Chung joined him. They walked maybe a hundred meters, then got in a taxi."

"Kim, it could have been another contact."

"Colonel, I don't think so. Two days later, the man's picture was in the paper. He was murdered!"

"It was the same man? Are you sure?"

"Yes, I saw him in the lights outside the nightclub."

"What did the paper say?"

"The victim's name was Kil Jon Hun. Married with two children, he worked in the Economic Planning Ministry. The paper said they valued him for his leadership in developing the five-year economic plan and incorporating civilian economics with the military defense budget. The paper didn't go into detail beyond that."

"Did the paper state how he was killed?"

"No, it said, 'savagely murdered'. It mentions another man murdered a month ago. It was similar in one detail. He was an importer with ties to the Economic Ministry."

Images of Chung flashed before Kim, the pistol and his eyes, so evil, his eyes.

"What else Kim, what are you leaving out?"

"Colonel, this man is evil. There is something about him that makes my skin crawl. When we arrived at the safe house, he wasn't there. There was food, clothing, reading material, and a radio. The keeper of the safe house told us to wait inside. There was only one overhead light in each room. Two days later, he appeared. We don't know how or when he entered the house. He was sitting in one of the dark corners, not saying a word, watching us. He's a ghost. We left the next morning. We stayed at several safe houses. The first one was in Seoul is near the street, Sunggyo-bang."

"Was there anyone else at these safe houses?"

"Yes, a woman that cooked and kept the house. The Sunggyo-bang house is a couple of blocks from the university and a large open air market. The market is as large as our parade fields. There are stalls filled with vegetables, pigs, chickens. The people barter with farmers. The market is a happy place. Back home, we have near riots over the distribution of food. In the south people have money and goods to trade, there're no shortages."

"Colonel, except for the University students, the people are content. Chung told us the students protest constantly."

"Enough Kim, enough! I don't need to hear about the capitalist lives of the American puppets! I suggest you don't put those observations in your report."

"Colonel, there is hope with the students. As you know, the April riots in 1960 ousted President Rhee, military rule followed. Park then declared himself President. We could make it happen again! We saw several demonstrations at the Seoul University. The students were demanding change. The students want the American soldiers out of their country. If we help the students protest and Park's government responds with violence, it may open an opportunity to further dissent among the people. The students want to unite the country. Then our Supreme leader Kim ll-sung will govern all of Korea."

"Between you and me, Kim, that is a dream. We need an overpowering force to conquer the people in the south. This is 1967, the world is changing.

Invading a country with a large army has become a thing of the past. This is the age of nuclear threats and insurgency. Look at the Russians and Americans. They could wipe each other off the face of the earth. Yet they maintain a cold peace between them. Over time, the Russians believe America will turn to socialism then to communism. Russia interferes in the politics of Europe, South America, and Cuban. Just as the Americans interfere in Korea and Vietnam. Each country trying to force its will on others without starting a nuclear war. We're able to get away with our attacks along the DMZ because Russia has our backs. If America or South Korea tried to invade or retaliate on a large scale, the Russians would come to our aid, but the threat of a nuclear war with Russia keeps the Americans at bay. The Americans and Russians play a game trying to expand their influence without destroying each other."

"Colonel, do we have a nuclear weapon?"

"THAT'S NOT FOR YOU TO ASK! You are aware of our reactor at Yong Byon. It's near the training camp. It is small reactor, but a start. Soon we'll have the worlds attention. Then no longer will we be the puppet of Russia or China. We can be more aggressive. The Americans will not risk a nuclear weapon being detonated. But for now, Kim, we are a small clog in the machinery. We must try to win over the people in the south. Chung is a hindrance to that goal."

"How is that Comrade colonel?"

"What I'm about to say must not leave this room."

"Yes, Colonel."

"Chung Jin Hein's real name is Jang Yong Son. He is the nephew of the Supreme leader's wife. While growing up, Chung was very close to the Supreme Leader's son and his aunt. Chung, and only Chung, is the only name you'll speak. Do you understand?"

"Yes, Comrade Colonel!"

"After Chung attended one of the elite schools, he joined the army. As a member of the Supreme leader's family, he wasn't obligated to serve. Chung has special talents, he trained as an agent. Those talents were exploited but not with a name tied to our Supreme leaders family. Chung developed into a superior agent, not only in gathering intelligence but as an assassin. He's successfully completed many missions. But now he is a liability."

"How is he a liability?"

"Let me continue. Think of the propaganda if they captured Chung, they would show he was one of our agents and link him to the heinous murders. We believe he has committed many. Worse yet, if they found out he was a relative of the Supreme Leader. Yi Hyo-sun was purged from the Liaison branch. He was head of anti-American and South Korean operations. He sent Chung on this mission. Yi was well aware of Chung's behavior but kept quiet. The leaders of the Workers Party are aware of Chung and his ways. Chung is more of a threat to our cause than an asset."

Kim was terrified of the thought that his orders were to kill a member of the Supreme Leader's family, even if approved by his commander. Who devised such a plan?

Kim's voice became loud as he felt a darkness wash over him.

"COMRADE COLONEL WHAT IF WE HAD KILLED HIM!"

"Don't fret Kim, we presented the facts to the Supreme Leader months ago. He came to the same conclusion: Chung either returned or be eliminated. You're in more danger for not killing him. I have been able to protect you. You'll have a second chance to redeem yourself."

"How's that?"

"Chung is a dangerous man. He may try to kill you and your team on your next mission. The information you brought back links Chung with the murders. Weeks before your last mission, a message from Chung was sent through a covert channel. He requested we train a team to help his return. Your team did train to bring him home."

"Or Kill him."

"Kim, the timing was perfect. He was requesting help. Yi's mistake was what he didn't tell us. Chung didn't want help for another six months. Yi knew the problems Chung was causing and wanted him eliminated sooner than later. Chung was tipped with you arriving sooner than expected."

"Why did Yi risk our lives and the mission?"

"Yi was desperate, but now he's purged. Who

knows what will become of him? Look Kim, we can only assume Chung was aware he was in trouble. We don't know if he believes he'll be killed for disobeying. We think he's on to something he considers important and wants it finished. Did he not tell you he has 'work' to do?"

"Yes, but why a team? He could come north by himself."

"I have no idea. The leader of the Liaison branch wants to see what Chung offers. You will have time to rest and train before your next insertion."

"So our mission is to return with Chung?"

"He returns or dies."

GP GLADYS

"God made me an Indian." Sitting Bull

Our third rotation on GP Gladys, another week of the same shit. A month ago, I spent my first night in this godforsaken country, dead dog tired and after being initiated by the attack on foxhole Charlie. Three dead men and no reprisal. Thirty days later, nothing changed. We load up a three-quarter ton truck with supplies and march the two thousand meters to the GP. A patrol walk rather than a march. Even with a hunter killer patrol providing security for our small convoy of a three-quarter ton truck, we were an easy target. The road to the GP cut between two brush-covered hills known as ambush alley.

The GP, one hundred meters from the MDL rested on a hill flatten by bulldozers. Our home for the next seven days consisted of a sandbagged trench encircling the hill with fighting positions every few meters. On the back of the hill, a concrete bunker with cots, a third of the platoon, rested while the rest stood guard. On the north side of the hill was the command Bunker, just six by eight-feet, big enough for one cot, shelves, and a footlocker to be shared with Sergeant Hicks. The foot locker served as our closet. Rats did not need to nestle in my spare socks.

We observed the North Koreans on what the

men called 'gook hill,' thorough a powerful spotting scope. The North Korean version of a GP was five hundred meters to the northeast. It was a boring, fretful duty. We watched them, watch us, my shifts to sleep haunted by vivid images of Boyd, Cook, and McElroy.

Sergeant Hicks and I were on the men's ass whenever they slacked off, but I had to admit we had a good platoon. We didn't have to do much ass kicking. Sergeant Hicks selected squad leaders based on their ability to follow orders, time in rank and their leadership. Battalion provided replacements, some good, some bad. We got rid of the fuck-ups. The new SOP had little effect on our mission. The changes allowed ten men in each platoon to convert their M-14 to full automatic with a selector switch. Carrying automatic weapons in the DMZ violated the 1953 Armistice Agreement. The Gooks violated the agreement using AK-47's and the PPSHs. Another good outcome, my platoon was near full strength.

But now, back to reality and our daily combat against the rats, using trenching tools. We thought we reduced the numbers during our last stint on the GP. But give credit to the enemy. They keep coming back for more. We killed over a hundred rats using poison and trenching tools. We suffered only one casualty. Private Rather reached into his pack for a snack and grabbed a rat, and the rat latched on to his hand.

The men have a running pool for the biggest rat

killed, now over two hundred dollars. The largest so far is twenty-two inches from the tip of the nose to the end of its tail. When we left the GP on the last tour, we thought we killed most of them, or the rats feared for their lives and defected to North Korea. I chuckled to myself as I pictured a battalion size horde of rats scurrying towards the North Korea outpost. Lieutenant Frank Richards stuck his head in the bunker. We were relieving his platoon.

"Hey Mike, we're just about finished loading. Questions?"

"I assume the log book noted anything important or different."

"It's noted, the same routine on the other side. The gooks are as bored as we are."

"How is the rat situation?"

"It's better! The fifty gallon garbage drums with lids helped, along with the poison."

"Okay, be careful going back. Looks like rain is on the way."

"Fine with me. I need a shower after a week in this stink hole."

Richard was right about a stink hole. The smell of two men living in close quarters hung in the still air. The platoon sergeant barked orders as the men loaded the last of the gear and garbage on the truck. The one truck convoy shadowed by the hunter killer patrol started the return trip back to base. Richards and his men no sooner left when the rain started.

The monsoon rains turned the packed trench mud into a skating rink. The pelting rain blew sideways, soaking the men in the covered positions. Ten minutes later, the sun broke through and steam started rising from the inundated ground. Mother nature continued to show her versatility with an hour of scorching sun, then ten-minute downpours. The rain blotted out gook hill. We expected up to fifteen inches of rain each month during the monsoon season.

"Sarge got anything interesting to read."

"There's a Stars and Stripes stuck up in the cubbyhole and Lieutenant Richards' entries in the logbook."

"I'll save the log book for when I'm bored."

The military controlled newspaper was a couple of weeks old, but one I hadn't read. Scanning the news stories little changed around the world; casualties in Vietnam increased, more protests, President Johnson met with Premier Kosygin in Sweden, China detonates their first hydrogen bomb, so on and so forth. Pages with Dear Abby, the comics and the crossword puzzle were still intact, but no sports page. Surprisingly, the last page, tattered, but complete, blessed the page with a full body pin-up of Playboy model, Elizabeth Jordan.

The sun broke through again. I handed sarge the paper and started out of the bunker, rifle in hand.

"Sarge, I'm going to walk the perimeter to check if we had a washout on the south wall."

"Don't fall on your ass, lieutenant. The mud is as greasy as goose shit."

At the north position Specialist Charlie

Ghostbear was looking through binoculars, scanning the field to the east of the GP. Specialist Riker and Kirst leaning up against the sandbags puffed away on a C ration Pall Mall or Camel. Damn things had me hooked. I never smoked till I got to Korea. Each C ration meal came with a pack of four cigarettes. The men traded the different brands: Salem's, Winston's, Camels, Pall Mall and Lucky Strike.

Ghostbear, one of the platoon's better soldiers, at six feet tall, solid as a concrete block. His dark eyes stared back at you when you spoke to him. Eyes that did not blink. He didn't mix in with the other squad members; he kept to himself. But he led by his actions. He followed orders, volunteered often enough, but most important he was a soldiers, soldier. Ghostbear was good sergeant material with a sense of humor.

Ghostbear let his fellow squad members know he did not want the moniker of Ghost or Bear.. He was proud of his Indian heritage and his name, GHOSTBEAR. A beaded leather pouch hung from his web gear.

"Ghostbear, what's with the pouch? It's not military issue."

"Apache issue, my father's side. My father is a full-blooded Apache and my mother, a Lakota Sioux. They met at the annual rendezvous in Oklahoma. My great-great-grandfather fought against the white man with Geronimo. My mother's bloodline goes to Sitting Bull."

"Wow, your family must tell some great stories."

"Nope, most are sad, not great."

"Did you carry the pouch in basic training and AIT?"

"Yea, and I took a lot of shit. One sergeant told me he was going to transfer me to the 7th Cavalry. It went over like a lead balloon when the Captain found out."

"What's in the pouch?" Reed asked.

"Powerful medicine! It protects me from harm and I can apply it to any wound. My grandfather made the medicine. My grandmother hand sewed and beaded the pouch.. LT, if I get wounded, make sure Moss uses the white man's medicine.

Grinning and staring, he said. "The pouch it's more like a white man's rabbit's foot."

Ghostbear raised the binoculars.

"See anything?"

"A lot of good eating is going to waste. There's a flock of pheasants down on the flat, sir."

"They have pheasants in Arizona?"

"No sir, but they do where my mother's people live. My grandmother lives on the Rosebud Reservation in South Dakota. The fields have a lot of pheasants.. My grandmother makes excellent pheasant cacciatore.

"Well, we can't shoot them. These pheasants belong to the Korean people."

"Yes, Sir."

I completed my inspection. The wall of sandbags held after the heavy rain. Three hours until dark, the boiling clouds forecasted more rain. A good night for the gooks to harass us.

"Hey Sarge, I'm going to open the C's." I flipped the cardboard case of C rations over, so I could see the meal description of the twelve boxed meals. I hoped for spaghetti and meatballs.

"I'm having ham and lima beans. You wanna trade sarge?"

"Fuck no, lieutenant, you don't want to be in the same bunker if I eat that crap. Trade with Sanchez. He treats C's like they're gourmet food."

"Well, Sarge, eat em now or eat em later in the week. I think I'll save the good stuff for Thursday."

"Sir, what good stuff?"

I opened the can with the ingenious p-38 can opener, and set the can on our kimchi rigged stove, an empty C-ration can. The heat tab warmed the ham and lima beans. Sarge broke out a can of beans and baby dicks, miniature hot dogs mixed in a tomato sauce. For dessert sarge we split a can of fruit cocktail and poured it over a tin of pound cake.

Our dinner conversation covered what was happening at battalion and in the country. Sergeant Hicks volunteered little personal information. I knew Sarge was in the Army for sixteen years; thirty-four years old and divorced. He earned his Bronze Star and Combat Infantry Badge on Pork Chop Hill. He didn't share his personal life, but he shared his knowledge. The man didn't preach. He taught and lead by example. Every day, I picked up something new. It was going to be a long week, and I wanted to learn more about the man, other than his favorite baseball team.

"Sarge, were you drafted or enlist?"

"I enlisted to get out of Baltimore, no work for the colored man. The Army guaranteed me three meals and a cot."

As the days dragged on, the sarge opened up. We took our turns watching and doing rounds, checking on the men, but in between Sarge was a chatterbox. He joined the army right after graduating from high school. They selected him for Non-Commissioned Officers' school. Went to Korea in 53' as a buck sergeant.

He spent most of the spring and summer on Pork Chop hill, a three-month nightmare. He explained how the Chinese attacked like a swarm of bees, blaring bugles from large speakers a half mile away. The attacks came at night. Few infantry tactics were necessary. You spent your time in a trench or foxhole watching during the day, shooting at night. The terrifying attacks occurred without the sound of bugles. In the quiet of a pitch black night, a flare would light up the ground, your rifle barrel and the Chinese faces just feet away. You didn't aim; you just looked over the barrel, pulling the trigger, shooting over and over, till they stopped coming.

After Korea, he was at Fort Benning as a drill sergeant and after five years got his E-6 stripe. The army was integrated, but racism prevailed. The white drill sergeants made E-6 after two years. In 1960, Sarge got busted to Private First Class. He got in a fistfight with his white First Sergeant. The First Sergeant was mistreating one of Sergeant Hick's colored soldiers. He explained the army has changed for the better, colored NCOs and Officers are being treated with respect.

"Why didn't you quit after they busted you?"

"They court marshalled me, but a few white officers stood up for me. The old guard saw it as a breakdown in discipline. The army was changing, so I took my punishment and stuck it out. I'm good at what I do and I love the Army. This is me."

"Who won the fist fight?"

"Hell lieutenant, First Sergeants are tough. I hauled off and smacked him. He dropped like the bag of shit he was, but got up and came at me like a whirling dervish. We both ended up with black eyes, split lips and bloody noses. It wasn't pretty."

"Sarge, it must be weird after Pork Chop hill, watching the gook's though the scope day after day and not shoot the bastards?"

"Scary is more like it. This is not the Korean war. Now it's cat and mouse. Are we the cat or the mouse, lieutenant?"

I didn't have an answer. Nightfall was on us. The magpies stopped their chattering, as did Sergeant Hicks. The North Korean loudspeakers started with the nightly propaganda. A woman spoke with a charming accent. Tonight her goal was to entice the KUTUSA'S to rise up against the American Imperialist.

Other nights, she tried to convince the

KUTUSA'S and GI's to defect. *"Good evening, GI. Life in North Korea is so much better. Good pay, beautiful girls, freedom to do as you wish in this great country of North Korea. Just walk north across the DMZ to our welcoming arms."* A couple GIs believed the bullshit and defected in the early 1960s. The nonsense continued spewing from the speaker. Sergeant Hicks went to sleep. Speaker blaring or not, he could sleep on command.

Time marched slowly. The darkness did not. The heavy rain-laden clouds made it darker than inside a cow's stomach. At 0200 hours, I noted in the logbook a convoy of ten vehicles using their blackout lights in Propaganda village, going east to west. They stopped at the far west end of the village.

At 0400 hours, the thump of grenades and rifle fire to our east meant the 1st of the 31st patrol was getting hit. Do I want to be here or on patrol? Not my decision to make, Rosie mentioned this will be our last rotation on the GP.

SCHADENFREUDE OR AE-SOOK'S SAFE HOUSE

"A fanatic is one who can't change his mind and won't change the subject." Winston Churchill

Chung picked up the Chosun Libo from the table. It was today's paper, July 29, 1967, the second page covered a story of the sadistic murder of Park Chang Wook. Police released the time of death as four days ago when the Wook family reported him missing. The story showed he worked for the government and was a respected man in his community. Police released very little information because the victim worked in a ministry, no motive offered. According to the article, the murder of Wook was the second murder of a government official. The police claim there's no reason to believe the murders were connected. It was a robbery gone bad.

Chung laughed, what idiots, I left them plenty of reasons to connect the murders of Wook and Yi. Mr. Wook and Mr. Yi did not carry any secrets to the grave; they gave them to me. Chung continued to laugh. The safe house's housekeeper asked what was funny.

"Chung, you're in good spirits. What makes you laugh?"

Chung wanted to tell her, but couldn't.

"It's nothing, just something I saw today."

She knew nothing of his missions and if she did, he would enjoy helping her take the secrets to her grave. Ae-Sook was a devout communist. She introduced him to others in Seoul that felt the same. She was an excellent cook and not bad looking at thirty-five. Chung chuckled. He remembered the number of times she tried to lure him into her bed. If she only knew. His chuckle turned to outright laughter. It took several seconds for him to regain his composure..

"What are we eating tonight?" He asked.

"I'll tell you if you tell me what's so funny."

He didn't answer her. Chung had two more days before he returned to his legal address, which he maintained for employment in the Ministry. Chung used the safe houses after an event like 'Wooks.' Over time, he developed a cover story for his neighbors. The periods of absence were because he was visiting his ailing mother, his nonexistent mother. After the murders, Chung checked his legal address to see if the house was being watched before returning.

He only met with his victims outside of work. First confirming they were from different ministries. He doubted if the unfortunate Mr. Wook, or Mr. Yi or the others would've mentioned his name at work. The meetings were something you didn't discuss with fellow workers.

He didn't want Ae-Sook to have the faintest idea about his self-imposed mission. She never let up with her constant prattle. Chung thought to shut her up, he should either kill or screw her. Either would be dangerous, besides she was a loyal party member, but vulnerable?

"Chung, tell me, what's so funny?"

"The Chosun Libo is what's funny, the paper is all lies. It would be closed immediately in Pyongyang; the editor drowned in his own ink."

"That is funny, an imperialist editor drowning in ink. That would make a good cartoon. Comrade Chung, I buy the paper to keep up with how these imperialist think. I buy it for you, hoping you'll show up more often. I dream of the day we'll be successful and kick the puppet pig Park out of the government and force the Americans to leave."

She went on and on. Chug was picturing his hands around her fragile lily white neck. Squeezing, making her eyes bulge and forever shutting her up. He cut her off.

"Ae-Sook, after we eat, please go visit a friend or something. I need time to think."

"I'll be quiet, I promise."

He wanted to use the radio without the chance of her overhearing the transmission, even if it was sent in code. The less she knew, the better. The Russian Oriol P350 radio was used only when necessary, sending messages in short bursts and late at night. Ae-Sook was aware of the radio and rules regarding the radio and the safe house. No one was to touch the radio except Chung. Ae-Sook was to have no visitors or friends at the house for any reason. Ae-Sooks' social life had to be conducted elsewhere.

"Please, after we eat, GO! I need to be alone."

The meal was excellent, rice, chicken and kimchi,

and a somewhat muted Ae-Sook. She left in a snit, dressed in her fine silk jeogori and colorful chima. The clothing was more colorful here than the code back home allowed. Her loyalty was beyond reproach. Frequently she left for several hours, returning with the smell of alcohol was on her breath. He asked where she was and the answer was always, 'out'. The next time, he was going to follow her. She seemed eager to be handed the money, perhaps to buy nice clothes, but she had a secret. He found among her things a nearly empty bottle of expensive foreign liquor. Constantly, she talked about her friends at work and music and lively bars. Was she developing an appetite for the decadent life of Seoul?

After she left, Chung turned the lights off and sat in a corner furthest from the windows. The darkness brought on an inner serenity that allowed Chung to ruminate over what he had done and to calculate his future moves.

He knew his mission in the south had to end. The unexpected visit by Kim and his team confirmed the Liaison Bureau wanted him back or dead. Chung was aware the party leaders had determined he deviated from his original assignment. They may consider him a liability, but his aunt is the Supreme leader's wife. The party wouldn't do a fucking thing.

The murders, in retrospect, were ill conceived. Without committing the murders, he may have been arrested by now. Just one person knowing is the best way to keep a secret, ill conceived or not. Chung felt great pleasure doing away with the unworthy men. But he was having a hard time extinguishing the hunger. Each time it became more difficult to stop with just killing, a powerful force fell upon him with more intensity after each killing. They needed to be punished, punished, PUNISHED!

Chung laughed as he thought, who am I to share this with? What's the word he picked up while training in East Berlin? Aah, schadenfreude, pleasure derived from another's misfortune.

Chung's mind reeled through the past few months and thoughts of the last victim. Poor Mr. Wook, a pathetic excuse for a man. Forty years old, fat and hanging out at a faggot bar. Another word he learned in Germany, faggot. Chung learned the meaning the hard way. He crossed into West Berlin trying to pick up an official in a bar who worked for the government. He had misjudged, the man wasn't gay, neither were his four friends. Germans had no use for 'faggots' as they kicked the shit out of him.

The first time Chung spotted Wook was in a bar in the Itaewon district in Seoul. Chung noticed Wook when he walked in the door. Wook had didn't remove his government ID fastened to his jacket. Wook was no newcomer to the faggot scene. He was at ease as he walked over and sat next to Chung. He had alternate choices, as there were several empty bar stools to his left and right.

Seoul's free society was a cesspool. Chung was all ears as Wook was talkative. Chung was a vociferous reader of the newspapers and the propaganda they spewed. He had no problem keeping Wook's interest and luring him to the path, Wook was eager to go down.

Wook liked his beer, and after 5 beers Chung could rest his hand on the back of Wooks. This technique helped Chung make his point and confirm the direction the relationship was going. Wook never pulled his hand away. Chung gained Wook's confidence by the end of the first meeting. After two rendezvous at the bar, Chung convinced Wook to a meeting at a discreet lovers' nest, a small house he rented, no questions asked. Within a month, Chung had Wook under his total control when Wook thought he was in control.

The color drained out of Wook's face when Chung showed him the strategically positioned F-21 Russian made camera. Chung loved the miniature camera. A KGB officer gave it to him. It had a wind up motor and a sharp fixed focus 28mm lens. Chung wanted to show Wook the graphic photographs, but getting them developed was not possible. Showing him the camera was enough.

Wook cried out, tears welling up, he realized; he had been seduced and deceived. Chung used his sexually, a mechanism he commanded at will, with no emotional ties to the victim. He used it to lure men or woman into a dark hole with no way out, but to follow his wishes.

"WHAT ARE YOU DOING WITH THAT!"

Chung had a story line prepared to make it easy for Wook to cooperate. Smiling and confident, he laid it out.

"Wook, I work for a large group of businessmen. We need information to help our businesses." Wooks' voice quivered as he responded.

"I work in the Ministry for Unification. I don't have access to financial information."

"Yes, you do, you just don't know it. We need to know the short and long-range plans for unification, they'll impact the economy. The government at some point will release the information. We just want a jump on the competition."

Wook's voice quivered as it increased a few octaves. "It's illegal. I'll go to jail, disgraced!"

"What will happen if I make these pictures available to your boss?"

"You'll destroy me. I'll end up in jail. I'm not a traitor, a thief."

"Look, you're not a traitor. The information will help our country grow."

"Maybe, but you want it for your own greed. To enrich yourself, not our country."

Chung had led Wook to where he wanted. Wook was thinking Chung was a corrupt businessman, not a spy.

"I will destroy the pictures if you cooperate. You'll be well paid."

"I can't do this. I'll go to the police, tell them everything!"

"No, you won't. You risk little by cooperating with me. No one will know of our trysts."

"I won't do it. I have not provided you with

any information. I can live with myself, being a homosexual. My family will disown me, I'll lose my job but I will not go to prison. I have friends that will support me."

"Yes, you may have friends. It's doubtful they will help you stay out of jail." Chung played his trump card. He walked across the room to where his jacket was hanging. Out of the pocket, he removed a camera. A Minox sub miniature camera. A camera designed to take photographs of documents. Wook gasped!.

"Friends, faggots or not, will not help if they know you gave away important information for sexual favors."

Wook shifted his gaze to his briefcase resting on the table, realizing he was done.

"Wook, you provided me with documents at each of our several meetings. Didn't they teach you not to take classified documents home? After a couple of beers and a romp in bed, you fall asleep. It was easy to pick the lock and photograph the documents in your briefcase. I even removed a few pages from the addendum section. Classified pages you didn't notice but will be during an investigation."

Wook sat on the edge of the bed, his elbows on his knees with his chin resting on hands folded together as if in prayer. A long silence before he spoke, whispering.

"How much money?"

Wook was pliable for the next couple of months. But started showing signs of becoming unraveled.

Ten days ago he showed up tormented, wringing his hands and no desire for sex. He handed over the roll of film, asked for his money and left. Five days ago, Wook showed up incoherent, babbling about needing to confide in someone. He was becoming self destructive and he no longer believed he was spying for a corrupt businessman. Chung couldn't trust Wook. He was emotionally exhausted. His last report did provide information regarding a high-ranking official in the Ministry of Defense. According to Wook, an aide in the Ministry provided the official with young men.

Chung snickered, thinking of Wook's last moments.

Wook was standing at the foot of the bed babbling about spying for the communists. Wook begged Chung to convince him they weren't spies. Chung stepped towards him as if to console and embrace Wook. Chung turned Wooks' torment to horror with a smooth fluid move and the flash of a five-inch blade. He grabbed the pathetic man by the hair, stepped to the left and then behind him.

Wooks' fear turned him into a limp doll. In one swift motion Chung clenched the long greasy, sweat wet hair, pushing Wook's head forward, forcing his chin to his chest. The blade pierced Wook's neck on the left side between the earlobe and collar bone. Chung stabbed rather than slashed to not get sprayed with blood. Wook gurgled a few unidentifiable sounds as the knife penetrated the windpipe. Chung twisted the knife. He could feel the blade cutting gristle. He lowered the quivering body to the floor.

Wook was dead in a couple of minutes. Chung thought of the tiger catching its prey and holding it by the neck. The prey gave in to the inevitable, much like Wook. Unlike the tiger, Chung could wallow in the joy and the release of his powerful urges. He placed his victims on their backs. He wanted to watch life leave the eyes of his prey. Wook's eyes asked, why? So pitiful.

Chung had covered his tracks. He rented the house under an assumed name. Wiping everything to remove fingerprints. He dropped the bedding off at the local laundry under an assumed name, never to be picked up. The rendezvous was at night. Dimly lit streets provided little opportunity for identification. The police would figure out the why Wook was in that 'kind' of house, but never the other side of the equation.

Enough musing about the past Chung. He needed to get close to the flesh peddler. The aide that acts as a pimp for the big fish. The big fish being a high-ranking member of the Defense Ministry. This official was far more discreet than Wook. It will take weeks to sort out where and how the pimp practiced his debauchery. Chung loved the hunt and the gratification that ended his powerful craving. One that he justified, a necessary part of his mission.

Chung pondered about the young woman Hyun-ae Bae, the University student, the leader of the student protests. Her organization April II, named after the April 1960 student protest in which the government killed 186 protesters. The protest caused President Rhee to flee to the United states. Hyun-ae Bae's April II had three tenets. They were against the current government, claiming they were a puppet of the Americans. The second was against the wealthy landlords who illegally were tenant farming. The most vocal argument was for the unification of Korea.

After a peaceful protest, he followed her to a coffee and tea cafe near the university. He introduced himself as a businessman and how he admired her ability to organize a protest. Chung looked younger than thirty-two years. His boyish good looks allowed him to mix with the students. During the second meeting, he offered financial help. It was accepted. Bae was a passionate leader and had potential. Just how he used her was the question.

The April II group was divided into different cells. Each cell had a different task. They never met at the same location. April II had a problem on the horizon. They were growing in numbers and the government was taking notice. More arrests of students were taking place, and they needed money. Fines had to be paid.

Supplying Bae with money to pay the fines and buy supplies helped gain her trust. His account at the Hana Bank in Seoul was getting low. To further compound the problem, they had cut the transfer of money from an Indonesia bank down to a third.

He still had enough money to complete his plan. He had been fugal while in the south, the wages from the Ministry helped. He decided Hyun-ae Bae was to become his primary focus, a pretty one at that.

OFFICE OF INTERNAL SECURITY

"Three things can not be long hidden: the sun, the moon, and the truth." Buddha

Jeong Cheol Won and Dong-Suk Yoo showed their ID to the officer guarding the scene. When they walked in the door, the homicide detective didn't seem surprised to see the agents from the OIS, Office for Internal Security. The victim, Wook, worked for the government.

Won did the introduction.

"Detective, inspector Yoo and I'm Inspector Won from..."

Both inspectors covered their nose with a handkerchief for protection against the overpowering and unforgettable stench of ripe bodies.

"OIS! I suspected you guys may show up."

"When was the body discovered?" Asked Won.

"The call came in at seven this morning, neighbors complaining about the odor. One of the other detectives recalled seeing a report of a missing person. We identified Wook from a photo at his place of work."

"No papers on the man, I take it. Said Yoo.

"No wallet, no money. If he wore a watch, that's gone. No belongings other than what the victim is wearing. The murderer stripped the bed. No recoverable fingerprints."

"Who last saw him?" Asked Won.

"Mr. Wooks' staff at work. A neighbor said the house has been dark for several nights."

"Did she see anyone come to the house?"

"The neighbors said there was no activity until after dark. No one could give us a description."

Yoo pointed to the Wooks' body lying on his back. Then asked.

"The cause of death?"

"Stabbed once in the neck. There is little blood splatter, so he must've fallen directly to the floor. There's a large pool of blood near the head."

"What's with the blood at his crotch?" Won asked.

"The cuts in his pants show someone has stabbed him three or four times. The autopsy will show us more."

"Does Mr. Wook own the house?" Yoo asked.

"No, the neighbors say it's rented. We're trying to contact the owner. Inspectors, this looks like a robbery with a perverted twist. We think Mr. Wook hooked up for sexual favors and it went south."

"You may be right, detective! Keep our office informed. Send over a copy of the autopsy." Won said.

"Yes, will do, inspector. Do you two always take turns asking questions?

"Your turn, Yoo!"

Yoo and Won returned to the car. Won spoke first.

"We have a sick bastard out there. Over four years, this makes it five, six victims?"

"Maybe Jeong, we need to read the homicide reports again. I bet there's more."

Jeong Won and Dong-Suk Yoo worked in the Sal-in unit at OSI, reviewing homicide reports in Gyeonggi providence and the city of Seoul. They investigated the murders connected to North Korea agents. Intelligence gathering by capturing the enemy agent alive was the main purpose of the unit.

The murdering enemy agent did not commit the Wook and five other murders while trying to flee north. There are no known witnesses. The victims were men between the ages of twenty-five and forty. One a known homosexual and now maybe two, depending on the background investigation of Wook. Yi worked for a different ministry. His murder took place two months ago. It's unlikely Wook and Yi knew each other. Wook's name never came up during the Yi's investigation.

Each murder occurred in a different police district. The murders were up close and personal. Two strangled, one with his tie and three by stabbing, all lying on their backs. Not on their side, or stomach. According to the autopsy report, they were stabbed with a sharp instrument, probably a knife with a 15 centimeter long and two and a half centimeters wide blade. The cause of death, one stabbed in the heart. Just one wound. Two were stabbed just once on the left side of the neck. The two victims stabbed in the neck were mutilated. They suffered several stab wounds to the groin. which appeared to be an act of rage. *"The weapon that caused the wounds to the neck, caused the wounds to the groin, but lengthened with a slashing motion, creating wounds five centimeters to ten centimeters long. It's unlikely the victim thrashed. The stab wound to the neck incapacitated the victim."*

The police haven't connected the two neck stabbings, Wook's in Seoul and one in the Gyeonggi. Won and Yoo had ferreted out the connections. The victims didn't know each other, but four had business dealings with either Yi's Ministry of Fisheries or Wook's Ministry of Unifications.

A short time after Yi's murder, OSI's signal division intercepted a radio transmission.. A message from a North Korea command center to the North Korea Navy headquarters stated the South Korean fishermen harvested 1,552,346 metric tons. Double the metric tons the North Korea fishermen harvested. The North Korean command center demanded to know if South Korean fishermen were fishing in North Korea waters. They ordered more patrols. The conspicuous part of the intercepted message was the North Korea command center knew the exact tonnage of fish. The South Korean ministry did not release the number to the public. It had just been compiled by Yi's staff and needed further review.

KIMCHI ALLEY

Dong suk-yoo drove on. The traffic was getting heavy. Jeong stared out the opened window at the mixture of shops in the busy Sewoon Sangga district. The district was booming. Men and women hustled by on the sidewalks, Jeong thought. Any of them could be the suspect. Jeong was concerned the suspect was shortening the intervals between murders. The savagery was accelerating. As a seasoned agent, he knew the murders were out of the ordinary.

North Korea's spies didn't operate this way. The murders riled the instinctive hunch in Jeong and Dong-suk. They had to convince their section chief this was the work of a North Korea agent turned homicidal maniac. Even with the intercepted fish quota message, Jeong pictured the Chief's words.

"There isn't enough proof to put more men on the case. This is work for the police."

"Dong-suk, pay attention to the damn road. You almost hit that woman."

"Jeong, why murder a person of such high profile? He had to know it would draw attention."

"How do know it's just one person? Also, sex is involved in two of the murders." Jeong said.

It was a hot, humid day. Grilled chicken, pork, and vegetable aroma spiced with Kimchi drifted through the street carried by the smoke from charcoal fires. The open air vendors were well known for tasty food. The nearby office and factory workers swarmed the narrow alleyway. He could taste the Kimchi and smoke-flavored chicken on his lips. That's their secret. The smoke carries the flavor; it lands on your lips and instantly you're hungry.

"Dong-Suk, pull over, let's get lunch."

"Good, I'm hungry."

The food vendors in the narrow alley used the bricked factory walls to anchor their smoke darkened canvas canopies. The canopies sloped towards the middle of the alley, nearly touching the opposing vendor's canopy. It was noon, and the crowded alley was noisy. The vendors yelled the orders to the cook because of the din created by customers and competing vendors. Yoo and Won jostled with other patrons for position to yell out their orders.

"What are you getting, Dong-Suk?"

"Pork and rice for me. Please, no Kimchi for you, your farts are deadly, the car will stink for a week."

"Sorry, but chicken and Kimchi a must. Spicy kimchi is good for the digestive track." said Jeong.

"Not good for my nose." As Dong-Suk said, pinching his nose with his finger and thumb.

"Lets eat at the park at the end of the alley. You won't have to fumigate the car."

At the crowded park, Jeong pointed to a bench under Kousa's dogwood shade. Dong-suk and Jeong sat on the bench facing the bustling alley. The scenery was excellent. Girls were getting away from wearing the traditional long jeogori. The new craze, skirts well above the knee. The narrow alley acted as a funnel, allowing more time to watch the slow walking short-skirted girls.

"Dong-Suk look, the girl with the black slacks. She is walking towards the alley."

"Ah, nice. She's a tall one."

"No, you nitwit?"

"Damn, that's the Bae girl!"

Jeong and Dong-suk were assigned to monitor Bae Hyun-Ae, a University student activist. Her organization 'April II' came to the attention of the authorities because of a dramatic increase in membership. The group was well funded. They had watched Bae at different rallies and investigated her background. The only unknown was how she funded the group. Before she got to the alley, she stopped and turned towards a man leaning against a building.

The conversation appeared to be lively. Bae was using a lot of hand jesters. Jeong tried to see the expression on the man's face. The volume of people passing behind Bae prevented Jeong and Dong-suk from getting a good look at the man. From what Jeong could see, he had no sign of anger or humor. Just a calm but chilling demeanor.

He was well dressed and young, about the same age as Bae. Her dossier put her age at twenty-seven. Bae and the man started walking towards the alley. The man looked towards the park with a trained once-over. He was looking to see if they were being followed.

"Quick Dong-suk, let's follow them."

"I haven't finished eating."

"Fuck the food, let's go."

The crowded alley quickly swallowed up Bae and the man. Jeong could glimpse them now and then. It didn't appear they were going to buy lunch. They walked at a steady pace, heading for the other end of the alley. Jeong and Dong-suk bumped their way through the crowd. Bae and the man kept disappearing and reappearing as they ducked under the vendor's canopies. Halfway through the two hundred meter long alley, Jeong and Dong-suk lost sight of them.

"Dong-suk, do you see them?"

"No, they just evaporated into the crowd." Dong-suk replied.

"SHIT! Let's hurry to the other end. Maybe we can catch them on the street."

Jeong and Dong-suk started pushing their way through the crowd in a polite but hurried manner. Near the end of the alley, they stopped. On the right side, there was a walkway between the two buildings.

"Dong-suk, let's take the walkway."

Many factory workers used the large courtyard where the walkway ended. The far end of the courtyard faced the street. A high wall blocked the view of the street. Three door size openings led to the street, one in the center and the others at the left and right corner of the courtyard.

"Dong-suk, take the right!"

Jeong and Dong-suk ran to the tree-lined street. Cars, taxis, trucks on the street and a sidewalk full of pedestrians. Jeong turned and walked back towards Dong-suk.

"WHERE THE FUCK DID THEY GO?" Jeong asked.

"I don't know, Dong-suk. We need to spend more time on this Bae woman. The man she was with, I recognized that face. Let's get back to the office."

Back at the office, Won Jeong and Dong-suk started pulling files of known or suspected enemy agents, collaborators that may have connections with businesses. There were over two hundred files generated in the past year. They pulled surveillance photos of student protests and suspected enemy agents. After a couple of hours, nothing and they had only looked at half of the files.

"Jeong, here comes the chief."

"What are you two numb skulls up to?"

"Chief, we tried to follow this woman, Bae, the college student. She gave us the slip in Kimchi Alley."

"A SCHOOL GIRL! Gave two experienced agents the SLIP? Jeong, you're better than that? What the hell happened?"

"She met a man, he appeared the same age, another student? My instinct tells me otherwise. They used the crowded alley to avoid being followed."

The chief looked at the four desks the men commandeered to spread out the photographs and files.

"What's with the files? Are you two trying to make

something out of Wook's murder.?"

Jeong let out a sigh of exasperation before he said.

"Chief, believe me, they're similar, connected, the autopsy proves it. The photographs and files are about the man and Bae. I saw that face before, somewhere in one of our files. I know it!"

The chief stood there, shaking his head from side to side before saying.

"You two are going to be the death of me. We're up to our ass with North Koreans sneaking into the country through the DMZ and by sea and you two can't follow a school girl. Stay on the Wook case, damnit."

Won tried to say otherwise. "Chief, she's not a school...."

"Enough Jeong! Dong-suk keep Jeong from going off the rails on this Bae thing. Concentrate on Wook. You two be here on time tomorrow. The KCIA and a US Representative of the CIA will be here at eight o'clock sharp, for the quarterly briefing."

"Ok chief, but Jeong is on the right track."

"You two be here first thing tomorrow."

Dong-suk watched as the chief walked away. He had just given them tactful approval to expand the investigation of Bae. Jeong and Dong-suk had the chief's approval so long as they stayed on the "rails" to follow up on Wook's murder. Dong-suk liked the chief. He let his agents do their work.

****

Dong-suk Yoo, valued Jeong, his mentor. At thirty-seven years old, Jeong Won had a lifetime of experiences. His average build and height were disarming. His bright smile charmed the ladies and interviewees, but beneath there was a different Jeong.

During the war, Jeong was a young lieutenant in the 36th Regiment of the South Korean 1st Division. His commander, Colonel Lee Yong Sun, a hard man and disciplined, rallied his troops to hold their positions against Chinese and North Koreans on Triangle Hill and later Sniper Ridge. They awarded Jeong the Order of Military Merit for bravery. Jeong spoke little of his wartime experience. He referred to the North Korea soldiers as people, Korean people, just like us. He had interrogated many of them. After the war, Jeong earned a bachelor's and a master's degree in political science.

Jeong was the departments trainer for Taekwondo and Hapkido. Several years ago, Jeong was jumped by two North Korea agents before he could pull his weapon. They had clubs, but didn't get to use them. The surviving North Korea agent spent a week in the hospital.

The agent said they used clubs because they wanted the attack to look like a robbery. One attacked from the front and one from behind. Before they could strike, Jeong disarmed one agent and used his club, hitting him so hard he could hear bones crack. The hospitalized agent said he hesitated. The hesitation cost him. Before he could react, Jeong was all over him, hitting, kicking him into unconsciousness.

Jeong counseled Dong-suk that the people of North Korea were not evil, it was the psychopathic communist leaders that whipped the people into a frenzy. Jeong told Dong-suk at least a hundred times, *"This will never end. The DMZ is a line on a map dividing good and evil. You can't separate good from evil by a line drawn on a map, just as you can't separate a people. Evil will continue to cross that line, and we must continue our work against evil. The Koreans in the north, our people, have two choices: follow or a bullet in the back of the head."*

After Jeong got his degrees, they selected him to go to the United States and train at Army Intelligence School at Fort Holibird, then on to Fort Bragg for counterinsurgency training.

Don-suk looked over at Jeong. He was flipping through files so fast, causing them to spill their contents on the floor.

"Jeong, are we eating dinner in the office tonight?"

"No, go home, get some rest and be here early. We'll check more files tomorrow."

"Maybe the man is someone you recall from a news story."

"No, he's here, in these reports. I'm sure of it, go home. I'll see you tomorrow."

VIPER AKA
CHUNG JIN HEIN

"There is no hunting like the hunting of man, and those who have hunted armed men long enough and liked it, never care for anything else thereafter." Ernest Hemingway

Jeong walked into the office at 7am, surprising Dong-suk who had files scattered on the floor.

"Good morning Dong-suk, find anything?"

"Not yet. There's fresh coffee. I asked the trainee to come in early. He is downstairs going though the microfilm looking for newspaper articles with photos of men involved in crimes or espionage."

"That's good initiative Dong-suk."

"Any luck last night?"

"No, he's somewhere here in our files!" Said Jeong.

The hour went by quickly. The chief looked at the files scattered on the floor as he entered the office.

"Where's the trainee? He should put these files away."

"We sent him downstairs to do research." answered Dong-suk.

"Get him up here. We can't leave files unattended. It is time for the briefing."

The windowless briefing room was on the third floor. The only furniture was an oval table with twelve chairs. Camera's tape recorders and briefcases were forbidden. No notes were to be taken. Before every briefing, they swept it for listening devices.

Nine agents from other departments filled the chairs. The two agents at the head of the table had an impatient look.

Jeong wasn't fond of the CIA from either country. They were a pompous bunch and politically orientated more than they should be for a national security agency. The KCIA agent started off with introductions. Jeong, lost in deep thought, tried to recall the fugitive information trapped in his head. Where did he see the man?

The introductions were over, and the American started his talk.

"Since our last briefing, there has been an uptick in activity..."

Jeong's mind flashed! It captured the information, the quarterly briefings. he asked Dong-suk to pull the last two months, not the quarterly KCIA briefings. Jeong bolted from his seat. As he raced towards the door, the chief grabbed his arm.

"Jeong, where the hell are you going?"

"Chief, I got it, I remember where I saw the man."

"It can wait, Jeong, after the briefing!"

"We'll want to share this with our guests. As Jeong nodded towards the front of the room. Give me five minutes."

"GO, Dong-suk can fill you in later."

Jeong raced down the stairs to his office. They kept the KCIA information in a separate file cabinet. Only the chief, Dong-suk, and Jeong knew the combination. He was so excited it took two attempts before he got the combination right.

The KCIA rarely disseminated written materials to OSI field offices. Jeong remembered it was a year, maybe more, since the KCIA had distributed a dossier with photos. Jeong grabbed the folders. There were only four. Hurrying, he flipped open two of the thin folders, no photos, he didn't bother to read; he wanted the pictures. The third folder proved a charm. The folder contained a three-page report and two eight by ten photos, showing the man he saw with Bae.

Jeong raced back upstairs. Dong-suk just walked out of the briefing room.

"The chief was getting concerned."

Nearly out of breath from running up several flights of stairs. Panting, Jeong pulled a picture from the folder and held it in front of Dong-suk's face.

"Son of a bitch, THAT'S HIM!" Yelled Dong-suk.

Jeong entered the room. The chief smiled. Jeong was on to something from the look on his face. The interruption flustered the CIA men.

Jeong walked to the end of the table where the two CIA men stood. He turned to the chief before opening the folder.

"Chief, we should be the only ones to share this information with the CIA. I can brief everyone later, on a need to know basis."

The chief pointed to the door and uttered one word. "Out!"

The chief waited for the door to close.

"This better be good, Jeong."

"It's better than good, chief." Jeong removed a

photo from the folder and panned it around to the chief and the CIA agents.

"Dong-suk and I saw this man at Kimchi Alley with the woman." Jeong placed a three-page document and two photos on the table. The first page listing the recipients was blacked out except for OSI, the second page was typed, listing security protocol.

TOP SECRET

WARNING

This document contains classified information affecting the national security of the United States, within the meaning of espionage laws, US Code title 18, Sections 793, 794, and 798.

CENTRAL INTELLIGENCE AGENCY

1. This document was disseminated by the Central Intelligence agency. This copy is for information and use of the recipient and of persons under his jurisdiction on a need to know basis.

2. This document may be retained or destroyed by burning following applicable security regulations, or returned to the Central Intelligence Agency by arrangement with the Office of Central

Reference.

3. When this document is disseminated overseas, the overseas recipients may retain it for a period not in excess of one year. At the end of the year, the document should either be destroyed, returned to the forwarding agency or permission requested of the forwarding agency to retain it in accordance with IAC-D-69/2 22 June 1953.

4. No action is to be taken on any ███████████ d which may be contained herein, regardless of the advantages to be gained, unless such action is first approved by the Director of Central Intelligence.

The third page had been single spaced and heavily redacted. Won read the heavily redacted page aloud.

"█████████: *The subject was photographed on* by███████ *subject is a trainee at a KGB facility. Subjects given and family name are unknown, KGB assigns names to trainees at the school. This subject was known as Viper. He has been seen in the presence of experience KBG agents. He is of Korean origin, served in the North Korea military. Believe to have trained with the elite North Korean 124th Regiment or the 17th Reconnaissance Foot Brigade. He has been seen at the* ███████*embassy by* ██ ███████████*on two occasion in*███████ *believed he was being trained to infiltrate and spy in South Korea. He is known to speak Russian and fluent English. The KGB mentors he has been seen with are skilled in spy craft methods. They include methods of entry, surveillance, evasion, recruiting, weapons and assassination. He attended few embassy functions, known to be aloof, extremely intelligent. No known vices, does not drink, use drugs, or gamble, sexual orientation unknown. Approximate height, five foot eight inches, weight approx. 160 lbs. Date he left the host country,* ▮▮▮▮▮▮ *is unknown. He was last seen on* ▮▮▮▮▮▮ *Elements of this report are deleted to protect the source. Information has not been verified using more than one source."*

"Chief, we can catch this guy by watching Bae. I'm sure they will meet again." Dong-suk said.

The American CIA spoke first.

"Hold on, paragraph four has to be adhered to and we don't know when the photos were taken. The report may be a year old, depending where and how the CIA received the information. It could be several years old."

"What the fuck does it matter? He was with a known student agitator. He's in our country, so screw your paragraph four."

The chief rapped his knuckles hard on the table.

"Jeong, hold on. We may need this to be a joint effort. Gentlemen, this falls under OIS's mandate. We'll do the field work. Please check for more information in your files. It would help if we could date the photos. We need to establish a time line when he may have entered our country, also any known alias."

The Korean CIA, who was a former OIS agent, spoke.

"Chief, this will not be a pissing contest. We'll help in any way, keep us informed as the investigation proceeds. It has to be understood if the investigation drifts out of your area of responsibility or involves another country. We need to be informed."

"That's understood." Replied the chief.

"I don't recall seeing anything come across my desk, but if something does, I'll send it over by courier."

"Thanks, anything will help." Said the chief before saying.

"Jeong, pick your team, use up to six men, but before you start surveillance, I want a thorough background check on this Hyun-ae Bae, including her family."

"It will take a day or two."

"Lets find out what we have on her regarding, property, relatives, banking and classes Hyun ae-Bae is taking, including names of her professors. We don't start watching her till we know who we're watching. This may involve more than a student dissident."

"Okay, Chief."

HYUN-AE BAE AND CHUNG

"The art of using deceit and cunning grow continually weaker and less effective to the user." John Tillotson

He had a feeling, a feeling he trusted. They were being watched when he met Bae at Kimchi alley. Two men sitting in the park got up and followed when he and Bae headed for the alley. Their actions hurried. As they passed a walkway off to the right, Chung's instincts told him they should separate. Chung explained to Bae he was late for a meeting. He handed her money and explained he wanted to buy her lunch. He pointed to a vendor at the end of the alley before asking.

"Please have lunch on me. Go to the vendor with the green awning. He has the best food. I'm sorry I have to leave. I'll be late for the meeting. Tomorrow, dinner with me, six o'clock at the Wooraeok restaurant?"

She gave him a puzzling but an accepting look before she said. "Yes!"

Chung hurried back to the walkway. The two men's heads were bobbing then and again, trying to look above the crowd. Were they looking for her or me? Maybe it was just a coincidence. Regardless, the next meeting will be where he could watch to see if she is being followed. The Wooraeok restaurant on the outskirts of Seoul was discreet, but well known. She should feel comfortable.

Chung arrived at the restaurant an hour before Bae. He watched as she exited the bus, dressed in a sky blue chimi and a dark blue flowered jeogori, as if she was on a date, taller than the average woman on the street. This was no date. Chung needed to convince her this was business. From his vantage point, Chung could see if anyone followed. She waited in front of the Wooraeok, looking aggravated. The past hour of watching the restaurant helped satisfy Chung that he wasn't being followed. After several minutes, he was satisfied no one was following Bae. Chung approached Hyun-ae unseen as she walked away.

Chung picked up his pace and caught her by the arm.

"Hyun-ae, I'm sorry I'm late."

She spun around, annoyed, saying.

"I'm not accustomed to waiting outside a restaurant for a man, any man. It's been fifteen minutes!"

"Why didn't you leave then?"

"I'm hungry and I'm curious. Who the hell are you?" She asked.

"Hyun-ae, let's go get the pyongyang naengmyeon. They make the best in town. Someone has rumored it that the recipe is from North Korea."

"That's not good. I'm at a restaurant with a strange man that likes North Korea food."

They both laughed, the ice broken.

Chung requested a table in the back corner of the restaurant, tipping the maitre'd handsomely. The restaurant was large and dimly lit. Sitting across from Hyun-ae, he was taken aback by her striking good looks. Her hair rested on her shoulders with long bangs that touched the top of her dark eyes, eyes that looked into you, not at you. An angular face, not round and full. A figure that turned men's heads. She walked with the confidence of a fit athlete and an attitude of, don't fuck with me.

"Hyun'ae, what do you want to drink?"

"A OB."

"Beer, few girls drink beer." He said with a raised eyebrow.

"OB's an excellent beer, better than the imports. They make OB from rice, Korean rice."

The waiter returned with two chilled glasses and bottles of OB after taking the order.

"Hyun-ae, I have been supporting your organization and know little about you. What can you tell me?"

"You first, I know less about you. You give a girl over three hundred thousand won, no questions asked? I don't even know your name. What do you want?" She asked.

"Fair enough. It is best we keep my full name out of it. Chung is sufficient. I am a businessman. My partners and I own a small manufacturing plant near Pusan. I travel to Seoul often on business. I have friends in the government. Our factory makes items that are controlled by the government. Under control, I mean they allow other countries to import the same items at a lower price."

"What other countries?"

"The Americans, but Japan is importing more. I despise the Ilbon-oe as much as I despise the Americans." He said convincingly.

"Why support my group? Don't businessmen just pay someone off to get what you want?"

"We are a legitimate business. We want good government to enable the country and businesses to grow."

"Chung, what business?" do you make something?

"Sorry Hyun-ae, the less you know, the better."

"Why, I will not reveal the source of the funding MISTER Chung! I could show the money came from small donations. It's not that much, 300,000 won is what an American soldier makes in a month."

Chung skipped the remark and asked.

"Hyun-ae, are you aware the government is watching you?"

"What! How do you know? So that's why you told me to get in a food line yesterday before you disappeared in the crowd."

"Yes, the two men were following you were from one of the government agencies. I can't, as a representative of my company, be seen with a student agitator. We must be very careful if I continue to support April II." He said.

"What do you expect to gain by supporting a bunch of University students?"

"Hyun-ae, your group has taken the name of April II for a principled reason. The protest in April

1960, got rid of a very cruel man. President Rhee had to flee South Korea. The students woke up the public. The protests caused the changes."

Hyun-ae took a long drink of her beer. She sat her glass on the table and folded her hands and leaned forward, glaring at Chung. With eyes he felt saw through his deceit. She said.

"Those protests cost two hundred lives. I will not let that happen. We're peaceful protesters. You and your fellow businessmen are foolish to think we'd risk everything for your profits! YOU! As Hyun-ae pointed a finger at Chung, she continued.

"YOU! want us to do your dirty work. We won't do it! Besides, I'm going to get my doctorate. Why should I risk everything?" As she raised her voice.

Chung was concerned she was going to make a scene. So he said.

"President Rhee was a barbarian. Park is trying to be a good leader. He doesn't want to squash student protests with violence. The police only charge your protesters with minor crimes requiring a small fine to be paid. We don't want violence. We want to change without violence. Yes, we'll profit, but so will our country."

"Why is someone following me?" She asked.

"The government, or the University wants to make sure you are not a North Korea spy!"

"I'm not, but you Chung with no last name. You may be the spy."

"I assure you I'm not a spy. I grew up in a small village outside of Pusan and attended Pusan

National University. My degree was in mechanical engineering. My partners and I started a small manufacturing business five years ago. It has grown but could grow larger and provide good wages for the workers 'IF' we didn't have to compete with the Americans."

Chung knew he tweaked her interest when she asked the next question.

"Your parents, where do they live? Are you married?"

"My mother died of an illness two years ago and my father died in the war. I am engaged to a lovely girl from my village. Her name is Ae-Sook." Chung saw the flicker of disappointment in Hyun-ae eyes.

"How do I know this is true?" She asked.

"I will show you my identity card. I'll hold my finger over my address and name. You can see my photograph, occupation, manufacturer, date and place of birth and here is a picture of Ae-Sook." Chung had Ae-Sook's picture taken in front of Namdaemun Gate in Seoul.

Hyun-ae continued to study the identification card.

"You're thirty two, you don't look that old."

She took the photograph of Ae-Sook and studied it for a moment. "Ae-Sook lives in Seoul?"

"No, she has relatives here. I took the picture during a visit." Chung explained.

"She is beautiful."

"Thank you. Now, your turn?" He said.

Just then, two American officers were being

seated a few tables away. They were talking loud. Hyun-ae cocked her head, listening.

Chung, speaking in English, interrupted her eavesdropping by asking in English. "You speak English?"

"Yes, I attended the University of California at Berkley for two years."

"How did that happen?" He asked.

"My physics professor attended Berkley, and he arranged a scholarship."

"Ahh, that was your training ground for organizing protests. Did you like America?"

"It's a nice place to visit. The country is divided. Not geographically, Vietnam and civil rights are big issues in America."

"Were the Americans nice to you or did they treat you like ah, what's the word, a chink or gook?"

"Most were nice. American men are brash, without sophistication, amusingly they stumble over themselves trying to court a girl."

"Certainly there are many suitors?"

"WHY DO YOU ASK? No, I don't have a lover in America or Korea."

"Sorry, I'll change the subject. You mentioned your doctorate. What's your field of study?"

"My thesis is using Nuclear power to produce electricity. Korea has few coal reserves, no oil on land, in the Yellow or Sea of Japan. We depend on the Americans for oil. I want to change that."

"Any brothers, sisters, your mother, father?" He asked.

"My only relatives are my uncle. He has two boys. Aunt Ju has no children. My father was an officer in the army. He died in the war, June 1952. My grandparents disappeared during the Japanese occupation of our country."

My mother is one of the first woman doctors in Korea. Raised by the Methodist missionaries. She attended Ewha University and went on to medical school, graduating with top honors. I was nine when she disappeared in1949. Because of my father's military career, my mother's sister raised me, Aunt Ju. She lives near Seoul and my uncle lives in Munsan near the DMZ.

"What do you mean, your mother disappeared?"

"From what Aunt Ju told me, a friend of my mothers, Kim dal-sam had moved to Jeju Island. We visited there when I was five or six. I remember the beautiful beaches and the Hallasan mountains. The people of Jeju respected Kim dal-sam. He was a teacher and a local political leader. My father liked him. They disagreed on many issues, but they agreed on one. Hyun-ae continued.

"The United Nations Temporary Commission rules made it hard to work towards unification of Korea. The Americans were the instigators. This was after the Japanese occupation at the end of WWII. The Korean people needed more of a say and President Rhee was heavy-handed. The Americans looked the other way."

"Yes, that was a bad time for our country" Chung said solemnly.

"My mother received a letter from Dal-sum asking for her help in 1948. The people on the island were rebelling. There were heavy civilians and military casualties. The people in Seoul were told communist insurgents had incited the rebellion. It was not till much later we learned our military played a role in the atrocities. Our soldiers killed thousands of innocent civilians suspected of helping the communist. The communists killed thousands of inlanders that sided with the government.

As Aunt Ju tells it, my mother was headstrong and determined to use her training as a doctor. In Seoul, the male doctors treated her as a nurse or aide. My father didn't want her to go. They had a big fight. He took her ID card so she couldn't travel. As soon as my father left for his unit, my mother took me to Aunt Ju's. My mother used Aunt Ju's ID card to travel. They could be taken for twins. She wrote to father and me. The letters stopped in May 1949."

"You said disappeared. You believe your mother is still alive?" Chung asked.

Her eyes watering up Hyun-ae continued. "In my heart, there's an ache that will not go away. As long as the ache remains, I'll believe she is alive. She is a strong woman. When she dropped me off at Aunt Ju's, she told me I must always be prepared to adapt. When she left, she held my hands with tears in her eyes told me to always remember, at the end of hardship comes happiness."

"Why didn't your father go to her?" Chung asked.

"My father's military duties kept him going after her. It wasn't until June 1949 my father could travel to Jeju Island. He talked to local villagers. They told him Kim dal-sam fled to North Korea. Unknown to my father, Dal-sam was the communist leader in the uprising. They revered my mother for her medical treatment of civilians. She remained neutral during the rebellion. Near the end of the fighting, a North Korea boat picked up the surviving communists.

The villagers told my father, Dal-sam and his henchmen kidnapped my mother. We never received confirmation because war broke out in 1950. My father was killed two years later, never knowing the fate of his wife. Dal-sam made it back to North Korea. He was killed in the battle of Jeongseon in 1950. The North Korean government refuses to acknowledgethe carnage on Jeju happened or if my mother is dead or alive."

"Aunt Ju told you this?"

"Most of it, during a break at the university, I traveled to Jeju. The people there don't want to talk about those times. Neighbors that opposed each other still live in the same villages. I found a nurse who was with my mother the night she was taken.. She told me my mother was a wonderful doctor and person. She saved hundreds of lives. On the night she disappeared, Dal-sam, 'the ruthless devil communist' as she called him, came into the makeshift hospital with ten or twelve armed men. The army was closing on the village. Dal-sam demanded that mother go with him. He had wounded men needing medical attention. She refused. He walked over to the man my mother was treating and shot him and then threaten to shoot everyone in the ward, putting the pistol to the nurse's head. My mother relented, never to be seen again."

"That's so sad, Hyun-ae, go to the United Nations or the Red Cross. Someone will help."

"Unlikely. My aunt and I tried for years. Our own government wants everyone to believe the bloodbaths never happened. The uprising, or whatever you want to call it, was swept under the mat. They told us they verified Dal-Sam had died in combat. The government wants me to consider his death as closure. I don't want to talk about it any longer. Let's get something to eat. I'm hungry. I'm ordering chicken and sticky rice and for desert rice cake. What are you having, Chung?"

"Naengmyeon for me."

It was obvious talking about her mother was difficult. Chung wanted to ask one more question.

"Hyun-ae, what was your mother's given name?"

"Ae-Jeong, why do you ask?"

"It's only right to know her full name after what you told me."

"That is very kind, Chung. Her name Ae-Jeong means to love. My mother is a very loving woman."

"Hyun-ae, we need to be very careful. We must make sure the help I'm giving your organization is not linked to me. I'll contact you with the time and place for the next meeting. I may not return to Seoul for a month or two. I have business at home."

"Your Ae-Sook misses you." She said with a hint of envy.

"Yes, and my business. I have money you will need for your coming protest. Also information I received from my friends in the government. I was told the Americans will send more soldiers to our country."

Chung almost slipped and said, your country.

"Chung, why must we be so secretive?"

"Your protests get our argument out on the street. The students take the protest home. The parents hear it, the newspapers print it. Our lobbyist used it to make our point. We can't be seen as instigating the protest."

"You have a lobbyist?"

"Yes, Hyun-ae, back to what I was saying. Part of the information was in the papers. Also the indications are, so says my friend, that the North has hinted they wanted to discuss unification. President Park wants no part of the talks, he wants the talks of unification kept quiet. Before I tell you more, you must promise you will use the information in a way the government doesn't conclude it came from government source."

"How am I to do that?"

"You never say you got the information from a source, couch it, so it seems you read it somewhere as common knowledge or rumors. Use the information to stir the pot, mix truth with fiction. Your followers will believe you, the government will accuse you of making it up. For instance, the North Korea radio station broadcasts fabricated information about the Americans and our government. You denounce the broadcast, but ask why our government hasn't countered the propaganda and throw in the information I'm going to tell you."

"That's foolish Chung. I don't think referring to North Korea propaganda will work, but I get your point. I promise I'll be careful."

Chung smiled, not at her comment. He knew he convinced her he was everything he was not. She is smart, self assured, beautiful and a future nuclear scientist, but naïve. A trait easy to exploit. Maybe I can turn her?

Chung thought of another angle. He must get a message to Colonel Choi. If Hyun-ae's mother is alive in North Korea, Choi will find her. It'll take a couple of months, but Choi will find Bae Ae-Jeong. Hyun-ae's mother will be my ace in the hole. In the years to come, as a nuclear scientist, Hyun-ae may be useful.

"Hyun-ae, we will meet in again early September. I'll get a message to you."

"The people following me, what should I do?"

"Just go about your business. Make sure you get permission from the University for your rallies. Don't let your followers break the law. If the government sees nothing abnormal, they'll stop watching you."

Hyun-ae finished her rice cake as they continued a pleasant conversation covering politics and the changes occurring in Seoul. Old buildings and market places were being demolished and replaced with skyscrapers.

Chung left the restaurant feeling good. Using the forged identity card was the safest way to convince Hyun-ae he was a legitimate businessman. By the end of dinner, he felt his charm mesmerized her. Chung's instinct told him he was successful in deceiving her. If the police did question Hyun-ae, they'll be looking for Chung in Pusan. There're thousands of men named Chung. Until he heard from Colonel Choi, he was staying at the Ministry.

UI'S, GOOKS, CHINKS AND LITTLE FUCKERS

"If you are far from the enemy make him believe you are near."
Sun Tzu

"HOLY SHIT! When did you get the bars, Rosie? Aaah Captain, congratulations!"

"You were on the GP when my orders arrived."

"Well, this calls for a beer, Captain!"

"That sounds great. But get your men ready to go on patrol tomorrow."

"Tomorrow? We just got back from Gladys."

"Sorry Mike, new orders. Headquarters wants the number of patrols increased. You got time to take a shower. The briefing is at fourteen hundred. Bring your platoon sergeant and squad leaders."

"Yes, Sir."

"Mike, I thought you wanted off the GP duty?"

"I did, I mean I do. I was expecting a break for the men, Captain."

He gave an understanding nod and walked away.

I went to see Sergeant Hicks before taking a shower. He had a separate room in the third and fourth squad's quonset hut. As I opened the screen door, one newbie yelled A TEN Hut. I countered with AT EASE. Two squads per hut allowed space between bunks and they didn't have to be stacked.

Everyone was in olive drab skivvies, glad to get out of the week old fatigues. Men were cleaning rifles, others were stuffing the weeks' worth of sweat soaked fatigues in their laundry bags. One man had an Akai reel to reel, blasting with the Box Tops new song.

"The Letter." *'Gimme a ticket for an aeroplane, ain't got time to take a fast train, Lonely days are gone, I'm a-goin' home, my baby, just-a wrote me a letter.'*

The morale was high. Six of the men in the platoon selected by the platoon sergeant and approved by me were going on a 24-hour pass. The rest of the platoon was looking forward to two days of limited duty. After my AT EASE, Sergeant Hicks poked his head out of room. He took one look, and he knew the news wasn't good. The music died.

"What's up LT? Aaah shit, I bet they want us to pull fence duty tonight?"

"Nope, they have selected us for the prestigious duty of patrolling the DMZ, starting tomorrow."

The eavesdropping third and fourth squad let out a collective groan, and more than a few mumbled fucks and fuck us, someone kicked a locker. The sarge didn't want to hear the bitchin.

"KNOCK IT OFF!" the sarge said in a booming voice.

"Sarge, be at the briefing room at fourteen hundred, bring the squad leaders. Inform the first and second squad."

"What about Sergeant Gomez? His orders just came through. He's going home in a couple of days."

"He stays behind. Bring Ghostbear."

"LT, is something big up? The patrol is not till tomorrow. Why a briefing today?"

"I don't know. See you at fourteen hundred."

Ten minutes before the briefing, my men started filing into the room. Sergeant Bob Betz was the first to arrive. He just turned twenty-two. A college dropout from Atlanta. Eight months ago, he graduated from NCO school. He took his duties seriously, a trait he instilled in his men. They respected him, nicknaming him sergeant BB. The nickname is not because of his name, it's because when he chews you out, it stings like getting shot with a BB gun. You wouldn't know he was a kick ass sergeant. He looked more like tall and lanky Barney Fife. Betz has been in the country for just two months.

Sergeants Ken Potter and Calhoun walked in together. Potter joined the Army in Erie, Pennsylvania, right out of high School. He screwed his knee up while at Fort Polk's advanced infantry course. After surgery and rehabilitation, the Army said he could stay but wasn't combat fit.

Potter made a career of getting transferred to an infantry division in Korea. He figured he could then finagle a way to get transferred to Vietnam. The CO twice denied his request. Potter, at six feet tall and a wiry one hundred and eighty pounds, is an aggressive leader.

Sergeant Sam Calhoun also joined the Army right out of high school in his hometown of Chicago. He scored so high on his aptitude test they wanted him to go to OCS. Instead, he opted for NCO school. He was a spit and polish man. After a week on the GP, his fatigues still looked fresh. Calhoun had come under fire. During his senior year in high school, two rival street gangs caught Calhoun and his girlfriend in a crossfire.. The shooting continued for several minutes. His girlfriend was hit in the thigh, he able to get her to cover and bandage the wound. He was street smart.

Ghostbear walked in the door with a somewhat bewildered look on his face. Unknown to Specialist, Charlie Ghostbear was being promoted to Sergeant. Sergeant Hicks and I both agreed he was an outstanding soldier. Though he had the attributes of a good leader, we won't know till he's tested. I motioned to him.

"Ghostbear, you know Sergeant Gomez will be shipping out. We're promoting you. The Captain approves and the first sergeant is finishing your paperwork." Ghostbear in true form was low key and humble.

"Thank you lieutenant, I will do my best."

"I know you will."

That was it, no questions. There was a smile on his face as he walked away.

Captain Hunt and Lt Mueller walked in the door. The sarge was right, something was going on. Just my platoon, no other Charlie company platoon leaders? Captain Roseman and Mo were a couple of steps behind the two staff officers.

Captain Hunt got right to the point.

"Men, Your CO has selected lieutenant Reed's platoon to conduct missions in the DMZ under the new orders and rules of engagement. The patrols are designated as hunter/killer patrols. I'm here to give you the basic changes in the operating procedure. Lieutenant Mueller will brief you tomorrow on current information. Open patrolling along the MDL is to cease. SHOW OF FORCE patrols are no longer part of our mission. Your new mission is to go on the offensive in the DMZ. Let the gooks think we no longer patrol the DMZ, become invisible in order to disrupt their infiltration and scouting missions."

"The most recent firefight involving the 1/31st resulted in one dead enemy soldier. Several made it back across the MDL. The dead son of a bitch had a hand-drawn map showing dates, times and routes of our patrols. During the firefight, they dropped a satchel charge. The same type of charge used last May at Camp Walley, in which two men were killed and eighteen wounded. It's been obvious they're scouting our patrols. We need to interdict their scouting missions.."

Sergeant Hicks raised his hand.

"You say no more SHOW OF FORCE patrols along the MDL. Should we stay away from the MDL?"

"Thanks sergeant, it's the platoon leader's call. The patrols will no longer be required to patrol along the MDL."

"Thanks Captain."

"The Patrols will be anywhere from twenty-four to seventy-two hours. On the longer patrols, you can send a patrol to the GP to resupply. We will stock the GPs with extra C's, ammo and water. The patrols are to use the terrain, trees as concealment, particularly near the gooks GPs."

"Lieutenant Reed, your platoon is to operate as five patrols. During the day, you will split your patrols to conduct sweeps and a blocking force. At night, you will set up five separate ambushes. We will issue each platoon one starlight scope. It's the smaller version, you can be mount it on an M-14. Questions?"

"You said we are to sweep the areas of interest. Who chooses the area, the time, and when do the men get to rest?" Reed asked.

"That is going to be your call, Lieutenant, unless we have intelligence that points to a specific area. You're to run the patrols in a way the North Koreans think you left the sector. No more bullshit patrols in the open! It's not deterring them!"

Mo asked. "Any changes to the rules of engagement?"

"Minor changes, the heavy mortar platoon and the QRF will support the patrols. Permission to use HE rounds south of the MDL will come from brigade instead of division. You can request Illumination rounds from the four duce. You can return fire across the MDL, into North Korea, without requesting permission. The operative words 'return fire.' The new directive from Eighth Army Headquarters states, all unidentified individuals, UI's are to be considered 'hostile' and are to be 'neutralized'. Quote and unquote."

Captain Hunt chuckled at the laughter and groans.

Before he said.

"Okay men, listen up. I was in the room when the division commander read the new orders. Someone asked what the hell, when the General explained."

"UI's, neutralize, it's my way of saying, '*kill the little fuckers.*' Captain Hunt's attempt to imitate the general got some laughs.

"The QRF will occasionally shadow the patrols."

Captain Roseman wasn't happy. "When are we getting replacement? My company is short, twenty men?"

"There will be an influx of replacements in the next few days. Your battalion will rotate out of the DMZ in late September. When you rotate back to the DMZ, your company will be close to full strength."

Our CO was pissed. "That doesn't help us NOW!"

Captain Hunt tried to soften the mood.

"Rosie, as I understand it, you and the rest of the company commanders are meeting with Colonel Williams after this briefing. The battalion commander is going to shuffle men around until the replacements arrive. Tomorrow morning at O nine hundred, Lieutenant Mueller will conduct the patrol briefing. Questions?"

Mo again, with half shit-eating grin, said.

"Captain, what are we to call the enemy, UI'S, Gooks, Chink's or Little Fuckers?"

"Call'em whatever you want. Anything else?"

No one had questions. Captain Roseman motioned me over.

"Reed, you Mo and Lieutenant Richards come up to

my houch after chow. I'm going over to battalion to see what the Colonel has to say about replacements. See you at eighteen hundred."

"Sure Captain."

"What happened to Rosie?" The new captain asked.

"Captain, you've earned your bars, you deserved to be addressed as Captain, get use to it."

"See ya, later, LIEUTENANT!"

The get together at Captains Rosie's houch was not much of a celebration. He had maps tacked to the wall. Beneath the map was a bucket with ice and eight cans of Hamm's beer. During two beers' worth of time, Mo and Richards briefed me on the ins and outs of running patrols in the DMZ. At twenty-one hundred, we called it a night. Tomorrow would be a long day. The two beers didn't help. It was a restless night.

THE FIRST PATROL

I met up with Sergeant Hicks after breakfast. We discussed what the men should carry. The squad, or I should say "patrol" leaders, instructed the men to get ready. Each rifleman was to carry at least eight, magazines besides the one in the M-14, two frag grenades, two canteens, poncho, extra socks, extra T-shirt, camouflage paint, three boxes of C's, bayonet, flak jacket, steel pot and one army issued blanket folded inside the poncho. The poncho blanket combo kept you from getting a wet ass while on a night ambush.

In addition, each patrol carried two claymores, four signal flares, two smoke grenades, four trip flares, a PRC-25 radio with extra battery, one pair of binoculars, a compass, a trenching tool. The RTO carried the M-79 and 18 rounds and a Colt 1911 pistol. The sarge and I, along with the patrol leaders, carried M-14's with a selector switch. This gave us the ability to fire on full automatic. A M-14 on full automatic was difficult to fire accurately. They assigned us one medic for five patrols.

Lieutenant Mueller's briefing was short and to the point. The weather during the first week of August was typical, hot, and humid. We assigned new call signs and passwords. RP's plotted. The highlight and alarming part of the briefing was the discovery of an unchartered Korean War era minefield.

One of lieutenant Richard's patrols stumbled on a dead gook, minus most of his lower body. The dead gooks' comrades didn't stick around. Dead men don't talk. They must have figured the explosion alerted the GIs. They didn't recover the dead mans weapon, an AK-47.

The engineers were called in and found another bouncing betty. The heavy rains were eroding the soil, causing the mines to be exposed. We now had another red lined minefield on our maps. I walked over to the staging area just as sarge exited his houch.

"Sarge, are the men ready?"

"Yes, sir."

"Feel free to fill in with whatever information I miss, or you want to add. Let's meet with the patrol leaders first, then the entire platoon."

"Sounds good, lieutenant."

The patrol leaders were kneeling, studying the map. Their packs in a row. Their weapons rested on top of their packs. The muzzles pointed north. Sergeant Hicks and I went over Mueller's briefing with the patrols. Sergeant Hicks pointed out the new minefield and the fact the gooks were now equipped with the AK-47.

"Listen up, men! Our mission is no longer 'a show of force.' Patrols should stay under cover as much as possible. Open areas are to be avoided. We will scout ambush positions during the daytime patrols.

We will coordinate the ambush locations at the rendezvous. The ambush positions should be three to four hundred meters apart. If the terrain prevents patrols from firing at each other, the positions can be closer. We'll rendezvous at fifteen hundred at charlie sierra 074951, chow down and rest before going on ambush. Questions?" Sergeant Calhoun spoke.

"What happens if a patrol comes under attack and needs help?"

"That's the purpose of coordinating our position at the rendezvous. Sergeant Hicks patrol will be situated where he can move to support a patrol. I will be with Sergeant Ghostbears patrol. We'll be able to support the other patrols. **No** movement at night without specific orders from Sergeant Hicks or me. Is that clear?"

A concerted, Yes Sir!

"The QRF is at our beck and call. Response time depends on our location. Field strip and bury your butts. The same goes for C ration cans, uneaten food, wrappers. If you have to take a dump, bury it. We need to be ghosts and the gooks' worst nightmare."

Sergeant 'BB' Betz, who was still kneeling studying the map, stood and asked.

"Lieutenant, how long will we be out?"

"As it stands now, two days. Listen up, I don't want the enemy to know we're in the DMZ. They can intercept our radio transmissions. I don't want any unnecessary radio traffic and none of that 'shorrrrt' bullshit over the air."

During the sweep, move your patrol and quietly. Look for signs of the enemy movement. Footprints, matted grass, food wrappers or tins, anything human and not GI. Make sure your men stay alert. Use hand signals as much as possible."

I picked up my pointer, a three foot long branch that Sergeant Hicks had removed the bark and traced our route on the map. Standing in front of the sergeants, I had mixed emotions. It was surreal, chilling, and exciting. I was responsible. It's up to me to lead thirty-seven men into combat. This differed from sitting in a fortified position, waiting for an attack. One that never came. Now our mission was to hunt a skilled and elusive enemy. How will I react in combat? The men, how will they react? I felt I could depend on my sergeants. They worked well together. Sergeant Hicks was the only one with combat experience. I was counting on teamwork and training. My stomach was churning. I continued with the briefing.

"When we get to the DMZ, we'll patrol as a platoon to just south of ambush alley. At that point, Sergeant Hick's patrol, along with Sergeant Calhoun's and Sergeant Potter's, will peel off and move to the vicinity of Charlie Sierra 140902. This will be the first leg of your sweep and block maneuver. At your objective, you'll select an ambush position with good cover and concealment. any questions?"

Okay then, I will be with Sergeant Ghostbear's patrol. Sergeant Ghostbear and Sergeant Betz patrols will hold for 60 minutes near ambush alley. After an hour, we'll sweep to a point just south of GP Gladys. Once we are south of Gladys, we'll swing east towards your position. Sergeant Hicks, you take the medic with you. Sergeant Potter's patrol will take the Starlight scope. Riker has experience with the starlight."

"Yes sir, at Fort Polk. It's a great scope when it works."Riker said.

We briefed the patrol leaders about the dead gook scouting our patrols. Sergeant Hicks emphasized the point.

"I better not catch any patrol on one of the old trails. If I do, your ass is grass and I'm a lawn mower!"

"Sergeant Hicks, let's get the men over to the test fire range. After we finish test firing, I want everyone back here for the last inspection and briefing. We have an hour before our ride is here."

"Yes, sir."

The test range was a bulldozed berm, six feet high. The test fire range was to insure your rifle worked. Each mission required a visit the range and firing your weapon into the berm. Each patrol lined up twenty-five meters from the berm and fired three rounds. We made test firing interesting by lining up empty beer or pop cans, one can per rifleman. The bet among the patrols was the most holes in the cans won. Sergeant Betz's patrol won the case of beer with sixteen holes.

During the last inspection of gear, you could hear

the APCs warming up their diesel engines, our ride the mile or so to the fence. Tower five was our entry point into the DMZ.

Each man carried or wore at least forty pounds of equipment and ammo besides their ten pound M-14 rifle. The United Nations Command issued a comical order we were to wear a black armband, declaring we were DMZ Police. To add to the bullshit, each man carried a DMZ POLICE ID card. They printed the card in English on one side and Korean on the back. *"THE BEARER OF THIS PASS IS AUTHORIZED COMPLETE FREEDOM OF MOVEMENT ACROSS THE SOUTHERN BOUNDARY OF THE DEMILITARIZED ZONE AND WITHIN THE SOUTHERN HALF OF THE DEMILITARIZED ZONE. THIS PASS MAY BE VOIDED AT ANY TIME BY THIS HEADQUARTERS. NOT VALID FOR ENTRY INTO NORTHERN PORTIONS OF THE DEMILITARIZED ZONE."*

I watched the men as Ghostbear and Hicks repositioned the map. The men were jabbering back and forth. Private Riker was holding the blue colored DMZ card up in the air to get everyone's attention.

"Guys, did you read this, *'not valid'*? Who the fuck wants to go there?" Someone yelled back. "If there's fresh pussy involved, you'll be the first!"

The men started taping the buckles on slings, tightening or loosening their flax jackets, and adjusting their web gear. I could sense anxiety and enthusiasm. A hunter killer patrol differed from marching to the GP and sitting on your ass for a week. The men knew the next two days were going to be intense. They continued to break each other's balls with wisecracks.

Most of the men had never been on patrol. They sat in a foxhole in front of the fence or on GP Gladys. Tonight, no foxhole, no sleep. Laying on our ponchos at an ambush site, watching a path waiting for the gooks. Placement of the claymores and trip flares was an educated guess. The gooks could attack from any of the points on a compass.

The mood changed. When I started the full platoon briefing, the joking stopped. The men became attentive and somewhat somber. The mission was different, more difficult and dangerous.. We now had to locate and destroy the enemy. Earlier in the barracks, the Kutusas added to the anxiety by passing along rumors that the gooks were crossing the MDL in larger units in the ROK sector, causing heavy casualties. Most of the Kutusa's had relatives or friends in the South Korean army, the stories had credibility.

Foxhole Charlie was still fresh in everyone's mind. Colonel Williams had ordered every company commander to send a contingent of men to the sendoff of the Boyer, Cook and McElroy. The men, including myself, watched as they loaded the body bags into the ambulance.

ELUSIVE ENEMY

"The most terrible job in warfare is to be a second lieutenant leading a platoon when you are on the battlefield." Dwight D. Eisenhower

Mo was sitting in our comfortable, beat up, decade old upholstered chair. A bucket of ice and beer by his side, Mo had eighteen hours off from QRF duty. I had just met with the Captain. I sat on the footlocker across from Mo.

"Wanna beer?" Mo asked, it was on the way, air bound, before I could say yes.

I caught the can and rolled it on my forehead. It felt good, cold and smooth. Using the church key attached to my seat with a lanyard, I opened the beer. I sat there with my elbows on my knees, staring at the top of my beer can, brooding.

We had ten patrols under our belt. There was no contact with the enemy in August. We knew every inch of Charlie company's area of operation after trudging over hill and dale, through woods, thick brush, and long abandoned rice paddies. The rice paddies were the worst. Over the decades, the paddies degraded into swamps. The grass wasn't as high as an elephant's eye, but tough to walk through and a good hiding place, but no one was hiding.

The men were wet, hot and tired, the dog days of August were a bitch, hot with rain and a wet chill at night. It was hard to keep their attention. I had a sense we were going to make contact, but I wanted it on our terms. Intuition was screaming, something was going to happen. Who's hunting who?

"Mike, what's bothering you?" Mo asked.

"Mo, we have been on ten patrols and not a hint of the enemy. Bravo Company was involved in a firefight last week. You and your QRF chased the little fuckers back across the MDL. The 1/31th got hit, two dead, three wounded. Every night along the DMZ, there has been contact with every unit but ours."

"Mike, that's a good thing! You run a tight operation. The gooks see there's little opportunity to ambush your patrols."

"That's the goddamn problem, they can see. Every move we make, the gooks know. At the briefing, they told us to be invisible, BULLSHIT! I know we're going to be hit, big time."

"You'll be ready for it." Mo said.

"I will, but will my men. It's getting difficult to keep them focused. They are falling asleep on ambush. Shit, last night, on ambush I had to bounce a couple of rocks off of Sillhammer's helmet. I'm ten feet away and he snores like a goddamn buzz saw!" Mike said.

"Hey don't worry, I got your back. If you get in a tight spot, I'll run the APCs right up their ass. Fuck the so called fucking Armistice agreement."

"I know."

"Mike, what did Captain Rosie want?"

"Oh yeah, I almost forgot. The word is we'll be rotating south of the river during the first week in September. Also, we go back on patrol tomorrow. This time it's for two days."

"Damn, good news with the bad, typical Army. Another beer?" Mo asked.

"No, we gotta get up early."

"What do you mean 'WE' I'm sleeping in till I wake up?"

"Change of plans, we go on patrol at O DARK THIRTY." Mike said.

"That means what for me?"

"The captain will brief us in the morning. You're to have your men ready for a daytime patrol."

"What the fuck time is O dark thirty?" Mo asked.

"Early, O four hundred."

"You got to be shitting me. Damn, no rest for the incorrigible."

****

O four hundred came fast. The strong coffee perked us up for the short briefing. The plan was simple. We were to enter the DMZ in Bravo company's sector, swing over into our normal area of patrol. Mo and his men were to shadow our patrols on foot. At eighteen hundred, they were to leave the DMZ and go back on mechanized QRF duty. Division intelligence picked up believable radio chatter showing "enemy activity". The men were not impressed at the predawn briefing. They heard it before, they knew the drill.

I stayed with Ghost Bear's patrol. Sergeant Hicks and Sergeant Calhoun's patrol maneuvered a couple hundred meters inside the southern boundary. Patrolling till they were east of the bombed out locomotive and then set up in a blocking ambush. I would take three patrols and maneuver far enough south of the MDL to stay out of sight. The QRF platoon trailed our right flank by two hundred meters. When we approached Hicks's and Calhoun's patrol, the QRF was to break off and set up on a nearby hill.

By noon, we completed the first leg of the maneuver and broke for chow. I weighed our choice of Ghostbear as a patrol leader. Sergeant Ghostbear turned out to be an excellent leader. He spoke quietly but firmly. Ghost bear was a stickler on covering our tracks. When we stopped for chow, he made sure they buried the trash, instructing the men to cut sod off the hole, set it aside, bury the cans, and then replace the sod. At night, the men were quick to set out the trip flares and claymores.

After chow we patrolled to our rendezvous and made plans for the nights ambushes. So far, the most excitement was a flock of pheasants flushing. The point man, Rodriguez, hit the deck when the cackling ringnecks flushed. He said he nearly shit his pant. We also kicked up three small Asian deer. Flushing game kept the men alert.

If the enemy was watching us, they were invisible. No footprints in the mud along the creek that ran east and west before bending across the

MDL. No sign of the enemy. A wlk in the park? My intuition was telling otherwise.

Our rendezvous was a hill covered with trees and brush, thick enough to hide five patrols. The patrols arrived at thirteen hundred. We made plans for the night ambushes while the men rotated between guard duty and sleep. Sanchez was sitting against a tree, holding up the mike indicating I was wanted on the horn. In the other hand, he held an open can of ham and Lima beans. The only soldier in the army that traded a can of fruit cocktail for ham and Lima beans.

"This is red moon, over."

"Red moon, this is sailfish six. Tomorrow's mission changed."

"Roger, out."

I spent the next twenty minutes deciphering the coded message using the code book I carried on a chain around my neck. I motioned for Sergeant Hicks to join me.

"Lets get the patrol leaders together. If any of them are sleeping, wake them. We just received new orders."

I spread out the map on the ground as the patrol leaders knelt in a semicircle.

"At O six hundred, the QRF will start a sweep at coordinates CS192220. We'll set up blocking positions in five different locations."

I pointed at the route on the map the QRF sweep would follow. The sweep was through a mixture of woods and swampy, overgrown rice paddies. We will spread our blocking positions on a series of small hills. G-2 had picked up information there were gooks in the area. After the sweep, the QRF will leave the DMZ. Headquarters thinking is an openly visible sweep will draw the gooks out into the open or force them into one of our blocking positions.

Sergeant Betz asked

"What if the gooks come across in a large force? We're broken up into small units. It's easy for them to hit and run because we are a couple hundred meters from the MDL."

"We'll set up like our night ambushes. If the shit hits the fan, we'll be close enough to support each other. Being daylight, we can move quickly." I said.

The map showed a series of small hills interlocked in a half circle overlooking a large rice paddy with woods on two sides. The hills were only hummocks covered with trees and brush, easy to defend.

"In addition, A company is on alert and ready to move as needed. Questions? Get some sleep. We're moving out in four hours."

I sat with my back up against a tree. Half the men were sound asleep. It amazed me how easily the men could drop off into sandman land. The temperature was around eighty, the men just spread out their poncho, rested their heads on their packs and goodnight. If there was a thick mattress to lie on, I couldn't sleep. I was ramped up. This patrol felt different.

At dusk, we moved to our night ambush

positions. The long night was disappointing in a good way. No enemy, but a son of a bitch in another way. At daybreak, it started raining. A torrential downpour that lasted for a couple of hours. Everything was not just wet, but waterlogged. To make matters worse, we had to set up the blocking force, coordinating with the QRF.

That meant dragging our wet asses and sopping wetgear fifteen hundred meters to the blocking location. Bogging us down even more was the water in every low spot. The small creek that was knee deep was now waist deep.

By noon, the clouds broke, and the sun felt like a blowtorch. The muggy air sucked the strength and morale out of the men.

The sweep was tedious for the QRF, trying to maneuver around the swamps. Once in position on the hillside, all we had to do was wait. The scorching sun summoned every flying, biting insect. The brush covered hillside provided shade and concealment. At least we didn't have to park our asses in the water. Looking to my left and right, the men were alert.

The QRF sweep didn't flush any gooks out of the brush. Bird-dogging didn't work. Two days and nights, nothing but wet feet and soggy gear. After the five-hour sweep, headquarters ordered the QRF to patrol just north of the minefield and exit the DMZ through tower five. We were on our own again.

We stopped on one of the interlocking hills and let the men eat. Headquarters wanted a five patrol sweep before sixteen hundred hours. We were to sweep the small rolling hills to our west. The hills were heavily forested, with small trees. Most of the trees sprouted after the Korean War and were fifteen to twenty feet tall. They were close together and provided excellent cover and concealment for friend or foe. Between the hills were more overgrown rice paddies.

After studying the map, I determined Sergeants Hick's and Potter patrols would be the shadow patrol and stay deep in the woods. I stayed with Ghostbear's patrol, Betz and Calhoun on the right flank of Sergeant Hicks and Potter. We moved west to our last rally point, the route previously plotted. We couldn't see Hick's or Potter's patrols. They were two hundred meters away. The thinking was we could patrol the thick cover on the hills and be above the open areas and any potential ambush.

I buried my empty can of beans and franks. It was twelve hundred, time to move out. Ghost Bear put Brown on the point of our diamond formation. The three patrols comprised twenty-two men. A formidable force considering Hicks and Potter patrols added another fifteen. The men, resting in the shade, stood on the order to move out! Swatting the mosquitoes along with the heat and rain smeared the greasy camo paint. The dark faces fit the mood.

The men were tired and quietly bitchin, I couldn't blame them. We were halfway through our misery for the day. We had to swing off the hill to a rice paddy. Once on the bottom, we could move inside a tree line to the next hill. The point man was ten meters inside the tree line when he stopped and was looking hard right towards the rice paddy. Brown held up his hand for everyone to stop and get on one knee. I moved up, eyeballing the grass.

"What's up Brown?"

"LT, something came through, crushing the cattails. I looked back, the men were on one knee. I motioned for Sergeant Ghostbear. The grass in the overgrown rice paddy was chest high, mixed in with cattails and flooded. The trail of crushed cattails crossed the entire paddy."

"Brown, you cover us. Sarge, take the trail on the left and I'll take the other. Let's see if we can find a track, human or animal."

The paddy had a few high spots. We might find a track. I had not gone fifteen feet when Ghostbear gave a low whistle. Then in a hushed voice said.

"Lieutenant, fresh gooks tracks, maybe seven or eight."

The hair went up on the back of my neck.

"Get Sergeant Hicks on the horn."

By now, Hick's patrol was across from us. I motioned for Sanchez to move to my position. I signaled to the men the number of enemy and the direction they were heading. Out of the paddy, the tracks disappeared.

"Steel jacket, this is red moon, over."

"This is steel jacket." replied Hicks.

"We have gook tracks in the mud. They're fresh,

seven or eight men. Move Calhoun's patrol in tight with yours. Stay in the woods. We'll stay inside the tree line until you get to the old trail at the base of the hill. Hold up there until we're across from you. There's another rice paddy at the bottom of the hill. We will stay in the tree line as far as we can. Once we are at the base of the hill, we'll move towards the top."

"Roger."

We moved out slowly, not wanting to get sucked into an ambush. The wet gear and the raised hair on my neck forgotten. This was on our terms. We know they're here. Even if they saw us, we may trap them using the QRF. Mo was moving to a supporting position. In order to comply with the Armistice agreement, they had to move on foot. That put them at least thirty minutes away. A long time if bullets are flying. Sergeant Hicks and his men were our flanking force if we came under fire and vice versa.

We were still in the tree line approaching a rice paddy between us and the next hill. "TAKE COVER!"

I heard the bullets whine by and hit the trees, then the muzzle blasts as I hit the dirt. Rodriquez was screaming in pain. Someone else was screaming "MEDIC I'm hit!" Two men down and the tempo of the incoming rounds was increasing. Shit! A lot of small arms and machine gun fire. The men were returning fire. It wasn't affecting the tempo of the machine gun fire from the side of the hill. The small arms fire was coming from the base of the hill, a hundred meters away. I was trying to get a fix on the machine gun when I saw five or six gooks running through heavy brush on our left. The fleeting figures appearing and disappearing. Riker also spotted them. We opened up, firing several rounds where they were and where we thought they went. Calhoun's patrol spotted them and opened up with their rifles and M-79.

The noise was horrific. We had to shoot through the same brush that was providing cover and concealment. The two-way firing range was causing more damage to the foliage than to flesh. Bullets were ripping through branches and small trees. The running gooks either hit the ground or were hiding in the brush. They were trying to flank us with the machine gun providing cover. Sanchez had flopped next to me, knowing I needed the radio. "STEEL JACKET, STEEL JACKET, OVER! GOOKS ON THEIR WAY TO YOU!"

"ROGER" Hicks replied.

JOHNSON, SANCHEZ GET SOME GRENADES ON THAT FUCKIN MACHINE GUN. TWO HUNDRED METERS AT ONE O'CLOCK!

I thought, how long before Mo and his men arrive?

"SPLIT SHOT SPLIT SHOT OVER!"

"THIS IS SPLIT SHOT, WE'RE ON THE WAY, ETA TWENTY MINUTES!" Mo said.

Sanchez's and Johnson's 40mm grenades from their m-79's started thumping near the machine gun. The rounds were hitting the trees and exploding before reaching the target. The incoming rounds from the machine gun were not decreasing. We were fortunate, the trees and the uneven ground provided excellent cover. Up ahead was a gully cut by run off water. It was deep enough to offer cover for a defensive position. I needed to get the men forward.

Sergeant Hicks men were engaged with the gook's trying to flank us. Grenades and rifle fire and the BRRRRRUP of the ppsh submachine gun. The small arms fire had the much louder crack of the AK-47.

"GHOST," I didn't have the time or breath to yell his title and full name. "GET YOUR MEN IN THE GULLY. I'LL HAVE CALHOUN AND BETZ COVER YOU."

"GOT IT."

I ran over to Betz and yelled to Calhoun. "GHOST IS GOING TO MOVE UP COVER HIM, GHOST GO! BETZ, WE GO NEXT."

Everyone that wasn't running forward started firing at the machine gun and the muzzle flashes in the shaded woods. In our dash to the gully, no one was hit. We now had a better angle to fire on the machine gun. Johnson and Sanchez were "jack-in-the-boxes" popping up to shoot, then ducking to reload their single shot grenade launcher. It was obvious there were more than eight gooks. I was guessing twenty. I called Mo.

"SPLIT SHOT SPLIT SHOT, THIS IS RED MOON, OVER."

"SPLIT SHOT HERE."

"THE MACHINE GUN IS AT CS178960. APPROACH FROM THE WEST, THEN SWING NORTH OF THEM. WE MAY TRAP THEM, WHEN YOU GET CLOSE CALL ME.

"ROGER,"

"RED MOON, THIS IS STEEL JACKET OVER."

"RED MOON,"

Hicks and his men cut off the gooks that were trying to flank us. "THEY PULLED BACK AS SOON AS THEY CAME UNDER FIRE. DO YOU WANT US TO MOVE FORWARD?"

"NEGATIVE, STAY PUT WE HAVE TO TAKE OUT THE MG FIRST. THE QRF IS ON THE WAY."

"ROGER." Hicks replied.

I yelled over to Calhoun to watch to see if the gooks that broke contact with Hicks showed themselves again. I rolled over on my back to reload. The machine gun rounds were ripping through the brush and trees just over our heads. The trees were being scarred, bark and branches rained down on our helmets. Sanchez was still playing jack-in-the-box. I called the Captain. "SAILFISH SIX THIS IS RED MOON OVER!"

"This is sailfish six over."

"WE ARE UNDER HEAVY FIRE FIFTEEN TO TWENTY ENEMY SUPPORTED BY A MACHINE GUN AT CHARLIE SIERRA 178960. REQUEST FIRE MISSION, HE AT CS178960."

"This is sailfish, negative on request. Alpha company is moving to give you more support."

The Captain had to go up the chain of

command before unleashing the four-duce mortars. Authorization was unlikely. I wasn't going to hold my breath. We had to quiet the damn machine gun.

I motioned for Johnson and Sanchez to follow me. As we ran up the gully, I tapped the backs of two riflemen, getting their attention to follow us. Once we were beyond the right flank of the men, the plan was to pop up and put as many rounds as possible on the machine gun before we started drawing fire.

It worked. Sanchez must have put a round right on the machine gun or damn close, it quit firing.

The small arms fire was decreasing. The sons of bitches were withdrawing. I ordered Betz's patrol to move forward, providing covering fire. Then Calhoun's and Ghost Bear's. Hick's and his men also moved forward, protecting our flank. By the time we were in position to attack, the incoming fire had stopped. A enemy trick? We used recon by fire. Every Tom, Dick and Harry moved forward on line, firing their weapon into the gooks hideout.

"CEASE FIRE, CEASE FIRE!" There was no return fire as we closed on the positions.

"Split shot, split shot, this is red moon over."

Mo's heavy breathing accompanied his reply. They were humping it to get here.. "This is Split shot."

"The gooks withdrew. Just watch coming up the backside of the hill."

"Roger,"

"Red moon, steel jacket over." Hicks said.

"This is Red moon over."

"We have one dead gook and a weapon at the base of the hill near the trail."

"Roger, pick up the weapon, check the body for any intel."

"Roger,"

The gooks had set up the ambush. We found empty brass scattered around the prepared positions. The positions camouflaged with cut brush. The enemy had planned to ambush a patrol along the old trail. They didn't expect us to come over the hill. We found bloody dressings at three positions.

Pieces of rice paper showed they had chow while waiting. Their screw up was our good luck. One of them opened fire. If they had waited, we would have been in the kill zone.

I called back to Moss, our medic, telling him we were sending men to move the two wounded men. We left them behind with a rifleman and a radio. Moss reminded you of Alfred E. Neuman of Mad magazine, the big ears, goofy smile and the freckles. He was an outstanding medic. The men liked him. Somehow, he earned the moniker Fuzzy.

Rodriquez was going into shock. He was hit in the left arm and hand. A bullet hit the first knuckle, went through the palm, exited just below the little finger. separating his fingers from his palm. Moss said just skin held the hand together. Blood was soaking through the bandages. I knelt and put my hand on Rodriquez's shaking shoulder. Moss stuck him with another syrette of morphine.

"Rodriquez, help is coming. We're getting you out of here!"

"MY HAND, MY HAND."

His dark eyes screaming fear. Morphine or not, he was terrified.

"My hand, my hand, why me?"

I didn't have an answer.

PFC Brown was the second man hit. He was unconscious on the poncho stretcher. Blood soaked banages on his upper chest and leg. Riker was holding a plazma bag hooked up to Brown.

"LT we have to get Brown air evac once we get to the fence. He might not make it!" Moss pleaded.

We will.I replied while cussing to myself, the goddamn rules kept choppers out of the DMZ.

"Split Shot, Red moon over."

"This is split shot."

"I need to evacuate one wounded asap and security while we police the site. What's your eta, over?"

"Just a couple of minutes. Two of my squads can take your men back."

"Roger."

"Sergeant Hicks, let's police up the gooks brass. Headquarters will be interested to know the gooks are using AK-47's The bastards will deny the entire incident at Panmunjom."

What a joke, Panmunjom, the North Korea delegation sits across from the United Nations delegation after every incident. The UN claims North Korea troops crossed the MDL. The North

Koreans deny it and accuse the Americans of crossing the MDL. No consequences, just a few harsh words, no retribution for what Rodriquez had just lost.

I watched my men as they moved among the gook positions, checking for booby traps and dropped weapons. I could see the adrenaline rush in the eyes, quick, sure steps with no sign of fatigue, no smiles or bantering. Our first taste of combat, a closeup look at where the enemy hid and waited to kill us.

Orders came over the radio as Mo and his men crested the hill. They ordered us to go to GP Gladys, resupply for another night on ambush.

"Mike, what's up? You look pissed."

"No rest for the wicked. I just received orders. Lucky us, we get to hump our way to Glady's, resupply and rest a bit. Then another night on ambush."

"What else do you want from us?" Two of my squads are moving your wounded."

"We used up a lot of ammo, tag along with us till we get to Gladys." I said.

"Ok, I don't think they'll try again. The 'little fuckers' got more than they were looking for and ran north to lick their wounds."

The mile march to the GP went quick. We moved through the brush and swampy areas with little bitchin; the men were alert. We were still high from fear and the adrenalin rush. Mo and his men dropped off before we reached the GP. Our approach to the GP was going to be observed by the gooks, no way around it. They know our location if they wanted to even the score.

"Sergeant Hicks, get the men stripped. I don't care if everyone is in their skivvies. We need to get everyone and everything dried out."

It took ten minutes for the GP to look like tenement housing with clothes lines stretched across every pole. The sun was out and a complimentary breeze from the north helped dry our gear. We had a few hours before moving out. The men chowed down and replenished their ammo. They felt secure at the GP. War stories were being bantered about with good nature ribbing untilBrown and Rodriquez's was mentioned.

Sergeant Hicks and I were sitting in the fortified position for the hidden 90mm recoilless rifle. It was against the Armistice to have a 90mm recoilless rifle in the DMZ. If the North attacked in force, the theory was the tank killing gun would be brought into play. The trouble with that theory is the GP is vulnerable to the heavy artillery. The North Koreans have enough cannons to flatten GP Gladys. Sarge and I made our plans for the night.

"Lieutenant, how do you think the men did today?" Hicks asked.

"They did great, everyone including you sarge. I don't believe the gooks expected you to be on our flank. They ran into a buzz saw."

"Did you get any word on Brown or Rodriquez?" Sarge asked.

"No, they'll take them to the medical unit near Seoul. Brown is shot up pretty bad, Fuzzy said he may not make it. Rodriquez gonna lose his hand."

"Shit, LT, Brown's brother is in Nam. Rodriquez's family are farmers. All he talked about was his cows. The men were calling him the milkman."

"I didn't know that, at least they out of here. You know what I also don't know?"

"What's that?" The sarge asked.

"Why the fuck the gooks can cross the MDL into this so-called neutral zone and kill us? They pick a spot, wait for a patrol, fire away and then beat it back north with no repercussions. It doesn't make any fuckin sense!"

"Lieutenant, we'll never know the answer. But it could've been worse. If we were on that trail, we would've been mincemeat. Fucking up their machine gun told them we were not someone to dick around with."

Sarge and I shot the bull for a while. He was divorced with two kids, a boy and a girl. They still live in Fayetteville, just outside Fort Bragg. He enjoyed bowling and fishing. Before he left for Korea, bought a used fishing boat and took his son fishing on Lake Wylie. His eight-year-old son caught a four-pound largemouth bass. Home for sarge was many months away.

Our ambush that night was as if nothing happened. No gooks, no combat. I asked the man upstairs to look over Brown and Rodriquez. Birds were singing at sunset and again at sunrise. They were out there, waiting for the next opportunity.

THE BLACK HORSE

"There could be shadow galaxies, shadow stars and even shadow people." Stephen Hawking

Hyun-ae was at Aunt Ju's cottage resting but in deep thought planning the upcoming protest

It was the middle of September and no word from her mystery man, Chung. She was wondering if Mr. Chung was who he said he was, thinking it may be better to distance myself from Chung. The money he provided was helpful. Could we get along without it? We need good information from inside the government, information that stirred the pot. Can Chung can supply it? He had sources in the government. The government getting into bed with the Americans was accurate. The newspapers printed that the government was taking money and military aid from the Americans, in exchange for what? Can I trust him? He's a capitalist with an agenda to further his business and help the country become independent of the Americans. One hand washes the other, so he will be useful to our cause. He can be our secret benefactor. We must move forward with our plans for the April II rally for September 29th. Aunt Ju will disapprove but will support me, even if I am arrested.

"Aunt Ju, when are you going back home?"

"Why do you want to know, Hyun-ae?"

Aunt Ju had two homes, one near the air base, Kimpo

and her cottage, as she called it, in the foothills of the Bukhansan mountains north of Seoul. Hyun-ae smiled as she remembered mother and the times they spent with Aunt Ju. Mother and Aunt Ju were so close, they were sisters and best friends. When my father was away with the army, we visited Aunt Ju. We played American music and danced. Aunt Ju taught me English and told funny stories. After the war, Aunt Ju fell in love with an American sergeant. Sergeant Joe Williams, he worked in the office that selected Korean companies providing services at the military bases.

Aunt Ju started out small, one contract for one American base. By 1955, she owned a large house near the Kimpo airbase. The house had the facilities and appliances of a modern home.

The cottage in the mountains was Aunt Ju's and Sergeant Joe's getaway. They had the cottage built in the traditional manner with a thatched roof and Ondol heating. The warmth of the floor in deep winter was soothing. Electricity and indoor plumbing are the only deviations they allowed. The cottage was high on the mountain. Seoul's city lights put on a dance every night. It was Aunt Ju's piece of heaven and starting to be mine.

Aunt Ju is a benevolent employer. She hired girls that worked the streets and provided them a place to stay. She paid a fair wage. In exchange, she demanded an honest day's work and a promise not to return to the streets. In return, she developed loyal, hardworking employees. The Americans noticed that work ethic. She now has contracts with ten American bases and close to one hundred employees and a modern laundry.

Her American sergeant returned to Korea after his discharge. Sergeant Joe had three good years with Ju. He died of a heart attack in 1961. He was a good man. He loved Aunt Ju and the Korean people. She buried him in a traditional Korean manner. It was a three-day ritual.

She washed 'her' Joe with incense and then dressed in a silk coat. They had taken the coat to the roof of the house and his name called out three times. The family prepared three bowls of rice, three vegetables, three soups, and three pairs of shoes. They were to be left outside for the messengers to the other world. As the wooden framed bier crossed the threshold carrying Joe's body, dressed for travel from this world to the afterlife, the men carrying the bier bowed three times. I can still picture Joe's and Aunt Ju's friends singing the sad song.

Arirang, Arirang, Arariyo, my love, you are leaving me, your feet will be sore before you go ten, just as there are many stars in the clear sky, there are so many dreams in our hearts, there're over there, that mountain is Baekdu Mountain, Where, even in the middle of winter days, flowers bloom.

Aunt Ju still believes in the old ways. She hired a shaman to perform a special ritual at the burial site to exorcise the evil spirits from the grave. Aunt Ju didn't allow the last part of the ritual. The oldest elder was supposed to stand on the coffin in the grave, then stomp on the dirt as friends and relatives tossed it in. She didn't want anyone dancing on Sergeant Joe.

"Did you fall asleep out there? Why do you ask Hyun-ae?"

"I'm sorry, I was daydreaming. It is so peaceful

here. I want to stay another day and plan my next protest."

"HYUN-AE! You're going to get yourself in trouble. Nothing good will come of these protests, especially if the University expels you? What about your doctorate?"

"They won't, most of my professors agree with me as long as the protests stay peaceful." Hyun-ae said.

"Hyun-ae, President Park and his henchmen will provoke violence. You have the professor's support because you are a treasure to the university and someday to your country. With that nuclear thing, you are smarter than your professors. Why do you think the Americans accepted you to go to their prestigious university in California?"

"The Americans didn't invite me. Professor Cheng arranged the scholarship." Hyun-ae said.

"Yes, but I had a long talk with Cheng before I let you go. He said your work caught the attention of scientists here and at Berkley. Hyun-ae you have to let this unification of our country go, let someone else chase the dream. It's never going to happen in our lifetime. If your mother was alive, she would want you to be happy, not leading a protest."

"SHE'S NOT DEAD! I feel it in my heart, SHE WOULD WANT ME TO DO WHAT I WANTED TO DO!" Hyun-ae yelled.

"Hyun ae, I miss my sister as much as a person can miss another. No word from her for eighteen years. She would've found a way, let her go! You have the world by the tail. It's time for you to find a nice young man and get on with your life."

"I could say the same of you, Aunt Ju. Joe died six years ago and at fifty you're still young and beautiful."

"I like my life and I don't need a man, especially a dominating Korean, and screwing up what I have accomplished."

"There are plenty of GIs." Hyun-ae said.

"THAT'S ENOUGH! Stay as long as you want. Just DO NOT scratch any of my albums."

Aunt Ju left the cottage and walked the half mile to the crossroads to the shops and a phone to call a taxi. The cottage was too quiet. I needed to plan my rally with music. I fell in love with his soft velvet voice while in California. Johnny Mathis was one American I could appreciate. Aunt Ju had acquired his albums dating back to 1957. The songs made me feel warm and happy. The languishing for my mother would not stop. Johnny's voice drifted throughout the cottage singing "Bye Bye Blackbird"

I collapsed into the comfortable western style couch Aunt Ju had purchased from the United States. It cost her a fortune, but was worth every penny. The music, beer and planning the protest made me drowsy. I didn't want to think about mother or organizing a protest. I gave up and drifted into a deep sleep, dreaming of a place with no buildings or trees, just open space.

The only visible things were the millions of stars in the black sky. They were close, close enough to touch. I reached out to touch them, but they swirled away like snowflakes across a frozen rice paddy. A loud huffing sound suddenly was close and hot breath was on my neck. With trepidation, I turned. A beast was staring at me with glacier ice eyes. Steam coming out of its nostrils, its body glistened with sweat. I was nose to nose with a wild stallion. I tried to look past the horse's head to see if anyone was riding. The horse reared, turned and galloped into the swirling stars. A soldier was riding the horse. As the horse disappeared into the stars, I tried to grab its tail. I awoke with a start. Someone was present in the room. I screamed.

"CHUNG WHAT ARE YOU DOING HERE? WHY, HOW? GET OUT!"

"Hyun-ae listen, please!"

"YOU SNEAK INTO MY HOUSE AND WATCH ME SLEEP, I'M CALLING THE POLICE! HOW DID YOU KNOW I WAS HERE?"

"Please, just give me a minute to explain."

"EXPLAIN WHAT! THAT YOU 'RE A PERVERT!"

"I'm looking after your interest. My acquaintances helped me with your apartment address. I wanted to make sure no one followed you. Your group passed out leaflets around the campus. I wanted to pass along helpful information."

Chung chuckled to himself. There were no "acquaintances" in the government to fetch addresses. They were all dead, but one. She didn't need to know that I had been following her for days. One thing was certain: she no longer was under surveillance by the government.

"You followed me here?"

"Yes, I paid the cab driver to follow your bus. He

thought I was a jealous husband."

"Or I was a cheating wife. How dare you!"

"Hyun-ae, I have information that will help your cause. President Johnson has agreed to give South Korea a hundred million dollars in military aid."

"In exchange for WHAT?" Wait! You sneak into my house after following me. You watch me sleep, it's disgusting, now you want to talk politics? Look at you, dressed as a university student. Where's your fancy clothes?"

"Hyun-ae, it's important that our relationship remains secret. No one must know. They will arrest us if they find out my partners and I are financing your protest. It's not just my partners that want change, many influential people support your protest. The protests in the past brought about change. Change that was better for the country. I want change for better profits, you want change for a better and unified country."

As her eyes watered, Chung saw a flash of acceptance.

"Can your acquaintances in government find out if my mother is still alive?"

"I don't know, but I'll ask."

Chung's suspicions were confirmed. Hyun-ae's weakness was her mother. Colonel Choi must not fail me in the search for Hyun-ae's mother.

"Thank you. Park's regime buried what happened on Jeju Island. Asking questions will be difficult." Hyun-ae said.

Chung lowered his voice just above a whisper as he

said..

"I know, we'll be careful. Hyun-ae, I have new information. South Korea agreed to send more troops to Vietnam and reduce tariffs on American products. The Americans, in return, will give South Korea vast amounts of military aid, including stationing units with nuclear weapons. Under the pretense of strengthening South Korea.. We're just their puppets. The Americans pull the strings that strangle this country."

"Chung, that makes little sense. Why would President Park send troops to Vietnam? We need them to fight the communist?"

"Park needs to show the Americans he is a powerful ally against communism, at the expense of South Korea's people. They will make the details of the agreement public in a week. There will be no talks of unification. The United States does not want President Park to speak with the north. The American's want to control our destiny. WE ARE A KOREAN PEOPLE. We must be one nation, not a country with an imaginary line cutting us in two. Before I leave, my partners and I want to contribute to your cause."

Chung removed a thick envelope from his jacket.

"We don't need your money. We need you businessmen to stand up to the government." Hyun-ae said.

"Use it, print fliers, posters, buy megaphones, whatever you think is necessary." Chung said, avoiding her point.

Chung handed the envelope to Hyun-ae as she asked.

"Why don't you use it to buy information about my mother from your government acquaintances?"

"They don't help me for the money, they feel obligated."

Chung smiled as he thought of poor Mr. Wook's last moments.

"No. I can't accept it." Said Hyun-ae.

Hyun-ae head was spinning. Chung showing up, offering money, talk of nuclear weapons? Who is this man? What businessmen? Maybe Aunt Ju is right. I'm biting off more than I can chew!

Hyun-ae handed the envelope and money back to Chung. Chung removed the money and placed it on the table.

"We earmarked the money for you and April II. If you don't want it, give it to the poor. I must leave. We'll meet again." Chung said.

"When?"

"We'll let circumstances determine when." Chung left the house smiling, a critical part of his plan folded in his pocket.

SOUTH OF THE RIVER

"It's been my experience that folks who have no vices have very few virtues." Abraham Lincoln

"Hey Reed, fuckin great fuckin news. We're moving south tomorrow. We leave at 1300. The Captain wants us in the briefing room in an hour."

The move the next day went smoothly. As a mechanized unit, each platoon had four APCs and a three quarter truck at their disposal. The new compound was a mile south of Freedom Bridge near Mun su ni'. South Korean contract guards manned the gate at the compound. They assigned a houseboy to each houch. Houseboy was a misnomer. These were men in their thirties and older with families. The Army vetted them through local contractors. They were hardworking, honest and respected by the GIs.

Laundry, polishing boots, house keeping was part of their duties. They kept the houch warm in the winter by making sure the diesel stove always had enough fuel. It was no simple task. The stove was a fifty-gallon drum fitted with a stovepipe and a bracket to hold a jerry can filled with diesel. The jerry can had a drip line that fed the fuel onto the burner. A five-gallon can last twelve hours. The houseboy arrived at 6 am. Kim, our houseboy, earned thirty dollars a month, enough to support his wife and three kids.

South of the Imjin river was a different world. The DMZ was a million miles away. We didn't have to wear combat gear. Fatigues and baseball caps were the uniform of the day. We stored our weapons in the armory. A high fence topped with barbed wire surrounded the compound. The men didn't have to pull guard duty. South Korean civilian guards provided security. They walked the perimeter day and night. At night, ferocious German shepherds accompanied them. The threat was not from North Koreans, but from well organized slicky boys.

It didn't take long before we realized we had a different battle on our hands. Drugs and alcohol were the new enemy. The men earned passes. Depending on the length of the pass, they could go to Seoul or the surrounding villages. The wares sold by the villagers were inexpensive and, most times, good quality. Koreans were enterprising, making everything from men's sharkskin suits or Japanese-style kimonos. They made brass ash trays and trinkets from spent military brass. The industrious Koreans gathered up brass at the firing ranges or they salvaged it after the Korean war. Sharkskin suits and brass trinkets soon fell out of favor.

The men found drugs, OB beer and the brothels inexpensive, available and far more intriguing. Alcohol and the brothels presented less of a problem than the drug of choice was called "REDS." The effect of the barbiturate lasted for days, unlike alcohol.

We were expected to keep a lid on the problem by

setting an example. They ordered the officers not to visit the whorehouses or the local shanty bars that surrounded the military bases. An order that was often disobeyed or not enforced.

The compound had an officers' club that was supposed to keep the forays into the village at a minimum. The quonset hut's plywood bar overlooked tables and chairs, suitable for a poker game or to have a drink and shoot the bull. We paid a barkeep, a houseboy that knew how to make a martini, tom collins, manhattan, white Russian and a potent old fashion. Drinks most of the young officers were not familiar.

The oldest lieutenants were Mo and I at twenty-six. The rest were 21 or 22 years old. Mo received his commission through ROTC. The rest of the platoon leaders in Charlie Company were OCS graduates. Rosie was one of two officers in the battalion from West Point.

Our drink of choice was beer. Our three days of rest ended tomorrow at O six hundred. Mo and I sat at a table in the O club having a Hamm's beer. Mo started earlier with beer and a couple of shots.

"Were you able to round up your men? I asked Mo. Top said, there were three men AWOL from B company. He told the Captain the MPs were looking for them in Kumchon."

"Yep, I tucked away my men in their houch. After three days, most had all the poon-tang and booze they can handle. And you?" Mo said as he took a sip.

"We're good. Sarge and I went looking for one

of our guys this afternoon. We found him in a shack just outside of Munsa ni'. You wouldn't believe this fucking place, a real shit hole. The shack had four or five different rooms. When we walked in, every Korean in the place disappeared. They must've thought we were the MPs. The floor was wall to wall mattresses. Three stoned GI's including Sillhammer, were sprawled out on the mattresses. PFC Sillhammer soon to be private Sillhammer, was so fucked up on drugs, he started swinging at us. Get this, while we were trying to get Sillhammer into the jeep, this mama-san comes up to me and demands payment for Sillhammer's stay. I told her to back off. She takes a swing at me. I ducked the punch but put up my fists as if I wanted to box with her. I was laughing because she was a little shit. Suddenly, five or six young, rough looking guys came out of nowhere. We got out of there. They scared the jeep driver shit-less. Fortunately, Sergeant Hicks had the foresight to borrow handcuffs from the MP at the gate. We handcuffed Sillhammer to a bunk up in the CP."

"What will you do with him?" Mo asked.

"Get him out of my unit. I'll trade you one Private Sillhammer for a PFC Smith."

"Fuck you Reed. Sillhammer wouldn't last a minute in my outfit." Mo said, as he leaned back in his chair.

"Hey, I'm just kidding. Top will take care of him. The first sergeant is good about that stuff. Something has to be done to control the drugs. The

Korean government might want to crack down on prostitution and drugs."

Mo breaks out in hysterical laughter as Lieutenant Richards, the second platoon leader, walks in. He watches as Mo tries to contain himself.

"Mike, what's so funny? Mo is going to piss his pants."

Mo, still laughing, slaps the table to trying to catch his breath and get our attention. He takes a swig of beer and downs another shot.

"Reed thinks the Korean government should stop prostitution!"

Richards cracks a smile, then laughs.

"What the fuck, guys? The shit hole I was at today, you wouldn't want your men there."

Mo stops laughing and gives me a serious look from across the table before he said.

"Reed, you still don't get this country. Prostitution is thirty percent of the Korean economy, nearly all of it, GI money. Think about it, fifty thousand GIs spending half their pay each month on pussy. The government sanctions prostitution by testing the girls for VD and even giving them shots. The Army provides the penicillin. I heard they deliver the penicillin to the clinic in a tanker truck." Mo laughs again as he explains his vision, half laughing, half talking.

"I can see it now, a five thousand gallon penicillin tanker. Instead of the fuel symbol, a red cross and a dripping dick with a syringe painted on the length of the tanker."

We broke out in laughter.

****

The next couple of weeks were easy compared to being in the DMZ. The company practiced maneuvers on the hills overlooking the rice paddies. We roared over dusty trails in our APCs, fighting an imaginary attack by the North Koreans. After the maneuver, we took a break. Waiting for orders to move or return to base, kids showed up out of nowhere.

The oldest was twelve years old. They were cute as hell, well dressed. One of our KUTUSA's, Do-ha, said they were from the nearby village or farms. They were a captivating and entertaining bunch of chatter boxes. The boys stood at attention and saluted as you walked by. They were looking for handouts of C rations and candy. The men got a kick out of handing out candy from their own stash.

On our last maneuver, we moved south of Munsa'ni. It was an all day maneuver, moving from hillside to hillside. Charlie's company cook's got to practice serving a hot meal in the field. The meal was ham with mashed potatoes, peas, and a chunk of cornbread, along with a half pint of real milk to wash it down. Kids started showing up, twenty of them dressed in raggedy clothes, unlike the well-dressed kids from the village. Do-Ha said they were from the nearby orphanage.

One pint-sized girl, six or seven years old with

a bright red sweater patched with different color yarns caught my attention. The once bright pink slippers she wore were now covered in brownish dust. She was as cute as the dickens with her hair in a dutch boy style. But it was her eyes. Her eyes said it all as she stood there. Do-ha spotted her and was kneeling by her side with a pint of milk. She broke out in a big smile and bowed to Do-ha, then to me, smiled and bowed.

Once the words, orphanage kids, spread among the men, they relinquished their cartons of milk. The kids' eyes got as big as saucers as the GIs motioned to the kids to get milk. Not missing a beat, the orphans took off their jackets and sweaters to use as sacks to transport their good fortune. The sad part was they stood nearby as we half heartily ate our tasteless ham and potatoes from the cold stainless steel trays.

Sergeant Hicks and I were leaning up against the command APC, observing the kids watching us. To us, it was just typical army chow. Their eyes told us otherwise. Sarge kept looking at me, then at the kids. I knew what he was thinking. There wasn't enough ham to dole out.

"Sergeant Hicks!"

"SIR?"

"Break out the C rations and make sure each kid gets at least one."

"On it Lt.!"

Each APC carried a basic load of ammunition and cases of rations on the odd chance we had to sprint off to war. We used the rations in this case as a gesture of goodwill. Do-ha had the kids line up to receive the meal. Do-ha was a good soldier. He not only spoke near perfect English, he fit in with the men. His sense of humor was good. He liked American jokes and music. If the men gave him any guff, they got it right back.

Do-ha loved his country and got upset when the men called Korea the armpit of the world. He was bigger than most Koreans at five foot eight, square jawed and wiry muscle.. When Do-ha joined the platoon, he got in a shoving match with Appleman, the biggest guy in the platoon, and a bully. Appleman took a swing at Do-Ha, missed and ended up on his back with Do-Ha's hand around his neck.

Do-Ha was making the kids guess what was in each box of C's. He had the kids giggling as he pantomimed what he thought of each meal. I got the impression that GIs passing out C's was common. The kids immediately looked at the top of the box and smiled or frowned. They couldn't read English, but they could associate the lettering on the box if it was a meal they liked.

The kicker was when the older kids pulled dog tag chains from around their necks. The chains held a p-38 army issue can opener. It was more comfortable finishing our meal watching the kids devour theirs.

MO showed up as I was talking to Do-Ha. With his shit-eating grin, he started giving me a hard time.

"Mike, it's against regulations to give away Army issue goods. Major Smoke will be up your ass."

"Goods, there is nothing 'good' about C's. You wanna give up some of your C's. I want these little buggers to take some to the orphanage."

"Yea, I'll have the men break out a few cases."

Do-ha was smiling as he pointed down the hill. A dozen were attacking our position. Word must have reached the orphanage that Charlie company was friendly.

"Do-ha, what's the orphanage like?"

"It's not a nice place. The Mun sa ni' Orphanage is run by a husband and wife. They steal many of the donations. They have three kids, the good or new clothes donated, don't end up on the orphans. The same with donated food. Much of it ends up on the couples' table, not the orphanages. Treatment of orphans is terrible.. If a child is born outside of a traditional family, they are outcasts. We, as a people, believe in bloodline purity. There're thousands of orphans."

"Do-ha, what the hell is blood line purity?" I asked.

"It's a bullshit belief that Koreans descended from a single ancestor. Since the Korean war, you GI's make a lot of babies. Not good, they're of mixed blood. Doesn't matter that my ancestors and other Koreans ancestors could be from Japan, China, Siberia or Mongolia! We're still considered pure blood, GI babies not so!"

"Do-ha, how the hell do you know so much about

the orphanage?" Mo wanted to know.

"I grew up in a very comfortable home. My father is high in management at the Bank of Korea in Seoul. Anyway, I felt sorry for the kids and I started stopping by when on leave."

"Why so many orphans? The Korean war was over fifteen years ago." Reed asked.

"The war killed thousands of parents. Many of the kids grew up on the streets. The mother abandons the kid, many being of mixed race. The girls turn to prostitution. Many more kids are born and abandoned. Sadly, Song-bun is still in our country. Song-bun is a caste system. The single mothers and orphans were considered low class. They have little chance of having a good life, no fault of their own. There is no government program to take care of them. As the orphans get older, they turn to crime or prostitution. It's what GIs call a cluster fuck."

Mo was leaning against the APC with a look of, I got a fuckin idea, when he spoke.

"What if I convinced the CO to let us sponsor the orphanage?"

"Good idea MO, but how the hell do you sponsor an orphanage?"

"Look Mike, we gather food and clothing and give it to the orphans. We can ask the men to ask for care packages from home. Since we'll be goodwill ambassadors, the captain will give time off to do stuff for the orphanage. He'll let us take his jeep or a quarter ton. We may have to make a run into Seoul!"

Mo said with a wink of the eye.

"Mo, you are one reprehensible son of a bitch! Let's do it!"

Mo pointed at Do-ha.

"Do-ha, do you want to be our spokesperson at the orphanage?"

"Yes sir, maybe I can get my dad's bank to help, unlikely but."

After chow, we headed back to the compound, after policing up our area. The kids did their own policing; they took everything, cans, empty cartons, stashing it in their jacket sacks.

The next day, the captain summoned Mo and me to the CP. We were thinking we were going to catch some shit about passing out the C's. The first sergeant, seeing the apprehension on our faces, added to our anxiety by jerking our chain.

"You two are in for it now! Go right in the captains waiting."

Instead, we got a pleasant surprise.

"Sir, you wanted to see us?"

"Yes battalion needs pay officers for the stockade. I'm assigning you two sorry asses to be the pay officers."

Mo poked me in the side and had that shit-eating grin. The captain gave him a dirty look before continuing.

"Currently, five men from the battalion are in the stockade. The men have to sign for their pay before it's put into their commissary account. You can stay overnight, just be back here by eighteen hundred the next day. Battalion will provide you with a jeep and a driver."

"Mo, you have been to Seoul, so I'm counting on Reed to keep you out of trouble. You're representing Charlie Company."

"Yes, sir!"

"You leave tomorrow. See the first sergeant for details."

Mo and I both stood at attention, saluted.

"Yes, Sir and thank you!"

"Get your asses out of here. Have a good time."

Sergeant Jackson was smiling as we walked over to his desk. He had the details for picking up the MPC. As payroll officers, we were required to carry sidearms, which was overkill. The total payroll totaled two hundred dollars, as most went to dependents or fines.

Outside the CP and Mo lets out a whoop and starts doing a jig, kicking up dust.

"Why so happy about going to the stockade?"

"The stockade is a bummer, over night in Seoul is bliss, paradise. We'll hit the Officers Mess at Kimpo and have a real steak with real potatoes served on plates, not a metal tray. The tables will have linen tablecloths, you can order wine. Then I'll introduce you to the Green Door."

"What's the Green door?"

"Never mind, just bring a couple hundred bucks from your stash.

STOCKADE AND SEOUL

"Between two evils, I always pick the one I never tried before."
Mae West

Mo and I went to the battalion to pick up the paperwork. PFC Eugene Slaydon was our driver. According to Mo, Slaydon knew Seoul like the back of his hand and kept his mouth shut.

"Slaydon, first to the stockade at Camp Tyler, then over the officer's mess at Kimpo. Pick us up at eighteen hundred hours. That should give you three hours to hit the PX, eat, and whatever else you want to do." Mo said.

"Yes sir! Anything you want me to pick up at the PX?"

"Mike, you need anything?" Mo asked.

"No."

"OK, let's hit the road." Mo pointed south.

The ride to the stockade at Camp Tyler took an hour. We pulled up to the gate, a MP checked our IDs. I was looking past him into the compound. It appeared deserted. A creepy place even in the afternoon, it made your skin crawl. A high fence topped with spiraling razor wire surrounded the compound. Inside the compound, there was another fence surrounding several quonset huts.

A warm wind picked up as we waited for the MP's okay to go ahead. The open ground was dirt and dust devils swirled and disintegrated when they hit the fence. Two of the compound's corners had guard towers, though occupied, the guards were not visible. The towers rested on telephone poles. Lights resting on the same poles ringed the compound. The scene reminded me of pictures of the WWII prison camps. The buildings that housed the prisoners were windowless. The guards directed us to a quonset hut that joined another hut end to end, making for one long quonset hut.

Inside we met with the cantankerous, bad ass looking MP Master Sergeant Kittle. His height and width made his desk look like doll house furniture.

"Lieutenants, place your sidearms on the desk. You'll leave the folder and the MPC on the desk. Take only the paperwork the prisoners are to sign and one pen. You can enter the secure part of the building through the door behind me. There is a desk with two chairs. You will take a seat and wait for the prisoner to be brought to you. The prisoner isn't to speak unless asked to speak."

The sergeant stood and placed the two 1911 Colt.45's in a secure locker.

"Follow me."

On the other side of the door, an MP stood to the right. Inside was a desk and two chairs. The linoleum floor had a foot wide yellow line painted in the center. The line ended three feet in front of the desk, a horizontal line the width of the desk crossed the top, forming a T. The floor glowed from the row of bare bulbs overhead and the constant waxing by prisoners.

I looked at Mo, he too was studying the floor. He shrugged his shoulders as we took our seats. The sergeant barked a command. The door at the far end opened. A prisoner advanced, walking on the yellow line. Two MPs, one behind and one to the right of the prisoner. The first prisoner to be paid was Private John Armstrong, formally Specialist Armstrong.

Tried and convicted by a Special Court Martial for assaulting a Korean worker at his base. They sentenced him to six months and forfeiture of two-thirds of his pay and reduction in rank from an E-4 to an E-1. There were no details of the assault on the paperwork. His base pay after two years of service was two hundred twenty-three dollars and twenty cents. After forfeiture, he was to receive seventy-three dollars and sixty-six cents.

Armstrong walked up to a top of the T. He stopped, stood at attention, raised his right hand to salute but caught himself, saluting by prisoners was forbidden.

Mo read the script. "Private John Armstrong, your conviction under Article 58b of the UCMJ includes confinement and forfeiture of two-thirds of your pay. The confinement facility will hold your remaining pay of seventy-three dollars and sixty-six cents. Do you understand, private Armstrong?"

The soldier looked barely eighteen and was about to burst into tears. There was a long pause as Armstrong tried to compose himself.

Finally, with a whimper. "Yes, Sir."

"Sign here." Mo asked.

The remaining four men walked the yellow line, each looking sadder than the last. It was a disheartening, twelve thousand miles from home and stripped of all self respect.

"Mo I felt sorry for Armstrong." Reed said.

"Why, he dishonored the uniform, our country. He got what he deserved. Let's go to Kimpo. We'll have an early dinner before the brass shows up."

Dinner at the Kimpo mess hall was a feast and, as Mo said, a waiter served the meal on china plates not steel trays, with cloth napkins and linen tablecloths. Cold Hamms beer, steak and lobster for the asking, for six bucks. To top it off, piped in dinner music. The bar was a half circle of polished wood with a brass foot rail. Its twenty seats were empty except for two lieutenants from the 7th Infantry Division. From what we could overhear, they were leaving the country. Their unit was on the DMZ. We were done with dinner and I could tell Mo wanted to talk to them.

"Mind if we have a beer with you?" Mo asked.

The two lieutenants turned, one spoke up. "No, we will even buy you one. We are out of here at 2200 hours."

"I'm Mike, this is Mo. We couldn't help but overhear you mentioning the DMZ. We're with the 2/23rd."

"This nut bag is Jack, pointing a thumb at his 7th division side kick, I'm Bill. Are you guys short?"

I replied. "NO, nine months for Mo and ten for me."

Jack said. "I don't envy you guys. It's going to

get worse. The North Koreans are going to screw with you. After a few more months, you get the sense the brass is letting them. The brass and the fuckin armistice rules put us grunts at a severe disadvantage. Korea is second fiddle to Vietnam.

"Yea, we have been hearing a lot of that." I said.

Jack chimed in. "They extended us for a month. There's forty thousand GI's in Korea and they couldn't find two replacements in the country. Why the fuck is that? They put a couple thousand GI's on the DMZ. The rest live in luxury south of the river. Why? They had Jack and I taking patrols out two days ago. Now, we're out of here. Even Major Ramos can't fuck with us."

"Was your unit in the firefight two weeks ago?" Mo asked.

Jack explained. "That was B Company. They lost one man and three wounded. That's what I mean, the gooks cross the DMZ and pick us off one here one there, but we can't go after them. Neither of us had contact with the gooks in over a month."

Jack and Bill heard the rumors the North Korea attacks were going to increase. Everyone was going to get extended. We exchanged stories and a couple of beers.

"Come on, Mike, time to hit the road. Our drivers outside by now." Mo said with a jab to my ribs.

The driver was waiting with the top up on the jeep. It looked like rain any minute.

"To the Green Door!" Mo commanded.

"Our weapons?" We had checked them in at the

Provost Marshall's office.

"We'll pick them up tomorrow."

There was no hesitation by the driver as he popped the clutch and off we sped. Seoul's streets were busy with a mix of small cars, buses, motor scooters, bicycles and people. In the center of the city, a few high-rise buildings towering over the older buildings, still with pockmarks from the war..

The people like busy ants hurried off to somewhere. There was a sense of urgency, the inhabitants bustling with energy which the light drizzle didn't dampen. The air cooled and a fresh breeze passed through the door less jeep. It was hard to envision just twenty miles to the north was a different world. Since the war, little had changed along the DMZ, meanwhile Seoul was becoming a metropolis.

Combat along the 161 miles of the 38th parallel had become a fact of life for US and ROK units. Combat was intermittent. One day a US unit was attacked, then it could be the next day or even weeks later, the gooks attacked a ROK outfit. The American press reported very little about the attacks. Did the people in America or even Seoul know a month ago, Brown nearly died and Rodriquez lost his hand or McElroy, Cook and Boyer, who gave up everything. Did the South Koreans, anyone, appreciate what they gave up?

"MO, do you think the people of Korea give a damn we're here?"

"Hell yes, for our money and the military shit we

give them. As long as they get stuff and money, they'll like us. It's when they can stand on their own two legs, they'll kick us out."

The driver turned off the main street into a series of alleyways. The rain had stopped, and the sun popped out from behind the clouds. We stopped in front of a high concrete block wall with a single door painted a navy blue. A thick hemp rope with a tassel dangled from the post, jutting out from the wall.

Mo jumped from the jeep, giving the rope a tug. A loud, long dong resonated on the other side of the wall. A moment later, the blue door swung inward. A good-looking woman stepped out to greet us. Her black hair tightly swirled in a bun held by a painted butterfly, showed her round face with dark eyes and red lips. She smiled, then her eyes flashed recognition of MO and her entire face glowed.

Mo bowed, An-nyong-ha-se-yo!

"Oh Lieutenant Mo, so happy to see you again. I thought maybe you were in big trouble!"

"NO, everything worked out."

"I see you brought a friend."

"Soo Lee, I present you, Lieutenant Mike."

"Pleased to meet you, Lieutenant Mike."

"Pleased to meet you Soo Lee."

"Come with me. We show Lieutenant Mike a pleasant evening and you too, Lieutenant MO!"

We stepped through the doorway into an incredible courtyard. Though it was late September, there were flowers in full bloom. Paths leading to benches under shade trees and a small pool of water with a nude statue pouring water out of a ewer.

We followed the shimmering Soo Lee through the courtyard on a stone path. Her silky black Kimono which was decorated with a large embroidered silver dragon with red eyes. The dragon's tail ended at her neck and the head was at her derriere. When she walked, the dragon was shaking its head back and forth.

A path lined with flowers saturated the air with a strong sweet fragrance, not the pungent smells permeating the city air.

Mo must have been reading my mind, as he said. "Hey Mike, now you know what the saying 'smells like a whorehouse' comes from."

Soo Lee turns and gives Mo a hard jab to the ribs.

"You not say that or I shut you off the rest of your time in Han-guk." She laughs and grabs Mo by the arm and snuggles up to him. They continue on as if on a stroll through a city park. Mo turned and winked at me.

Mo said. "She saved my ass when I first got to Korea."

I'm thinking, what else don't I know about this guy?

The path led to an enormous and impressive house by Korean standards, with masonry walls painted a sand color and a roof with red tiles. The double doors were four feet wide each and at least eight feet high. Large metal straps held them to the frame. Each door had a brass handle, a foot long and shiny as a soldier's belt buckle on inspection day.

The doors were painted in a rich forest green. The lyrics to the song, "Green Door" drifted through my thoughts. A song from the 1950s about piano music and laughing, on the other side of the "Green Door". The singer wanted to find out what secret it was keeping. I was going to find out.

We stepped into a foyer to the sound of Korean music. A female was singing with a voice that sounded like a wind chime in a gentle breeze. The foyer opened to a large room with several chairs and love seats. A mural of a nude couple embracing covered one wall.. At the far end of the room, five girls were at the bar.

The glass shelves behind the bar held brand name liquor rivaling the officers' club. Three of the girls dressed in stateside style clothes, tight skirts, and flowery blouses. The other two were wearing Japanese style silky kimono's, one was lime green the other sky blue.

Soo Lee said. "Gentlemen, these ladies will be your hostesses for the night and welcome you to the Green Door. Ladies, Lieutenant Mike and you may remember, Lieutenant Mo?"

Soo-Lee bowed, turned, and the head shaking dragon disappeared in the hallway.

Four of the girls approached Mo and I.

The tallest one spoke first. She was the tallest because of her super high heels. "I am Joo-Eun. This is Da-hee, Jin-Jo, and Mi-Jung. We will be your hostesses tonight. Come and tell us about yourself. What state are you from? Do you want a drink or something to eat? Up close they looked older than they did from across the room, but they were Korean beauties with charm, pretty smiles and intense dark eyes."

Joo-Eun's english was nearly perfect. As we walked to the bar, the girl in the sky blue kimono continued to stare at me. The Kimono hugged her hips and covered her legs except for the ankles. The staring was mutual. She cracked a smile and slid off the bar stool and sashayed towards me.

"Hi Lieutenant, Mike, I am Ha-Neul. I see you have met my friends, but when you are ready to go to bed, it's you and me!"

The other girls started giggling, Joo-Eun turned and gave them a stop the giggling look. I was hooked, line and sinker. I could only utter two words.

"You bet."

"Gee Mike, you must've got something special for Ha-Neul to choose you."

Ha-Neul spoke.

"Lieutenant Mike is better looking than you MO!" Besides, Mike is a much better name than "MO."

We laughed, Joo-Eun fixed everyone a drink, and the girls started asking questions. They wanted to know about our home towns. What music we liked and did we ever see the Beatles. We danced and laughed as three of the girls tried to sing the doo wop song by the Casinos *then you can tell me goodbye.*

The Akai reel-to-reel tape had the Stones, Sinatra, Chubby Checker. Ha-Neul was an excellent dancer, whether it was the jitterbug or the monkey. It was obvious the girls liked American music.

Ha-Neul took my arm and led to the center of the room just as Johnny Mathis started crooning his song Misty, "helpless as a kitten up a tree." No doubt I was. When the song ended, Ha-Neul slid her arm around my waist and gave a tug, smiling.

"Come, I show you my music collection."

I looked back as we headed towards the hallway. Mo was at the bar. He saw the direction we were heading and raised his glass and with a big shit-eating grin.

"Good night Mike, mind your manners and I'll see ya in the morning."

Ha-Neul's room was down the hall. The boudoir was more than I expected. It was large, there was a sunken blue tiled bath, large enough for two. Opposite the tub was an enormous bed with an ornate, dark wood headboard. Next to the bed, a dresser, chair and a shelf with an Akai reel to reel. Shear curtains covered the window on the other side of the room. The setting sun bathed the room in a soft light. Under the window was a table, two chairs, and a vase filled with flowers from the courtyard.

"Mike, you want a drink?"

"No thanks, I had enough, its been a long day, I'm ready for lovin' and a good sleep."

"You'll get both with me. What music do you want?"

"You pick Ha-Neul."

She fast forwarded the tape and the Four Tops were

singing "Baby I Need Your Loving."

The day's events were catching up. The bed was soft with sheets that had to be silk, felt cool to my bare back. Compared to what I had been sleeping on, this was pure heaven.

Ha-Neul was standing at the side of the bed, her kimono slid off her shoulders showing her perky breasts. She smiled and seductively let the Kimono slide down her arms until it was below her waist. The Kimono hid a sculptured body. Smiling again, she crooned in a beautiful, crazy, Korean accent, "Baby, I need your lovin" as she laid beside me ever so gently. Lovin was right, nothing but good loving. Ha-Neul was not shy about what she liked, and I loved every bit. After wards we lay there shoulder to shoulder, letting the coolness of the room bring our body temperature and breathing back to normal. We made small talk. I soon passed into the sandman's land.

A dreamy, soft voice whispered in my ear.

"Lieutenant Mike, time for bath and morning meal."

Half awake, I could feel Ha-Neul warm breasts against my back. As she snuggled up closer, she nibbled on my ear. Her soft touch succeeded in fully wakening me to a before breakfast round of lovemaking. Now I'm as hungry as a bear.

"Did I hear you say breakfast?"

"You, Lieutenant, get a bath, then we feed you."

The water was tepid as I sat in water up to my chest. Ha-Neul's hand worked wonders, massaging my neck and back as she sat on the edge of the bath behind and above me. Playfully, she wrapped her legs around to the front of me, forcing her heels into my chest. Teasing and laughing, she soaped up my hair with a shampoo and gave me a wonderful massage. I couldn't believe that I could be so lucky, damn this was nice.

Two girls brought a breakfast of scrambled eggs, toast with jelly and real coffee. Ha-Neul and I sat at the table across from each other as if we were an exclusive couple. We were making small talk about California and San Francisco. She wanted to visit, but not live in America, "too violent." Ha-Neul liked to read the newspapers from America. Sipping my coffee, I wanted to ask her how such a beautiful girl ended up here. Where did she learn to speak and read English? I was afraid she would tell me she had been an orphan, making me picture the little girl in the red sweater begging for the milk. Ha-Neul was smart, beautiful. Why this?

"Mike, you look sad. Something wrong?"

"Ha-Neul, I had a fantastic time. It was an incredible night."

It was time to leave. She didn't ask for any money. Mo said to bring a couple hundred bucks. I left all of it on the dresser. The night was worth every penny. I wanted to leave it at that.

"Mo will be in the main room. I hope you will return soon. *Anjeon hage gada,* it means go safely."

"Thank you Ha-Neul. I hope you get to California."

"Lieutenant, you say, *da-nyo-o-gess-sumni-da,* it

means, see you later."

"*Da-nyo-ogess-sum-ni-da.*"

Mo was waiting. He smiled and started towards the door; we stepped out of the green door and into the brilliant sunlight.

"Well, Mike, what do you think?"

"About what?"

"Come on, you knucklehead, the Green Door."

"It's a cool song and Ha-Neul is a beautiful, smart young lady. We talked all night, solved the world's problems, and she taught me to speak Korean." We exited the courtyard and were walking with the sun at our backs in a narrow alley.

"Mike, you're so full of bullshit."

"Where're we heading?"

"We have a couple of hours before the driver shows. I thought we would tour the university. It's supposed to be a nice campus."

After a fifteen-minute walk, we arrived at the campus. The grounds ran parallel to one of the main streets. There was a lot of activity. A large group of students gathered in an open park. The students were dressed in white shirts. The girls were in skirts, or black slacks, to go with their white shirts. Groups of students suddenly started appearing on the side streets and streaming out of the alleys, filling the park. They were chanting, many were carrying signs. It appeared to be a rally.

"Mo, what do you think they are up to?"

"I think it's a protest. It's confined to the park. We should be okay."

We turned left then right, walking on side streets, passing small shops on each side with many of their wares on the street. Owners and customers were haggling over the price of goods in a unfamiliar language. I felt like a tourist.

"Mo, where are we going?"

"Don't worry Mike, I was told there's a block of nice shops in this neighborhood, the brass and embassy officials shop there."

"How the hell do you know all this, and how did Soo-Lee save your ass?"

"That's a story to tell over a beer."

As we moved through the streets, we could hear the din of the students and an intense woman was on a loudspeaker, speaking excitedly. Where was Do-Ha when you needed him? It would be interesting to know what it takes to whip up Korean students.

As we turned another corner, police wearing riot gear were double-timing in a column of fours towards the small park.

"Mike, let's get the hell out of here. They are going to bust up that demonstration, and we don't want to be in the middle of that shit. Let's go back the way we came."

This part of Seoul wasn't off limits, but getting caught in a student demonstration showed a lack of good judgment.

We started half running, jogging back the way we came. The shop owners were moving their wares into their shop. We rounded a corner, police armed with M-1's, and billy clubs, barricaded the narrow alley with a jeep. One of them saw us and motioned for us to turn back.

"Come on, Mike, let's take this ally. It might lead us back to the main street."

POP! POP! POP!

"Shit Mo, that sounds like tear gas canisters."

The crowd noise was getting closer, and we didn't know what street we were on and whether it lead us out of this mess. Students were now running in the street in front and behind us. Two, three of them popped out of an alleyway, running, looking back over their shoulder with fear in their eyes. We put our backs up against a wall as a group of eight or ten students sprinted by with a gang of cops on their heels. The cops glanced at us but continued the chase. They knew who they wanted. It wasn't us. We headed the opposite way at a fast walk and entered an open market. Around the perimeter there were six alley ways like spokes on a wheel.

"Which way Mo?" I asked.

Mo pointed straight ahead. As I reached the corner of an alleyway, I looked to my left. A shop owner distracted me with a yell, a warning? Before I could react, I sensed something or someone was coming from my right. I half turned when a body slammed into my chest. The impact knocked me off my feet. I was falling backwards. I instinctively wrapped my right arm around the girl's waist as we both plummeted to the pavement. My left arm tried to break the fall. We fell as if in a lover's embrace, face to face.

My shoulders hit the pavement hard. A split second before my head smacked the pavement, I saw stars. I tighten my grip on the girl's taut, slender body. She gave a guttural yell, her eyes just inches away from mine. They were the most beautiful, dark, angry eyes I had ever seen. Her long black hair was dancing across my face. The girl was trying to pull away from my grip. Her left arm is trapped between our bodies.

Stunned, I continued to hold on to her. The girl used her left arm for leverage to separate our bodies enough to haul off and slap me with her right hand. I released my grip and watched the tall, shapely girl run towards a narrow alley. Just before she disappeared, she turned and, in perfect English, yelled, "GO HOME GI!"

A split second later, the three-man team came around the corner. They were in a tizzy, yelling in Korean, I assumed, about losing sight of the girl. There were six alleys and only three cops. I was sitting on the ground and received a befuddled look from the three keystone cops. I pointed to a different alley, opposite from where the girl had disappeared.

The keystone cops took off running.

Across the way was a mama-sun who watched the entire incident bowed towards me with a smile of approval for sending the cops in the wrong direction.

"Mo, did you see her? She's beautiful!"

"Jesus Mike, you just got laid in the best whorehouse in Korea and now you want to chase school girls."

"She was no schoolgirl."

"Forget her. You can't just go over to the student union or a sorority house to meet her. They don't do things that way here. Let's get the fuck out of here."

We found the main street and walked as fast as we could away from what must have been a chaotic scene.

TURNING POINT

"Democracy don't rule the world, You'd better get that in your head; This world is ruled by violence, But I guess that's better left unsaid." Bob Dylan

Today was Hyan-ae's big protest. Chung had seen the flyers posted around the campus. Eavesdropping on students convinced him of a big turnout. The police were going to show up in force. He was going to add his own twist. He arrived early at the campus, searching for the right place. The neighborhood surrounding the campus was unaware of the coming pandemonium. Chung chooses a narrow alley without shops and less traveled. There were many nooks and crannies he could tuck himself. He knew from the start it was a doomed protest. Chung observed the police moving to different staging areas near the campus hours earlier. He was counting on a student to use the alley as an escape route.

When Bae started her megaphoned verbal assault on the government. *"Park's regime must work to unify the Korean people, North and South,"* the pop of tear gas guns started. The panicked students ran single file by Chung's cubbyhole. He wanted a lone student, one student fit his purpose, and he didn't care if it was male or female. He slid the pipe out of his sleeve, then gripped it for a practice swung. The weight of cool steel felt good.

A few seconds later, he got his wish. A male student, moving at a slower pace than the earlier group, kept looking over his shoulder. Chung waited until the victim was cross from his hiding place. The young man turned back as Chung stepped out. Chung took delight in seeing the surprised and horrified look in the man's eyes. The heavy steel pipe struck his forehead with such force the head burst like a melon. The impact stopped the students forward momentum. For a split second he stood there, then dropped, with his face smacking the pavement.

Student Lee Sook lay on the ground quivering. Chung struck the back of Lee's legs and shoulders, adding insult to injury. Chung stood over the body, smiling, knowing the police were going to get blamed for the killing. He wanted to turn the man over and enjoy the moment life left his victim. Staying longer was foolhardy.

He moved along his pre-planned escape route. Chung wiped the pipe of blood and brain, discarding it in a pile of rubbish, the cloth further down the alley. Chung felt charged. He had not been this aroused since Wook. If he had a soul, each death he presided over, replenished it. He chuckled, recalling an old Buddha proverb, *"it is a man's own mind, not his enemy or foe, that lures him to evil ways."*

Chung popped out of the alley on to the main street. He turned away from the commotion. Two American officers were thirty meters to his front, hurrying. If he had caught them in the alley, they were dead. Several streets away from the university, he hailed a taxi. For a week, he decided to lay low.

One man he recognized from the food alley was at the protest. The man was talking to police officials in the staging areas. Were they hoping I would show up or were they watching Bae?

He knew it was time to move to a safe house away from Seoul.

****

Won and Yoo and twelve agents from OIS were at the protest, each with a photograph of a man know as the viper. Won was certain the Viper would show. They negotiated with the police to allow the protest to go on for thirty minutes. Won wanted a chance to scan the crowd to see if Viper mixed in with the students. The five police units, forty men each, were to break up the protest and detain the unruly students. He had argued against police wearing riot gear, let the students have their day, but lost. President Park would not let students harangue the government.

The protest barely begun when one of the police commanders jumped the gun by moving close. An elderly shop owner tried to move his wares out of the way, but not quick enough. A policeman was spotted by students, pushing him to the ground. They rushed the police. Pure bedlam broke out with students and police running in every which direction. Hyun-ae Bae disappeared from the park. Radio chatter between police units picked up. Then an ominous call came over the airwaves. They found a body in an alley.

Won and Yoo hurried to the scene. The victim was a male student. Won had a gut feeling. This was the Vipers' doing. Won and Yoo watched as police forensics processed the scene. A police team is unlikely to ambush a student in a narrow alley, more suited for a calculating, demented son of a bitch.

Won arrived at the office the next day with a copy of the Chosun Ilbo under his arm. The paper alluded to the police being involved in the student's death. The police were claiming no police units were in that alley. President Park's spokesperson stated the protest was communist inspired and the leaders of the protest had Lee's blood on their hands. Arrest of Bae was being considered. The chief pulled up a chair next to Won's desk; he threw a folder onto Won's desk.

"Won, your input PLEASE?" The chief asked.

"Chief, I know the Viper set up this entire mess for us to end up in a pile of shit."

"You are probably right. Here's the preliminary autopsy report. Because of the heat from the press, they gave it priority. Though it doesn't let the police off the hook, it lends credence to your theory. The victim was struck with a round object three point eight centimeters in diameter. About the same thickness as a nightstick. The impact to the skull was with such force, a nightstick according to the coroner doesn't have the weight to cause such damage. He thinks something heavier, a pipe? We are awaiting lab results to come back from a pipe found in the alley."

The chief opened a second folder as he spoke..

"Won, I'll spare you the technical details. I'll hit the high points." *'The impact to the skull was with such force the weapon carried through the frontal lobe, fragmenting the brain pan into several pieces, stopping at the Parietal, destroying the basal ganglia.'* A narrative at the bottom of the page did not surprise Won when the chief read. *'The angle and depth of the wound suggest the person who swung the object was tall. There was no damage to the victim's face below the forehead. It was straight on. The victim's height is one hundred sixty centimeters.* I think you get the point!"

"Chief, this confirms it! The bastard needs to be caught!" Won said, raising his voice.

"Won, hold on, I agree, we have a manic on our hands. A clever and dangerous man that enjoys butchery, along with his espionage. We're going to catch him. We need to put together a plan without those fucking numb skull police. I'm authorized to keep our suspicions quiet. The forensic evidence shows the police were not involved. If they tie the murder to the protest, they will bring charges against the instigators. They will charge Bae and others with organizing an unsanctioned gathering that resulted in a death."

"Chief, the public and the press will not buy a bullshit cover story."

"Look Won, if we say a North Korea maniacal agent is involved, he'll disappear. This Hyan-ae Bae is involved. She may not know Viper is a spy, we can't afford to scare him off. She is our best lead."

"Want us to pick her up, chief?" Yoo asked.

"No, use her as bait. Try to prevent him from killing her. This sick bastard doesn't hesitate when it comes to killing. Put together a schedule for surveillance, seven days a week. Don't tip her off by talking to her friends or relatives. Won, I want to remind you her University records show she is a genius, destined to be a scientist in nuclear energy. She is very close to getting her doctorate. She attended Berkley in California for a year. What contacts she made are unknown. Use your best men and be careful."

"We will chief, Yoo is doing a discreet check on her Aunt Ju's home near Kimpo and the uncle in Mun-su ne. Do the police suspect the North Koreans are involved?"

"No, they would've leaked it to the press. So get your ass to work."

"Yes, sir!" Won and Yoo replied.

AUNT JU'S HIDEOUT

"Judgment comes from experience, and experience comes from bad judgment." Simon Bolivar

Hyun-ae arrived at Aunt Ju's mountain retreat with a bruised knee and scraped hand. She couldn't shake the image of the American GI, flat on his back, staring up at her as if he was going to kiss her. She used a towel and cold water to clean up the deep scrapes to her knee and hand before stretching out on the couch. Her thoughts were spinning as she spoke to the walls.

"I need to concentrate and figure out what I did wrong. Why did the police attack us? We planned the protest for weeks, posting flyers around the campus. Why didn't the police tell the school to refuse us permission? Was Chung there? Maybe protests are the wrong way to get the attention of the government. My escape was fortunate. The injury to my knee prevented me from running fast. Why were the police no longer chasing me after I ran into the American? What was he doing there? He pulled me to his body so tight, his body felt so muscular, so much for GIs being soft. Maybe Aunt Ju's right, I should find a lover?"

She could hear the hurried steps of Aunt Ju on the stone walkway leading to the back door. Her expensive high heels made a click-alee clack when she walked fast on a hard surface.

"Hyun-ae, are you okay?"

She hurried over and sat at the end of the couch, removing the wet towel from Hyan-ae knee. "Your knee needs attention. Bits of stone are in the cut."

"Why are you here, Aunt Ju? This is a workday."

"I own the company. I work when I want. It's on the radio about the police breaking up the protest. I'm concerned about you. The radio is saying they found a murdered student in an alley near the campus. They haven't said the name of the student."

Hyun-ae face suddenly had a tortured look as tears streamed from her eyes.

"NO, NO, it's my fault, NOOOO!"

Hyun-ae body shook as she sobbed hysterically. Aunt Ju moved closer to hold Hyan-ae. After several minutes, the sobbing stopped.

"Aunt Ju, I knew better, the protest should've been canceled. I should've known the government would do this. Why didn't I listen to you? It's my fault."

"You can't blame yourself. You didn't advocate violence, you always strive to have peaceful protests. We don't even know if they connected the death to the protest. We wait until we find out what happened."

The next day, Aunt Ju buys the newspaper. After seeing the headlines, she regrets buying it and thinks of telling Hyun-ae they were sold out. But to what end, the radio carried the story.

Hyun-ae was sitting at the table. She hung her

head when Aunt Ju placed the paper in front of her. The large blocked letters, **STUDENT MURDERED AT PROTEST**, dropped the weight of a mountain on her shoulders. Hyun-ae head fell on her folded arms on top of the front page. She opened her eyes to a dead Lee Sook's student photo, staring back at her. Hyun-ae pulled away and stared out the window..

"Hyun-ae, did you know him?"

"No, Oh Aunt Ju, I'm so sad. This is my fault!"

Aunt Ju felt Hyun-ae's pain. Resting her chin on top of Hyun-ae head and wrapping her arms around Hyun-ae shoulder. The newspaper article was ambiguous, listing different scenarios who murdered Lee. They hinted that a rogue police unit or a robbery giving little information as to the cause of death. Hyan-ae eyes opened wide when she read, *"if the death is connected to the protest, the police will file charges against the organizers."*

"Aunt Ju, they're going to arrest me?"

"The government's not that foolish, it would create more unrest. There is nothing to lead them to believe your group had anything to do with the murder, right, Hyun-ae?"

"AUNT JU! how could you even think..."

"Hyun-ae, no I don't, I'm sorry. You must stay here. This can be your hideaway."

"I'm not running from the police."

"They are not looking for you. Use the house as a sanctuary. Stay here until I find out what happened, the police do not know about this house. Sergeant Joe purchased it through a corporation. It will take time for the police to unravel any connection. Take a break from school, you have your entire life ahead. Do something fun, fall in love again?"

"Aunt Ju, how could bring that up?"

"It's been three years, Hyan-ae. It was a terrible accident, but it's time to find someone else. Your mother would've wanted you to be happy and in love."

"Stop talking as if my mother was dead. She's not DEAD!"

"Your boyfriend is dead and you need to get on with your life. Hyun-ae, you are brilliant, beautiful and I love you dearly, but on some things in life, you have poor judgment. You need a good man to add balance to your life."

"You have someone in mind, AUNT JU!, if not, there has to be one unmarried pig farmer on this mountain."

"Stop it, Hyun-ae, use that intellect and marry it to common sense. Listen to my advice. Whether or not you use it, it's up to you. I'm leaving. You have the place to yourself and the pig farmer. Stay as long as you want."

"Aunt Ju, I'm sorry. I will think things through."

"Good, stay through the winter. This house is cozier than your apartment. Mr Yi, the elderly gentleman across the way, will keep you supplied with fuel. He'll watch out for you. I will be back in a week. Try not to listen to the news. I will come to you when there is real, confirmed news."

"Thank you. I love you Aunt Ju!"

Training and the Orphanage

Camp Lawtons was just south of the river on a hillside. It was the second night after our return from the Seoul, it had been raining for hours. Then it became still with ground fog. The highest point in our compound was behind our hooch.

Mo and I were returning to our hooch. Suddenly, the muffled thumps of grenades, the sharp crack of the M-14 and the brrrrp of the PSH-41 reverberated across the river.. We ran to the top to see if we could pinpoint the firefight. Popped flares made it easy to surmise OP Mazie was under attack. Mazie is north of the river, but south of the DMZ. The fighting intensified, red and opposing green tracers arching through the sky.

"Jesus Mo, that's a lot more green than red tracers. Mazie taking heavy fire."

"Fuck me, they have only a squad guarding Mazie. Shit! There's a road to it and my guys would've been there in a fucking minute!"

"Mo, Let's get to the CP."

At the command post, everyone was listening to a terrified squad leader calling for help..

"RAZOR! RAZOR! I HAVE TWO MEN DOWN, WE ARE TAKING HEAVY FIRE, WHERE THE FUCK IS THE QRF?"

The company commander in a calm voice replied.

"They're on the way son, how many?"

"I DON'T KNOW MAYBE TWENTY, FUCK THEY'RE BEHIND US, I HAVE TO FIGHT!"

The commander called the QRF. *"Chariot, what's your eta?"*

"Less than a minute. We're going to ride in on these little fuckers. Less chance of my men getting hit in a crossfire."

"Roger."

A long four or five minutes passed.

"Razor Razor, this is Chariot over!"

"This is Razor."

"The gooks withdrew when we pulled up. We need med-vac asap, over."

"They are on their way. Secure the area."

Sanders, the Company commander and the QRF leader continued to plan for the med-vac.

"Captain, do you think we should alert the men?" I asked.

"Yes!"

"First Sergeant!"

"Sir."

"Alert the civilian guard commander. We'll have one of our men outside each hooch for the rest of the night. Leave the civilians guards on the perimeter. I don't want another Camp Walley."

"Yes, sir."

"Mo, Mike, set up a schedule and put guards on your houch."

"Yes sir, Captain, what happened at Camp Walley?"

"Another fuck up. Camp Wally is five or six klicks

south of the DMZ. A team of North Koreans made their way through the DMZ to Camp Walley. They threw satchel charges in a hooch. They made it out of the camp without being shot at."

"What were the casualties?"

"Two killed and seventeen wounded. The gook's got away, back north, or who knows. Now get out of here."

"Yes, sir."

"Fuck Mo, you going to sleep tonight with both eyes closed?"

"Come on, Mike, those pricks are in North Korea by now!"

"I'm going to the armory and draw a sidearm."

"Go ahead, you draw a sidearm and I'm going to draw me a stiff drink."

We got the scoop on the firefight the next day. One GI dead, two wounded. One North Korea, KIA and one WIA. The gook that died got within twenty meters of the squad's position. The estimate as to the number of gooks ranged from fifteen to twenty. It was a planned attack on a specific target, Mazie.

The North Koreans cut the fence between two manned positions in B company's sector. The positions were a hundred meters apart. All the space in the world for someone to slither through. Whether the gooks went south or back north is unknown. That was it, 'we got the word' no retaliation, just go about our business.

"Mo, fuck this! We suffer three casualties and that's it. We are not going to retaliate?"

"Mike, the shit's going to hit the fan and the shit is going to hit us."

"What?"

"If I know the Army, they are going to bust our balls. I see a lot of time on the firing range, practicing marksmanship, night fire, improving night patrol and ambushes. In three months, we go back across the river and we'll be training right up to the last day. When we get our chance, it's up to us to even the score."

****

"What did the captain say about the orphanage?" Reed asked.

"He said, only two hours one day a week. We can use his jeep." Mo replied.

The trip to the orphanage became an emotional roller coaster of yin and yang. The kids, especially the little ones, swarmed the jeep when we arrived. Happy, laughing, shouting out our names, they too seemed to have caught on to Mike and Mo, but without the M, it sounded more like Ike and OO. The sad part, we never had enough to give every kid something.

The men in Charlie company took to the kids. The men had toys or stuffed animals sent from home. There are thirty-two ten years old or younger. We never had enough toys or stuffed animals. There were sad faces when their name wasn't called. The kids stood in a row, waiting to see if the headmistress called their name. She kept track of who had last received a toy. When it was obvious, their name wouldn't be called, their arms drooped to their sides as they walked away with their chins resting on their chest.. After these heartbreaking scenes, we kept the toys at the camp until we had enough for every the kids.

Mo and I played soccer with the older kids. Over the years, different Army units put in a soccer field, swings, tilled up a garden to grow their own vegetables. Judging from the ropes hanging from the branches of apple, cherry and persimmon trees, they were used for more than a food source. We were heading inside to check the pantry when a jeep with two MPs skidded to a stop. branches

"Are you Lieutenant Reed?"

"Yes, Sergeant, what's up?"

"Your CO wants you two back to camp now! He didn't say why."

As we got close to camp, we could see the Brigade Commander's glass bubble helicopter in the field next to the gate. The platoon leaders and sergeants were gathered outside the Company CP. Lieutenant Richards was leaning against a jeep with his arms crossed with a face in a scowl.

"Frank, what's going on?" Reed asked.

"We don't know, the Brigade Commander is here. You can bet it's not good. They're going to extend our asses?"

Just then, the CP door opened and, leading the charge, was the Brigade Commander. We snapped to attention, and he returned our salute. He didn't miss Mo and me in our rumpled fatigues, covered with dust from head to toe from playing soccer and the dusty ride back to camp. He gave us a dirty look and grimaced. Captain Roseman noticed. The brigade commander spoke.

"Listen up men, brigade has chosen Charlie company to undergo additional training before your next rotation north. We are up against the North Koreans' 124th Regiment. A highly trained unit of officers and a special forces unit known as the 17th Foot Brigade. The enemy has been crossing the MDL with impunity and it has to stop! Captain Roseman will fill you in on the details."

****

We spent several weeks training with the emphasis on counterinsurgency. Marksmanship with the M-14, two times a week and Quick Kill Fire training. They selected Mo and me to conduct the Quick Kill training.

"Mo, how's the hand?"

"Screw you Reed. It hurts, he shot me right on the knuckle. At four feet, that hurts, BB gun or not."

The Quick Kill course taught the men to shoot instinctively without aiming, but with reasonable accuracy. The trainer stood in front and to the side of the shooter. We armed the shooter with a Daisy BB gun. The trainer tossed a three-inch disc in front of the shooter. The shooter raised the BB gun to his shoulder, looked over the barrel and shot. All within a split second. One of Mo's men was anxious and didn't move the gun to the target, hitting Mo's knuckle as he tossed the disc.

"Hey, your guys can't shoot for shit. You better wear a helmet, flak jacket, along with the safety glasses."

"Screw you again Reed."

"Mo, the training helped at the range today. Four of my men qualified as experts, eighteen as sharpshooters and the rest, marksman with the M-14.."

"How did you do, Reed?"

"I kicked ass! Two short of a perfect score. The only platoon leader to qualify as an expert. When do your men qualify?"

Mo answered. "Tomorrow morning, and thanks for leaving room for me to beat your score. After the range, we're going on maneuvers?"

"Yep, it doesn't look like fun. Night maneuvers to a hill supposedly under attack?"

"That could turn into a cluster fuck real fast." Mo said.

The next several days we ran the APC's to various ridge lines outside of Munsa-an-ni, reinforcing different line companies under attack by imaginary North Korea forces. It was mid-October and the attacks in the DMZ had decreased. Probably because of the lack of foliage that provided the gooks concealment. Our training increased using the APCs in tactical situations in the surrounding hillsides, day and night.

Moving through the villages without a mishap with four diesel driven boxes of steel weighing thirteen tons each, nine feet wide, was becoming more of a miracle each day. People, bikes with piglets strapped to the back, carts, honey wagons, taxis, and buses, entered the mix on the village's narrow streets. As platoon leader, I was the track commander of the second APC in a column of four. My headset allowed communication with the other APCs over the din of the engines. Riker was driving the APC in front.

"RIKER SLOW DOWN! A TAXI IS TRYING TO GET AROUND!" I yelled into the mic!

Before I could finish my sentence, a yellow taxi smaller than a Volkswagen darted by us and was alongside of Riker's APC. At that instant, Riker had to pivot the APC to the left to avoid a kid who had fallen off his bike. The left front of the APC caught the side of the taxi, like a flipper on a pinball machine. It was no contest. The taxi ricocheted off the APC, crossed the road, jumped the ditch, then smashed through a cinderblock wall. Surprising a flock of chickens and a couple of pigs. The taxi crashed into a tree in the courtyard.

"Shit, fuck, goddamn fucking, son of a bitch, mother fuckin cluster fuck!" The entire platoon knew I could cuss up a storm.

"EVERYONE STAY WITH THEIR TRACK! Sergeant, get the medic and Do-Ha, radio the company, and have them contact the MPs."

"Yes Sir,"

I ran up to the taxi. The driver was trying to force the door open. The impact jammed the hood into the driver's door. Do-ha and I pulled the driver through the broken window. His head was bleeding, but from the verbal barrage leveled at us told me he was not seriously injured. Moss and Do-ha tried to calm him.

"Do-Ha, tell him we'll pay for his taxi and medical bills."

The Army's policy has been to cover damages regardless of fault to promote good relations.

He wasn't about to quiet, now yelling Korean obscenities. A crowd was gathering, and I was looking over my shoulder for the MPs. Suddenly an old man appeared and raised his hand to the taxi driver, as if to shush him, speaking in an even voice. The driver stopped talking bowed to the gentleman. The gentleman turned to Do-Ha and me and introduced himself, speaking Korean in a soft-spoken manner. Do-Ha told him the name of our unit and translated the old man's words.

"I am Bae Jung-Hee. This is my home and property. The wall, chickens and dead pig can be replaced. The taxi damaged the tree to the point it will not recover."

Mr. Bae walked over and knelt by the tree, sliding his hand over the damaged bark and shattered trunk. The old man continued.

"It is a cherry tree I planted fifteen years ago to celebrate the end of the war and in honor of my wife, who died in 1953. During the fall and winter it reminded me of the hard times, but come spring it brought life with its beautiful blossoms. It was a reminder that we can survive harsh times. By the middle of summer, the tree provided pleasure with its fruit and memories of my wife making her delicious sweets. It's very sad to lose the tree."

"Mr. Bae, I'm sorry. We will do whatever it takes to fix the wall and plant a new tree and pay for the chickens and pigs." Do-Ha Translated!

"To plant a tree as mature and beautiful will not be possible. Such is fate. I'll find out the cost to repair wall and let your commander know. Your unit is at camp Lawtons?"

"Yes, Mr. Bae. The CO is Captain Roseman. Do you want my men to stack the concrete blocks and remove the damaged tree?"

"No, I'll get help." Do-Ha translated.

Do-Ha then turned to getting the contact information from the taxi driver. Just then, two MPs arrived.

"Lieutenant, you're going to have a shitload of paperwork."

Hyun-ae Bae meets Reed

"Love is a trap. When it appears, we see only its light, not its shadows." Paulo Coelho

The next couple of weeks went by fast. Training intensified with joint operations with other units. Mo's prediction of never ending training proved accurate. Charlie company was in the field for three, four days at a time. We were missing the hooch. Everyone was issued a winter parka, heavy itchy wool underwear along with wool pants and shirt. For wind protection, we had nylon shell pants. Capping off the gear were mittens with inserts, a wool skull cap and rubber pacs. They earned the nickname mickey mouse boots. They were black and over sized, like Mickey's feet.

The winter gear added twenty pounds to our equipment. It was the first week of November. Night came faster and colder.

My platoon of four APCs was pulling into the motor pool when the first sergeant flagged me down. It was 0900 hours, we had been out the entire night, we were beat. He was shouting over the roar of the engines.

"LIEUTENANT, THE CAPTAIN WANTS TO SEE YOU ASAP!"

"FIRST SERGEANT DON'T YOU KNOW ANY OTHER TIME FRAME OTHER THAN ASAP!!"

"YES SIR, HOW ABOUT, NOW!"

Shit, something's up. As I got to the CP, Mo was coming from the hooch.

"What's up, Captain?"

"Tell me, did you two knuckleheads commandeered an engineer's backhoe and dig up and steal a cheery tree from the orphanage?"

"Sir, we.."

"I know you did. Why the fuck didn't you two tell me? Never mind, just never the fuck mind. I will not chew your asses out, matter of fact, you amused Colonel Williams and impressed him with your relationship building with the citizens of Munsa-an-ni."

What deal did you make with the orphanage? It's my understanding the cherry tree you dug up was full size. Who the fuck operated the backhoe?"

Mo took the honor.

"Sir, I worked for a contractor while going to college. The orphanage is happy. We took up a collection and arranged for two cherry trees to be planted in the spring. We didn't tell you, guessing the punishment wouldn't be as bad if we just did it. Mike said the old man was heartbroken about the tree, so we came up with a plan."

Captain Rosie broke out in a smile.

"The Colonel said the villagers respected the 'old man' known as Mr. Bae. He's a decorated colonel, during the Korean War, he was involved in some of the heaviest fighting. He has invited you two as his guest for dinner tomorrow. Colonel Williams is sending the payment over for the damages. Mr Bae agreed to eighty thousand Won, which is just about a hundred dollars, so there's no need to negotiate. Just enjoy the evening."

"Thank you sir, should we take Do-Ha as an interpreter?"

"The colonel said Bae has someone in the family that speaks English, but take Do-Ha just in case. By the way, the MPs cleared your platoon in the accident. Apparently, that taxi driver has been terrorizing the village for weeks. A couple of mothers spoke up about his reckless driving. You two better be on your best behavior. Talk to Do-Ha about the local customs. On your way out, tell Sergeant Jackson I want to see him."

"Yes, Sir."

"Sergeant Jackson, the Captain wants to see you ASAP!"

The next day, our house boy Sung-ho, we called him Sam, pressed and steamed our issued wool pants and shirts. Shoulder patches sewed on, boots and belt buckles shined. We were ready to have dinner with retired Colonel Bae. Do-Ha and Sam filled us in on the customs, instructing us not to cross our legs, eat slow, don't finish your meal faster than Mr. Bae, bow when arriving and leaving. If he offers to shake hands, hold your right forearm with your left hand. If a Korean woman is present, don't extend your hand. They don't shake hands with men, just bow.'

Do-ha parked just inside the repaired wall. The

cherry tree appeared to be healthy, but difficult to tell without leaves. Mo and I walked towards the house when Mr. Bae came out to greet us dressed in black slacks and a starched white shirt, open at the collar. Maybe it wouldn't be the stuffy affair Mo and I were expecting. We bowed and shook hands as instructed. Colonel Bae smiled.

Bae motioned to Do-ha for him to come. The exterior walls of the house were a gray stucco with a red tilled roof pagoda style. Two enormous wooden doors adorned with wrought iron hinges and large door handles comprised the entrance. Inside was a small foyer with a mat to place our boots. Colonel Bae slid open the translucent rice paper door covered with wooden filigree to the main room.

The large room had a high wooden ceiling supported by large wooden beams. The walls were covered with wood panels. The walls had many glass windows covered with rice paper screens radiating a soft golden glow on the walls. It was a warm room sparsely furnished, with a long, low table in the center of the room.

Positioned on the floor around the table were five large cushions. The only other furniture was a couple of low tables with lamps. Framed oriental art and shelves with ceramic figurines decorated the walls.

Just then, a young lady in traditional dress entered the room. She had a floor length pink chima with a yellow jeogori as a jacket. She pulled her thick black hair back and held with a yellow ribbon. We bowed in return as she came to a stop. As we raised our heads from the bow, our eyes met with instant recognition. I saw the flash of anger in her big, beautiful almond-shaped eyes.

"YOU, YOU!!!"

A tirade of words in Korean followed, many of which I knew the meaning, were not ladylike. I turned to Do-Ha as Mr. Bae spoke to the angry young lady.

"What did she say?" I asked Do-Ha.

"As you Americans say, she called you every name in the book."

Colonel Bae then spoke in English.

"Gentlemen, I apologize for Hyun-ae's outburst. Also, for misleading you whether I spoke English. I prefer the Korean language, even if I have to suffer from the inconvenience of an interpreter. Hyun-ae, meet Lieutenant Mike Reed and Lieutenant Morgan Ashforth."

Mr Bae, looking directly at me, said.

"Lieutenant Reed, it seems you have met my niece under unusual circumstances?"

We bowed again at the introduction, feeling uncomfortable.

Hyun-ae eyes locked onto mine, the anger in her dark eyes seemed to melt away. I thought I saw a hint of a smile cross her face.

"Yes sir, we crashed into each other in the market near the University."

Mo had a smirk on his face and I gave him a dirty look. Mr. Bae started chuckling.

"So you're the Lieutenant that caused my niece to hurt her knee and saved her, by sending the police off in a different direction."

"Yes, sir."

"Come, let's sit." He motioned for us to sit on the cushions around the table.

Hyun-ae moved towards the cushion between her uncle and me. As she sat, the air stirred, carrying a subtle, delightful, mysterious fragrance. Mr. Bae's houseboy appeared and served drinks with ice. Mr. Bae explained.

"It's a liquor made from wild pears." It had a mellow taste but with a kick. Hyun-ae sat with her hands folded on her lap. She spoke in perfect English.

"Morgan and you Mike, I suppose, are the 'OO' and 'Ike' the kids at the orphanage talk about?"

"Yep, Charlie company adopted the orphanage. The men get a kick out of helping."

"Good, because our government doesn't help. Uncle Bae and Aunt Ju donate to the orphanage. Do you know there're no government agencies dedicated to helping the orphans?"

"Hyun-ae! Please forgive her. She likes to talk politics." Hyun-ae continued over her uncle's objection.

"The government believes in bloodline purity, as if mixed race is a threat to Korean racial and ethnic purity. Incredibility, they believe mixed races are a threat to our national security."

"HYUN-AE!"

"I'm sorry, Uncle, I wanted to explain why the donations and the work the Lieutenants do is important. It is no fault of the kids they're orphaned. About a third of them are mixed. So thank you for your generous work."

The conversation ranged from where we lived in the states, our education and what we thought of Korea. Whether it was the second drink of pear liquor or Mo's ability to make pleasant conversation, Hyun-ae relaxed and talked freely, describing her time in California and her quest to earn a doctorate in nuclear physics. Do-Ha and the Colonel were having a lively conversation about the army and the life of a KUTUSA. The Baes practiced Confucianism, which Hyun-ae described it as more of a philosophy or way of life than a religion. Dinner was served and Hyun-ae explained the dishes.

"The main dish is *Jeonju bibimbap,* a rice dish with many cooked vegetables mixed with Gochujang shredded red peppers, fried egg, minced beef, *kimchi* and rice cakes."

The delicious meal ended with a pot of coffee, real coffee. A drink I acquired a taste for since being in Korea. This coffee was not an army brew. The aroma filled the room. My delight must've shown on my face as I sipped.

"Lieutenant Reed, you enjoy the coffee.?"

"Yes, it's excellent."

"In Seoul, there's an importer that sells coffee from Sumatra. You must take some back with you."

"Thank you, Colonel. I will enjoy every cup. I

might even share with Mo."

I was getting anxious. The evening was going to end. I wanted to see Hyun-ae again. I didn't know how to ask her.

"Gentlemen, before you go, I want to show you photographs taken by my wife. Photography was her hobby, and she became quite good at it." We followed the colonel to an alcove off the main room. My eyes followed Hyun-ae as she diappeared into another room. Mr. Bae had covered the walls of the alcove with black and white photographs of farmers in the fields, villages, Seoul, mountains and family members. His wife took them in the forties before the war. Hyun-ae appeared at my side.

"The photograph in the middle is of Uncle Bae, his wife and my mother and father."

Hyun-ae eyes started tearing up. Colonel Bae moved behind Hyun-ae, gently holding her by her shoulders as he whispered in her ears. He then turned to us.

"I had a most enjoyable evening. Hyun-ae has something for you."

Hyun-ae returned from another room after a couple of minutes, presenting wrapped gifts to Mo and Do-Ha. She handed me a small book tied with a ribbon. She smiled as our eyes met and hands touched.

"Lieutenant Mike, please read. The book has the Sayings of Confucius."

We bowed and said goodbye. As we pulled away, Mo started laughing.

"Damn, there must be karma in your life. You said you wanted to meet her again and I'll be damned. It happened. Mike, you couldn't make it any more obvious. You're head over heels for that girl."

Do-ha chimed in.

"I think she likes you. She gave us a box of rice cakes. She gave you something personal."

Back at the hooch, I sat on my bunk and removed the ribbon from the book. Inside the cover was a folded note. *'I am staying at my Aunt Ju's place. You are welcome to visit next Saturday or Sunday afternoon. The directions are in English and Korean in case you have to ask someone.'* Hyun-ae.

Suddenly, I was on cloud nine!

WON AND DONG PICK UP THE SCENT

"Chief, we located Bae. She's staying at her uncle's in Munsa-an-ni."

"Last month you determined she wasn't at her uncles?"

"We continued watching the uncle's house and the aunts."

"When did you see her?"

"October 24, two days ago. We have confirmed it's Bae. We have a team watching the house. If the Viper tries to make contact, we'll have him."

"You saw her two days ago and not since?"

"She's hiding out."

"BULLSHIT WON! Colonel Bae wouldn't let his niece get involved. Viper won't go to that house. She's not hiding out at the Colonels. If you haven't seen her in two days, she gave you the slip!"

"What do you want us to do, Chief?"

"Find her, be careful. She must not suspect she is being watched."

"Chief, the village of Munsa-sa-ni is small. Everyone knows each other. It's difficult not to draw attention."

"Spread your men out, cast a larger net. The villagers won't know who or what you are watching." Said the chief.

"Chief, the Viper? Do you have anything new?"

"Nothing, he is hiding, or he went back north. We

can't take the chance he hasn't. What about her aunt, any activity at her house near Kimpo?" the chief asked.

"No, she works seven days a week, a busy lady."

"She also is wealthy. Does she own other properties?"

"We checked, and she has several buildings in her name and her company's name. They're work shops, nothing suitable for hiding." Won replied.

"Keep checking. My guess is Hyun-ae is staying someplace owned by the uncle or aunt."

LAND OF THE MORNING CALM

"Love is too young to know what conscience is." William Shakespeare

The weekend was slow in coming. On Saturday, we had a battalion inspection. Everyone in pressed fatigues and shined boots. Battalion staff officers scrutinized everything from weapons to the company clerk's records. Charlie Company impressed the battalion commander with the number of field exercises we completed, along with the improvement of the men's rifle skills. We scored the highest among the battalion's companies.

We pleased Colonel Williams with the maintenance on our tracks after the Sergeant Major, a stickler for detail, examined our maintenance records and test driving three APCs. When the Sergeant Major exited the last APC, he gave Colonel Williams a thumbs up.

We stood at parade rest as the Colonel and Captain Roseman discussed the results of the inspection. As Colonel Williams walked away with his staff, Captain Roseman turned to the men of Charlie company with a big smile on his face.

"Men, we passed the inspection with flying colors. WELL DONE! tomorrow we will issue day passes. Platoon leaders, I want to see you in my office."

We followed Captain Roseman to the office,

anticipating he had something in mind other than a day off for the officers. He sat down and glanced up with a quizzical look on his face. "What's with the sad faces?" Mo spoke up first.

"Damn it, Rosie, Captain! We were looking forward to the day off tomorrow, but it looks like you have something else planned."

"JESUS! cheer up, you'll get the day off. I just wanted to thank each of you for the hard work you and your men put in for this inspection. The Colonel was more than happy. He said we're ready to go back to the DMZ."

"Shit, maybe we should have flunked!" Mo said.

"MO, the colonel said we go back in two months. The training has to continue. Tomorrow he wants the company commanders at battalion. Thus, I need one of you to babysit the company. Lieutenant Richards, you're the short timer, so you're it. The rest of you 'WILL BE' back in the compound by 2100 hours. Sergeant Jackson is arranging for truck transport for the men that want to go to the PX. Sorry Mo, I need my jeep. The company's quarter ton is available."

I left the meeting trying to figure how I was going to get to see Hyan-ae. Mo interrupted my thoughts.

"Mike, you know who's allowed to drive the quarter ton?"

"No, who?"

"Do Ha, we can ride with him, drop the men off at the PX, then we can go to the..."

"Sorry Mo, but I have other plans. I'm going to meet

Hyun-ae in Ujeongbu."

"What the fuck? How did that happen? Mike, she's a beautiful woman, but do you know what you are getting yourself into? The army doesn't want its officers to fraternize..."

"Screw you! We can't fraternize, but you can fuck them! Go to your Green door Mo, go to timbuk fucking tu, for all I care, I'm going to Ujeongbu."

Mo broke out laughing. "TIM BUCK FUCKING TU?" He continued laughing then said.

"Mike, I'm sorry. I was just trying to explain, Colonels and such discourage officers from getting involved with Korean women. If you're planning on staying in the Army, you.."

"Jesus Mo, right now I don't have a clue if I'm staying or leaving. This thing with Hyun-ae feels good and I'm going to see her."

"How do you know she wants to see you, and why Ujeongbu?"

"She put a note in the book she gave me. She is staying at her aunt's place."

"Alright, Alright, Uijeongbu is somewhat on the way to Kimpo. I think we can convince Do-ha to take a slight detour."

"Thanks Mo."

****

Do-ha dropped me off in a small cluster of shops and homes halfway up the mountain, which was more like a large hill. The note said to take the path lined with white stones, count off six houses, then take the path to the left to the last house. The air was crisp at 2500 feet elevation. Wisps of gray smoke spiraled up from the houses lining the small intersection.

It was a beautiful November afternoon, with a chill in the air. The sky was bright blue. It was quiet in this little corner of Korea, with no military trucks roaring by. I could hear the cheerful sing song of a woman tossing feed to her chickens across the road. There were a couple of young boys walking in the center of the road, tossing a soccer ball back and forth, heading for the field. Peaceful, small town Korea, serenity. No wonder they call Korea, Land of the Morning Calm.

I was started towards the stone lined path when a Kimchi cab stopped in front of me. What caught my attention was the fare. The woman was giving the driver hell as she opened the door, her yelling broke the calm. She paid, and the cab sped off. The resemblance to Hyun-ae was striking, and the look she was giving me wasn't good.

"Lieutenant, are you lost? This village, not for GIs." She said in perfect English.

"No, I'm going to see a young lady, Hyun-ae Bae! She is staying at her aunt's place and I'm guessing you are Aunt Ju?"

"Where did you meet Hyun-ae?"

"At her uncles we.."

"So, are you, Mike or Mo? She told me about the dinner at her uncle's and the work you two do at the orphanage. Hyun-ae didn't tell me she was seeing you?"

I extended my hand but pulled it back and with a half bow, I said.

"I'm Mike Reed. I assure you, Hyun-ae invited me."

"Well, if that's the case, come with me, Lieutenant. This will be quite interesting. She isn't expecting me."

The fifteen-minute walk covered a lot of ground and Bae family history. Aunt Ju explained she was upset with the cab driver because he drove too fast. The cab was filthy and it smelled of dead fish. As we continued up the path, she told me she was Hyun-ae's aunt on her mother's side. It surprised her that Hyun-ae invited me to the cottage. I learned Aunt Ju was married to a GI, who had since passed away.

She asked if I knew Hyun-ae was a student at the University and was working on her doctorate, which I did. We passed the sixth house and turned left on the path leading to Aunt Ju's place. A quaint cottage set apart from the other houses up against a forest of pine trees. The bright red-tiled roof glistened in the sunlight. The view was spectacular looking out over the city. When we got close to the door, Aunt Ju turned and put her hand out for me to stop.

"Lieutenant, please wait here. I want to announce your arrival!"

"OK, please call me Mike." She turned and gave me a steely look. I had forgotten first names in Korea are only for close friends. After what seemed an eternally the door opened and Hyun-ae appeared at the door.

"Lieutenant, please come in. My aunt is rude, making you wait outside."

After crossing the threshold, I could feel the warmth in the cottage and the electric charge between Hyun-ae and me. Aunt Ju was standing in the far corner smoking a cigarette, watching us. She was smiling. I took it as meaning, she perceived the connection between Hyun-ae and me.

CHUNGS LOOSE ENDS

"Silence is a true friend who never betrays," Confucius

Won was thinking about Bae as he walked into the office. They need more investigation into the Bae family. It was January, and Viper hadn't surfaced, nor the Bae girl. Won walked to the fresh pot of coffee as he said.

"Good morning Chief, what brings you to the office so early?"

"Homicide called. A double murder occurred over in Sewoon Sagga district. Take Yoo and get over there. Here's the address."

Won and Yoo arrived at the small house at the end of an alley. It was one of the few areas in the district untouched by rebuilding. The same homicide detective investigating the Wook murder was standing at the door.

"Inspectors Won and Yoo, I'm glad they sent you. I believe you'll find the circumstances of these murders very similar to Mr. Wooks. The house is being processed, be careful what you touch.

Apparently, the killer caught the man and young lady in bed. Time of death occurred around midnight using their body temperature, but with the door open, that alters things. This morning a neighbor noticed the open door. He looked in and saw the male victim and called the police. The man is eviscerated like a pig. We don't know if he slit the man's throat before or after. Perhaps the medical examiner can tell. My guess is he wanted the victim to suffer before he cut his throat."

The naked body was lying face up on a floor smeared with syrupy blood. Intestines had spilled as the man struggled. Yoo rushed out the door, holding his hand over his mouth. Yoo later told Won, the spilled intestines reminded him of a coil of sausages.

"Signs of forced entry?" Won asked.

"No."

"Who was murdered first?" Won asked.

"The man.

we're guessing, no sign of a struggle." Said the detective.

With an exasperated look, Won said.

"Why didn't the woman run? She had time."

"Either she knew the killer, was too terrified to run, or drunk. There's an empty liquor bottle on the table. The killer strangled and separated her neck. When the medical examiner moved her head to examine the bruising, he discovered the only thing holding the head on her neck was skin and muscle. The killer separated the vertebrae at C5, C6. Her name is Yim Ae-Sook.

She told her neighbors the occasional visitor was her brother. No one saw his face. He always arrived and left when it was dark. Yim lived here for several years. The male victims' wallet and ID are missing. In the bedroom, there is a hiding place for something the size of a briefcase. The detective continued.

"The killer removed the panel after the butchery, leaving bloody fingerprints. A mistake by the killer? There's more intrigue. A photograph was taped to the back of a drawer."

The detective removed a photograph from an evidence bag. Won put on his gloves. Yoo returned, still looking green around the gills. The black-and-white photograph showed four young ladies wearing the same uniform style of a dress. Yoo commented that the girls and the victim were pretty and looked happy. Won studied the background in the photograph.

"Damn it! Look at this! Is that a North Korea soldier?"

The detective went over to the medical examiner's bag and remove a magnifying glass, handing it to Won.

The images in the photograph were ordinary civilians, except for the soldier leaning on a lamppost, watching the girls. Nothing appeared out of the ordinary. There wasn't enough background in the photograph to determine the location. The magnifying glass showed a soldier in a North Korea uniform.

"It is. We checked Yim Ae-sook's identification. She claimed she was a war refugee from North Korea when she was twelve. Her story to authorities back then was she lived in various orphanages near Seoul. She ran away several times and lived on the streets. They believed her story. They granted her papers when she was twenty-five. The photo contradicts her version. In the photo, she is at least twenty and in North Korea."

Yoo jumped into the conversation.

"She's a North Korea agent and if."

Yoo stopped talking, as the police were not aware that Won and Yoo were chasing a spy, a very proficient and prolific killer.

"Inspector Won, is there more?"

"Detective, there's no proof connecting the other murders to Wooks. We found no fingerprints at Wooks' scene. We need to determine if there's a connection to Wook. Who is the dead man? Whose bloody prints are on the panel? Is he Ae-Sook's so-called brother or was he her lover? There's nothing to show there's something more. There're the similarities to Wooks' murder, but until there's evidence, I have nothing to share.

I'm taking the photograph of the girls. When we have something, I'll let you know. We don't want the press knowing Yim's connection to North Korea or this murder's connection to the North Koreans. Tell the press you are investigating a love triangle."

"Inspector WON!, you can't tell me how to conduct my investigation!"

"No, but my boss will call yours. I'm warning you what not to say to the horde of reporters outside. They go for murder stories with a love triangle twist. They'll eat it up. We'll be sending a team over to help with the forensics. They will not interfere with your men."

On the way back to the office Won thought, Yim Ae-Sooks name was familiar, not one of his cases, but part of someone's case. Yoo was non-stop with his theories and conclusions interfering with Won's train of thought.

"Yoo, you are worse than a flock of magpies. Yes, Viper was probably the murderer, but why? Who is the unidentified male? Was it a safe house? Why kill the girl if she was the keeper of the safe house? How did she get into the country? If the same fingerprints are throughout the house, we can assume it was his safe house. It will confirm he's in Seoul. Why did he eliminate the girl? Was the viper the unknown brother, or the murdered male? Something else struck me. Wook's murderer rented the house, paid cash. On a table there was a week of stacked newspapers. In Yim's house, a stack of newspapers, it's just an odd coincidence, but!" Do you recall Yim's name on our radar?

"No, I don't recall the name, but I'll check as soon as we get back. Won, take the photo straight to the technical bureau. They can blow the picture up to show better detail. The other girls, who and where are they?"

"The chief will want to see it before it goes anywhere."

****

In the Chief's glass cubicle, the leader of Bae's surveillance team was talking excitedly. The Chief motioned for Won. Yoo left to check if they had a record on Yim Ae-Sook.

"Won, they located Bae. She is staying near Ujeongbu in a house owned by the aunt. She used two different corporations to buy the land and build the cottage. We didn't catch it during the first search of the records. The surveillance team determined Bae was not hiding. She is out and about. Even more surprising, they saw her with an American officer, a lieutenant. The team followed him back to his unit near Mun sa'ni, which is where her Bae's uncle lives."

"What do you want to do, Chief?"

"Talk to his battalion commander, get background on the lieutenant, if you get him to swear to secrecy about our concerns with Bae fill him in on the some details."

"Chief, I should take the American military intelligence men I worked with a while back, Kowalski and Meyers. I believe they're still in the country."

"Good idea. Set it up as soon as possible. Meanwhile, we'll monitor Bae." The chief said.

Won used his Rolodex to get the number. He wanted to go this afternoon.

"Kowalski, inspector Won from OSI."

"How you doing, Won?"

"Fine, we need to talk to an officer with the second of the twenty-third. We believe he's with Charlie company."

"What's his name?"

"We just know he's a lieutenant, and seeing a girl named Bae, Hyun-ae."

"Why do you want to talk to him?"

"We'll explain when we meet. It's best if he didn't know we were coming. Can you arrange it?"

"Yes, but we're part of the discussion!"

"I understand. This is a delicate situation. Discretion is necessary."

"The earliest it can happen, let me check, is January 22, in the afternoon."

"Why not tomorrow?" Won asked.

"Meyers and I are testifying at a court martial. I'll get back to you with the details." Said Kowalski.

Yoo rushed into the cubicle.

"Won! We had Ae-Sook under surveillance. A neighbor reported suspicious activity a month ago. We checked her background, interviewed neighbors put her under surveillance for a few days.. We blew it, we never interviewed her. Coworkers liked her. Ae-Sook liked to party, but they found nothing suspicious. They discontinued the surveillance. Get this, one of the surveillance reports states she met a man in the marketplace near the university. They just exchanged pleasantries and kissed. The description in the surveillance report fits the male victim, her lover."

"Good work Yoo, why did he kill her and what's the connection between Viper and Hyun-ae Bae?"

Blue House January 21, 1968

"The quality of decision is like the well timed swoop of a falcon which enables it to strike and destroy its victim." Sun TA

I couldn't sleep so I tried to read. Mo was snoring loudly at the far end of our hooch. I had a scratchy army blanket wrapped around my shoulders. My thoughts kept drifting. November and December had been cold with rain. It was now January. Hyun-ae and I had been meeting once, sometimes twice a week, the past two months. The training had dwindled to three days a week. The other days we pulled maintenance, prepped for inspection and did PT.

Mo and I made our weekly trips to the orphanage. In November, we put on a push to gather winter clothing and boots for the kids. Aunt Ju solicited used winter clothing and cash donations from her female employees. She was the conduit for setting up my dates with Hyun-ae. I called Aunt Ju at her office and tell her the day I could see Hyun-ae. Aunt Ju then called the shop owner near the cottage to relay the message to Hyun-ae.

I had only a few hours off during the day. But Hyun ae and I managed to get to Seoul and the Changdeokgung Palace and the Gwanghwamun Gate. I was learning, Korean has history dating back thousands of years. Our next planned excursion was going to be the Jingwansa temple, built in 1000 BC. The pocked marked buildings in Seoul showed the ravages of the war between the north and south fifteen years earlier.

There's one day in November that runs through my mind over and over. The Captain issued Mo and me a twenty-four-hour pass. Mo's destination was Seoul. Aunt Ju's was mine. I arrived at the cottage on our Thanksgiving day. Koreans celebrate a fall harvest in October. I knocked and heard a faint call.

"Come in door unlocked." Hyun-ae walked out of the bedroom decked out in a full length red and black satin dress that showed off the curves of her body. She had pulled her hair back into a bun, with wisps of her black hair along each side of her face. She smiled.

"You like!"

I was staring at a beautiful woman. My jaw dropped as I uttered.

"You're beautiful!" I wanted to take her in my arms. We had kissed on earlier dates with each time being more passionate but always the push back with her saying. 'lieutenant you must go or they will mark you AWOL.' The steamy embraces and kisses kept me coming back. Hyun-ae smiled, then spoke.

"This is a special day in America. You have a big feast with the Indians and family, right?"

"Family yes, no Indians."

"I know, Thanksgiving. I'm just as you say, pulling your leg. We're going out to have a fancy dinner on me. I have a very special restaurant picked out in

Seoul. If we leave now, you'll have time to get to your base tonight."

"Hyun-ae, I have a twenty-four-hour pass."

She smiled. "Good, let's go. We can enjoy more time in Seoul and a relaxing dinner." Holding hands, we entered the Wooraeok restaurant. The decor was warm with dark wood paneling on the walls broken up by painted screens dividing the restaurant into several areas. Paintings on the wall depicted Korean history.

Flowers in glass vases, white linen table clothes, classy. The menu had a mix of Americans and Korean entrees, most being Korean. There were a few American officers seated, with what appeared to be their wives. A few units could bring the family.

Twenty miles north, as the crow flies, is a very dangerous place. No civilians, no first-class restaurants. The DMZ had none of this. The few thousand US soldiers stationed in and along the DMZ were in purgatory, a couple of steps from hell and only twenty miles from heaven. What a country!

We followed the mait're de, Hyun-ae turned the heads of the male diners. I received dirty looks from an Air Force colonel. I couldn't remember what I ate at the restaurant, what I remember, it was good. We finished dinner and were waiting for dessert when she reached across the table and took my hand. I vividly recall the smile and her bright dark eyes, her exact words and the warm rush through my body.

"Mike, I like you very much. I want you to stay with

me tonight."

We made love that night. She had an athletic body but was soft and gentle in her touch and kiss. When on top, Hyun-ae body was as light as a feather. She wrapped her arms around my neck and squeezed, not just with her arms. We were entangled in each other's body as if we were wax, fused together.

That night, we fell asleep in each other's arms. I woke up first. She was lying on her side, facing me. Her long black hair resting on her shoulder. During the night, the cottage cooled. The bed was soft and warm. Outside, the morning was calm. The early light of the day through the window gave her hair a sparkle. I couldn't believe I was in bed with such a fascinating woman. As I pulled the blanket up over her shoulder, she opened one eye as if winking at me, smiled, then wrapped her arms around my neck and slid on top. Her long black hair danced on my face, smelling as fresh as roses in a garden.

Over breakfast Hyun-ae told me about Ji-Hoon kwon, her fiancee. They met at Berkley. He also was an exchange student. A car hit him while crossing a street in Seoul two years ago. She realized she must 'move on' as Aunt Ju keeps reminding her. She enjoyed her time in California. Hyun-ae loved the giant Redwoods, Yosemite, her professors, but most she loved the freedom. Students could protest without fear of reprisal. Unruly classmates protesting hauled away by the police were released without being fined or beaten. There were no soldiers or police on the street corners checking identification.

"Mike, did you play football?"

"Yes?"

"What position?"

"Why do you ask?"

"Because American football is fun to watch. Our team at Berkley, the Golden Bears, was not very good. They won only half of the games they played."

"What year was that?"

"Nineteen sixty-five. I loved going to the games, seeing the fans in school colors, everyone having a good time, even when we lost. It was colorful, loud and fun to watch the strategy. Watching giant men knocking each other over sounds barbaric when I tried to explain the game to my friends in Seoul. So, what position did you play?"

"Linebacker."

"Middle or outside?"

"Middle, you know the game."

"Yes, my favorite middle linebacker before you was Sam Huff. He played for the Red Indians."

"You mean the Redskins."

"Yes, he was a smash them bash 'em linebacker."

She jumped up and scooted into the bedroom, returning a minute later.

"See!"

She held up the Cal gold and black pennant with a bear.

"I kept the Cal Bears hidden away, but now I'll put him on the wall."

She described how she devoted her time to her

studies and protests against the government. It was the first time she opened up and told me her ambitions, find her mother, develop nuclear energy for Korea and see it united. She believed her mother was very much alive. She could sense her mother reaching out to her.

"I know I'm obsessed with finding my mother. My dreams haunt me. In them she is alive and determined to come home."

She told me she believed the North Koreans were using her mother's talents as a doctor. Refusing to acknowledge she is alive. The North Koreans and even her own government deny the communist rebel Kim dal-sam, kidnapped her. The 1949 uprising on Jeju island was so long ago, no one cares.

She explained her friend Chung, a wealthy businessman, made a promise to get information on her mother. He had made donations to her April II protest group. I thought the wealthy businessman part didn't fit. She was going to get her doctorate in nuclear physics. Her plans changed. She doesn't know when she will go back to the university. She dropped out of school because of the student murder during the last protest.

"Mike, the protest had a terrible ending, but good came of it. I met you."

She told me her feeling were in a turmoil. In a dream, she came face to face with a black stallion ridden by a soldier. The stallion then galloped off to the stars. In the dream, she tried to grab the horse's tail, but the horse disappeared into the night. Was I the soldier on the horse?

She knew I was leaving for home in a matter of months. Korea was her home. Sitting across the table over tea that morning, she again used the word like. Her words were etched in my mind.

"Mike, I like you very, very much, but in a few months, you'll leave Korea. The answer is no if you ask me to go to America. I don't want to hurt you, but I never could leave Korea, Aunt Ju and Uncle Bae. You calm me and make me feel new again. I want to be with you. I wish we could just go on and not worry about the future."

We stared at each other across the table. Her dark, teary eyes pierced my soul. I knew then, her family and country were her anchor. I couldn't break that bond. Did I want to? I knew her warm embraces and sensual kisses kept me coming back, along with her mysterious intrigue and kind heart. It's going to be hard to let go. I told her what I thought she wanted to hear.

"We should take each day as they come. The near and distant future is not ours to control."

****

I had just fallen asleep after musing about Hyun-ae. It midnight and cold as a witch's tit when Private Beier burst into the houch with blowing snow following him.

"LIEUTENANTS WAKE UP, GET UP! The captain wants you at the CP now!"

"What the fuck, Beir! What's up?" I found my wool

pants at the foot of the cot and stood to put them on, my bare feet hitting the ice cold concrete floor.

"The battalion is on alert. North Koreans attacked the president's house."

"THE WHITE HOUSE?"

"NO, THE KOREA PRESIDENT!"

Mo and I hustled to the CP. The wind was blowing from the north, two inches of snow had fallen. At the CP, Captain Roseman was in full battle gear. His M-14 was lying across the desk.

"Men, the first Sergeant has alerted the platoon sergeants. We are to move out by O three hundred. A unit of North Koreans attempted to breach the Presidential palace. They attacked at 2130 hours. They were unsuccessful. There are many casualties, including civilians. Most of the North Koreans got away, it's believed they'll travel north, trying to go through the DMZ. We will try to intercept them in the Tae-Bak mountains."

After a four-hour ride, the battalion reached its rally point with units of the 2nd Division. We were on the western edge of the Tae Bak mountains. Ten miles south of the DMZ.. The headwaters of the Han river flowed by our bivouac area. As the sun peeked over the mountains, they briefed us on our mission.

We were to patrol in platoon size units and conduct night ambushes. The North Korean commandos were traveling in small units of two to four. There was a dusk to dawn curfew for civilians. Any suspicious persons were to be challenged before taking them under fire. We were told that the trained commandos will fight to the death, armed with the submachine guns and grenades. They're dressed in long overcoats which helped conceal their weapons. Our mission was to find the enemy and warn and protect the civilians. Using the KUTUSAs to explain the reason for the curfew.

The residents living in the grid assigned to us did not have electricity. Few owned a transistor radio. No villages or roads, just small family units perched in the nooks and crannies of the mountains. They scratched out a living raising pigs, chickens and scouring the mountainside for ginseng and wood to make charcoal, the primary fuel for heating and cooking.

"Sergeant Hicks, let's make sure the men take enough winter gear, we'll be in the mountains for more than a day or two.. We're going to be humpin rough terrain and we'll need to change out our socks, long underwear and make sure everyone packs their winter headgear. The helmet is not enough at night. The temperature drops into the teens at night."

"Lieutenant, we're going to sweat, then freeze our ass off after humpin the five miles uphill to our patrol area."

"Sarge, get the men ready."

"Yes sir, Lieutenant, the cold in Korea has no mercy."

"We can dress for it. The CO will set up a supply depot near the top. We won't have to come off the mountain for supplies. At three thousand feet elevation, think of the view."

"Okay lieutenant, I'll jack up the men's attitude and convince them we are on a sight seeing hike through the magnificent Korean mountains."

"Sarge, just be thankful it snowed only a couple inches, lets get the men ready to move out."

Our area of responsibility was two klicks wide and three long, running east to west. To the south was Mo's platoon to our north a ROK ranger unit. The terrain was rugged, with steep trails and large rocky outcrops. There were few trees for protection from the wind or cover for our ambushes. The first day was pleasant, with deep blue sunny skies which helped the morale despite humpin fifty pounds of gear to our patrol area.

The familys living in the hollows of the mountains comprised of grandparents, parents and grandchildren. They lived in a cluster of two or three thatched roof homes. Do-Ha talked to the grandmother of the first family we met. The men and wives were gathering wood or tending to the animals. She didn't know an attack occurred on the presidential palace or that a curfew was in place. The grandmother, with eyes wide open and flailing her arms, feared the 'bughan gun-in' would kill her family. She wanted us to stay. Do-Ha calmed her down. She told us her husband may be near the trail that leads to the next family a twenty-minute walk. She walked over, looked up and smiled with a couple of missing teeth, in English said.

"Lieutenant, you got Lucky Strike?"

I didn't, but Sergeant Hicks rounded up C ration cigarettes. Do-ha said she thanked us profusely not only for the cigarettes but for fighting during the Korean War. We found the grandfather, and he said he would warn the others. The next few days were the same. Word of the curfew spread, we didn't have to worry about civilians walking the trails. No suspicious men had been seen in the area.

At night it was cold to the bone, the wind was raw. The weather was our enemy. After four days and nights, the men were becoming lackadaisical. Routine patrols, catch a couple of hours of sleep and set up ambushes for the night. The mountainous terrain looked the same. Sarge and I were on them about being alert. We sweated during the day, froze our ass off at night. Changing out socks and long underwear was essential. Soldiers bitch no matter how good or bad the situation. Appleman got a chuckle out of the men.

"Lieutenant, my dick is gonna get frostbit and fall off. I just pissed, and it turned to ice before it hit the ground. When are we getting off this fucking mountain?"

The sarge answered him.

"Appleman, your dick isn't big enough to get frost bit and if it did, you wouldn't miss it. Stop being a pussy and change your goddamn socks before you lose your toes, which are a lot bigger than your dick."

Sarge and I knew we had just tonight and tomorrow before being relieved. We didn't tell the men until we received the actual orders.

I set up our ambush that night on a series of trail junctions. Half the platoon with Sergeant Hicks just one hundred meters to our west. We set up where two trails intersected. We contacted the ROK unit, they were north of us on the other side of the ridge. The top of the ridge was the dividing line between our areas of operation.

The sky was so black and clear you felt you reach out and touch the stars. Millions, billions of them. Mother nature's way of showing her beauty. As midnight came and went, I couldn't help but sink into thoughts of Hyun-ae, her warm bed and soft touch.

Finally, a hint of morning showed as the eastern sky turned from jet black to a red, orange hue. What was that old saying, "red sky at night sailor's delight, red sky in the morning sailors take warning." The crisp air was dead still, 'land of the morning calm' was a fitting aphorism for Korea.

The trail below our position was still in the shadows of the mountain. From around a bend in the trail, three figures appeared. They were walking single file. The trail was wide, they could walk abreast of each other. At two hundred meters, they appeared to be men in long overcoats. Sergeant Ghostbear and the rest of the men also spotted them. I motioned for everyone to keep down. I had picked our ambush position because of the huge rocks for concealment and our elevation above the trail.

Daylight was coming fast. They had to be on the

trail before daybreak. The nearest family was at least a mile away, meaning these guys were moving during curfew. Looking through binoculars, I could see their clothing fit the description. It was still too dark to see any bulges under their coats.

If we were to fire on them and they weren't gooks, I would be in deep shit. I watched as they walked another fifty meters before coming to a stop. They were having a discussion. They were getting off the trail and moving towards the rocky outcrops uphill from the trail. Once in the rocks, they would have a good defensive position. We couldn't open fire. They had to be challenged first. I signaled, get ready. The three figures were in the shadows as the sun peaked above the mountain and lit us up like a spotlight.

I yelled halt in Korean, JEONGJI! In response, we received bursts of fire from their submachine guns. We returned fire. The three men disappeared into the rocks.

"SERGEANT GHOSTBEAR, GIVE US COVERING FIRE TILL WE REACH THE OTHER SIDE OF THE TRAIL."

Ghostbear and his men started peppering the rocks as the commandos disappeared. Do-Ha alerted the ROK rangers what was happening. Ghostbear and his men were receiving only sporadic fire, which told me the gooks were trying to outrun us, using the rocks as cover. A ten-man squad could not catch up with the three fleeing gooks. Hopefully, by pursuing them, they would run into the ROK unit. Halfway up, we came under fire.

One commando stayed behind to slow our pursuit. He underestimated the range of the M-14. Ghostbear's men, still in the ambush position, were elevated enough to see the gook firing at us. Ghostbear's men provided heavy covering fire. As we fired and maneuvered.

In short order, we closed on the vacated enemy position. We found his shell casings and blood. He was hit, but not enough to prevent him from running. The blood trail led to the top. Do-Ha was on the radio with the ROKS when intense gunfire broke out. The gunfire lasted less than five minutes. Do-Ha confirmed they killed the three commandos.

Appleman picked up the spent enemy cartridges as souvenirs. No one wanted to walk over the ridge to view the carnage. We backtracked the commandos to determine where commandos came from, to no avail. Battalion ordered us to stay on the mountain until morning. One more night and in the cold hell.

Interrogation

"When anger rises think of the consequences." Confucius

After coming off the mountain on January27th, we learned the North Koreans captured the USS Pueblo. War appeared imminent. The North Koreans killed two crewmen and towed the ship to their port at Wonsan. The entire country was on ALERT! We were ordered to move up to the DMZ in four days. I wanted to see Hyun-ae, but it was going to be impossible. The entire country was on a dusk to dawn curfew. We had to pull maintenance on the tracks and get our gear ready to move north. The captain wasn't going to give out passes..

I was in the motor pool going over the checklist for the APCs when Private Beier came running over to tell me the Captain wanted to see me "RIGHT NOW." Beier was becoming the bearer of bad news.

"What for Beier?"

"I don't know, but he sounded pissed. He had just hung up the land line then yelled to me to get your 'ass,' Lieutenant, Sir, over to his office."

"Do you know who he was talking to?"

"The Colonel."

"Shit, what did I do now?" I walked into the captain's office and I could see he wasn't happy.

"Captain, what's up?"

"Close the door Reed."

"Captain, I.."

"The COLONEL called! Not the battalion clerk. The Colonel wants you at headquarters within the hour to be interviewed by military intelligence. **What** are you involved in with that Korean woman?"

"Captain, believe me, we're not involved in anything. We're dating, that's all, nothing to do with the military or secrets. I know better and wouldn't even consider going down that path."

"I believe you Mike, it's just that the Colonel sounded pissed. Beier will take you over and wait for you."

I walked into battalion headquarters with my heart in my throat, not knowing what to expect. The Sergeant Major walked out of his office and with apprehension in his voice.

"Lieutenant, they are waiting for you in the briefing room."

The Colonel and four other men were in the room. Two Koreans dressed in civilian clothes. The other two were wearing khakis with no stripes or bars to reveal their rank. Both had the serious look of bad asses, but Kowalski stared at me with a mean pit bull look. The two Koreans I didn't know who or or what they represented. The Colonel began the introductions, gesturing towards the two Koreans.

"Lieutenant, Mr. Won and Mr. Yoo from the Office of Internal Security and Mr. Kowalski and Mr. Meyers from Division Intelligence."

No one stepped forward to shake hands, only a nod of acknowledgment. The colonel pointed to a seat as he spoke.

"Take a seat Lieutenant."

"Yes, Sir." I could feel the four of them staring at me, trying to read my body language. Was I sweating, nervous, no they did not rattle me, just curious. Hyun-ae and I did not break any laws, military or civilian.

The taller Korean spoke first.

"Lieutenant, when did you first meet Hyun-ae Bae?" Won asked.

"Mr Won, may I ask what this is about?" Kowalski, who was leaning against the wall, took a step towards me and bent at the waist before he spoke. I was the only one seated.

"You may not, Lieutenant, answer the damn question."

The Colonel stepped between us.

"Mr. Kowalski, I expect you to treat my men with respect. I have no reason to believe he has done anything wrong."

"Lieutenant, Mr. Yoo and I have concerns regarding Bae and her role in leading a protest group. Mr Kowalski and Meyers are here as observers. We don't suspect wrongdoing on your part. Now, when was the first time you met her?"

"It was in October at her uncle's house. We were there to pay for damages caused by one of our APCs. We had dinner. Lieutenant Morgan, Do-Ha, a KUTUSA and her uncle were present."

"How did the relationship continue?"

"She got word to me to meet her at Aunt JU's place.

We met a week later."

"Didn't you find that a little unusual?" Won asked.

"No, we kinda hit it off during the dinner."

"How many times have you seen her since October?" Won asked.

"Maybe fourteen or fifteen times."

"Where did you meet?"

"It was always at her aunts, we would go out. I had only a few hours off duty, so we stayed local."

Kowalski chimed in. "Local, meaning her bed, where she screwed your brains out, setting you up."

"Screw you Kowalski, you don't know a thing about her. She has more class in her little toe." Reed said, raising his voice.

"Did she introduce you to any of her friends, fellow students?"

"No, Mr. Won, I met her aunt and uncle, no one else. Look, she comes from a well-respected family. She is close to getting her doctorate in nuclear physics. Her father died in the war, her mother kidnapped by the North Koreans in 1949. Her Uncle is a retired colonel. The Army has vetted aunt Ju because of her business.

Won you must know all this, what the fuck? We don't discuss my duties. I doubt if she even knows my unit's location, let alone our mission. The DMZ is not part of any conversation. I'm not going to reveal our movements! It could get my men and me killed."

Kowalski jabbed again with his mouth.

"Maybe she hasn't screwed you enough to make you feel comfortable. Tell Mr. Won about your pillow talk."

Now I was getting pissed and tired of sitting with five men standing over me. I started to get up, clenched fists. I wanted to deck Kowalski, but thought better of it, realizing they were doing the good guy-bad guy routine.

"Kowalski, you're a pig and a horse's ass."

Won held up his hand, meaning for Kowalski and me to stop.

"Lieutenant, you obviously are fond of Bae. What do you talk about?" Won pressed!

"We visit Korean historical sites. she explains Korean history, ancient history. Nothing concerning current politics. She is teaching me the Korean language. We listen to music. Her aunt is fond of American music, life in the states, her time at Berkley."

"Did she ever take you to tour the gardens at the Presidential Palace?" Won asked.

"No, it's winter."

"Did she ever mention President Park and whether she disagreed with his policies?"

"She said she wanted changes in the government, but used the word government, never referred to President Park by name."

"How did she want to change the government?"

"Peacefully, she's against violence?" Reed replied.

"Was aunt Ju there during any of these discussions, **changing the government**?"

"NO! Damn it! We talked politics, maybe two times. We were having a good time. Why would I want to go down that road? She was taking a sabbatical from her studies." Reed replied , now in a staring contest with Won.

"Did you know she was the organizer of the riots at the University?"

"Yes, she told me. It was supposed to be a peaceful protest, but something went wrong and someone killed a student."

"Did she tell you they may charge her with inciting a riot?" Won stated with a tone of doom.

"No, she told me she was taking time off because of the protest."

"How often was aunt Ju at the cottage?"

"A couple of times she stopped by or was there when I arrived."

"What did you talk about?"

"Aunt Ju was interested in where I grew up and life in the United States. She married an American Sergeant from Rochester. I'm from Buffalo, so we made small talk. The sergeant had passed away. She wanted to know about my family, where I went to school, that kind of stuff. She let me know she's an independent woman, something apparently rare in Korea. Aunt Ju asked nothing about the military. She's a nice lady looking after her niece's interest."

"What about her Uncle?"

"I met him only at the dinner in October."

"Does Bae talk about her mother?"

"She told me she believes her mother is still alive. The North Koreans kidnapped her back in 1949. Hyun-ae said the government will not help her.

Apparently, what happened on the island of Jeju is a dark spot in Korean history."

"Did she talk about her friends?"

"She mentioned a friend of hers, some guy named Chung. She said he was a businessman. He had friends in government and he could get information about her mother and he helped her out with money, a small amount to finance the demonstration."

"When was that?"

"We didn't talk dates, I suppose, before the demonstration."

"How much money did he give her?"

"I don't know, I didn't ask!"

To me, her protest group did not differ from the college kids protesting back home. Not some revolutionary group. But, I could tell from Won's body language, he was interested in Chung.

"Did she say his full name?" Won continued his questioning.

"No."

"What type of business?"

"No."

"Did she say what branch of government he had friends?"

"No!"

"Did she say if he was young, old, a family friend, anything about him?"

"No, No, No and No!"

Did you ask anything about this Chung?

"No."

"Why not!"

"Why would I?"

"Are you sure she used the name Chung?"

"Positive."

"When you went out, did you meet anyone? Did she talk to anyone?"

"No."

"Lieutenant! It's hard to believe you two are out and about and never ran into her university friends?"

"We stayed away from the university."

"Did she buy you any expensive gifts?"

"FUCK NO!"

"Did Hyun-ae seem to have a lot of cash?"

"NO!" LOOK, Mr. Won, you are barking up the wrong tree. Hyun-ae wants to become a scientist and help Korea develop self sufficient energy. She would like to see the Korea united as a democracy and if I'm guessing right, so does most of the country. If I thought for a moment she was on the other side, I would tell you. She is not a "Jane Bond."

Kowalski almost lost his front teeth when he said.

"You thought! The only real thinking being done is with your dick."

Won shook his head and put his hand out to stop me from getting out of the chair. He turned to the Colonel. "Colonel Williams, may I have a word?"

"Lieutenant, wait in the other office. "

"Yes, Sir."

For fifteen minutes, I paced between the Sergeant Major's office and the Colonels. The clerk buried his head in paperwork, trying to avoid talking to me. My head was spinning. Here it was, at the end of January, and my armpits were soaked with sweat. I did nothing wrong, but I felt like a man on the first step to the gallows. The Colonel stepped out of the briefing room.

"Lieutenant, they want to talk with you. I have to be somewhere. When you are done, report back to your unit. Good luck Lieutenant, and be careful."

As I walked to the briefing room, I was even more puzzled. "Be careful." I didn't want to open the door.

"Come in, lieutenant and have a seat." They were all seated in chairs arranged in a circle. I took a seat in the empty chair, now more concerned than curious. My chair was across from Mr. Won, our knees were about a foot apart. It was apparent he was going to do the talking. The atmosphere in the room had changed. Cigar smoke obscured Kowalski's face. He seemed less hostile. Won was more relaxed as he started talking.

"Lieutenant Reed, may I call you Mike?"

"Okay by me."

"Mike, we believe Hyun-ae Bae is associating with a North Korea spy. We don't know if she is aware he is a spy. His name is unknown. It may be this 'friend Chung'. We know the spy has been in the country for several years. We don't know if he was involved with the attack on the Presidential palace."

Won picked up a large envelope from his lap and slid out an eight by ten photograph and handed it to me.

293 |DENIAL OF CONFLICT

My expression said it all. Instantly, I recognized the man. The last time we were together, Hyun-ae wanted to buy something for her aunt. We had gone to a series of shops. At the last shop, I noticed the same man lurking nearby on three occasions. One time I could've sworn he took a picture of us. I turned to point him out to Hyun-ae, but he was gone.

"SHIT!" I said.

"Where did you see him, Lieutenant?"

I told them about the time shopping.

"Did you ever see him again?" Won asked.

"No."

"How did Hyun-ae respond when you told her you thought you were being followed?"

"She asked what he looked like. I told her he appeared to be young and taller than most Korean men and well dressed. She said it might be a government man because of her involvement with the protest."

Kowalski chimed in.

"You let it go at that! You are pussy whipped."

I let Kowalski's remark slide. My thoughts were slipping down the slippery slope. What the hell was I involved in? Did Hyun-ae lure me into some kind of conspiracy? I couldn't believe she was involved. No, I didn't want to believe. FUCK, FUCK!

Won changed the subject.

"Kowalski tells me you completed an intelligence course at Fort Holibird before becoming an officer. After OCS, you got screwed by the Army. They assigned you to the infantry instead of back to intelligence."

"Something like that." I replied.

"I also spent some time at Holibird. I liked the training, but Baltimore is a pigsty for a city. Does the Army still have the off limits area called 'the block'?" Won asked.

"You should ask Kowalski. He probably spent a lot of time down there."

Mr. Meyers spoke. He apparently was senior over Kowalski.

"Knock it off Lieutenant, you too Mark. What we're about to ask of the Lieutenant is very serious."

"What's that, sir!" I replied.

Meyers smiled. I guessed he was a captain and partnered with Mark Kowalski to be his attack dog.

"We want you to continue to see Bae with the approval of your battalion commander."

"We're moving up on the DMZ in a couple of days. I won't have time to see her." I said.

"The colonel will see to it. You'll get days off here and there." Meyers said.

"Wait! You want me to spy on her?"

"Yes, we do and I wouldn't go along with the plan if I thought you couldn't help Mr. Won catch this guy. Mr Won can explain further. Before we go any further, you're not being ordered to continue to see Bae. We are asking you to volunteer. If you choose not want to work with us, then you can't see Bae. It's all in or nothing." Meyers explained.

"Can I think about it?" I asked.

"For about ten minutes, we need an answer now."

"So I'm going to the DMZ and may get my ass shot. On my days off, I'm supposed to help you guys catch a spy, who may kill me?"

Won stood and walked by, patting my shoulder. He walked over to the large map of Korea. His back was to us as he studied the map.

"Do you love her, Mike?"

The question caught me off guard.

"I don't know, I mean, I haven't asked her to come back to the states with me. Look, I care for her a lot. I have several months left in the country. Who knows which direction our relationship would go?"

"Does she love you?" Won asked.

"Why do you keep going down that road? What's my love life got to do with it?" Mr Won turned from studying the map, again we locked eyes before he spoke.

"Hyun-ae is a beautiful, brilliant woman. She's a genius. Her IQ is off the charts. In the academic world, she is being closely watched. We have talked to officials at the University. They compare her to Lise Meitner, one of the scientist that created the first self-sustaining chain reaction. Bae's work with top nuclear scientists has the attention of our government and others. Did you know her theory of generating electricity from nuclear fusion is viable?

No! I said, astonished.

"Let me explain, scientist worldwide are working on using nuclear fusion to generate energy rather than splitting the atom. Fusion powers the sun.

Fusion uses deuterium, hydrogen of which water is the source. A cleaner, more efficient way to use nuclear power. Korea has little in the way of natural resources, the country needs her. We're just trying to get a sense of why she picked you."

"I was starting to like you, Mr. Won. She didn't pick me. The meeting was coincidental at her uncles, remember? We never discuss nuclear energy or military stuff."

"Sorry Mike, I didn't mean it that way, it's just you and Bae...."

"Since when does one's intellect determine who you like or love? A lot more goes into a relationship than a person's IQ. Just what do you want me to do? I'm in on your scheme. She's not involved, so I'll help her."

Meyers nodded in agreement before he spoke.

"You're right, Lieutenant. Bae may not know she is associating with a North Korea spy. By working with Won, you may save her from getting into trouble and perhaps her life. Mike, what we're asking you to do is dangerous. Mr. Won and Yoo have reason to believe this man has committed several murders. He murdered those he dealt with. The details of his relationship with the victims are not important to you, but you need to know he is a dangerous man."

"How many people did he kill? Should I carry a sidearm?"

Won had sat back down and was watching me. He raised his eyebrows as he spoke.

"Carrying a sidearm is up to you. I wouldn't

recommend it. We don't know for sure if the man connected to Bae is the murderer. If he is the murderer, it's unlikely he would risk further exposure coming after you. Bae would also wonder why you're suddenly carrying a gun."

I had my doubts I was getting the entire truth from Mr. Won, but I went along with their suggestion. We spent a few minutes on contact information. All reports regarding my dates with Hyun-ae were to go through Meyers or Kowalski. Hyun-ae was being watched 24/7. We would be under surveillance no matter where we went. They assured me that Mr. Won and his men were discreet and would be at my side in an instant if I were in danger.

I'm thinking how are they going to be at my side if I'm in bed with Hyun-ae. In the middle of the night, Chung, whatever his name, could slip into the cottage and slit my throat. My throat? I should be worried about our throats! But, what if she is part of some crazy plot? No, no, that's not Hyun-ae. She would not be mixed up in shit like this.

"Mike, Lieutenant! You still with us?"

"I was just thinking, Hyun-ae isn't involved in this shit. It's not in her. If she was, Aunt Ju would know and stop her."

Meyers leaned forward, resting his elbows on his knees, staring at me.

"That's likely, Lieutenant, but we have to confirm if Hyun-ae is involved with this guy before we approach her. So let's go over what to watch for and how to get her to talk about Chung. I shouldn't have to remind you, not a word to anyone, especially Hyun-ae. Before you go back up north to the DMZ, Colonel Williams is going to allow the line companies some time off. You will see Bae."

Chung on the Run

"Quick decisions are unsafe decisions." Sophocles

Chung sat near the window in deep thought. Since killing Ae-sook two weeks ago, he changed safe houses twice. Chung was upset with himself. He should have expected Ae-sook to have a lover, a friend, someone. He should have left the house as soon as he saw the man's winter coat on the chair. Instead, he lost control, curiosity got the better of him. He had to snoop around and go through the man's coat. When the man woke and walked into the room, the knife instinctively came out.

It was over quickly and silently, his hand over the victim's mouth as the knife sliced through the naked man's neck. Chung didn't know what came over him. He should have let Ae-Sook live. Maybe the man wasn't her lover, just a pickup at a bar? But why did she bring him home, against all the rules? Would she let it go if he killed someone she cared for? She was loyal, how loyal? Chung tried to rationalize. There were many times he wanted to wring Ae-Sook's neck because of her incessant talking, but never thought he would.

He was fortunate in one respect the newspapers were playing up the murders as a love triangle. Colonel Choi would learn of Ae-Sook's death and blame him. Chung could use her indiscretion as a reason or, as the paper called it, a love triangle.

Chung's poor decision forced him to resign from his the ministry. He did it the morning of the killings. It would be better to resign using an excuse of an urgent family matter in Pusan. Better to leave on good terms rather than suddenly disappear.

Since the raid on the President's house, it was hard to move around the city. The police constantly checked his papers. The caretakers of the safe houses were becoming fearful they would be swept up in the ceaseless government raids. He had enough money stashed to last several months, but security wise, he had to get out of the country as soon as possible. Going after the defense minister was no longer an option!

Chung kept thinking he had to take back something other than the classified documents stolen by his victims. The detailed drawings and photographs of key military bases provided good information. The workings of the ministry he worked for had only marginal value as intelligence. He needed more.

The work of a master spy would be to convince the Bae woman to defect. A brilliant nuclear scientist in the making. It would be a propaganda coup and maybe enough of an accomplishment to get him hero status or at the least save him.

Chung watched the snow fall and melt as it landed on the city street.The wet shiny street was dark, lit only by the streetlight on the distant corner. It was an empty street. It looked cold, lonely, and dangerous. His imagination was getting the better of him. Government agents were hiding in the shadows.

He had panicked at Ae-Sook's. He needed to calm down. Chung knew they eventually would compare his fingerprints against all government employees. They would have a picture of him to splash all over the papers. It would become impossible for him to move around. It was just a matter of time, probably weeks, maybe a month.

He decided waiting was worth the gamble. He needed to know if Colonel Choi found Bae's mother. Maybe the next radio contact or the one after he would know. Chung needed definitive proof she was alive. The mother would be an incentive for Hyun-Ae to go north. If he can't convince Hyun-ae, then she will become a kidnapped victim, just like her mother. Chung laughed as he pictured Kim and his team dragging her through the DMZ to North Korea.

Return to the DMZ

"Just as courage is the danger of life so is fear its safeguard."
Leonardo Di Vinci

As Mr. Won stated, the Colonel gave the battalion a day off. I had to admit Won's men were good. There was no sign of them watching Aunt Ju's place. I thought the surveillance team would stand out like a sore thumb. Fortunately, on my arrival, Aunt Ju was at the cottage. Her being there helped buffer my mixed feelings. I was anxious. Could I act the same knowing what Mr. Won told me?

The man in the photos looked dangerous. Won, Kowalski and Meyers were not telling me everything. I was in love with Hyun-ae, but now my stomach was turning inside out. My head spinning as I walked in the door.

Hyun-ae scooted over and threw her arms around my neck and gave me a hug and a long kiss. She had the habit of placing her thigh cunningly between my legs sensually for just a couple of seconds. Frank Sinatra was singing "Witchcraft."

"Hey you two, I'm here."

"Hi Aunt Ju!" I moved towards the couch. I wanted to sit down. Aunt Ju sat by the desk, giving me the once over. Hyun-ae sat down beside me with her feet curled up under her and hugged my left arm.

"Mike, Hyun-ae and I just learned your unit is going back to the DMZ."

"HOW! did you find out?" I snapped.

"Mike, it's no secret, Hyun-ae, and I stopped by the orphanage and all the kids knew Charlie Company was going back to DMZ."

"I'm sorry. I didn't mean to."

"That's okay. Aunt Ju and I were talking about returning to the university. You won't be able to come here as often. I'll stay in Seoul during the week and come back here most weekends. I feel much better about going back to the university. Aunt Ju arranged a meeting with the parents of the student. They don't blame me for his death. If you get time off on a weekend, contact the shop and I'll make sure I'm here."

It sounded all too convenient. I could feel Aunt Ju's eyes on me.

"Mike, you seem uncomfortable?"

"It's just a lot of stuff going on back at the base, Aunt Ju. Hyun-ae, I'm glad you're going back to school. I will not have much free time until we rotate south of the river, my time in Korea will almost be up."

I immediately knew I had touched a nerve when I mentioned my tour in Korea would end after thirteen months. Hyun-ae let go of my arm and got up from the couch.

"I'll make some tea."

****

Two days later, we were on our first patrol. It was a

twenty-four-hour mission to set up night ambushes and patrols during the day. There were few changes to procedures. The biggest change was we didn't need permission to return fire across the MDL. The other change, we now received combat pay.

Our mission was to locate and ambush the gooks. Also, try to determine if there was a pattern to the routes they choose. What type of weapons did they use and the size of each unit we encountered? Were they attempting to infiltrate or ex filtrate through the DMZ, all typical combat intelligence?

They assigned me eight replacements. We divided them among the patrols. Six of the eight men took part in the training we had just completed. The two nineteen-year-olds missed the training; Jim Fox and Billy Dallas. Neither one knew their ass from a hole in the ground. I split them up between Hick's patrol and Potters. I went with Sergeant Potters patrol on the first mission.

The temperature was going down to fifteen with twenty miles per hour winds. The FB-172 army issued cold weather card calculated a below zero wind chill.

A half moon reflected light off two inches of fresh snow. Visibility was good in the moonlit woods. The plan was to rotate each squad to GP Glady's for an hour warm up. Patrolling to and from the GP would also keep the men warm and alert. The moon was low in the sky; the trees cast long ominous shadows on the snow. Sergeant Hick's patrol was the first to rotate for a warmup. It was 2300 hours as they moved towards the GP.

"Razor six, this is razor four over."

"Go ahead four."

"We just cut some tracks. Looks like three men moving east. They are walking, not running, over."

"Razor four, what's your position, over?"

"We are about two hundred meters north of our ambush position, near the creek. Over,"

I notified the other patrols to hold their positions but be ready to move. Even with some light from the moon, maneuvering all five patrols could cause a friendly fire incident.

"Razor four, hold your position. We will approach your position from the south. Do you roger over.?"

"This is four, affirmative, over!"

The approaching patrol would use a flashlight with a red filter, the waiting unit would flash back. The link up went without incident. I decided we would follow the tracks while Hicks and his men would be on our left flank, less than one hundred meters away, and still maintain visible contact. I notified the company's mortar squad to be prepared to fire illumination rounds. It would be cool to call for some HE mortar rounds, but fire support in the DMZ needed authorization from god or a bird colonel. Neither deity would allow it. We still had to follow the rules of the 1953 Armistice. The goddamn gooks didn't.

The QRF, Charlie Tango, was on the same net. Mo cut in, "cut em up razor, we are ready to roll."

We moved out with my men on line. The half

moon was behind us, casting eight long, eerie shadows. The terrain was flat for the first hundred meters, with low brush and trees. Up ahead, two hundred meters or so, was a brush covered knoll. It would be from there if we took fire. The tracks were heading straight for the knoll.

"Razor four, over."

"This is four over."

"Four, the tracks are heading for the knoll to our front. Move forward and set up just below the knoll. Over."

"Roger."

I followed the center track of the three. We moved another twenty meters when the hair stood up on the back of my neck. The footprints showed the three men had turned and faced our direction. The three gooks then ran towards the knoll. I motioned for my men to get down.

"Razor four, over."

"This is four, over."

"Four, it looks like they may have spotted us. Hold your position, over."

"Roger."

I had to decide fast. Were we being sucked into an ambush with more than three gooks on the knoll? We couldn't charge up the hill, we would be exposed. Our white pull overs consisted of white pants and a white jacket made of a denim like material. The jackets for most of the men were too small, the flak jacket was on the outside diminishing the camo effect.

The creek where we had hooked up with Sergeant Hicks meandered through the DMZ and now it was sixty meters in front of us, running just below the knoll. The banks of the creek would provide some cover. Riker was checking the creek out with the starlight scope. It's unlikely they would try to use the creek bed for an ambush. The gooks would probably wait for us to cross the creek and start up the hill. "Probably?"

"Sergeant Potter, let's maneuver up to the creek, two at a time. I want Riker with the starlight to go second. I'll be the third with Dallas, then you come up last."

"Got it LT."

Dallas was my RTO. I turned to get the mic to call Hicks. Billy Dallas was shaking like a leaf in a Texas storm. It wasn't from the cold.

"Dallas, just stick with me, run like hell, it'll be alright." Dallas nodded and handed me the mic. His eyes, highlighted by the black camo paint and as big as saucers, told me he had his doubts. I alerted Captain Roseman and battalion. I requested the QRF to move to a location to provide support.

"Sierra six the is Razor six over."

"This is Sierra six, over."

"Sierra six request Charlie Tango to Romeo Papa Zulu, over."

"Charlie Tango, this is Sierra Six. Move to Romeo Papa Zulu, Over."

My other three patrols were to form up at the GP and then make their way to us.

"Razor four, over."

"This is four, over."

"Move forward to the creek and hold up."

"Roger Razor six."

I signaled Sergeant Potter to send the first two men forward. They zigzagged their way, stopping a couple of times behind what cover was available. Then they disappeared into the gully cut by the creek. Dallas and I followed Riker, jumping down into the narrow, shallow gully, making a racket as we crashed through the ice. The gooks had to see or hear us.

I looked down along the bank; we lined up with our weapons pointing at the knoll. Our overheated breath coming out in short, quick blasts vaporizing in the cold air, like racehorses at the gate.

I hushed at Riker. "Get the scope up and check out the hill." He never got the chance.

Sergeant Potter and Appleman were rushing towards us. Twenty-five meters from the gully, the gooks opened up. We returned fire at the three muzzle flashes. The flashes seemed a lot closer than seventy to eighty meters. They must have had good cover, as our tracers were dead on their position. The gooks kept firing, the green tracers hitting opposite bank, kicking up the snow, stone and dirt, making us duck for cover.

Sergeant Potter was dragging a screaming Appleman into the gully. Fuck, Moss was with Ghostbears patrol. Magruder's M-14 was on full automatic, and he wasn't concerned about running out of ammo. I ducked down to call Hicks. Dallas was curled up, almost in a fetal position. His M-79 grenade launcher cocked open to load, lying in the snow. I grabbed the mic from his shaking hand.

"RAZOR FOUR MOVE, MOVE! OVER"

"WE WILL BE ON THEM IN A MINUTE."

I radioed the rest of the patrols to hustle to our position. We needed the medic.

Just then, over the sound of our rifles, I could hear Sergeant Hicks men firing as they advanced on the gooks from our left flank. I yelled to my men.

"CEASE FIRE, CEASE FIRE!"

The gooks switched from firing on us to Hicks. He was closing on their position. In seconds, the firing stopped. The bastards pulled out.

"Razor four over!"

"This is four, nothing here but empty brass, no casualties, over."

"Four, hold your position, Out."

The rest of the patrols arrived with Fuzzy. Our medic started working on Appleman. He took a bullet to the shin and was in incredible pain. Fuzzy was trying to calm him down. Even the morphine didn't keep him from screaming a string of cuss words any sailor would be proud of.. 'Son of a bitch, those Goddamn, cock sucking, dog eatin, mother fuckin shit heads, goat fucking bastards, oh fuck me it hurts.'

His cries were from pain or fear, or both. By the time we got him out of the DMZ, it was 0200 hours. We had to use a stretcher made out of ponchos because no choppers were allowed in the DMZ. Keeping warm wasn't an issue after getting Appleman out, no need to alternate patrols to Glady's. I combined all five patrols on high terrain, rather than try to set up five separate ambushes.

****

February was cold, wet and miserable. The good thing was, no further contact with the enemy. The ROKs were involved in firefights almost daily. They were suffering significant casualties, as were the North Koreans. The Gooks were staying away from the 2nd division.

Towards the end of the month, the weather warmed, and they extended patrols from twenty-four hours to thirty-six and, occasionally, forty-eight hours. It was at my discretion how often the men spent time at the GP, warming up. The routine rotations to the GP were becoming a prime target for an ambush. We set up an ambush to ambush the ambushers. Nothing happened. It was becoming difficult to keep the men focused. After two weeks in the hospital, they sent Appleman home with screws in his leg and a purple heart.

I visited Hyun-ae just once in February. Won, Kowalski, the interrogation, seemed like a dream. I knew in my heart Hyun-ae wasn't a spy. She wouldn't betray her country, her family. I walked in the cottage door, not knowing what to expect.

"MIKE!" Hyun-ae charged me, flung her arms

around my neck and wrapped her legs around my waist.

"Mike, I missed you." At that moment the DMZ, Mr. Won, Kowalski, Appleman, the cold misery of the patrols faded away.

We spent the best part of my six hours off in her warm, soft bed. Feeding off each other's desires, her long legs tightly wrapped around my hips, pulling me deep inside her, our bodies melding together, moving in unison. There was a lilt to the sounds we made as we made love. Then lying there, face to face, staring into those dark eyes, searching for what's deep in her soul.

"Mike, what do you see?"

"A beautiful, caring woman!"

She slid out of the bed as she said. "You forgot hungry, let's make something to eat. I'm starving."

I was lying on my side propped up on an elbow, watching the most perfect body move in the most perfect way. Her long black hair hung down over her porcelain like skin. Unlike porcelain, it was warm to the touch and parts jiggled as she walked. Not only was Hyun-ae smart, beautiful, a kind soul, she could cook.

"Hyun-ae, what's the meat? It's delicious."

"You don't want to know."

I put my chopsticks down, thinking she cooked some dog, I knew Koreans liked dog meat. She broke out laughing.

"No, Mike, it's not gaegogi, not dog. It's pork, a family recipe my mother used. My mom is an excellent cook, doctor and mother. Each night as she combed my hair, she would sing joyfully, as she took her beautiful gold hairpin and put it in my hair. The pin had been in the family for generations. Someday it will be mine. I was her little Mugunghwa, or rose. She would then put me to bed with stories about our ancestors. When I sit in front of the mirror combing my hair, I see her standing behind me, smiling."

"She would smile if she could see how beautiful her daughter turned out."

"I see her smiling in my dreams but never singing. Why is that Mike?"

"She doesn't want to wake you."

"Good answer. My mother will always look after me."

"Did you hear from your friend Chung about your mom?"

"Mike, do you think I'm crazy because I dream of my mother?"

"No, you say the dreams are pleasant, nothing wrong with pleasant dreams."

"No, I haven't heard from him. He must have gone back to Pusan. That's where his business is located."

"What business is that? I thought you met him at school, a close friend, you date him?"

"Mike, are you jealous? Don't be, he is engaged and an honorable man. He has the same ideals for Korea as I do."

"Well, can you call him or get in touch with him?"

"No!"

I dropped the subject. I at least had some

information to pass on to Kowalski.

We talked about her going back to the university. She told me government officials from the Energy Ministry approached her. They wanted to recruit her to work with others on a government project after she gets her doctorate. She was to be interviewed next week. I'm thinking Won and his men are at work. They arranged the interview. God knows I wanted to say something, warn her. We kissed goodbye as the afternoon daylight faded. It was a dismal ride back across the river. I was spying on Hyun-ae.

Bae's Mother, Alive and Well

"I found the paradox that if you love until it hurts, there can be no more hurt, only more love." Mother Teresa

Colonel Choi smiled. Chung's last message said he was ready to return to the north. The cryptic messages requested a woman named Ae-jeong Bae, if still alive, be located. She had a medical degree and could be working as a doctor. The messages said a Kim Dal-Sam kidnapped her from Jeju Island. Choi was to send back with Kim's team, proof that she was alive. The burst of cryptic messages didn't explain what Chung was going to do with the information. It was intriguing. Besides, the team will insure Chung returns or they will eliminate him.

Ae-Jeong Bae, a respected doctor, was alive and well living in the northern mountain town of Kanggye. During the battle for the Changjin Reservoir in 1950, she set up medical facilities for wounded soldiers. The town of Kanggye became a refuge for the government officials fleeing Pyongyang.

She had won the praise of officials, but she couldn't be trusted. After the war, she tried to escape to China on several occasions. After spending years under house arrest, she had accepted her plight. Her ability as a doctor allowed her to travel among the northern providences. But always under the close watch of her personal aide assigned by the party.

The photographs showed she was still an attractive woman. The report detailed her life since being brought to North Korea, brought? She wasn't 'brought' Kim shanghaied her under the threat of death to her co-workers on Jeju.

At the beginning, she was a strong willed, belligerent woman. Her medical skills, and saving the life of Han Ik-su, kept her out of prison. She stopped talking about her daughter and family ten years ago. The photographs and information gained from her interview last week should be enough proof for Chung. Unfortunately, she became hysterical after being interrogated regarding her daughter and family. She had to be sedated, screaming, 'NOT MY LITTLE MUGUNGHWA, NO, NO!'

What was Chung up to? What did the mother sense? The Mugunghwa, a flower of eternal blossoms that never fades.

Short Timer

"It's not what happens to you but how you react to it that matters." Epictetus

March was a bone chilling month. The temperatures fluctuated between the thirties and forties with a dampness in the air that seeped into your bones. Nights were raw. Our Hunter Killer patrols were long and grueling. Still March went by fast. The only contact with the enemy was a brief firefight near the MDL. We spotted four unidentified individuals. UI'S is what the brass wanted them called. We gave chase to the four gooks. They returned fire but disappeared into the brush along the MDL. Later that day, my men and I could've been killed.

Billy Dallas was getting better at being a soldier, clumsy as hell but a good kid, with a sense of humor, solid with the radio, little athletic ability, and constantly attacking the ground. After each face plant, he tried to make it a joke, saying he's practicing 'taking cover.' Against my better judgment, I kept him as my RTO. During the enemy contact earlier that day, he loaded his M-79. He didn't unload it, as ordered.

An hour later, Dallas was fifteen or twenty feet behind me as we moved up a steep hill. He slipped, why the safety was off, and his finger inside the trigger guard, I'll never know. I heard the characteristic bloop and felt the grenade burrow into the ground, a foot to my left. The grenade didn't explode because it didn't travel the number of revolutions needed to arm. It scared the shit out of the men and me. Dallas had to go.

April was tedious, patrolling, a day off, then back out. To keep the morale up, I requested passes for the men on our day off. Two men from each patrol were allowed six hours to go south of the river. If they came back high or drunk, no more passes. Captain Roseman approved, and it worked. The men began performing better, trying to impress their patrol leader. The sergeants picked who got the passes. I felt less guilt when I saw Hyun-ae.

I was getting short, four months to go. Despite the miserable weather, getting shot at and nearly killed by my RTO. I felt comfortable leading my platoon. Maybe the army was a career choice? Then my thoughts drifted to Hun-ea and my weird nightmare.

Hyun-ae and I were in her soft, warm bed, staring into each other's eyes. When Aunt Ju walked into the room. Aunt Ju removed her clothes and slid into bed behind me. In the dream, I felt her warm naked body against my backside. Aunt Ju pressed the cold steel blade against my neck. Hyun-ae smiled. In the morning Mo said, I woke him up screaming, NO! No! During my visits with Hyun-ae, I didn't mention the dream.

The April air smelled of spring and gunpowder.

Many of the 2nd Divisions units along the DMZ were being hit. The gooks used hit-and-run tactics on targets of opportunity, killing four Americans, one KATUSA and wounding six. The ROKs suffered twice as many casualties.

Sappers attacked again, like the attack on Camp Wally, this time at the 1/31st compound. They cut the wire and avoided the guards. They tossed satchel charges into two hooches. Fortunately, one charge didn't detonate. In the other hooch, two were wounded, most of the men were in the field. The guards killed one sapper.

I just sat down with a cup of coffee when Mo and the newest platoon leader walked in the houch. Danny Slattery, or Slats, as he liked to be called. Thin as a bed slat, with his red hair and fair skin, he was as Irish as you could get. After two months in country, he proved to be a good platoon leader. He loved his whiskey and was good natured. His platoon rotated on and off, GP Gladys.

"Hey Mike, want a drink?"

Danny held up a bottle of Crown Royal.

"Where the hell did you get that?"

"My uncle sent it over. It's hard to find in the states. He lives in Canada.."

Mo turned on his reel to reel and the first song on the tape by the Doors, "Light My Fire," didn't help my mood. The album version was the longest damn record. *"OUR LOVE BECOMES A FUNERAL PYRE"* hit home. My first Crown went down fast. A couple of drinks later, my body and mind settled into the raggedy overstuffed chair.

Danny told us on the gooks side of the MDL there's increased activity. Small units were coming and going from the Gooks position every day. It made little sense. They usually rotated every three days. Danny said he advised the S-2, but they made little of it.

The Crown pushed away where we were and what was ahead of us tomorrow. Three friends, three guys, not soldiers, in our own space. We debated the outcome of the Championship game in which Green Bay trounced the Oakland Raiders 33 to 14. Bart Starr outplayed Lamonica.

Danny and I believed in the AFL. I liked the Buffalo Bills even if their record was dismal at 4 and 10. Danny was a Jets and a Namath fan. Mo didn't have a favorite team, he argued the AFL players were not NFL caliber. We talked about girls and the bars we hung out in the states and cars and bikes. Danny had a Corvette he bought right out of OCS. I had a MGB and Mo had a 1966 Bonneville Triumph. He boasted there wasn't a bike on the street that could beat him racing or picking up girls. Out of the blue, Danny asks.

"Mike, you still seeing the Korean chick?" His question was more curious than disrespectable.

"Yea, why?"

"After the last rotation, I went to camp Casey. They have a big PX there."

"No shit Danny, a BIG PX." Both Mo and I shot back, laughing.

"Come on, guys, you know what I mean. I was looking for something to buy my girl back home. The sales clerk was a nice Korean girl. She spoke excellent English. We hit it off."

"So, is there a question?"

"Yea, what's it like, you're dating a local.? How do you get a date? They don't have phones, or do they?"

Mo rolled his eyes before he said.

"Jesus, Danny, you're here two months and you want to marry someone?"

"Hell, no! It's nice to see someone when we're not in the DMZ."

"Well, don't ask Mike, he's up to his eyeballs with that 'Korean chick.' I've met her and can't say I blame him. But there's a huge slew of shit that goes with dating a Korean, especially if you're an officer. My advice, come with me. I will guarantee you a good time. Right Mike?"

"Right on, Mo."

I called it an evening and hit the sack. Mo was "right on" loving Hyun-ea laid an abundance of shit on my shoulders. Accepting it and continuing like a good soldier was the only choice. The Crown Royal put an end to more painful thoughts and washed away the possibility of another dream involving Aunt JU. I drifted off into a deep sleep.

****

Danny's platoon was to rotate back on GP Gladys the next day. We were to provide security escorting Danny's platoon, then the same old shit, patrol and ambush. April weather was one of the best months to be in Korea. Rainfall was supposed to be sparse and temperatures mild, as we advanced into the DMZ in mud up to our ankles with Danny's platoon.

"Sarge, what did the S-2 Captain say about enjoying Korea's weather in April?"

"Hey lieutenant, there's an old saying 'there's no such thing as bad weather, just soft people' and we ain't soft."

"Lets move out!"

It was 0700 hours and raining cats and dogs, windy and cold. We completed the soggy escort to Gladys without a problem. By late afternoon, the sun came out and our gear dried out.

The DMZ was transforming with the warming days and rain. The trees had a hint of green. Leaves were sprouting, the grasses were growing out of their winter brown. Birds were chirping and the tiny brown frog was croaking. The frozen crunchy ground was gone. As the leaves sprouted and the grass grew, visibility became limited. We moved slowly, looking for signs of the enemy. We covered a lot of ground and slept for a few hours. Hopefully, enough sleep to stay awake at night. We knew the enemy was here. Who was the better hunter was the question?

Sergeant Ghostbears patrol located a Korean War era pillbox on the side of a brushy hill. I was with Belz's patrol. We swung over to the pillbox.

"How did you find the pillbox, Sarge?"

"We stumbled on it. Fox was on point and tripped

on old barbed wire. From the ground, he was looking at a small opening into a pillbox."

"Sarge, anything in it?"

"From the looks of it, the gooks used it as an observation post. Dried grass inside for matting and the brush stacked against the front. There're no leaves sprouting on the branches. See these."

Ghostbear pulled a couple branches out of the ground, covering the front of the pillbox. Taking my bayonet, I shaved the bark off the branch. It smelled sweet and fresh. Old cuts turn gray as the branch decayed. A chill ran down my back. They cut the branch within the last few days. We were being watched. I held the branch out towards Ghostbear. He nodded and bent over to smell the branch. I knew what he would say.

"Those fuckers had a good view. We're going to get hit!"

"I agree Sarge, set up an ambush with trip flares and claymores above the pillbox. Let's see if the bastards come back tonight and we hit them first. You take the Starlight."

"Yes, Sir!"

"Lets not mention the pillbox on the radio. The gooks have us tuned in."

I wrote the coordinates for the S-2 debriefing. Tomorrow we'll have to escort the engineers to take care of it with C-4. It was getting late and time to have chow before moving to our ambush positions.

Sunset tonight was 1836 hours. Sunrise just over twelve hours later at O648 hours. The weather was going to hold. With a full moon, visibility won't be a problem for us or them! Sergeant Hicks and his men were two hundred meters north of Ghostbears' ambush position. Hicks and Ghostbear were on the same ridgeline. They couldn't fire on each other during a firefight because of elevation change.

Potter set up in the flats, an overgrown rice paddy. The paddy jutted out towards the MDL. The dikes surrounding the paddy tied into an old railroad berm. A locomotive, shot up during the Korean War, still rested on the bent and twisted rails a hundred meters south of Potter's position. Potter and his men had excellent cover and concealment among the trees. Potter's patrol was within a hundred meters of the MDL.

Sergeant Calhoun was three hundred meters further to the east, near the Mayor's house. I stayed with Sergeant Betz and his patrol, setting up to the west on a knoll overlooking a creek. On different occasions, we found enemy tracks along the creek. The slow-moving creek originating in North Korea twisted and turned through the DMZ, crossing the MDL.

The set up felt good. Sergeant Hicks could reinforce Ghostbears men in short order and Calhoun's, only a few hundred meters beyond Ghostbears' position. We could get to Sergeant Potter within minutes. I dreaded the thought of having to move men at night during a firefight. Keeping the ambushes close but effectively apart lessened the worry. We hunkered down on the north side of the hill. My stomach was churning with butterflies. I had an uneasy feeling.

Below our position the creek was about twelve feet wide, peaceful and soothing, a ribbon of mercury in the moonlight. Quicksilver flowing through a field of grass and a forest on the north bank. The moon casting shadows off the trees, painted twisted black arms and fingers across the creek's silvery surface. The mountains to the north seemed to lurk. The moon was not high enough to illuminate the south face of the mountain, only highlighting the peaks. In the mountain's shadow, there was enough artillery to blow us off the face of the earth.

Thankfully, tonight, the 'lady' wasn't on her loudspeaker broadcasting her bullshit. *'So Sorry your girlfriends, wives are running off with their lover, you GI should be back in the states, not in Korea.'*

As always, the night dragged. As the moon sank into another night, the painted, blacken faces obscured under the helmets disappeared. With the moon gone, the stars filled the sky. It was quiet. So quiet you could hear the soft rustle the men made as they shifted their body. I shivered. We're going to get hit.

The night dragged on until the horizon turned to a reddish orange, the sky went from black to a tint of blue. Sunlight was erasing the shadows. The creek went up in value from silver to a gold ribbon. Jesus, I muttered under my breath. We made it through another night.

"SHIT!" A rattling of gunfire broke the silence. Potter's 12 gauge riot gun loaded with double OTT buckshot boomed among the clatter of automatic rifles. I shouted to Betz's patrol.

"WEAPONS AND AMMO ONLY LEAVE YOUR PACKS!" Double OO, Jimmy Otto, my new RTO, was trying to jam the mic into my face. I could hear Potter's RTO screaming. "THEY'RE ALL OVER US, HELP!. SARGE IS HIT!!"

I grabbed the mike. Screw radio protocol.

"WE'RE ON OUR WAY!"

As we double timed off the hill, I called Sergeant Hicks told him to link up with Ghostbears and Calhoun near the wrecked locomotive and move on Potter's position from the south. We were approaching from the west.

At the bottom, we got the men on line. We had two hundred meters of open ground to the tree line. We could get ambushed, there was no other choice, bee lining it was the quickest way to the fight.

The tempo of the gunfire increased, along with the explosions of grenades. We moved on the double through the woods towards the raising sun, covering a hundred yards. We broke into the open at a run, racing to the next tree line.

The sharp crack of the bullets cut through the air. A split second later, the rattling of a heavy machine gun as we hit the dirt. The spring grass was'nt tall enough to provide concealment, let alone cover. The men realized the hump offered cover. We slithered towards it. The machine gun, just north of the MDL, was zeroing in, its bullets smacking the ground. Tufts of dirt were being tossed in the air. The hump in the middle of the field, an old excavation, provided protection. We needed to move now.

"SANCHEZ, TEN O'CLOCK, 300 METERS, GET SOME ROUNDS ON THAT GUN!!" He had to get on his knees to fire his weapon over the brush between us and the machine gun. Betz and I realized he needed cover. We both raised up on our knees and began firing. Double O got into the act and the two thumpers were effective. In less than a minute, the five 40mm grenades launched by Sanchez and Double O sent the machine gun crew diving for cover.

"GO, GO!" We scrambled over the protective hump, continuing our bat out of hell race for the tree line. We made it to the trees when the machine gun started firing, but it stopped after a brief burst. We had disappeared from sight into the trees.

The gunfight ahead was intense and must have been a north, south exchange. No errant rounds were hitting the trees. Potter's men knew we were coming from the west. We moved forward over small mounds thick with trees and brush. We slowed to a fast walk as we moved towards Potter's position.

Suddenly, to our left, four or five gooks appeared at forty meters. They were running left to our right. We saw them first and after a fusillade of gunfire, two gooks fell. The others turned and ran north with rounds, chasing them.

"ANYONE HIT?" Betz responded.

"NO! TWO GOOKS DOWN!"

I grabbed the mic and told Potters RTO we were coming in.

"SARGE! GRAB THOSE WEAPONS. LETS MOVE!"

Sergeant Betz picked up the PPSh-41 of one of the dead gooks. Otto picked up the other weapon. The second soldier was lying face up, eyes and mouth open, as if he was going to say something.

"LETS MOVE, SINGLE FILE!" I didn't want Potter's men getting itchy fingers. As we moved, the firing diminished. The gooks we ran into made it back to command central two men short with information reinforcements had arrived.

We arrived at Potter's position ahead of the rest of the patrols. The chaos of the firefight had subsided. The North Koreans were pulling back and Potter's position was taking intermittent fire. Potter's men were returning fire toward unseen targets. Sergeant Potter was lying on the ground behind his men, his left shoulder wrapped in a field dressing.

Next to him were the patrols two claymores. They must have retrieved them before the attack, which was unfortunate. The claymores would have shredded the gooks. Bent at the waist, Fuzzy raced over to Potter. The arriving patrols were on one knee, looking to me for orders.

"SERGEANT HICKS, GHOSTBEAR, TAKE THE RIGHT FLANK, TIE IN WITH POTTERS MEN, CALHOUN GO LEFT WITH BETZ'S MEN, PUT A COUPLE MEN TO WATCH OUR REAR!"

The men moved towards their respective positions, crouched at the waist. Except for Riker, whether he thought he was impervious to bullets or just instinctively stood up, the bullet spinning him.

"MEDIC!" As long as we stayed low, we had excellent cover. The trees growing out of the dikes were taking hits, bark was flying. Whether it was the noise of men shooting and shouting or my brain was too busy to process sounds, I didn't hear the bullets zip by or hit the trees.

Two men wounded within fifteen minutes. Where the fuck was the QRF? I had yet to hear Mo's call sign on the net. Riker wasn't making any sounds, not good!

"RED-EYE, WHERE THE HELL ARE YOU? OVER?"

Before Mo could answer, the company commander, Red-eye six, did.

"Red-eye two, hold your position, help is on the way, over."

What I didn't know, a battalion staff officer was an observer in a tower. At dawn he saw something suspicious through binoculars, just east of GP Beryl. The Captain ordered MO to check out what he thought he saw. Which placed Mo and his QRF on foot a mile from his APCs and over an hour away.

"ROGER, WE HAVE WHISKEY INDIAN ALPHA'S, WILL NEED APC'S TO EVACUATE! WE ARE TAKING FIRE, IT WILL BE HARD TO PULL BACK WITH WOUNDED! OVER!"

"RED-EYE TWO, WE'LL GET THERE ASAP!"

Captain Roseman was in a tight spot. Charlie company's other platoons were guarding the fence or a GP. He rounded up mechanics, clerks, men just coming off night duty, anyone who could carry a rifle, to act as a QRF.

I no sooner handed the horn back to double OO when the firing picked up on our right flank. Sergeant Hicks and Ghostbears men were burning through ammo. I stuck my head over the berm and I could see the gooks firing and moving. The enemy was trying to close on our position.

"EAGLE SIX PERMISSION FOR FIRE MISSION ENEMY IN THE OPEN, COORDINATES, CHARLIE SIERRA 074950, OVER!

"NEGATIVE, RED-EYE TWO! Hold on your position!"

Fuck me, we're on our own, too close to North Korea for mortar support. The battalion CO didn't have the authority to start another Korean war. Fucking Armistice, fucking politicans are in denial.

"FOX, SANCHEZ, DO-HA COME WITH ME, OTTO STAY HERE!"

The gooks were using the shallow gully, thick with brush, in front of our right flank. The gully curved around towards the rear. They were going to use it for cover and flank our position. Running couched, we slid into the gully. To our surprise, a couple of gooks were there, fifty meters away. Our M-14's barked against their submachine guns, brrrrrrrp! They ran up the top of the Gully, giving the men targets.

I turned, and Sanchez was down, screaming in fear and pain. I yelled over the edge of the gully. Fuzzy was just 30 meters away.

"MEDIC! DO-HA, STAY HERE!" Fuzzy dropped into the ravine.

"FOX GIVE US A HAND!"

We got Sanchez over next to Riker. Fuzzy had Sanchez's shirt cut open. Blood was pumping out of a small hole in Sanchez's right side, no foaming blood.

"OTTO WITH ME!" We moved up behind Sergeants Hicks. The enemy was pulling back.

"GOOD MOVE LT, WE HIT THE SOB'S THAT POPPED OUT OF THE GULLY."

"GET THE MEN RELOADING THEIR MAGAZINES. HELP IS A WAYS OFF. THIS ISN'T THEIR TYPICAL HIT AND RUN!"

I required the riflemen to carry a bandolier, an extra sixty rounds of ammo, besides eight magazines. The sixty rounds refilled three magazines. The men had burned through most of their basic load from the number of empty magazines on the ground.

"LT, THEY WANT OUR ASS, THEY ARE GOING TRY TO OVERRUN US!"

"TRY IS RIGHT, SARGE!"

We were still receiving sporadic fire, the trees were taking the hits. Otto and I did our crouched sprint over to Sergeant Betz. Betz and Calhoun's men were facing west. The woods and brush made it difficult to see over fifty, sixty meters. I needed a plan to get the wounded out. The gully we just chased the gooks out of sliced through the woods in a southerly direction behind our position. It provided cover for a hundred meters. We could use the gully to move the wounded.

"SARGE, USE THE GULLY BEHIND US TO GET THE WOUNDED OUT. WHEN THAT TIME COMES I WANT YOUR MEN TO HOLD THIS POSITION, I'LL BE WITH BETZ'S MEN ON YOUR RIGHT TILL WE GET THE WOUNDED OUT.

"OKAY LIEUTENANT."

"OTTO GIVE ME THE MIC. RED-EYE SIX, OVER! RED-EYE SIX OVER!" Nothing but static. "OTTO IS THE BATTERY GOOD?"

"YES, JUST REPLACED IT." He slung the radio off his back to check if the antenna was loose and the frequencies were set.

"TRY EAGLE!"

"SAME LIEUTENANT, STATIC! WE ARE BEING JAMMED!"

"KEEP TRYING!"

Betz screamed! "HERE THEY COME!"

I looked over the grass and brush covered dike and saw a line of men running towards us. Their bodies blurred by the brush, no question of who they were, the muzzle flashes showed their intentions. Sergeants Betz and Calhoun were firing, but the men lying against the dike were ducking for cover. The only way you win at a two-way firing range was to get more rounds down range than the enemy.

I ducked over to Magruder and Kirst. Magruder was lying on his side, bug eyed, clutching his rifle at the forearm. Kirst was on his stomach, but was well below the top of the dike. He turned his head, his face was ashen with fear.

"LT, SOMEONE IS GOTTA GET KILLED!"

"NO SHIT KIRST, GET UP, RETURN FIRE, NOW!" To make my point, I extended my body above the dike and fired two short bursts at ducking and weaving figures. I had switched my M-14 to full automatic. Sergeant Calhoun saw what was going on and urged his men to return fire. Just then Sergeant Hicks and Ghostbears men let loose with a volley. The gooks were making another run at the gully. We were being hit on two sides.

"LT, I HAVE SIX ON THE HORN!" Otto had switched to the alternate frequency.

"SIX THIS IS RE-EYE TWO!"

"We are on our way!" Captain Roseman said calmly. He was at least thirty minutes or more away.

"WE ARE UNDER ATTACK BY ENEMY FROM THE EAST AND WEST, GET HERE FAST!" I didn't wait for an answer. The strong acidic gunpowder smell permeated the air, along with its deafening sound, as the entire platoon returned fire at the advancing enemy. Otto and I bolted back to Sergeant Hicks' side of the perimeter. I grabbed his web gear to get his attention and pull him back from his firing position.

"SARGE SEND ANOTHER MAN TO HELP FOX AND DO-HA TO COVER THE GULLY. WE MAY NEED TO PULL OUT."

As the Sarge moved to send one of his men to the ravine, Otto and I made a run up to Potter's position. Specialist Robinson had taken over for the wounded sergeant. The dikes of three overgrown rice paddies protected his position. Two dikes ran north to south, thirty meters apart. They tied into the east, west dike, making a three-sided box with the gully at the south end.

The impromptu defensive position was too damn close to the MDL. The enemy had quick access to ammo, reinforcements, and medical care. If they overran us, they would drag the survivors across the MDL. Maybe the gooks wanted more prisoners to enhance negotiations. They still had the USS Pueblo crew. No matter what, we're fucked if they rushed us with an overwhelming force.

The woods were not as thick in front of Potter's position. The field of fire was larger. Robinson's men were firing at gooks who were trying to advance on his position. A frontal attack was too open. There was a small hill a hundred meters north of the MDL. I could see the gooks running down the hill disappearing into the brush. The hillside was well within the range of our M-14's and grenade launchers. They were using the cover at the base of the hill for staging.

"ROBINSON GET SOME ROUNDS ON THOSE BASTARDS COMING OFF THE HILL! Betz's position was taking the heaviest fire. Otto and I did our crouched run back to Betz's side of the perimeter. I had to try for mortar support one more time.

"EAGLE THIS IS RED-EYE TWO, OVER!"

"This is Eagle."

"THEY'RE STAGING JUST NORTH OF US, WE ARE UNDER ATTACK FROM THE EAST AND WEST,

REQUEST PERMISSION FOR FIRE MISSION!"

"NEGATIVE, RED-EYE TWO, NEGATIVE! The Colonel knew after an hour into the fight, we had wounded and running low on ammo."

Meanwhile, the powers to be were trying to stop the fighting. They convened an emergency meeting at Panmunjom. They were exchanging harmless and meaningless words across a felt-covered table, as bullets ripped through bodies and the trees just above our heads.

Our return fire had slowed the gooks. Their attack stalled at sixty meters from Betz's position. On Sergeant Hicks and Ghostbear side of the perimeter, the enemy was backing off. They weren't retreating on Betz's side. The men were holding their rifles over the dike and firing without exposing their bodies. I yelled over to Robinson.

"I NEED JOHNSON AND BROWN WITH ME!"

"HOW MUCH AMMO DO YOU HAVE?" Brown had four magazines, Johnson three, plus one bandolier. I still had five magazines and a bandolier. I gave one mag each to Brown and Johnson before yelling to Sergeant Hicks.

"SERGEANT HICKS! WE ARE GOING IN THE GULLY AND TRY TO FLANK THEM."

We were going to use the gully that ran south, then leave it and move to our west and north. With luck, we would roll up the gooks flank.

"LET'S GO, OTTO YOU TO!"

We slipped into the gully just south of Do-HA and the others guarding the gully from a westerly attack.

We ran about a seventy meters before I halted. The gully was getting deeper as we ran south. I had to crawl to the top, pulling myself up by grabbing the brush. I couldn't see them, but the brrrrrrp of their sub-machine guns told me they were close.

I signaled to the others to join me. On one knee, I motioned for Otto and Brown to be on my right and Johnson to the left. We went thirty meters when we made contact. Johnson's and my M-14 were on full automatic. Otto was able to get a couple of his 40mm rounds through the trees. Brown was a good shot and was making use of his marksmanship. We took them by surprise. In less than a minute, they started withdrawing, returning minor fire.

Johnson and Brown continued raking the fleeing enemy.

"JOHNSON, BROWN, MOVE OUT, BACK TO OUR POSITION."

We raced back to the gully. The gunfire backed off to an occasional crack of M-14's as men fired at the retreating gooks. We reached Betz's position. Fuzzy was tending to a screaming Magruder. The bullet smashed into his forearm, shattering the bone. Fuzzy was trying to get a sling up around Magruder's neck.

The rest of the men turned their heads, the look on their faces said, let's get the hell out of here. I couldn't agree more. Scattered on the ground were hundreds of spent cartridges and more discerning, empty magazines.

"SERGEANT HICKS HOW ARE WE FIXED FOR

AMMO?"

He went around to the sergeants, then back to me.. The firing had stopped.

"Three magazines per man and ten 40mm rounds for each M-79. Most of the men have two hand grenades. Lets hope those chicken shits never got close enough we have to lob grenades."

"Not good. If they come, we'll run out of ammo. I don't want to be lobbing grenades."

As I said, "Six should be getting close", Otto was tapping my arm with the mic.

O'DANNY BOY

"A true friend is someone who is there for you when he'd rather be anywhere else." Len Wein

"RED-EYE TWO, THIS IS BLACKHAWK, WE ARE APPROACHING FROM THE SOUTH USING THE GULLY." Danny was breathing hard, telling me Slats was hoofing it from GP Gladys, a click away. There was no shooting, so I had to assume they were undetected.

"SERGEANT HICKS, LET FOX AND DO-HA KNOW FRIENDLIES ARE APPROACHING IN THE GULLY!"

"WILL DO, LT!"

I ran over to Fuzzy, tending the four wounded men near two larger trees. Sanchez's olive tone face looked as if someone had dusted it with flour. The others were lying on their sides, scared and in pain.

"Fuzzy, how are they doing?" He moved closer and in a low voice.

"We gotta get Sanchez out of here. He's bleeding internally. The others are hurtin' but will be okay."

"OTTO!" I reached back for the mic.

"RED-EYE SIX, RED-EYE SIX, WHAT'S YOUR ETA? OVER."

Again the static, broken message. Otto had the radio off his back and was adjusting the squelch. The captain's voice came over the airwaves loud and clear.

"RED-EYE TWO ON OUR WAY, TWENTY MINUTES."

"Fuzzy, twenty minutes, get him ready to be moved."

"Will do Lieutenant!"

Just then.

Slats and three men popped out of the gully, carrying several bandoliers slung over their shoulders. Captain Roseman also was getting close with reinforcements. Things were looking up.

"Jesus, Slats, how the hell did you get?"

"YOU'RE WELCOME, MIKE!"

"Sorry Danny, thanks. Glad you made it. We need the ammo and extra men. The gooks will rush us again."

"Hey, I'd rather be here than anywhere else."

"That's a crock of shit! Let's get the ammo distributed."

"Where do you want my men?" Slats asked.

"Two with Sergeant Hicks and two with Sergeant Calhoun."

We passed out the bandoliers of ammo. There was no talking. The steady metallic clicking was the only sound as the men refilled their magazines. I moved back to Robinson's position. I pointed to the thick cover at the base of the hill.

"ROBINSON, if you see any gooks coming off that hill shoot them, I don't give a fuck if they're in North Korea. They are staging their attacks at the bottom of the hill."

Fuzzy was preparing a stretcher for Sanchez. The

other wounded men could walk with help.. An unnerving calm settled over our position. The gooks had stopped shooting. As I looked around, Sergeant Hicks looked my way, nodded, I assume, approval. Specialist Dusenbury gave a thumbs up. Our orders were to hold our position till Red-Eye six arrived, then pull out. Suddenly, Sergeant Ghostbear let out a war cry, then yelled.

"HERE THEY COME!"

The enemy was attacking using the trees as cover. I moved up to the berm. It was different this time. Every man, plus Danny's men, had their rifles and grenade launchers up on the dike and ready to fire. "FIRE! FIRE AT WILL, FIRE!" With that command, I opened fire, firing short bursts at the weaving and darting enemy. The fusillade of gunfire was deafening. Over the gunfire, I could hear courage on my left and right; the vociferous screaming of men as they stretched above the berm to fire at the approaching enemy. I could see the dirt and tufts of grass being kicked up as the enemy bullets tried to whittle away our protective berm. The curtain of fire we were laying down was effective. The enemy was suffering the consequence.

It was a coordinated attack from the northeast and northwest. They were using the thickest cover to our east and west. The gooks tried to drive a wedge into our position. They tried fire and maneuver, advancing, dropping to the ground and firing. It wasn't working. After several minutes, they fell back. They realized the price was going to be too high. The sergeants and I started screaming, "CEASE FIRE, CEASE FIRE!" Once you get a GI firing his weapon, he didn't want to stop.

"ANYONE HIT?" No cries for the medic. Otto was trying to hand me the mic.

"Red-eye, this is Red-eye six, over!"

"This is red-eye, over!"

"We are approaching from the south. Be there in zero five, over."

"Roger."

"FOX, DO-HA, MORE FRIENDLIES COMING IN!"

Captain Roseman sent a ten man squad. The rest of his men were holding a position to our south. The wounded were to be moved back to an APC. We were to hold our position and give cover for the evacuation of the wounded. After the wounded evacuated, we were to drop back to the locomotive.

"Slats, it looks like help will be here in a couple of minutes. Are you going back to the GP?"

"Hell yes! The captain will have my ass for abandoning my post!"

Sergeant Hicks was pouring water on his left hand. I crouched and ran over to see what he was doing.

"Sarge, what the hell! Damn! that must hurt!"

A thick splinter an inch long was under the skin on the back of his left hand. A bullet smashed into the forearm of his rifle, driving the splinter into his hand behind the knuckle of the middle finger. I turned to call the medic.

"Don't, Lieutenant, he has his hands full. This can wait till we get back."

"Okay, I'll take Betz's men to see if there's any wounded gooks we can take as prisoners. Stay here, make sure Fox stays alert on that ravine. I'll take Do-Ha with me. Alert the men we are going to be out front."

"Okay lieutenant, be careful."

I moved over to Betz's position.

"Sergeant Betz, we are going to backtrack to where we entered the woods to see if there's any wounded gooks. Keep the men on line and close. If we make contact, we'll beat it back here."

"Got it LT."

We moved slowly through the woods. I was hoping there were no gooks playing dead. I didn't want to be surprised by one raising up out of the grass. The gooks had closed within sixty meters of our position. We saw why they pulled back. Our curtain of fire was effective. Strewn about were several bandage wrappings, their medic was a busy man.

They dragged the wounded or dead away, leaving only six bloody trails. No weapons were left.

"Sarge, let's move on to where we shot the two gooks."

Sergeant Betz signaled to move forward. The bodies were only fifty meters away. I motioned for the men to form a perimeter. I walked towards the body to my left.

"Sergeant, check the other one, watch for booby traps, see if he has anything of intelligence value. Remove any patches or insignia on his uniform. G-2 wants to confirm what outfit we're up against."

"Yes, sir!"

I walked over to the dead soldier and knelt to check his pockets. His body was still warm. No insignia on his jacket. The left side pocket had a bulge. I suspected it was a grenade. Without unsnapping the pocket, I gripped the bulge. It was a grenade and I could feel the safety lever through the heavy material. I unsnapped the pocket. The grenade's pin was still intact.

His wide canvas belt held only a pouch with a compass. I tugged at the snap on the left breast pocket and it popped open. The cloth was coarse, similar to a ten-ounce canvas. The pocket held sheets of folded paper. I handed them to Do-Ha. He scanned the paper with a sad look on his face.

"What's it say?"

"It's a letter from his girlfriend."

"Okay, hand it here."

I put the letter back, snapping the flap. I put a lot of pressure on the snap. It was creepy; the body was still soft. His dark eyes, surrounded by an ashen face, stared up at me. He looked as if he wanted to say something. I had a fleeting thought of the dead gook suddenly clutching my hand to tell me, 'I didn't need to push that hard.'

"Do-Ha, how old do you think he is?"

"Twenty five, maybe older."

"No rank, no dog tags, strange! Let's get out of here!"

We made it back to our position. The firefight was over. Hundreds of spent bullet casings covered the ground. Enough brass to make more than a few trinkets and ash trays. I wondered how many words they exchanged at Panmunjom compared to the number of bullets fired in anger here. For certain, the generals and colonels spilled no blood on the green, velvet-covered table.

Sergeant Hicks was grimacing in pain. Flexing his hand had caused the splinter to touch the bone.

"Sarge, move your men to the rear. I'll stay here with Sergeant Ghostbear. I'll send the rest back, one patrol at a time. Get that hand taken care of ASAP."

"Roger Lieutenant."

Otto and I moved over to Sergeant Ghostbear.

"That was one hell of a war cry, Sarge!"

"Apache side of family!"

"Get your men ready to pull back. We'll wait till Sergeant Hicks makes it back to the locomotive."

"Okay Lieutenant."

The DMZ went quiet, no screaming men, shooting, crackling of radio static. The remaining men looked over the berm, expecting another attack. Most had lit a cigarette. Two magpies joined us and were chattering away. The smell of wild lilac replaced the acid odor of gunfire. The breeze stirred the tall grass and trees with newborn leaves.

My mind drifted back to the Wiscoy creek, my favorite trout stream, sixty miles southeast of Buffalo. The water was pristine, a rarity in Western New York. The stream held wild brook and brown trout. On a day like today, I would fish with nymphs, or a wet fly. It's amazing how the DMZ went from a place of sheer terror to peacefulness. The ten pound M-14 reminded me it could change in a moment's notice. Double O interrupted my train of thought.

"Lieutenant, six ordered us to pull back. He said everyone at the same time."

THREE BY SEA

"The guerrilla must move amongst the people as a fish swims in the sea" Mao Zedong

Kim and his team landed on a beach between Goseong and Sokeho. The incoming tide swept away any signs of men coming ashore. Kim was glad to have his feet on the ground. The voyage in the cramped Yugo class submarine was smelly and claustrophobic. Then a harrowing ride in the inflatable boat to the uninhabited shore. The seas were to be calm, instead they had to buck five foot waves. Kim hoped the inflatable and operator made it back to the sub. If not, his capture could compromise the mission.

The plan was to bypass the seashore villages moving cautiously through the countryside because of the midnight to six am curfew. Once in the mountains, the team could rest until daylight, then follow the valley to the villages of Hongcheon and Yangpyeong. Kim felt comfortable and confident traveling through the terrain. Lee and Park seemed relaxed. They traveled separately and met at prearranged locations. The final destination was a safe house north of Seoul, two hundred kilometers away. In Seoul, Kim would board a bus headed to the village of Yangju, Lee and Park, following on separate buses.

Kim was confident the papers would pass scrutiny when traveling by bus between Hongcheon and Yangju. Thanks to a recent South Korean defector, Kim and his men had the latest in identification papers. After the raid on the Presidential palace, the South Korean government issued new identification papers. The bureau duplicated the papers and even the South Korean manufacturer's labels in their clothing.

They carried no weapons. Just harmless travelers from the countryside. Kim carried a forged letter showing he had a job waiting for him. Lee carried letters from his betrothed and Park was traveling to his grandmother's funeral. Kim was convinced the IDs with the letters as backup would pass inspection at checkpoints. This proved true at the bus station. The officer gave his papers a cursory glance, asked him why and where he was going, then motioned him to move on.

It was comical when three GIs boarded the crowded bus in Yangpyeong. Kim was sitting on the aisle end of the seat to discourage other passengers. The bus was full and one of the GIs walked down the aisle and stood next to Kim. He looked down and smiled, motioning for Kim to move towards the window. Kim hesitated, but moved. He knew Americans were big. This man took up more than his share of the seat, pressing Kim against the window. The GI smelled of alcohol and sweat. Probably headed back to his base after visiting one of the many whorehouses in the south. For the next fifty kilometers, Kim thought of the many ways he could kill the GI.

Travel to the safe house was easy, almost too easy. Chung was there upon their arrival.

"Kim, good to see that you made it."

Chung reached out and shook Kim's hand. He then turned and nodded to Lee and Park.

"You must be tired and hungry after your journey. Mi-Sook will make something to eat for you and your men. Our cover is the four of us are Mi-Sook's brothers. We'refrom Seoul, if anyone asks. Mi-Sook came south with Ae-Sook many years ago."

Mi-Sook was aware of Ae-Sooks death and how she died. Her only comment was 'she should've been more careful'. As the evening went on, Kim was having a hard time believing this was the same Chung. He was cordial, friendly, warm. Kim and his men weren't in danger from a depraved killer?

"Kim, do you have the photos I requested?"

"Yes! Colonel Choi was most interested in your request."

"Let me see the photos, and then I'll explain."

Kim removed his jacket from the hook near the door.

"Mi-Sook, I will need a sharp knife." Kim asked.

Before he finished the word knife, **thwack**! A knife suddenly appeared stuck in the wooded floor. Mi-Sook smiled as she said.

"Be careful. It's very sharp you don't want to damage the material."

Kim used the tip of the stiletto knife to remove

stitches from the jacket liner. Several photos sheathed in plastic were sewn into the lining. In a separate envelope, a letter from the mother addressed to Hyun-ae.

Chung studied the photos. He was smiling as he said..

"Hyun-ae looks like her mother. Both are beautiful woman."

He removed the letter and read, then hesitated, looking at Mi-sook.

"Mi-sook, as a young woman, read the letter. What do you think? Does it sound believable if you had not seen your mother in nineteen years?"

Chung handed the two handwritten pages on hospital stationery to **Mi-Sook.**

Dr Ae-Jeong Bae, Administrator, Kanggye Hospital was in bold print across the top. Mi-Sook read only the first page before laughing.

"This letter is garbage. No mother writes a letter like this. An intelligent daughter would believe none of the lies."

"What part do you find not believable?"

"Chung, you have been here long enough. People in the south don't believe there's a good life in the north."

Mi-Sook, in a mocking voice, read a sentence. *"My Mugunghwa, I miss you so much, but I love our leader and my work here as a doctor. I could never come back to the repressive South Korean government.* This letter is a load of pig shit! Whoever put the letter together must have their head up their ass! Don't show it to the girl. You are better off showing her the photographs and convince her with that silver tongue of yours."

Kim was stunned that Mi-Sook, a keeper of a safe house, knew details of the mission. Apparently, she was privy to more information than Kim. She was showing disrespect to the bureau. Kim was about to say something when Chung saw the look on his face.

"Kim, I trust Mi-Sook more than I trust you. She's a key part of this mission. I was her instructor and mentor. She'll be of great help. The photographs and the letter were to be used to convince a young lady, named Hyun-ae Bae, to defect to the North. Her mother, kidnapped during the uprising on Jeju Island nineteen years ago, is still alive."

"Kim, what did Colonel Choi tell you about the doctor?"

"During the war, Hyun-ae's mother treated many officers and now they are high-ranking members of the party. It's known that Han Ik-su owes his life to her. He was wounded at the battle of Changjin Reservoir. They appointed him director of the General Politburo. He watches out for her." Kim continued.

"They respect her as a doctor, but not as a good comrade. She tried to escape to China frequently. It's been ten years since her last attempt. She has accepted her fate. Pyongyang continues to deny she was ever in the country. Years ago, the South Korean government stopped asking about her."

Lee stood up before he spoke.

"Comrade Chung, why all the trouble to take a young woman with us? We know little about her? We can't cross the DMZ with this woman. She has no training. What if she cries out or decides she doesn't want to go? There's enough danger without complicating the mission."

"Comrade, she's not your typical young woman. Her genius is in physics and she is a specialist in nuclear energy. If she hadn't been involved with the protest group, she would have had her doctorate a year ago. She attended Berkly University. She'll be an asset and good for the propaganda machine." Kim jumped up and stood next to Lee, his fists clenched.

"SHE'S A UNIVERSITY STUDENT? ARE YOU INSANE? You will not convince a twenty-year-old to go through the DMZ, mother or no mother!"

Kim realized he was yelling at a very dangerous man.

"I apologize Comrade Chung, I.."

Chung held up his hand, signaling Kim to stop. Mi-Sook was standing in the corner and stifled a giggle. Chung removed a folder from a satchel marked CONFIDENTIAL and handed it to Kim.

"Kim, I obtained these documents from a contact. They're from the Ministry that plans South Korea's future energy needs. The document mentions our young lady twice, she is twenty-seven, not twenty. She has put forth theories that are workable for converting nuclear energy to electricity. The report states that Hyun-ae is considered a treasure. The government is going to overlook her involvement in politics. They don't believe she's going to start an insurrection."

"Comrade Chung, why would she leave her family and the opportunities here?"

"One reason is her mother. She is obsessed with the belief her mother is alive. I believe, no, I'm positive, she would risk her freedom and life to see her mother. She has a psychotic obsession, she lives with the constant thought of being with her mother. We all have desires, wishes, some good, some evil. It is a matter of degrees.

With these photographs, I can convince Hyun-ae her mother is alive and well. In her mind, she believes it. The photos will confirm it."

Kim calmer unclenched his fists before saying.

"That may only spur her to go to the government to ask them to reopen her mother's file and she'll tell them about you!"

"Kim, my comrade, after I show her the pictures, she either agrees to come along, or we kidnap her just as her mother was nineteen years ago. If she gives us a hard time, she will no longer exist as the 'treasure' for the south. If we can't have her, neither shall the south. I'll slit her throat."

"Chung killing her would be bad for the propaganda machine."

"Not so. This is where Mi-Sook's role is important. Just before we move north, Mi-Sook will visit Hyun-ae apartment in Seoul. She will plant a pistol, plastic explosives and propaganda material, along with an envelope containing money. It's an envelope

I handled. The OSI will the process the prints. They will match the fingerprints I left at Ae-Sook's safe house. Hyun-ae's fingerprints are also on the envelope. The police or OSI will conclude she is working with us as a traitor, whether she is dead or alive."

"But Chung, what if the police pick her up before.." Mi-Sook spoke.

"I have been watching her at a home north of Seoul. She's there nearly every weekend. She is alone most of the time. On the weekends, she sees an American soldier, a lieutenant. It's obvious they're lovers. He stays the night. Sometimes a woman shows up and stays with Hyun-ae. I'll plant the evidence in Hyun-ae's apartment in Seoul, then meet you and your team in Uijeongbu."

Mi-sook continued with confidence.

"The house is under surveillance. One man watches the house. They rotate every four hours. Same time every day. We don't know why the surveillance, but suspect her involvement with the protest. The car is six hundred meters away on a side road. Using binoculars, they can see who comes and goes. At night, the surveillance car moves to an alley across from the path that leads to the house. Only the front of the house is visible. They don't want to get any closer, fearing the neighbors would talk."

Chung suspected the reason for surveillance. They saw her with him in the alley months ago. The government men stood up too quickly in the park and started in their direction. The fingerprints on the envelope will confirm she's working with us. Chung laughed.

"You don't agree with the way I tell the plan?" Mi-Sook asked.

"No, No Mi-Sook, go on, I was just thinking how stupid they are."

Mi-sook walked over to the corner of the room after removing the knife stuck in the floor. She slid the blade between two floor boards and, giving the blade a twist, the board lifted. From the space beneath the board, Mi-sook removed a rolled map. She unrolled a two foot by two-foot hand-drawn map on the floor, placing a tea cup on each of the corners.

"The house Hyun-ae is using is secluded. It's near the top of a large hill. Beomgol-ro road goes by the path that leads to the house. The road winds down the hill into the city. Where the road reaches its highest point, there're a few houses and shops. It will be easy for your team to find this spot if we get separated.

A shop in the center of the cluster of buildings sells food and other goods. Across from the shop, a path goes up the hill, marked with white stones. After you pass the sixth house, a path leads to Hyun-ae's house. The house backs up to a forest of pine trees. It is not a large forest, but big enough to hide."

"Mi-sook, why not come from the other side of the hill and avoid the possibility of being seen?"

"Kim, if we use the backside of the hill, it would draw attention. People do not walk there, it's steep and rocky.

"What about the surveillance? If they've been watching the house, they'll know we're strangers."

Mi-Sook smiled as she spoke, confident in the plan.

"No worry, Kim. The path goes to the top of the hill and ends at a small park. There are benches, a small shelter and a trail leading into the forest behind Hyun-ae's house. Many people go to the park to watch the sunset or to view Uijeongbu's city lights. We'll go there as brothers and a sister and take pictures of the city. After dark, your team will take the trail to the forest. I will go to the house. By then, Chung will have shown Hyun-ae the photographs of her mother and told her if she doesn't cooperate, her mother will be in great danger. My presence may help keep Hyun-ae calm. I will show her the photographs of planted evidence I took in her apartment. The silly girl doesn't even lock her door. Kim, your team will stay in the woods as our security."

"Mi-sook, what if the other woman or the American is there?"

"If the American is there, the operation is off. We can't afford to have the entire American sector on alert. If the woman is there, I will take care of her when I know you made it to the safe house with Hyun-ae."

"Questions?"

Lee asked.

"When is this to occur?"

"The days of April 27-28 or our secondary dates are

May 3-4. It will depend on which weekend Hyun-ae visits the house."

"Chung, how are you getting to the house without being spotted?"

"That is my concern, not yours, comrade Kim!"

WISE AND LOVING

"When you come to a fork in the road, take it." Yogi Berra

"Captain, you wanted to see me?"

"Mike, you need to get your men ready to move out in a moment's notice! Battalion expects more attacks tonight. Your platoon is the battalions reserve until 0800 tomorrow."

"The men are busy cleaning weapons and getting resupplied with ammo. It will take an hour. We will be ready to move well before dark."

"Good! By the way, your men performed well this morning."

"We had some good luck, captain."

"Luck was a small part. Your leadership saved the day. From the debriefings, seems the gooks tried to overrun Potter's patrol. Your quick response stopped them. You did a damn good job."

"Thanks captain, I would like to write up commendation for two men."

"We'll see, write up a brief description."

"Captain, may I barrow your jeep to see Sanchez and the other men in the hospital this afternoon?"

"Sorry but no!"

"Captain, I want to see my men. Besides, it's my birthday tomorrow."

"Happy birthday! Look, it's too late, it's 1500 hours and I want every swinging dick here and ready to roll. Battalion wants you at headquarters, 0900 tomorrow. You can go to the hospital afterwards. Take my jeep as your birthday present and Do-ha as your driver. I want you back here by 1700 hours."

"Captain, Do-ha performed well this morning. He could use the time off. I don't need a driver."

"Mike, your ass needs to be here by 1700, no if and or buts. I know damn well you're going to Uijeongbu after the hospital. Do-ha will make sure you're back here on time and no one steals my jeep while you visit, ah what's her name?"

"Yes sir! Her name is Hyun-ae."

The night couldn't pass fast enough even after a couple of drinks of Slats Crown, Mo and I appropriated. Slats was stuck out on Gladys for a couple more days.

"Mike, you're quiet tonight."

"Jesus Mo, this is the first chance I had to relax since this morning's firefight. My stomach still doing fucking flips. Five of my guys wounded, no fire support and no reinforcements. Did I do everything right? Fuck! Sanchez might die. I ordered him to get in the ravine. I got him shot. If it wasn't for Slats, we would've been in deeper shit. We're out there ALONE AND NOBODY GIVES A FUCK! WE KEEP TAKING BULLETS WHILE THE BRASS AND POLITICANS EXCHANGE WORDS."

"Mike, we were called out on a wild goose chase."

"I'm sorry Mo, I got carried away. What happened?"

"We were just east of GP Beryl and shit, there were five, maybe six gooks. We pursued them in a running gunfight. They went straight for the MDL. It definitely was a diversion. As soon as we made contact, they attacked Potter's men." Mo went on..

"Look Mike, Sanchez getting shot isn't your fault. It's combat!"

"Don't worry about it, Mo, it's just the way it is. On top of this bullshit, I'm to report to battalion tomorrow and guess what?"

"What?"

"Tomorrow is my birthday."

"That calls for another drink! How the fuck old…?"

"Twenty seven."

"Damn man, that's old for a lieutenant."

"Hey, fuck you, I joined the army when I was twenty-four as an enlisted man."

"Come on Mike, I'm just bustin' your balls. Here's to ya, to live another day to fight the communists bastards! The second tall drink was smoothing things out.

"The captain gave up his jeep so I could visit the hospital. I'll be back by 1700 hours. Wanna come along Mo?"

"I can't. I'm on duty tomorrow."

"Too bad. I'm going to see Hyun-ae tomorrow and I don't know what the fuck to tell or ask her."

"Mike, you're not going to ask her to marry you, are you?"

"I don't know what I'll say. I love her but, we live in two different worlds. She's going to be a scientist. I don't know an atom from an acorn. I don't know if I'm going back to school or staying in the army. Fuck,

I may end up working in a factory like my old man. I have two brothers and sisters back in the States. She has family here. Would she be happy in the states, would I be happy living here? How do you reconcile these differences with just love? When I'm with her, the world is perfect. Now I just don't know!"

"Mike, you don't realize it, but you are still coming off an adrenalin high. Combat screws with your head. You can't catch up to the shit that's racing through your mind. What you did this morning was no small thing. Look, I knew this was coming. I have a friend at division personnel. We were in ROTC together. I ran into him at the Green Door."

"You and that Green Door, you should partner up with Soo-lee."

"Mike, there's a ton of paperwork and bullshit, to marry a Korean?"

"Really?"

"He told me it takes months to get the paperwork approved. Besides the paperwork, you need permission from your commander. Hyun-ae has to pass a background check and a physical. My buddy says it takes five to six months for it to be approved. What do you have left, three months?" Mo asked.

"No, four in Korea and thirteen months in the army."

"My advice, finish your tour, get settled in the states then send for her."

"She wants to get her doctorate. I have no idea where I'm going to be stationed. I'll be in Nam in a matter of months if I stay in the army. She'll be stranded in the states by herself."

"Do you think she would go?"

"No, I don't know! I want to know now, not later." Mo poured another drink, handing the bottle to me before he spoke.

"Lets have another drink. It will help to settle your nerves. Tomorrow will be a better day. Que sera sera!"

The last drink was smooth and deadening. It was 1900 hours, too early to sleep. I sat on my bunk, intending to finish a book left by an earlier officer. "Einstein Intersection" a science fiction novel where an alien named Lo Lebey searches for his love, Friza, among the earthlings and their different cultures. It seemed familiar to "Orphaus and Eurydice" which was the only Greek mythology story I ever finished. I could see Hyun-ae and myself on the pages. I drifted off into a deep sleep. It was a dark sleep.

Where ever I was, it was pitch black. I was on Hyun-ae's black stallion, racing through the darkness. I was bent at the waist, hanging on to stallion's mane. The long hairs of the mane were whipping in my face as we effortlessly cantered through the night. Up ahead, a person seemly suspended in midair was reaching out from under a hooded cloak. My mind raced. It was Hyun-ae! The stallion galloped faster, my legs locked on to the beast's bare sides. We moved synchronously. I wanted him to slow, but I had no control. I could feel his stride increasing. Gripping the mane tightly with my right hand, I reached down with my left hand. I was going to swing her on to the back of the stallion like they do in the cowboy movies. The other hand grasped my wrist so hard it made me look at the face. It was the dead North Korean soldier, his dark eyes staring at me, his lips moving, 'what will be will be.' I woke, startled, to Mo's gruff voice.

"HAPPY BIRTHDAY YOU OLD MAN!! Time to get up!"

****

"Do-ha, when we get to battalion stick close, as soon as I'm done, we're heading for the hospital at Yongson."

"Ok LT. The mess is just across the way from headquarters. I'll be there."

The cigar smoking Sergeant Major greeted me as I walked into Headquarters..

"Lieutenant, the spooks are in the debriefing room. Only two of them this time. Be careful."

I thought to myself, be careful, what the fuck did that mean, he's gotta be jerking my chain.

I walk into the room, Mr. Won and Kowalski are sitting at the far end, they stood.

"Congratulations lieutenant, I heard you and your men taught the North Koreans a thing or two!"

"Thanks Kowalski, can we get this over with as soon as possible? I want to see my men at the hospital."

"Lieutenant, my country and I also want to thank you."

"Thank you, Mr. Won."

"Lieutenant, I wanted to tell you in person, officially we're no longer watching or even suspect Hyun-ae Bae being involved in any seditious activities."

"What brought about the change of heart, and what does 'officially' mean, Mr. Won?"

"There're many reasons, but the main reason Bae was under investigation was because my partner and I saw her meet with Chung. We believe Hyun-ae didn't know Chung was a North Korea agent. We suspect he may have gone underground or back to North Korea. Nothing has turned up to suspect she is involved in subversive activities."

"So now what!"

"Well, lieutenant, you don't have to report to Kowalski, but I wanted to tell you personally we were ORDERED to stop surveillance. We have other cases to work. We haven't turned up any further contact between Chung and Bae, so we're ordered to stand down. But my gut feeling tells me there's a connection between Hyun-ae and Chung, especially after that day in the alley. I don't know what, but you should be careful. He's a very dangerous man. I brought along photographs of Chung to refresh your memory. If you see him, call Mr. Meyers or Kowalski."

"Thanks, I'll remember that, if I see him again."

"Look lieutenant, I'm serious. My boss pulling us off this case doesn't mean shit. Chung is still involved with Hyun-ae. He's going to surface again and I'm giving you warning!"

Kowalski, who had kept his mouth shut, spoke. "Listen to him lieutenant, I have worked with Won on other cases and his hunches are usually right."

"None of this sounds right. Hyun-ae and I are being set up as bait. YOU SON OF BITCHES, THAT'S WHAT THIS IS ABOUT!"

Won held up his hands as if to calm me before he spoke.

"It's not lieutenant, I can assure you Kowalski and Meyers will not disobey orders."

"He's right lieutenant."

"Screw you Kowalski, what makes you think Mr. Won told you everything!" Kowalski raised an eyebrow, a flash of doubt crossed his face before he spoke.

"Reed, it took a lot of string pulling to allow you to play house with Bae. They approved the operation because you were under twenty-four-hour surveillance when you were with her. No way in hell is the brass is going to allow you to risk your life in a Korean intelligence operation without safeguards."

"What the fuck's the difference? I risk my life every day I go into the DMZ?"

"We're done here. There's nothing else I can say. Won you have anything more?"

"No."

"We're leaving. I can give you a ride to the hospital."

"Thanks Kowalski, after the hospital, I'm going to

see Hyun-ae. I assume I don't have to report to you."

"That is correct. If I were you, I would finish my tour and go home and forget Hyun-ae."

"I'm not you, Kowalski!"

"See ya lieutenant, be careful!" Kowalski said as he walked towards the door.

Mr. Won stood and walked towards me.

"Mr. Won, why not show Hyun-ae the photographs and see what she has to say about Chung?" Kowalski stopped at the door, waiting for the answer.

"Lieutenant, if we show her the pictures and she is not working with him, it would be dangerous for her. She may act differently. He may kill her because he suspects he's compromised or she will warn him. It's imperative that you say nothing to her, you risk her life as well as yours!"

"But you're not watching her anymore, so what's the difference?"

"There are many ways to keep track of somebody without surveillance."

Mr. Won extended his hand. We shook, he stepped back and gave me a half bow. Without saying a word, he turned and followed Kowalski. I slumped on a metal fold up chair. I tried to piece together what had just happened. Were they really done with Hyun-ae? Why not? I'm know she's not involved in spying. If Hyun-ae had a onetime encounter with this Chung, there's no way she knows he's a North Korean. the Sergeant Major interrupted my chain of thought.

"Lieutenant, is everything okay? I need the room. A

patrol is coming in for a debriefing."

"Okay, Sergeant Major. By the way, what did you mean when you said, be careful?"

"Kowalski and I go back aways, before he switched to intelligence. I asked him what's up. He said the lieutenant, meaning you, I suppose, got your tit caught in a ringer. He said they were going to back you out?"

"Do you trust him?"

"Kowalski, yes, the Korean no!"

"Well, don't fret Sergeant Major, my 'tit' is not in the ringer."

Do-ha was sitting in the driver's seat with his head back sound asleep, enjoying the unusually warm day.

"Do-ha! Wake up! Let's get to the hospital."

We stopped at the PX and bought some Playboys and Oreo cookies for the men. I didn't know what to say, what was the protocol? They shipped Rodriguez, Brown and Appleman out before I could see them. Did you walk into their rooms and say, hey guys, here's some magazines and cookies for your bravery? I was worried about Sanchez. He didn't look good when they loaded him into the APC.

Sergeant Potter, Riker and Magruder were in the same ward.

"How you guys doing?" Magruder was sitting on the edge of his bed, Sergeant Potter and Riker were in bed propped up in a sitting position.

Magruder was first. "LT the food fantastic. We get real mashed potatoes, steak and real eggs none of

"Here's something to go with the milk."

Magruder's face lit up like a Christmas tree. "Thanks, hey guys, we got titties to look at and Oreos to dunk!"

"You have been here barely twenty-four hours with an arm shot to hell and in high spirits, you are something, Magruder."

Potter and Riker were sitting up in their beds, shaking their heads.

"Don't mind him, Lieutenant, he just got his happy medicine. We are being treated as heroes. The food is great and they're taking good care of us."

"Well, heroes you are! The head nurse said they will discharge you in a couple of days."

Potter looked concerned as he said. "Do we go back to Charlie company?"

"I don't know sergeant. I asked the CO, and he didn't know. He's coming tomorrow, he'll have an answer."

"Home would be nice, LT."

"Sarge, is it true that you moved away from your men to take a crap when you spotted the gooks?" Reed asked.

"Yep, I took Dusenbury with me. I only went twenty meters when I spotted the bastards crawling in the high grass. There was a bunch of them, fifteen or more. I shot the point man and Dusenbury opened up on the rest."

"You were lucky you hadn't dropped your drawers!"

"I forget about taking a crap." Potter said.

"I want to commend each of you for your courageous actions yesterday. Not only did you fight well, you held your shit together. You're good men and I'm honored to serve with you." The three men nodded as Riker spoke.

"Lieutenant, we were talking earlier and we agree your actions saved our ass."

"Thanks Riker, it was everyone doing what we were trained to do that made it work. How's Sanchez doing?"

"Not good LT, I stopped in to see him this morning. He's in and out, the nurse said he had a high fever last night."

Arthur Sanchez had a separate room because of the machinery plugged into his body. He was awake when Do-ha and I walked into the room. A IV was in his arm and a monitor above his bed measured his heart rate. He was as pale as when they loaded him into the APC.

"How are you feeling, Art?"

"Hi lieutenant, Do-ha. I'm nauseated and my side hurts like hell. They keep me doped up. They tell me I'm going to be okay. The bullet went clean through. The doc said the bullet just nicked the liver, no permanent damage. I was hoping for a piece of lead as a souvenir."

"You'll have a souvenir, a Purple Heart."

"Gee thanks lieutenant, but you should get a metal. You kept the gooks from overrunning us."

"The entire platoon did."

A nurse Major, businesslike, walked into the room.

"Lieutenant, we limited visitation to a few minutes. He's supposed to be resting."

"Major, how's he doing?"

"He's going to be okay, but he needs his rest. We are concerned with infection and his blood count is very low. He's on a special diet, don't give him any food from the PX. Please keep your visit very short. By the way, your CO called. He said you have to be back by 1600 hours."

"Thanks Major."

We visited with Sanchez and the other men for a few minutes before heading to Hyun-ae's place. It was nearly 1400 hours, which meant I had less than an hour. We pulled up to the shop across from the stone lined path.

"Do-ha, I won't be long, the shop across the road has good rice cakes, cold drinks. Please don't leave the jeep for more than a few minutes. It's a safe area but.."

"Don't worry LT, I'll wait in the jeep."

I hustled up the white stone lined path. I had mulled over and over what I was going to say. Half of me said, do it, the other half said don't. When I walked in the door 'don't' lost the arguement.

"MIKE!" She charged across the room and wrapped her arms around my neck. After a long kiss and warm embrace, she released her tight grip and clasped her hands behind my neck and, leaning back at arm's length, asked.

"Mike, what's wrong?"

It always amazed me how women could sense something different with the slightest of nuances.

"I can't stay, Do-ha's waiting in the jeep. I want to talk, ask you something before I leave."

"Do you have time for tea?"

"A drink would be better."

"Okay, a scotch for you and a beer for me. Why is Do-ha with you?"

"We just came from visiting my men at the hospital." She tilted her head with a quizzical look.

I blurted out. "Five of my men were wounded in a firefight yesterday."

"MIKE YOU OKAY!

"Yes, I'm fine."

"Oh, I'm sorry your men got hurt. Will they be okay?"

"Yes."

"Mike, I worry about you. I don't know what you do, but I know the crossed rifles on your collar say infantry. Aunt Ju told me five of our soldiers were killed in the DMZ last week. Tell your commander I request you not be put in harm's way."

I pictured going to the captain and saying 'Captain, my girlfriend who may be in cahoots with a spy, who would slit my throat, requested that you do not put me in harm's way.

"Why are you laughing?"

"I don't think the captain will take your request seriously."

"Why can't you stay and why do you need a drink?" She sat across from me with a bottle of OB beer, sliding my glass of scotch across the table.

While Do-ha was busy perusing the playboys at the PX, I went to the jewelry department and bought a ring. Not a diamond, didn't have the money to honor such a quick decision. For a seventy bucks, the PX had a ring with a blue topaz stone.

"Hyun-ae, I want you to go to the states with me as..." Her eyes grew as big as saucers. I put the small velvet-covered box on the table.

"MIKE! I thought we agreed to take it one day at a time?"

"We did, I have four months to go. If you want to come with me, it takes months to process the paperwork."

"I know, I spoke to Aunt Ju."

"So you want to.." She reached across the table, putting her hands on top of my hand holding the ring box.

"Mike, oh Mike, my heart gets so heavy when I think what's to happen in four months."

"If we get married we, wait you asked your aunt, what did she say?"

"She will help, no matter my decision. Mike, I will not say yes, but I will not say no. I'm in love with you and want to be with you. You'll be going back to your family. If I go with you, I'll be leaving mine. My education, my country, my mother are here. I'm torn between them and you. My heart will ache for you if I stay and it will ache for my family if I leave."

She squeezed my hand as tears rolled down her cheeks.

"I'm sorry Hyun-ae I should not..."

"No, I understand. If the shoe was on the other foot, I would do the same."

"No matter what happens, I want you to have this." I peeled her hands off mine and placed the ring box in her palm. She stared at the box as if she was asking herself, do I open it?

"It's beautiful." I could see it in her eyes. She liked the ring, or maybe the meaning or both.

"I will wear it always. It will make me feel we are always together."

She rose from her seat and walked around to my side of the table and wrapped her arms around my neck as she whispered, then nibbled on my ear.

"How much time do you have?"

I reached around her waist and pulled her onto my lap. I glanced at my watch, it was fifteen twenty.

"It's late. I will barely make it back in time." She smothered my forehead with kisses, allowing her breasts hiding under her thin top, to caress my face.

"I must go. The captain will have my ass."

"You stay and you can have my.."

"I know, but the captain was adamant I make it back by sixteen hundred. I'll be getting time off soon. If I have to, I'll come to Seoul or hell and back to see you."

I slid her off my lap and took her hand and walked to the door. She was staring up at me with teary eyes.

"Lieutenant, please be careful. I want nothing to happen to you."

She wrapped her arms around my neck, standing

on her tiptoes planted a kiss. I wanted it to last forever.

"Mike, I love you! 'I'll never find another you'."

I left feeling as if she had removed a ton of bricks from my shoulders. We were in love. She even asked her aunt, which was a good sign. She was at least thinking of going to the states. Hyun-ae just gave me the best birthday present and without knowing it was my birthday.

TRAPPED

"A liar will not be believed, even when he speaks the truth."
Aesop

After hiding for hours on the hillside overlooking Hyun-ae's cottage, Chung confirmed there was no government surveillance. Did they give up? Was it a trap? If so, they would've cleared the neighbors from the surrounding houses. How would they know today was the day? Chung concluded, No, they gave up!

Through his binoculars, he observed the American lieutenant come and go five hours earlier. It was a quick visit. The likelihood of him returning was slim. The sun had set. Mi-sook and Kim's team were in place. It was twenty hundred hours. Chung knocked on the cottage door.

"Who's there?"

"Chung!"

Hyun-ae had a questioning look on her face as she opened the door.

"What are you doing here?"

"May I come in? I have good news about your mother."

"I don't receive callers at night."

Chung thought better of mentioning the lieutenant. He needed to get in the cottage. He bowed his head.

"I promise to be a gentleman."

Hyun-ae opened the door and walked towards the center of the room with Chung on her heels. He saw two beer bottles on the table.

"I see you still enjoy your OB."

"What information do you have about my mother?"

"You were right in believing she's alive. She is in good health and works as a doctor near the China border. She has accepted her life in North Korea."

"I don't believe you!"

"Sit down. Let me explain. She's not only the lead doctor in the providence, she is the administrator of the hospital."

Chung read her expression of doubt but also of, tell me more. Chung embellished the mother's deeds even further.

"As a doctor she saved lives during the war, including high-ranking officers. She enjoys many benefits because of her service. She is a loyal member of the party."

"That's not so. You're a liar. My mother despised the communist! WHO ARE YOU?"

Chung could see Hyun-ae's eyes widen with fear and doubt. He stepped behind her, placing his hands on her shoulders. He could feel her body trembling. She tried to stand.

"SIT! I want to show you something."

Chung released her shoulders and removed from his coat the photos and placed them on the table. Hyun-ae stared down at the photographs of her mother. She started shaking violently and weeping.

Hyun-ae asked, knowing the answer.

"WHO ARE YOU?"

"I am who you think I am. Your mother requested I bring her Mugungnwa home with me."

Without warning and with the quickness of a cat, Hyun-ae grabbed a beer bottle and in one motion stood, turned, swinging the bottle at Chung's head. He got his arm up, partially blocking the bottle. The blow to his head knocked him backwards as Hyun-ae bolted towards the door with the bottle still in her hand. The door opened with Mi-sook blocking it. Hyun-ae, startled, hesitated, then charged Mi-sook, swinging the bottle. She ducked the as she threw her shoulder into Hyun-ae's midsection, driving her to the floor. Hyun-ae dropped the bottle from the force of the impact. Mi-sook straddled Hyun-ae and tried to grab her flailing arms. Chung recovered enough to smile. He wanted to let them continue fighting, but he couldn't risk alerting neighbors. He knelt at Hyun-ae head and grabbed her arms.

"STOP IT! YOU'RE NOT GOING ANYWHERE."

"What do you want of me? WHY ME!"

Chung stood over the two women as he ordered Hyun-ae. "Get up, try to run or scream, I'll bind you like a pig on a farmer's bike. You understand?"

Hyun-ae nodded her head in agreement. Chung led her to the chair at the table.

"Your mother is alive and living a comfortable life. The pictures are a month old. She is holding a recent newspaper quoting President Park about the unification of Korea. It proves your mother is alive."

Hyun-ae screamed with spittle flying.

"PHOTOGRAPHS, YOU MEAN FABRICATED BULLSHIT!"

"Quiet or I'll gag you." Chung said. "She calls you her little flower, 'Mugungnwa'. How would I know that?"

She burst into tears while looking at the photographs. Her mother's long hair was up in her usual style, held with the gold hairpin. The hairpin was convincing. Her mother looked distinguished and healthy, smiling with co-workers in front of a hospital. There was no doubt she was Aunt Ju's sister. Mi-sook handed Hyun-ae a handkerchief. "I should slap you."

"FUCK YOU!"

"OH! you speak like the filthy GIs!" Mi-sook said with a devious smile.

"Ladies stop, we need to get ready to move. Soon we'll be taking you across the DMZ."

"Kidnap me? My government will not stand for its people to be shanghaied."

"They'll be glad to see that you defected. A student troublemaker, trying to overthrow your government. Your last protest caused the death of a student."

"I never advocated for the overthrow of Park's regime, only for change!"

"Tell her Mi-Sook."

"My 'Little Flower', you never lock your door to your apartment. It was easy to hide the gun, explosives and literature urging your group to turn to violence at the next protest."

Mi-sook placed four photos on the table showing her apartment, and the planted evidence.

"I had no protests planned!"

"Of course not Flower, you'll be in North Korea. Your April II people will be hunted down and charged with sedition."

"The police won't believe it. They'll figure out you put the gun and other shit there. You're crazy, both of you!"

"Hyun-ae, remember when I handed over the money?"

"I gave it to the orphanage."

"Do you recall the exchange? I handed you the envelope filled with cash. You held the envelope, looked inside and gave the envelope back to me. I put the cash on the table and the envelope in my pocket. That envelope is now in your apartment filled with new money and our fingerprints. The authorities have my prints."

"YOU SON OF A BITCH."

"They have been hunting me and had you under surveillance, so now the connection. I'm a known spy and you're a collaborator. Do you think they'll give a shit or believe we kidnapped you? Your government will not pressure ours to get a defector back."

"You'll have to drag me out of here. I will disprove your so-called connection?"

A click clack grew louder. Someone was coming

up the stone path. Hyun-ae heart sunk. From the sound, it was Aunt Ju's high heels. Before she could utter a warning, Chung clamped his hand across her mouth.

The door opened, Mi-sook was standing to the side, she latched on to Aunt Ju's arm and hurled her into the room. Aunt Ju fell off her high heel shoes, hitting the floor hard. Chung released his hand from Hyun-ae mouth and grabbed a handful of hair. He jerked her head back, exposing the front of her neck. His other hand brandished a knife. In a loud whisper, he said.

"NOT A WORD OR SHE IS DEAD! Don't scream. Who is she?"

"My aunt, Ju!"

Aunt Ju sat there stunned with a bewildered look on her face before muttering. "Who are you?"

"Aunt Ju, are you alright?" Hyun-ae asked.

"Shut up!" Chung hissed.

Chung pulled harder on Hyun-ae hair, flashing the knife for Aunt Ju.

"Listen ladies, I don't wish to hurt anyone, but I will if you don't cooperate. Why are you here, Aunt Ju?"

"This is my house. I come and go as I please. Take my money, anything, just go away!" Chung burst out into laughter.

"Aunt Ju get up! We don't want your money, we want your niece. She will be with her mother."

Aunt Ju stared at the photographs spread out on the table.

"NO, NO, NO! YOU BASTARD!"

"You look like your sister." Mi-sook said with a smirk.

Ju looked at Hyun-ae, then at the remaining beer bottle on the table. A split second later, the bottle was flying at Chung's head, with Ju right behind it. Hyun-ae dashed for the door, only to be tackled by Mi-sook. This time Hyun-ae used her momentum to roll and end up on top of Mi-sook, smashing her fist into her face.

Ju charged, Chung dodged the bottle. He instantly recognized Ju's fluid movements. Ju had training. He stepped to the left, avoiding her low kick and parried her punch. He stepped back as Ju expected, but she did not expect his body becoming airborne as he brought his left leg up and around in a high crescent move. His shoe smashed into the side of her face. Like a rag doll, she fell to the floor. Chung's knife came out.

"HYUN-AE STOP OR I WILL SLIT HER THROAT! Get over here." Aunt Ju was coming too.

"Mi-sook, call Kim. We need help control these two tigers."

Mi-sook was bleeding from the nose and lip. "You come at me again, I'll kill you."

"Fuck you, bitch." Hyun-ae said with a snarl baring her teeth.

"We'll see who gets fucked!"

"MI-SOOK GET KIM IN HERE."

Mi-sook closed the partially open door, out of her shoulder bag, Mi-sook removed a handheld radio.

"Lion, this is Lily. Come on in."

"Hyun-ae, you fight well. You'll make a good comrade." Chung said with a smile.

"Screw you!"

"Do you screw your American lieutenant as hard as you fight? Both sides have watched you. I saw him leave this afternoon. You cooperate and your aunt and your lieutenant get to live. As a bonus, you get to be with your mother and become a scientist. Your government considers you a treasure, hope for the future of nuclear energy. Behave, do as I say." Chung demanded.

"You do not know where he is."

"He's with the 2/23rd. He'll be an easy target when he comes back, not knowing you've gone. My men will be waiting."

Kim's team walked in. Chung continued the lie to add more fear to the tale.

"Kim's team is just one of many teams in the south. Now get up, help your aunt. Park, keep an eye on them. Lee, see if there's ice in the refrigerator for Ju and Mi-sook. We can talk in the other room."

"What are we going to do, Chung? Hyun-ae will not cooperate. She will give us away the first chance she gets." Kim said whispering.

"No, she won't. If we use her aunt as the carrot, Hyun-ae will cooperate. It's too late to head back to the safe house. We'll stay here for the night. We have the entire night to convince Hyun-ae we mean no harm to Ju.

We spell out to them we're spies. It's no benefit for

us to harm anyone. We explain to Hyun-ae that Mi-sook will stay behind for another day to give us time to cross the DMZ. When we cross the DMZ, we'll call Mi-sook on the radio. Mi-sook will then leave aunt Ju bound, gagged and drugged, time to get away. We persuade Ju and Hyun-ae that if our mission succeeds; they get to live. That is an incentive to cooperate. Keep your gloves on, the police or OSI should find only Ju's, Hyun-ae's the lieutenants and my fingerprints." Mi-sook held up the radio with a question.

"The radio range is only a couple kilometers. I can't receive a call from the DMZ, besides Ju has seen my face. I'll still be in the country, THE POLICE WILL HUNT ME DOWN!"

"CALM DOWN MI-SOOK! Hyun-ae doesn't know the range of the radios! As far as Ju, after Hyun-ae and I leave, kill the bitch, then your identity is safe. they'll think I did it. Kim, before daybreak, take Park and Lee, use the forest as cover, go to the main road, then split up. We'll meet back at the safe house as soon as possible. Hyun-ae and I will catch the early bus. Mi-sook, after we leave, take care of Ju. Tomorrow night, we cross the DMZ."

SAFE HOUSE

"He who has a why to live can bear almost any how," Friedrich
Nietzsche

"You did well, Hyun-ae. I felt the tension in your hand when three of your countries soldier's got on the bus. I remind you to continue to cooperate. If you said anything, I would have shot the soldiers and you. Tomorrow morning, your aunt will be free and you'll be on your way to see your mother. We're safe here. We're a kilometer from the Imjin. The five of us will rest till night. We must cross the river well before daybreak. Can you swim, Hyun-ae?"

"You're mad! The water is cold, the river is wide, and the current is strong."

"The rainy season has not begun. Tomorrow at 0400, the tide is low and the crossing place is waist deep. I asked if you could swim in case something changed. Can you swim?"

"Yes,"

"Good, Mi-sook bought clothes. They're in the bedroom. They will be more proper for tonight's mission. Get changed while Lee fixes us a meal. Fix your hair so it fits under the hat."

"Why? I'm a trivial matter in the scheme of things. I have no government secrets. I'm a student with a life to live. Why drag me into your oppressive world? I have no wish to help your great so-called leader?

He's a murderer, a tyrant!"

Chung's brow furrowed, his eyes flash anger.

"That comment ten miles north of here will get you shot on the spot! Hyun-ae, don't forget your mother. She is alive, and as I told you, she is a respected doctor. You will see her in a couple of days. Your dreams, ambitions, whether you are north or south of the 38th parallel, stay the same. You are an intelligent woman. Don't let a boundary dictate your life. You'll be with your people, Koreans, not the lackeys in the south that lick the boots of the Americans. Science, nuclear energy, unification, things you can do and be with your mother. Did you not tell me you dream of your mother?"

"You are insane! Chung, I'm not trained!"

"Once we get through the fence, it's a walk in the woods. There are very few patrols. Our goal is to avoid the GIs and cross the DMZ. Now go get changed."

"NO! I'm NOT GOING! HOW DO I KNOW MI-SOOK DIDN'T ALREADY KILL JU! CALL YOUR BITCH ON THE RADIO AND LET ME TALK TO MY AUNT!"

"Calm down or we'll gag you. We must maintain radio silence. We're too close to the DMZ. They will intercept any radio transmissions. Once we cross the DMZ, it doesn't matter. I will call her. When the authorities get to your aunt's house, Mi-sook will be gone. They'll find your aunt safe."

"Park, Lee, this foolishness. Life in the south is better. Why do you support a regime that starves its people, imprisons them or murders them? You're watched where ever you go, there's no freedom." Hyun-ae beseech.

Kim stood, crossed the room and stared at Hyun-ae before speaking.

"You didn't address me, Hyun-ae. I speak for my team. Park, Lee and I have been together for several years. Chung, I can't speak for, but the three of us come from small villages with brothers, sisters, mothers and fathers. We love our families. We grew up working together with other villagers, learning we're part of what binds the family to the village to the province and from that we develop the love of our country. Patriotism isn't about the bright lights of Seoul. We work together with our Great Leader to make our country strong!"

Kim continues, raising his voice.

"Your government kowtows to the Americans. In your Korea, you also must carry identification papers. In the first April I protest, hundreds of students were killed. During the last protest, the police killed a student! Yet you continue to allow yourself to believe your government's bullshit!"

"You're full of bullshit Kim, your so called 'great leader' uses patriotism to punish his people. He blames others for his failings. The "GREAT LEADER' of yours would've mowed the students down with machine guns! Your people are suffering because of him. Open your eyes, your mind. Compare what you have seen in the south to the everyday events in your country. There's no comparison!"

Kim stepped closer, his face inches away from

Hyun-ae's.

"You were going to be arrested."

"I would get a fair trial. In your world, all I would get is a bullet!

Chung stopped the debate.

"Enough! Hyun-ae go change, Lee, prepare something to eat."

Chung looked outside to see if the loud talk aroused suspicion among the nearby houses. It started to rain.

"We will leave at 2300 hours. The rain will provide cover. Kim get the weapons hidden under the floor in the other room."

DARKER THAN

"Thoughts are shadows of our feelings-always darker, emptier and simpler." Friedrich Nietzsche

"Mike, how was your visit to the hospital today?"

"It went well. The men are doing okay. Sanchez is hurting, but the head nurse said he'll recover."

"Did you give Hyun-ae the ring?"

"How the hell did you know?"

"Do-ha saw you go over to the jewelry department. I just guessed you bought a ring. A diamond ring?"

"No, a topaz."

"What's her family going to say when they find out?"

"We're going to work it out. Her aunt is on board with whatever decision we make."

"And the colonel, uncle Bae?"

"I have no idea. We didn't mention him. Why do you think Colonel Williams wanted to eat dinner with us? Do-ha and I had to haul ass to get back here in time."

"He was checking you out! I heard he's looking for a new staff officer at battalion, S-2. You have intelligence training."

"I don't want to be a Mueller. I'd be bored!"

"Hey you got a few months to go. It will look good on your record. Also, there's a rumor the captain put you in for a medal."

"For what? I did what they trained me for."

"Don't knock it. If you stay with the Army, it will help with your career and with Hyun-ae. Want a beer? Slats hid the good stuff."

"Thanks, but no, gotta get up at 0330 and get the men ready. We have to be at the fence by daybreak."

"Suit yourself, but I gotta have a beer or two to get a good night's sleep. See ya in the morning."

O three thirty, came quick, I started walking down to the CP in the rain. It was darker than the inside of a cow's stomach. Funny, that thought came to mind. Wayne, a fishing buddy back home, would say that when we went fishing at night.

"Mike, shine that light back here before I fall down these fuckin steps. They're slicker than owl shit!"

I turned with the light.

"What the fuck are you doing with a goddamn umbrella? You look like Mary Poppins, man. You're going to catch some shit at the CP."

"Hey it's raining cats and dogs. Damn poncho's don't keep your arms dry, your pants get wet. I just wanna stay dry in the APC. I can the open the hatch, pop the umbrella, get some fresh air, so don't give me anymore shit.

What cha gonna do for a platoon sergeant? Did you decide if you're going to replace Sergeant Hicks?"

"I'm thinking Ghostbear as a temporary, Hicks will be back on duty in a week. Are you really going to walk into the CP with that umbrella?"

"Screw you! Let's get to the briefing so we can go eat. I'm hungry."

The briefing was short and sweet. The QRF would leave their APC's and shadow our movements. So much for Mo staying dry. During the day, they would try to remain within five hundred meters of our movements. At night they would go back to being the QRF. The thinking was that the gooks may try to exact revenge. Apparently, the ASA spooks had a listening post on OP Dort. They intercepted a communication saying the gooks suffered three dead and seven wounded in our firefight.

The company clerk interrupted the briefing with an **urgent message** from division TOC to battalion TOC to Charlie company. "**To all units in the area of interest,**" followed by a list of coordinates. "**A South Korean security team raided a home at 0100hrs. The raid took place two kilometers southwest of Freedom bridge. Items left behind confirm the house was being used by the enemy. The house was empty, as many as five individuals were seen at the house just hours before the raid. It's unknown if the occupants went north or south.**"

The heavy rain ruled out using dogs to track the enemy. There hadn't been a recent breach of the fence. I cautioned the men to assume the 'enemy' was on the move and headed north. They needed little encouragement to keep their shit wired tight. Our last encounter was more than enough. I wondered what 'items' the gooks had left behind.

The morning had a distinct feeling. The darkness

of the night, the rain and the surreal image of six foot two helmeted Mo under an umbrella heading for the CP gave me a chuckle. He's going to get his ass wet. The urgent message had me concerned.

No replacements for my wounded men left me with thirty-two men reorganized into four patrols instead of five. There was no bitchin' this morning. The men didn't have to be told to carry extra ammo.

Mo and I coordinated our movements. We would conduct a sweep and block operation east of GP Gladys along a low ridge that ran east to west. I would keep one patrol near the top and one on the south slope. The other two patrols would act as a blocking force to the west.

Mo's QRF would set up three hundred meters south, halfway between the blocking force and the patrol sweeping.

CROSSING THE IMJIN RIVER

At the west tip of Crab island, a bend in the river allowed a sand bar to form. The river at this spot was only chest deep. Chung's band had to wade the river only once, as Crab island became a peninsula at low tide.

"Lee, you and Park cross and secure the other side. Hyun-ae, you'll follow me with Kim behind you. Stay within an arm's reach. We don't have to worry about footprints. The rain will wash them out. You ready, Hyun-ae?"

"I'm scared, it so dark. What if the water is deep?"

Chung removed his backpack and pulls out a coil of rope, tying one end around his waist, then made a loop and slipped it over Hyun-ae's head, cinching it tight around her waist. He tossed the remaining rope to Kim.

"Kim, tie it around your waist. Hyun-ae don't even think about it. Kim and I are strong swimmers."

The river's current was barely visible. In the blackness of night, the river drained of light flowed like spilled ink across a flat surface. Chung waded in when he felt the tug. Hyun-ae wasn't moving. Kim pushed her forward with his weapon, then stepped up behind her, whispering in her ear.

"Move bitch!" Chung turned and reached out for her hand.

"Hyun-ae, focus! The river is only a hundred meters wide. Soon you'll be on the other side. In a matter of hours safe, on your way to seeing your mother and Ju being set free."

The river crossing went as planned. A hundred meters south of the fence, Chung and his wet band hid in a tangle of wild lilacs and Korean rose.

"Kim, you reconnoiter the fence. It's 0200 hours. I want to cross the fence at 0330 hours. Colonel Choi's men will start a diversion just east of the position the Americans call Gladys. We'll stay with Hyun-ae. Take your radio in case we get separated, go!"

Fifteen minutes later, a parachute flare lit up the sky a couple hundred meters away, too far to be looking for Kim. No shots fired, a jumpy GI?

"Hyun-ae, there's a jacket in my pack. Maybe it will stop your teeth from chattering."

"I'm wet, cold, what the fuck did you expect?"

"Our ladies don't talk that way."

"Fuck you!"

Kim returned thirty minutes later. The rain wasn't stopping. Hyun-ae sat on the ground with her knees pulled up to her chest. Chung's jacket pulled over her head.

"Chung, we can't use the gate. They made changes. They fortified the foxhole. There's barbed wire, and they have elevated the position using dirt and sandbags."

"What about that flare?"

"I don't know, but it lit up the position well enough. I could make out at least four GIs."

"SHIT!" Kim send a message to the colonel to hold off on the diversion.

"WHAT ABOUT MY AUNT!"

"QUIET HYUN-AE!"

"Call Mi-sook!"

"We have time when we cross."

Kim spoke.

"Chung, while scouting for our first mission, we looked at a secondary crossing point. It's four hundred meters west of here. The rain may be an asset. The fence crosses a gully, the gully runs though the minefield."

"Lead the way. We'll scout it at daybreak."

As the sodden band started moving west, Hyun-ae turned and ran, getting only thirty feet, when she tripped, falling flat on her face. Chung was on her back before she could get to her knees with his hand over her mouth and his knife at her throat. She felt his hot breath as he whispered in her ear.

"You try that again, you're dead as well as your beloved aunt and lieutenant. Where the fuck do you think you're going? The GIs will kill you, they shoot anything that moves north of the river. You understand, there's no second time. You try again and everyone you love is dead!"

Hyun-ae shook her head in compliance.

"Kim, let's go."

The team moved quietly through the brush well behind the GIs positions until they were near the gully. With the hint of daylight on the horizon, Kim and Chung eased up to the gully seventy meters south of the fence. The gully ran northeast towards the fence. It was more than a meter deep, filled with water and razor wire. The wire crossed the gully, then turned north to the fence, preventing them from circling around the wire. The east side had another foxhole. The problem was with the foxhole on the edge of the gully. Cutting the razor wire would alert the GIs.

Chung's thoughts turned to attacking the position. One of the team had to cut the razor wire. Another watch Hyun-ae and two to attack. Not enough. It was too dark to determine how many GIs were in the large foxhole. Attacking was too risky. They had to wait for more light.

Kim and Chung inched up closer. The rain had stopped and ground fog formed. In the fog shrouded dawn, they could make out three helmeted figures in the T shaped foxhole. Two were facing the fence and one was facing the rear. The men were alert. Chung spotted the two sandbags in front and at the rear of the position. The sandbags were behind the claymores to shield the defensive position. One claymore covered the gully, the other killing zone was along the fence.

Over the years, rain had cut a gully through the minefield. The foot deep rushing water would cover any sounds they made. It's unlikely the GIs placed the so called 'toe popper' mines on the bottom of the gully. It was worth the risk.

"Kim, didn't you say around 0700 hours the replacements for daylight hours leave every other position empty?"

"Yes, and the GIs are careless during daylight."

"Okay, we wait. To attack is suicide. You stay here till they make the change. I'll wait with the others."

Chung made his way back to Lee, Hyun-ae and Park, hunkered in a cluster of pine trees. The fog was getting thicker, visibility was less than a hundred meters. Chung continued mulling over his plan. The fog will provide concealment. We can do it.

The magpies in a nearby tree were busy with their morning chatter. Lee was smiling. Chung asked.

"Why are you smiling?"

"The magpies brought us good luck the last time."

It was 0720 hours when Kim made his way back to the thicket hideout.

"Here comes Kim."

"Chung, we're fortunate. They abandoned the foxhole at the gully. There's at least a hundred meters between the two occupied positions with three GIs in each one. We should leave before the fog clears. Did you alert the Colonel?"

"No, the Russian piece of shit of a radio died from the rain. Use yours."

"Chung, maybe we should go now. It will take the colonel an hour to set up a diversion. The fog may lift by then."

Before he spoke, Chung stared at Hyun-ae, then broke into a smile, sending a chill down her spine.

"I agree. Let him know we'll be coming through four hundred meters west of the original plan. Lee, you'll cut the wire. Kim will be the first through, followed by Hyun-ae, me, then Park. Lee, you cover us until we are through the fence, then follow. Everyone must stay in the middle of the gully. It's unlikely they placed mines where they would wash them away. Kim watch for trip wires. We must stay below the sides of the gully. The minefield is only fifty meters wide. Hyun-ae you follow Kim no matter what happens. He can run like the wind. I'll be behind you. We have one purpose, and that is to make it home. We don't want contact with the GIs."

"Look at me, Hyun-ae!" Her dark eyes were wide with fear, wet strands of hair hung from under the ill-fitted hat. Chung reaches out to wipe the mud from her face. She recoiled, her eyes flashed hatred as she spit at his hand. Standing up, she whispered with as much insolence as she could muster.

"I understand! I want to talk to Aunt Ju now!"

"NOT TILL WE ARE SAFE, let's go, Park, lead the way."

The fog was getting denser as the morning warmed. Using wire cutters covered with a heavy cloth he cut through the razor wire, Lee crawled to the chain-link fence. While on his back, he quietly, cut an opening. The GIs were oblivious to what was happening fifty meters away.

Kim, Hyun-ae, then Chung made it through the opening crawling on their bellies. As Park started through the fence, Lee peeked over the edge of the gully. Out of the fog, a GI appeared. He was walking straight towards them. They saw each other simultaneously. The GI got off a couple rounds and

Lee fired a short burst. Both men were hit, Lee fatality. Chung realized the GIs were running to the wounded GI, they were sitting ducks.

"KIM RUN, GET OUT OF THE GULLY!"

The GI didn't run to the hole in the fence. The firing was futile. They were shooting at the hole in the fence or Lee's body. The GIs continued firing blindly. The dense fog prevented them from grasping what was happening. Chung and his band were through the minefield in seconds and into the thick reeds and knee deep water. Chung moved up close behind Hyun-ae.

"You did good, Hyun-ae. You'll see, you made the right choice."

"Fuck you! You just lost one of your men and you're worried about my feelings. Lee's back there all shot up. You're a demented son of a bitch!"

"Kim, let's use the cattails as cover till we get to the woods."

****

Mo and his men entered the DMZ at tower five. My platoon was now reduced to four patrols and without Sergeant Hicks. At dawn we crossed into the DMZ at foxhole Charlie. Surprisingly, the engineers hadn't changed the path through the minefield. On the other side, Ghostbear and Calhoun's patrols would split from Betz and I. They would set up ambush positions deep in the DMZ.

Betz and I, with eight men each, were going to move west for several hundred meters before turning north, stopping a couple hundred meters south of the MDL. We would then sweep east towards Ghostbear and Calhoun along the low ridge.

Mo and his men would move to coordinates north of foxhole Charlie, setting up as a large blocking force on a north, south axis. They would also act as a QRF. Except for the objective, to kill men, the operation wasn't different from a organized deer drive back home.

"Sergeant Betz, let's hold up till 0700 hours before we move west. It will give Ghostbear and Calhoun time to reach their position. We'll move in wedge formation."

The fog was thick as we started to move slowly along the northern edge of the minefield. The tall wet grass along with the fog made it difficult to move much faster than a snail's pace. We were nearing a gully that cuts through the minefield; the gully drains into a large marshy area. Gunfire broke out. Up ahead, I could see tracers slicing through the fog.

"DOWN!" A order unnecessary, as everyone was down on one knee or their belly. The firing was along the fence at the gully. Double OO handed me the mic to the platoons radio. Perkins, carrying the radio for the company and battalion net, ran up beside Double OO.

"Lt, they hit foxhole delta, one man down and gooks through the fence."

I called Betz, told him to move as I motioned for my patrol to move at a quick pace. The shooting had stopped. Mo was moving towards our position.

I ordered Ghostbear and Calhoun to change plans and move west. We might trap the SOBs. After informing tower five, we arrived where the gully emptied into the swamp. We followed the broken reeds in a northwesterly direction. It appeared from the minimal damage to the reeds a small group was traveling single file. A hundred meters further, Do-ha on point, finds a hat. They were staying in the marsh for cover. The cattails were thicker than the hair on a cat, it was difficult to move fast. The marsh hooked around to a wooded area that extended almost to the MDL.

I ordered Betz to move to our position and to stay on the trail. The marsh reeds were thinning. Without cover, the gooks would swing back towards the woods. The woods would provide them cover to make a run for the MDL.

****

"Chung, GI's two hundred meters behind us!"

Chung knew they had to get out of the marsh before they were spotted. The GI's rifles were far more effective at long range than their PPSh-41s. The woods would provide cover. After the woods, they still had to cross a stretch of open terrain. If they moved fast, they could make it across before the GIs could fire at them.

"Park, take cover and delay them, then head for the

woods."

Less than a minute later, a volley of shots rang out. It wasn't a good sign. The telltale Brrrrp of the ppsh was short. Either Park panicked and was running for the woods or they shot him.

"KIM, WHEN WE GET TO THE WOODS YOU AND HYUN-AE RUN STRAIGHT FOR THE MDL, DON'T WAIT FOR ME. I'LL HOLD THEM UP LONG ENOUGH FOR YOU TO GET ACROSS!

"CHUNG! THERE'S MORE GI'S CUTTING ACROSS THE MARSH!"

"GIVE ME YOUR WEAPON AND GET MOVING!"

The tall grass and brush prevented the GIs from spotting them near the edge of the woods. Kim, Hyun-ae and Chung broke out of the marsh, sprinting for the trees and heavy brush, only to be spotted by the GIs a hundred meters away.

****

I was behind Do-ha, the rest of the men following single file. It was hard to move fast. The water was thigh deep in places. Betz called on the radio, they had killed one and spotted three more running for the woods. Mo called and had passed Ghostbears blocking force and was approaching the woods from the east.

To our right, three gooks broke into the open, running for the woods. The middle one had long hair, it was whipping about as the body moved with familiar agile movements. WHAT THE HELL! It was

Hyun-ae!

Do-ha raised his rifle.

"NO!" As I slogged by Do-ha, wishing the thigh deep water would part. I pushed the barrel of his rifle down. Abandoning all caution, I headed for the woods. My men hesitated, stunned by my actions. I churned through the water, leaving them behind. My legs moved as fast as my mind raced. She wasn't being dragged, she was running with them! She was one of them. NO, NO! I made it to the woods' edge.

In a frenzy, I ran jumping ditches, dodging around bushes. Up ahead, I glimpsed two bodies running. I couldn't chance a shot. I ran with branches slapping my face. What I was doing was insane, deserting all common sense, but I didn't care I had to catch her. I wanted to know WHY?

Was it adrenalin or insanity? The trees were a blur as I ran to catch them. On the other side of the woods, they would be exposed. I could shoot the one gook, SHIT! it hit me, where was the third one? Before I could completely process the thought, he stepped out from behind a large tree, one that survived the decades of wars.

I could see the grinning face. In one quick motion, he raised the ppsh to his shoulder. Still running, I started to raise my rifle to my shoulder. It felt like I was in a slow-motion movie. The rifle was halfway there when I saw the flash from his muzzle as I went down. I fell into one of the deep irrigation ditches hidden by the tall grass that grew on its banks.

I hit the bottom, dropping my rifle. I felt no pain

from the bullets, realizing I wasn't hit. I picked up my rifle and ran a few feet bent at the waist, then stood up. My M-14 already at the shoulder caught Chung looking at the spot where I had gone down. The split second was all I needed to pull the trigger. I continued pulling the trigger before I climbed out of the waist deep ditch and ran up to Chung, laying slumped up against the tree. I kicked away the ppsh. He was hit several times in the upper body. He smiled. Despite the labored breathing and the blood bubbling out the side of his mouth, he managed to say, 'dangsin-eun neuseunhae,' I shot him again and took off after Hyun-ae.

They were already halfway across the field, Hyun-ae leading the way. I yelled.

"HYUN-AE!" She turned her head. The remaining gook ran forward, grabbing her arm. I started after them. I only took a few steps when someone slammed me to the ground.

"REED WHAT THE FUCK YOU DOING!" It was Mo.

Bullets from across the MDL started ripping through the grass. "IT'S TOO LATE, SHE'S GONE, WE GOTTA GET OUT OF HERE!"

We made our way to where I left Chung. The incredulous looks of my men brought me back to my senses.

"Thanks MO! I don't know what I was thinking!"

"NO FUCKIN SHIT! Mo knelt down to remove the satchel slung over Chung's shoulder."

"Jesus, how many times did you shoot him?"

"He had it coming! We have to take the body.

Korean intelligence will want proof."

"Are you sure it was Hyun-ae?"Mo asked.

"Hold off on the questions till we get back. The shit is gonna hit the fan."

****

It was early afternoon when we reached the compound. There would be a debriefing before hitting the bottle and trying to figure out what happened. My mind was reeling with different scenarios. She said she loved me. It felt like she did. How could she be so convincing? Aunt Ju was okay with our relationship? Was Ju part of this? Where was Won, Kowalski? I knew they weren't telling me everything? Was last night's raid on a house south of the river connected? So many fucking questions.

The debriefing was long and thorough. The battalion S-2 didn't know Hyun-ae was one of the gooks. Shit, I'm thinking she's a gook?

They passed around kudos, three dead gooks, one wounded GI. Do-ha mentioned one of them was a woman. The S-2 shrugged his shoulders. Mo was keeping his mouth shut! By tomorrow, Won, Kowalski and the whole fucking battalion will know she played me for a fool.

The satchel Chung was carrying was filled with film canisters and documents from different ministries. Many of the documents were marked secret. The S-2 droned on with more praises. I needed to call Kowalski. The briefing room door opened, no phone call was necessary. In walked the Colonel, Kowalski, and Won. Shit! Tomorrow had arrived.

"Captain, wrap up the debrief. We need the room."

"I'm done, sir."

"Everyone out, Lieutenant Reed, you stay."

The look on my face gave me away.

"Not to worry, Lieutenant, you and your men are to be commended. Chung's bag holds many secrets."

Kowalski broke in with a serious tone.

"We're not here to congratulate you. We have some bad news."

"What? SOME BAD NEWS! It couldn't be worse than..."

Kowalski didn't wait for me to finish.

"He murdered aunt Ju Sunday."

"What! Where?"

"In her cottage, he stabbed her multiple times and we can't locate Hyun- ae."

"NO! Who why! Then you don't know."

"Know what?"Kowalski asked.

"One gook was a woman. It was Hyun-ae!"

"What the fuck! You saw her, you sure?"

"Yes, why, why would she do it?"

"Do what, lieutenant?" Won asked.

"Defect to the north."

"What about murdering her aunt?"

"She wouldn't, she couldn't do it, she would'nt let him do it! She loved her aunt."

Kowalski piped up.

"Just like she loved you, Reed. We warned you not to get involved. You just called her ONE OF THE GOOKS."

"Lieutenant, my men found four sets of prints, yours, Hyun-ae, Ju' and Chung's. There was no sign of a struggle. We looked for Hyun-ae at her apartment in Seoul. We didn't find Hyun-ae, but we found a pistol, explosives and money. The money was in an envelope with both Chung's and Hyun-ae's fingerprints. When was the last time you saw her?"

"A couple of days ago, just for a few minutes."

"Was her aunt there?"

"No! No one was there. Do-ha, my driver was outside waiting.

"What did you talk about?"

"Won! We didn't talk about anything political or military, we never have. She was trying to decide if she was going to the states with me."

"How did you and your men kill Chung?"

I reiterated the mission, adding a few details not covered at the briefing. I could have shot the gook and Hyun-ae, but didn't.

I also told them when I yelled her name, he grabbed her by the arm and dragged her forward. I didn't know if she was a captive or going willingly.

The colonel chimed in, speaking to Won and Kowalski.

"The lieutenant had no input on this mission. Battalion staff set it up just an hour before the mission.

Reed and his men were at the right place at the

right time. Unfortunately, the lieutenant used poor judgment in his selection of a girlfriend.

Lieutenant, until Kowalski and Won finish their investigation, you're confined to the compound."

"Yes, sir."

I was making my way to the hooch when Do-ha flagged me down.

"LT, here's the hat I found that Hyun-ae was probably wearing. Do you want it?"

"You knew that was Hyun-ae but didn't say anything!Thanks Do-ha, but no to the hat."

"Okay."

"Do-ha, what does dangsin-eun neuseunhae mean?"

"Say it again."

I repeated the words with a clear image of Chung lying there with the dying smile.

"It sounds like, you lose."

Epilogue

I sat glued to my chair for over an hour, holding the paper but not reading it. Kowalski's call was like getting kicked in the nuts. I wanted to throw up, and I was in pain. Fifteen years ago, none of it made sense, none of it makes sense today. Alice knocked on my office door before poking her head in and half whispered.

"Mike, are you alright? You're as white as a ghost."

"I'm fine. Just close the door."

"There's an oriental guy out here. He asked to see you. His name is Mr. Won."

"FUCK!" I pounded my fist on the desk as I stood up, startling Alice.

"Mike, I can send him away!"

"I'm sorry Alice, I didn't mean to startle you. Give me a minute, then send him in."

Mr Won walked in the door looking much the same as he did fifteen years ago. I'm guessing, now in his mid-fifties, he still looked trim and fit. His jet black hair was now mostly gray, dressed in a ban-lon shirt and sports coat. He looked like a businessman.

"Mike, so glad to see you." He walked towards me, extending his hand. I hesitated but, courtesy got the best of me.

"What brings you to Buffalo, Won?" He glanced at the broken phone base and the newspaper on my desk.

"I see you read about the airliner."

I gestured to him to have a seat. "Yes, and Kowalski called."

"That's interesting. I thought he was out of the game."

"Are you still in THE GAME, Won?"

"Mike, may I call you Mike?"

"That's fine."

The look on Won's face was ominous. "Did Kowalski tell you what's not in the paper.?"

"No!"

"The Russians did not force the plane to land. We have confirmation the plane was shot down, no survivors."

"NO, No, I thought she was still.. As I slumped into my chair thinking Kowalski didn't have the fucking balls to tell me.

"Look Mike, I'm sorry! Hyun-ae is a hero and was a very brave woman. I'm here as a favor to Hyun-ae."

My mind was reeling. "You came all the way from Korea just to see me?"

"No, I escorted Hyun-ae from West Germany to Langley. My official duties ended there."

Alice stuck her head in the door.

"Would you and Mr. Won like coffee?"

Won nodded his head yes.

"Okay, make a fresh pot."

"Already done."

"What do you mean, you escorted her from Germany?"

"Let me start from the beginning." Won said.

Alice came in carrying a tray with the coffee, cream, sugar and her homemade cookies. I pulled the bottle of scotch from my bottom desk drawer.

"Mike, it's a little early for that, besides scotch doesn't go well with my homemade cookies." Alice said in a scolding manner.

"I'll just set the bottle here for backup."

Won watched as she turned and walked out the door, closing it behind her.

"I see you still have good taste in women."

"The beginning Won!"

"After crossing the DMZ, we couldn't get any information about her. North Korea denied she even existed, claiming we made the whole thing up. Our government went by the evidence and considered Hyun-ae a defector, traitor and a accomplice to murder. The North claimed Chung was a South Korean and American soldiers murdered him while he was trying to defect. By the way, we learned from a recent defector that Chung was a nephew of Kim Il-sung's wife. Chung's real name was Jang Yong Son.

So what! Did you believe Hyun-ae was a traitor? A murderer?" Reed asked.

"I had my doubts, but the case was closed and they forced me to take on new cases. We were aware of North Korea agents kidnapping people from the south and even Japan. But they never tried to cover the kidnapping by planting evidence. In 1970, we interviewed a defector who made his way through China to Mongolia. Mongolia has a policy of helping North Korea defectors. He worked at a hospital in the town of Kanggye, in a providence of North Korea bordering China. He told us a doctor by the name of Bae helped him through her contacts to escape. Apparently, doctor Bae had tried to escape in the early years after being taken hostage. She told him she would try again, under the right circumstances, but she..."

"Bae's MOTHER!"

"Yes, Bae's mother. She refused to go with him because her daughter had a son too young to make the attempt. In order to get to Mongolia, it required a dangerous journey across the Gobi desert."

I couldn't get the words out fast enough, my head exploding, my stomach churning, first Kowalski's call, now this on top of the strong coffee and early morning egg and bacon breakfast.

"A SON! Did you see him? Meet him. What's he like? He had to be…"

"Yes, he's your son. He was on the plane with Hyun-ae."

I sat there with my head in my hands.

"O my god, why, what did I do? This is all fucked up!" I reached for the bottle and poured two fingers of booze into my coffee. I held the bottle out towards Won. He shook his head no.

"What was his name?"

"Min-jun, it means quick, gentle and handsome."

"I'm sorry Mike. Do you want me to go on?"

"Yes."

"Do I have your word that this remains between the two of us, Mike?"

"YES!"

"About six years later, the CIA let us in on information they started receiving from a source in North Korea. Black Stallion is the code name used by the source. The information was very specific regarding the North trying to build a nuclear weapon. Black Stallion used an ingenious method to get the information out of the country. The method is classified."

I thought of the dream she told about the Black horse.

"Did they know then, it was from Hyun-ae?" I asked.

"No, information continued to be passed to the CIA for the next seven years.. I wasn't in the loop and didn't learn any of this till this August. Apparently Black Stallion was invited to a conference hosting many prominent communist experts in using nuclear energy. The conference was in East Germany. It turns out Black Stallion was doctor Bae Hyun-ae, a nuclear physicist. She wanted out; she wanted to defect. They then bought me into the fold. The CIA snatched her and her son out of East Germany in mid-August."

"She was in the states in August? They, you, wouldn't let her call me, WHY?" I shouted.

"The CIA protected her and controlled her every move. I had little to say. I was at Langley at their invitation. She asked me to inquire about you, where you lived, what you did and if you were married. I was not to contact you. She wanted to go home and see her uncle and visit Ju's grave. She would contact you in her own way.

I was getting impatient.

"Let me go on. After crossing the DMZ, they took Hyun-ae to her mother. She was a doctor at a large medical facility and had connections."

"Then her mother was alive! Hyun-ae never gave up hope. Where is her mother now?"Reed asked.

"She died in 1980, cancer."

The mother convinced the authorities to let Hyun-ae keep the baby. The party could use the son as collateral. Hyun-ae would not try to escape without taking her son. Very lucky for Min-Jun and Hyun-ae, normally the regime would force her to have an abortion or, when he was old enough, ship him to a work camp. Min-jun was not of pure blood.

As time went on, she completed her education at a University in Moscow under renowned physicist Andrei Sakharov. There was always the threat that harm would come to her mother and son if she tried to defect. Where ever Hyun-ae went, a matron traveled with her.

As the son grew older, it was clear to the schoolmates he was different. He was constantly being roughed up, shunned. Even as Hyun-ae's status improved, her son still couldn't go to the better schools. In 1975, she married a professor at the local university. She told me it was a marriage of convenience. He was a widower in his late 50s. His brother was a high-ranking party official. After Hyun-ae escaped her husband and his brother were accused of treason and executed.

The brothers were close, so favors were easy to secure. Soon after the marriage, they accepted her son at one of the better schools. He played sports and was accepted by classmates.

"It sounds like she was accepting her fate in life. Was she kidnapped?" I asked.

"Yes, and a witness was located to verify her story. The witness, Mi-sook, was one of the perpetrators. At Langley, Hyun-ae told us that a woman by the name of Mi-Sook was left with Aunt Ju. She was supposed to leave her tied up and unharmed. Mi-sook turned herself in as a defector in 1981. My partner, you remember him? Dong-suk, interviewed her?"

"Yes, you two still partners?"

"No, anyway Mi-Sook gave him a lot of important information back in eighty-one, but said nothing about Chung and Bae or Aunt Ju. We had nothing to connect Mi-Sook to Chung. We were under the impression that Chung murdered your aunt.

Under our 'Special Law' in 1982, they granted Mi-sook refugee status. After interviewing Hyun-ae at Langley, we arrested Mi-sook. We offered her a plea deal if she talked. She did, and she told the entire story. It matched Hyun-ae's. Hyun-ae was going home as a hero!"

"Why weren't you on the plane with her?"

"My job was done. I wanted to play tourist. Hyun-ae asked that I give you this after she left for Seoul."

Won pulled from his jacket a small package wrapped in paper with a simple ribbon tied in a bow. He handed it to me.

"Mike, I'm sorry for what happened, believe me. My country extends its gratitude for what you did."

I shook his outstretched hand.

"Thanks, I believe you." I walked Won to the door. The room became quiet as I closed the door. It was as if the world stopped making noise, no street noise, it was as though I was deaf. My mind was reeling, images flashed, I could feel the rain, the fog, smell the gunpowder. I could hear and feel her sweet voice saying. "I'll never find another you."

I sat down and took a big swig of my boozed up coffee and open the package. A book on Confucius, a picture of Hyun-ae and our son. She was as beautiful as ever. Min-jun towered over her. He looked more Korean than GI.

In the pages of the book a note 'My love, here is the direction where I'll be staying, written in Korean and English in case you have to ask someone.'

Hyun-ae

****

Made in the USA
Middletown, DE
14 October 2023

40546252R00235